Merryn Allingham was born into an army family and spent her childhood on the move. Unsurprisingly, it gave her itchy feet and in her twenties she escaped from an unloved secretarial career to work as cabin crew and see the world. The arrival of marriage, children and cats meant a more settled life in the south of England, where she's lived ever since. It also gave her the opportunity to go back to 'school' and eventually to university.

Merryn has always loved books that bring the past to life, so when she began writing herself, novels had to be historical. She finds the nineteenth and early twentieth centuries fascinating to research and her first book, *The Crystal Cage*, has as its background the London of 1851. The Daisy's War trilogy followed, set in India and London during the 1930s and '40s.

Her latest novels explore two pivotal moments in the history of Britain. *The Buttonmaker's Daughter* is set in Sussex in the summer of 1914 as the First World War looms ever nearer, and its sequel, *The Secret of Summerhayes*, forty years later in the summer of 1944 when D Day led to eventual victory in the Second World War. Along with the history, of course, there is plenty of mystery and romance to keep readers intrigued.

If you would like to keep in touch with Merryn, sign up for her newsletter at www.merrynallingham.com

Also by Merryn Allingham

The Crystal Cage
The Girl from Cobb Street
The Nurse's War
Daisy's Long Road Home

Merryn Allingham

The Buttonmaker's Daughter

ONE PLACE. MANY STORIES

This novel is entirely a work of fiction. The names, characters and incidents portrayed in it are the work of the author's imagination. Any resemblance to actual persons, living or dead, events or localities is entirely coincidental.

HQ
An imprint of HarperCollinsPublishers Ltd.
1 London Bridge Street
London SE1 9GF

This paperback edition 2017

2
First published in Great Britain by
HQ, an imprint of HarperCollinsPublishers Ltd. 2017

ISBN: 978-0-00-819383-6

Printed and bound by
London CR0 4YY

Our policy is to use papers that are natural, renewable and recyclable products and made from wood grown in sustainable forests. The logging and manufacturing processes conform to the legal environmental regulations of the country of origin.

To the Lost Gardens of Heligan,
the original inspiration for this novel.

Chapter One

Sussex, England, May 1914

Her father's voice ripped the silence apart. It burst through the closed doors of the drawing room, swept its way across the hall and rattled the panelled walls of golden oak. From where she stood on the staircase, the girl could just make out his figure shadowed against the room's glass doors. A figure that was angry and pacing. Carefully, she made her way down the last remaining stairs, then tiptoed to a side entrance. The air was fresh on her skin, cool and tangy, the air of a glorious May evening. A sun that had shone for hours still lingered in the sky and a few birds, unsure of when this long day would end, continued their song.

She walked purposefully across the flagged terrace and down the semicircular steps to an expanse of newly mown grass. Its scent was enticing and she had to stop herself from picking up her skirt and dancing across the vast lawn. It was relief that made her feel that way, relief that she'd escaped the house and its hostility. From a young age, she'd been encircled. Family discord had been a constant. Her parents' union was what was once known as a marriage of convenience, but whose convenience Elizabeth had never been sure. Their ill-assorted pairing had been a blight, an immovable cloud which hung over everything within the home.

Uncle Henry had done something bad, it seemed. Something to do with the stream that couched the perimeter of both their estates. An act of calculated spite, her father had roared. Whatever it was, she wanted no part of it. She shook her mind free and strode across the grass as swiftly as her narrow skirt allowed, her speedy passage disturbing one of Joshua's prize peacocks. The bird squawked at her in annoyance and flew up onto the ridge of the stone basin that sat in the centre of the lawn, fanning his feathers irritatedly. He was lucky the gardeners had yet to prime the fountain, or he might have ended more ruffled still. The warm weather had arrived without notice and caught the staff racing to catch up. The roses crowding the pergola that linked lawn and kitchen garden were already unfurling, their scent strong.

She passed beneath the grand arch leading to the huge swathe of land that grew fruit and vegetables to feed the whole of Summerhayes, and felt its red brick humming with the heat of the day's sun. The tension she'd been carrying began to slip away and her limbs relax into the reflected warmth. Today had been difficult. Her father's temper, always erratic, had exploded into such fury that the very walls of the house had trembled. At such moments, she was used to finding solace in her studio, paint and canvas transporting her to a world far removed from the sharp edges of life at Summerhayes. But today, painting had failed her. And miserably.

She stopped to listen, the sound of young voices floating towards her across the still air. From behind hoops of sweet peas planted amid the potatoes and cabbages and onions, she could just make out the figures of William and his companion. They were making their way along the gravel path that lay at right angles to where she stood. It was late, too late for them to be out. They were defying the curfew imposed when Oliver had first arrived to spend the long school holiday with her brother.

'You'd better get yourselves indoors,' she called out to them, as the boys made their way along the cruciform of gravel that bisected the kitchen garden. 'Papa is in a towering temper and you'll be for it if he sees you're still out.'

'We've been down to the lake,' Oliver said. 'We wanted to check on progress, but not much has happened. In fact, just the opposite, the site looks a mudbath.'

'The stream has stopped flowing,' her brother put in. 'At least, I think that's the problem. The lake isn't a lake any more. It's a mess.'

They were near enough now for her to see their grubby trousers and flapping shirts, no doubt a result of the check on progress. 'You look hideous. If Papa sees you, you're bound to be punished. Make sure you creep in quietly.'

'Why is he in a temper?'

Often there seemed no rhyme or reason to her father's outbursts and, when she didn't answer, William said, 'Is it Uncle Henry?'

She nodded.

'He must have done something to the stream,' he continued. 'He did warn that he would if the gardeners kept taking water.' In the muted light of evening, her brother looked older than his fourteen years.

'I can't see why he should,' Oliver said spikily. 'There's a stream three feet deep flowing along the edge of both estates – plenty of water for everyone.'

'You don't know Uncle Henry,' William said.

But if you did, she thought, you would understand his actions as perfectly consistent. Whatever Henry Fitzroy could do to hinder or destroy his brother-in-law's plans, he would.

'Go on, both of you. Make haste and use the side door. With luck you won't be seen.'

'Likely the old man will still be shouting and won't even notice we've even been out.'

William was becoming cheeky. That was the influence of his more forthright friend and her father wouldn't take kindly to it. Or to any show of rebellion. Joshua ruled him with a rod of iron and so far her gentle brother had bent himself to his parent's will, retreating to his mother for comfort. But now Alice appeared to have a rival for his affections. Oliver had become William's closest confidant. Her brother had been wretched at school, a school their father insisted he attend – until Oliver had appeared at the beginning of the winter term. But Olly, as William called him, had proved a saviour and the change in her brother was astonishing. She could see why they liked each other, why they had come to depend on one another. At school, they were both outsiders, despised by their fellows and teachers alike: William the son of a button manufacturer and Oliver, the son of a Jewish lawyer.

'Are you coming back with us?' The light was fading fast and William had begun to look anxious.

'In a short while. I'd like to take a look at the lake for myself.'

'You'll need boots,' her brother warned.

'And a dress that's a few yards shorter,' Olly quipped.

'Don't worry. I'll not be long.'

She shooed them away with a wave of her hand and carried on along the narrow gravel path that skirted the various outbuildings: past the boiler house, the bothy, the dark house that forced Summerhayes' rhubarb and chicory and sea kale, and, finally, the head gardener's office. She glanced across at the huddle of buildings. Nestled together, they made a charming picture but afforded little comfort. The one time she'd visited – for some reason, she had found herself in the tool shed – she'd seen immediately that light was not to be wasted on the workers. The interior had been gloomy, with small windows and little daylight. It was damp and cold, too, since only Mr Harris enjoyed a fireplace, his one luxury in a room of bare boards and battered furniture.

Through another grand brick arch and into the Wilderness. That was the name she and William had given it. Her father insisted it should be called the Exotic Garden but from the start it had been the Wilderness to them, a place where they spent as many hours as possible, hiding from their nursemaid or later their tutor and governess, and hiding from each other.

She came to an abrupt halt. Something was wrong. She stood for a moment and then realised what was missing: she should be hearing the splash of water against stones. A stream flowing to her left, flowing down from the encircling bank and into the lake. But there was no sound of water, no sound at all. The garden seemed to have come to a standstill and an uncomfortable quiet reigned. She took a long breath, then walked through the laurel hedge, the living arch that marked the entrance to her father's most cherished project, and saw immediately what William had meant.

A little of Joshua Summer's plan had already been realised. A flagged path had been laid to provide a gentle promenade in a space that was made for the sun, and aromatic herbs planted in the cracks between the paving stones. Beyond and behind the path, bed after bed of Mediterranean plants would find their home and eventually flourish in profusion. On one of the long sides of the lake, a small summerhouse made of Sussex flint and stone had been built, its wooden seats looking out across the water to the terrace and the pillars of what would one day be a classical temple. She could see its foundations from where she stood. They were complete and several of the pillars had already been fashioned and were lying to one side, like giant marble limbs that had somehow become detached from their body. But the magnificent lake, designed to reflect the temple's elegance, was now little more than a muddy pond, and the statue her father had commissioned – a dolphin whose mouth spouted a constant stream of water – rose, strange and solitary, from out of the ruin.

Somewhere a dog howled. It was an unworldly sound funnelling its way to her through the thick evening air. The hairs at the nape of her neck stood to attention, but almost immediately she realised the noise had come from Amberley, from one of her uncle's hounds, and gave it no more thought. Picking her way along the flagstones, she had to lift her skirts clear of the sludge before gingerly circling the large oval of dirty water. She had reached the west corner of the temple when a noise much closer to hand startled her. Wildlife in the garden was prolific and for a moment she thought it must be a fox moving stealthily through the tall trees that grew behind the temple, making his way perhaps to the Wilderness to find his tea. But then she heard a cough. A man. And footsteps, soft but unmistakable. The lateness of the hour was suddenly important. She shouldn't be here. Her mother had warned her often enough that the estate was not secure, that there was nothing to stop a curious passer-by from scaling the six foot wall and enjoying Summerhayes for himself. She took a step back, poised to flee. The gloom of dusk had settled on the garden and the overhanging trees behind the temple workings cast an even deeper shadow across her path. There was a crackle of twigs, a swish of undergrowth.

She turned abruptly.

Chapter Two

'Forgive me, I've startled you.'

A young man's slim form appeared from behind one of the prostrate columns. At the sound of his voice, she half turned back. He was hardly the threatening figure her mother had warned of. She fixed her eyes on his face, looking at him as closely as she dared, and was sure she had seen him before. She *had* seen him before, if only from a distance.

'Are you the architect?' she said uncertainly.

'Not quite.' He gave a slightly crooked smile. 'I'm the architect's assistant, at least until the end of this summer.'

She found herself smiling back. 'And what happens at the end of the summer?'

'My apprenticeship will be over. I'll be the architect you took me for.' He strode towards her, holding out his hand. 'I should introduce myself. My name is Aiden Kellaway.'

'Elizabeth Summer,' she said, trying not to think what Alice would say to this unconventional meeting. Aiden Kellaway's grasp was firm and warm.

'I know who you are. I've seen you on the terrace when you take a stroll with your mother.' He had an attractive face, she couldn't help noticing. He was clean shaven but his light brown hair was luxuriant, falling in an unruly wave above soft green eyes.

Those eyes were resting on her and she said hastily, 'You seem to have met a problem here.' She waved a cuff of shadow lace towards the quagmire.

'The gardeners have certainly. Mr Simmonds and I will keep supervising the building work, but a temple without its lake is a sad sight. Do you know why this has happened?'

'Why there's no water?'

'I know why there's no water – I walked upstream for half a mile and saw the dam that's been built.'

The Amberley estate lay above Summerhayes and Henry Fitzroy had evidently used this advantage to divert the river and render Joshua's beloved garden a sad joke. Elizabeth felt intensely sorry for her father. He was a rough man. A life devoted to making buttons had not conferred the polish needed to succeed in the highest circles, but for all that her father possessed a deep and instinctive love of beauty.

Aiden Kellaway was looking at her enquiringly. 'I meant why your uncle – I'm presuming it is your uncle who ordered the diversion – why he should wish to ruin the most beautiful part of a very beautiful garden.'

She wasn't sure how to answer. She knew the reason only too well but Mr Kellaway was a stranger and she had no wish to confess the family feud. Something in his face, though, invited her to be honest. 'There is enmity between Amberley and Summerhayes. There has been for years and most local people know of it. Anything Uncle Henry can do to upset my father, he will.'

Aiden shook his head. 'That's sad. And to hurt his own sister, too.'

'I doubt he cares much about my mother. He's not that

kind of man.' She stopped abruptly. Honesty was one thing, gossiping in this unguarded fashion quite another. 'In any case,' she hurried on, 'the Italian Garden is my father's idea. Mama never ventures further than the lawn.'

'Why Italian? Does your father have connections there?'

'None that I know of, but when he was very young, he travelled to Italy and spent several months journeying northwards from Rome. He still talks of it. He told me one day that it was a revelation to him, how people all those years ago had created a beauty that endured for centuries. I think it made him want to create something himself – something that would delight people for generations.'

Her father's one Italian excursion, it seemed, had crystallised a yearning that until then had lived only in his heart.

'Your father is a visionary man. Summerhayes is a wonderful project.' Aiden said warmly. 'He can be rightfully proud of creating a glorious site out of what was once barren pasture. Or so I understand.'

'The gardens *are* my father's pride and joy. But the barren pasture, as you call it, once belonged to Amberley.' She would not spell out her uncle's jealousy, she had said too much already, but she saw from the young man's expression that he understood.

He simply nodded and looked out across the swathe of mud to the laurel arch, now faded to shades of grey in the disappearing light. 'I wonder, though, why your uncle is so opposed. Having such a magnificent garden as a neighbour must add distinction to his own property.'

'I doubt he'd agree. Amberley is an old estate and Uncle Henry clings to its past glory. My father has the money to indulge himself with projects such as this.'

'And your uncle does not?'

She would say no more. The subject was too intimate and too painful. Any more and she might reveal the whole sorry business, the transaction between Amberley Hall and her father. A transaction of which for years she'd been only dimly aware.

'I see,' was all he said. But she knew that he was thinking through the answer to a question he couldn't ask: why her mother, a Fitzroy of Amberley, with a family history stretching back to the Conqueror, had married a man like Joshua Summer.

The dusk was closing in and the crêpe de chine dress she had donned for dinner was proving uncomfortably thin. She shivered slightly and he noticed. 'It's getting chilly. May I escort you back to the house?'

'I won't trouble you, Mr Kellaway. You will wish to be getting home and I can find my own way back, even in the gloom. I know the gardens too well to get lost.'

'I'm sure.' He smiled the slightly crooked smile again. 'But I'm walking your way. My bicycle is waiting for me outside the bothy, though I must be quiet collecting it. The boy on duty has to be up and dressed before five.'

She hadn't noticed the bicycle when she'd passed by, but that wasn't surprising. How her father's men came and went barely impinged on her. Why would it? She lived in a bubble, an affluent bubble, but real life went on elsewhere. Or so it had always seemed.

'Do you live far from Summerhayes?'

The bicycle had prompted the question but she was genuinely interested. Then she worried that she had been too personal. The rigours of a London Season had not cured her of the candour her mother deplored. Alice's strictures rang loudly in her ears. They had been repeated often enough for her to know them by heart: *A girl should keep her distance from anyone who is not family or a family friend.*

Aiden seemed to find nothing amiss with her question and answered readily enough: 'I have lodgings in the village. A room with board in one of the cottages by the church.'

'And is it comfortable?'

'Comfortable enough. Though the cooking could be better.'

'It's late. You will have missed your evening meal.'

'I will. But I'll get cold meat and pickles instead – my favourite supper.'

She wondered for a moment how cold meat and pickles tasted, and how wonderful it must be to sit at a kitchen table, still in your work clothes, and just eat. No dressing for dinner, no servant hovering, listening to a stilted conversation, and no trudging through course after unnecessary course before escape beckoned.

'Allow me,' and before she could protest, he'd tucked her hand in his arm and was steering her along the flagged pathway and out beneath the laurel arch into the Wilderness.

'This is an amazing place,' he said, as they followed the winding path towards the walled garden. 'So many rare and beautiful plants.'

'My father chose every tree and shrub. They come from all over the world, I believe. He told me that it was plant hunters in the last century who brought them back to this country, and made a fortune doing so.'

'And each with an adventure attached to it, I'd swear, and a story to tell.'

She wondered what Aiden Kellaway's story might be. In the cool of late evening, the warmth of his body as they

walked side by side was unnerving her, and she tried hard
not to think of it.

'Do you often walk in the gardens?'

She grabbed at the mundane question. 'I take a turn on
the terrace – where you saw me with my mother. Sometimes
I venture a little further.' When I can, she thought. When
I can be free of parents, free of servants.

'Like tonight. What tempted you to wander so far?'

'I suppose because it was such a wonderful evening.'

They had reached the kitchen garden and in the silvery
spread of a just risen moon the most humble of vegetables
had taken on a majestic air.

'I thought it wonderful, too. There was no need for me
to stay behind. I could have finished the few tasks I had in
the morning, and Mr Simmonds urged me to leave with
him. But this evening was too good to waste behind the
door of a poky cottage.'

'Do you enjoy working with Mr Simmonds?' It was
something else she genuinely wanted to know. Questions
seemed to be tripping off her tongue tonight, far more than
she'd ever needed to ask.

'He's a brilliant architect and an excellent mentor. I've
worked with him for five years and learnt a great deal. I'm
lucky he's one of the old school. He likes to work on site
from his own drawings, rather than sit in an office and
direct others. And that suits me very well. Since my uncle
organised the apprenticeship, I've never looked back.'

He stopped walking for a moment and looked down at
her. It was as though he needed to dwell on his own words.
'You know it was a huge piece of good fortune for me that
he met Jonathan – at a race meeting, would you believe?'

'Racing?'

'Jonathan Simmonds is a bit of a gambler,' Aiden admitted, walking on once more, 'but don't tell your father. He might not like to think his architect has such a weakness.'

'And you? Are you a gambler?'

'No, indeed. What would I gamble with? Mind you, my uncle has hardly a penny to his name. But then the Irish can never resist a flutter.'

'He's Irish?' She was learning something new every minute. Right now, though, the Irish were not the most popular of nations. Only yesterday, she'd heard her father fume against the 'Irish trouble' and predict that a civil war there was all but inevitable.

'It's not just my uncle that's Irish. I am too.'

'You don't sound it.' He didn't, though now she was aware, she thought she could detect the slightest of lilts to his voice.

'That's because I've been in England too long. And my aunt and uncle even longer.'

'How long? Why did they come to England? Where do they live?'

The bicycle was propped against the bothy wall, as he'd said. He took hold of the handlebars and wheeled it onto the path that led to a side gate and out onto the village road. She stayed where she was and he turned back to her.

'So many questions, Miss Summer.' She blushed hotly. He was right. She'd been intrusive to the point of rudeness. 'But am I allowed one?'

'Yes, of course,' she said hastily. 'I'm sorry.'

'Then, what are you doing deep in the Sussex countryside? Shouldn't you be in London, having a fine time?'

'I've had a fine time,' she was quick to counter.

'Still… you might enjoy a very different kind of company,

away from Summerhayes.' He pointed to her hands where the faintest traces of paint were still visible. He was far too acute.

'I daub, that's all. And I'm happy enough here.'

'Are you?'

His face glimmered beneath the arc of moonlight and she could just make out his expression. He was considering her intently, as though wanting to drill down into her deepest thoughts, and she found it discomfiting. It was time for her to leave.

Chapter Three

Alice was on alert and heard the side door of the house click shut. She hoped her husband had not. But Joshua was still talking, still vehement, though a good deal calmer now. He seemed to have talked himself out of his anger and she had no wish to provoke a further outburst. She looked through the uncurtained diamonds of window glass and saw only darkness. What was Elizabeth doing walking in the gardens so late? At last her husband's voice dwindled to a stop. He would return to her brother's perfidy soon enough, but, for the moment, she could breathe freely.

'Shall I call Ripley for tea?' she asked hopefully.

He didn't answer but shuffled to the edge of the sofa, then heaved himself to his feet and trod heavily across the polished oak floor. He enjoyed using the telephone, she knew. It was modern and efficient, two words that were his touchstone. His hand had reached for the instrument when she said, as casually as she could, 'Did you think any more about the finishing school?'

'I did not. And the answer is still no.' He turned to face her, a grimace enlivening his otherwise stony expression. 'I thought I'd made it plain that Elizabeth has no need to attend a foreign school. In my view, she is perfectly finished already.'

'She is a credit to the family.' Alice used her most emollient tone. 'But would it not be a good idea to allow her to travel a little before she settles down? You have said yourself how wonderfully foreign travel broadens the mind. And, in Elizabeth's case, it would be particularly beneficial. She would have a new setting in which to paint.'

'She can paint here. She has her own studio, dammit. And as for travelling, she travelled more than enough last year and didn't like it. This is where she belongs.' He stomped back across the polished boards and spread his bulk along the printed velvet of the sofa. The effort pulled the Norfolk jacket tightly across his chest, its buttons looking ready to pop.

'She travelled to London,' Alice said mildly.

'Exactly. And isn't London the greatest city in the world? Even greater than Birmingham, though some would argue differently.' His lips pulled back into the slightest of smiles. When his wife failed to acknowledge the pleasantry, he glared at her. 'Where else should she go?' he asked belligerently. 'I don't want her in Europe. Europe is a dangerous place – more so with every month that passes.'

'But how is that possible? You are still in touch with Germany, are you not? Surely people there won't want trouble. Or in France or anywhere else for that matter.'

'Trade is one thing, war another. I'll keep contact with Germany as long as it remains a good customer. The old factories do well from it. But it doesn't mean I trust them. I don't trust the man who leads them. The Kaiser is a swaggerer and he's unpredictable; he'll make trouble, mark my word. It may appear quiet at the moment but the Germans have the greatest army in the world – that's something we should never forget. And now it has a navy to rival ours.

They've been building a fleet large enough to threaten us at sea. Did you know that?'

She shook her head. She was hazy about the politics of Europe and could not argue. Not that she would, if she'd been Emmeline Pankhurst herself. It was not what women did. But, surely, Elizabeth would be safe in one of the best schools in Switzerland? And her daughter would gain so much from the experience. Different people, different customs, and encounters that could prove important. Introductions. Introductions that could lead to marriage and put the wild ideas Elizabeth had out of her mind. It was typical of Joshua that he couldn't see the need for his daughter to widen her horizons. Summerhayes was the only horizon he could contemplate and what was right for him must be right for Elizabeth. But if the girl were to remain here, things could not stay the same. She approached the subject tentatively.

'If Elizabeth is not to go to Switzerland, we might look for a suitable husband.'

'She had the chance to find a husband and chose not to.'

He wanted to keep his daughter here. Keep her under his fond but watchful eye. And part of her sympathised. Marriage wasn't the gilded promise that mothers held out to their daughters. She, of all women, should know that. But the girl's future had to be considered. Joshua wouldn't always be here and neither would she. Far better that Elizabeth had a home of her own long before that happened. And her daughter would have choice; she would not be forced to marry for money, as her mother had been.

'London may have been the wrong place,' she persisted. 'The men she met there were not perhaps right for her.' Though goodness knows what kind of man would attract her wayward daughter. 'Someone closer at hand, someone from our own county, might suit her better.'

Joshua's shoulders tensed in an angry fashion and she began to think it wise to abandon the conversation, when a quiet knock on the glass doors of the drawing room heralded Ripley and the tea tray. Her husband was forced to swallow his rancour but, when the footman had poured the tea and departed, he said, 'Why can't you leave the girl alone? She's still young. She is happy here. Let her be.'

'She is nineteen years old, Joshua. In a few months' time, she will be twenty. She is in her prime, a time of her life when she should have the pick of husbands.'

'Not like you, you mean.'

The warmth crept into her face and she took hold of the teacup with an unsteady hand. She hadn't wanted the pick of husbands. She'd only ever wanted one, but a solicitor's clerk was never going to match Fitzroy ambition. She had loved Thomas with the purity of the very young, and known herself loved in return. But their fate had been inescapable. Once discovered, the boy had lost his position and been harried out of Sussex. By the time she was despatched to London – a last-ditch attempt to save Amberley – her place was already reserved on the shelf for redundant spinsters.

She could still feel the humiliation of that summer in London. The Season had cost her family dear but failed to attract any offer of marriage, let alone from a man with money. That hadn't surprised her. Since she'd lost Thomas, she had made little effort to please, and she knew she was judged unattractive and insipid. But her family had seemed strangely unprepared for her lack of success, her brother in particular. He'd been a stripling then but it hadn't stopped him from reminding her, whenever opportunity offered, that she was an unwanted daughter. There had been a barrage of unkind comments – on her appearance, on her lack of personality. And it hadn't stopped at taunts. On occasions, he'd grabbed her by the shoulders and physically shaken her or pinched an arm or a hand as he'd passed her chair, just to make sure that she wouldn't forget the family's disapproval. When she'd returned from London, it was with little hope of ever finding a husband. And even less hope of Amberley ever securing the money that would ensure the estate remained in Fitzroy hands. Until Joshua arrived in Sussex.

'No, not like me.' She had taken time to recover her composure. 'Elizabeth's situation is very different. There is no need for any kind of business arrangement.'

'Considering how our business arrangement has worked out, it's as well.' He glowered at her and she was fearful that he would start once more on Henry's most recent act of malice. But he was too busy brooding over past insults.

'I saved your family from bankruptcy, poured thousands into Amberley, and what was my reward? It took me years to wrench land from your brother, land I was owed, land that your father had signed over. I had to go to law, expend even more money to get what was rightfully mine. And the result? Your brother has made trouble wherever and whenever he can. It's clear he won't be satisfied until he reclaims Summerhayes for his own. And, good God wouldn't he like to! A ramshackle manor house and the poorest of ground transformed. He longs to get his hands on what my wealth has created.'

There was a long silence while he drank his tea and looked through her at the wall behind, William Morris's manila daisies seeming to grip all his attention. Whenever her brother acted badly, the old bitterness broke out anew. First her father, then Henry, had attempted to renege on the marriage agreement, and every tactic, every subterfuge, every gambit used to prevent her husband taking possession of land that was rightfully his was engraved on Joshua's heart.

She had picked a bad time to raise the subject. She smoothed the creases from the messaline silk, one of the many expensive dove-coloured gowns Joshua insisted on buying, and took the empty teacups to the tray. He looked up as she did so, coming out of his studied gloom.

'You must drop this idea of brokering a marriage, Alice. It will spell disaster. And there is no need for us to do a thing. Elizabeth will stay at Summerhayes and one day a young man will come along who takes her fancy. I'll be able to inspect him, make sure he's the right sort. And if he is, I'll make him welcome. He can join me in the management of the estate, take some of the weight off my shoulders since William looks unlikely ever to do so.'

'William is only fourteen.' In defence of her youngest, she lost her timidity.

'He is old enough to take an interest, but he remains a child. He hasn't a serious thought in his head. And that boy you've invited here – Oliver, isn't it? – if anything, he's worse. Playing tricks on the servants, laughing in your face. The boy has no respect. But what can you expect coming from a family of Jews? That's a little matter you didn't tell me about.'

Oliver's family was something to which she'd given no thought before agreeing to the boy's stay, and she felt guilty at her oversight. But then there was rarely a moment when she didn't feel guilty.

'Once we can send him packing,' Joshua pronounced, 'he doesn't come again.'

She wasn't going to argue for Oliver. She wasn't at all sure herself of the young boy's suitability. Instead, she steered the conversation back to Elizabeth.

'You wouldn't wish Elizabeth to get into trouble,' she said cautiously.

'Of course, I wouldn't. What are you talking about, woman?'

'She's young and headstrong. All this nonsense with the suffragettes – it's had an effect on her.'

Joshua gave a loud tsk. 'Don't mention those women in my presence. They are a scandal, a disgrace to their sex.'

'Elizabeth reads the papers. She is aware of what is happening beyond our sleepy corner of the country.'

'Is she intending to create a disturbance, too, then?' He gave a snort of derision. 'In parliament perhaps or maybe at the racetrack. Should I give her a little hatchet, do you think, so she can join her sisters in slashing the nation's works of art?'

'I'm sure Elizabeth has no such ideas,' her mother said seriously. 'It's their talk of female independence, female equality, that has caught her imagination.'

She saw that at last he was paying attention. 'What has she been saying?'

'Only that she sympathises with their aims. And that a woman should be able to decide her own future.' This latter sentiment was barely murmured.

Despite his corpulence, Joshua bounced up from the sofa, his annoyance lending him flight. He began to pace up and down the drawing room, backwards and forwards across the soft tufts of the Axminster, until he had bruised its thick pile into a clearly marked track. He came to rest, towering over her.

'And what precisely does that mean – decide her own future?' His growl threatened trouble. 'Doesn't she have future enough here with me? I've been a good father; some would say too good. I've let her twist me to her wishes more times than I care to remember.'

'You have,' she soothed. 'But perhaps as a good father, as good parents,' she corrected, 'we should take time to look for a suitable husband. A man who could guide her and guard her from getting into – trouble.'

'And where do you propose to find him?'

She was glad he didn't question the nature of any trouble. In some ways, she knew their daughter better than he, knew her wilful nature, the passion of which she was capable. For a clever man, he could be amazingly blind. He had only to look to himself to see his daughter mirrored there. The hours Elizabeth spent in her studio could only go so far in sublimating such feelings, Alice reasoned, and the thought of trouble was never far from her mind. Elizabeth's solitary walks did nothing to calm her. A gently reared girl did not walk alone and certainly not after sunset – her daughter knew the rules well enough, but took no heed of them.

When she didn't answer, he warned, 'If Elizabeth should ever marry, it must be to a man of stature. I'll not have her marry beneath her – a tradesman or some such.'

It was a perfect irony. Joshua was such a tradesman, a very rich one it was true, but a tradesman nevertheless. The fact that he appeared oblivious to the contradiction gave her the courage to confess what she had in mind.

'We should, perhaps, look to family connections. My family connections.'

'I married you for your connections, remember, and where has that got me? And since you are all but separated from your family, it's not likely to get us anywhere now.'

She ignored his jeering tone and took a slow breath before she said, 'Henry might aid us.'

He gave a bitter laugh. 'Aid us! The man has done nothing but cause harm, or try to, since the moment I dared to reclaim what was mine from his penniless estate.'

She disregarded the slight to her family home and pushed on. 'But this might be something with which he would be willing to help.'

The Fitzroys had saved their estate through marrying her to Joshua, but they had also lost caste. Another marriage might help them regain it. Henry had hated the necessity that assigned her to Joshua – she'd sold herself, he had said – even though it was he who had encouraged their father to sign the contract. He who had placed the pen in the older man's hand. Might this be an opportunity then to salvage some honour from a bad deed?

'Elizabeth is his niece,' she went on, 'and a good marriage would redound to his credit as much as ours. She is a beautiful girl and there is nothing to say she could not make a very good marriage.'

Joshua was silent. She had given him pause. Last year, he had been furious with his daughter for rejecting two acceptable suitors, but his anger hadn't lasted. Deep down, she knew, he'd wanted to keep his daughter by his side. But if, after all, Elizabeth were to make that splendid marriage, it would be a crown to his career. A trumpet call announcing to the world that here was a man who was as good as any of his neighbours.

He walked slowly over to the blank window, a new pair of balmoral boots creaking beneath his weight, then turned and frowned at her.

'You'll have to tackle him then. He's your brother. His latest act of spite makes it intolerable that I should exchange even a "good morning" with the man.'

She was not a courageous person, but where her children's welfare was concerned, she could fight as well as the next woman. Any suggestion that Joshua had not thought her brother worthy of consulting on such a delicate family matter would antagonise Henry even further. If that were possible.

'The approach will only be successful if it comes from you, Joshua,' she said firmly. He didn't, as she expected, immediately rail at her and she was emboldened to continue, 'We will see the Fitzroys in a few days – at morning service. And church might be the very place to make peace with them.'

Again, Joshua said nothing. She had no idea what he was thinking. All she could hope was that her words had hit home and, come Sunday, he would unbend sufficiently at least to speak to his brother-in-law.

The difficult evening had taken its toll and her head had begun its familiar ache. She rose from her chair, stiff from sitting so long. 'I'm feeling a little weary. And I need to check on William before I retire.'

'At his age! Ridiculous! You mollycoddle the boy,' were her husband's parting words.

She said nothing in reply but walked out into the hall. She would look in on the boys before she slept. Satisfy herself that all was well with her youngest and dearest. As for the business of Elizabeth's marriage, she hoped she'd said enough to begin some kind of thaw. The Summer family led a lonely life and if Henry could be persuaded to introduce one or two likely suitors to their restricted circle, then youth and proximity might do the rest. It was important that her daughter find the right man, a man she could love and respect. Not for Elizabeth the pain of an ill-assorted liaison or the indignity of being bought and sold in a marriage made by others for others. Not an arranged marriage, but an encouraged one. That was a more comfortable thought.

Chapter Four

William's door was slightly ajar and she pushed it open a little further. The room was large and high-ceilinged, its tall windows giving onto a rolling expanse of green and filling the space with light and air. It was the room William had chosen for himself when he'd emerged from the nursery. She remembered how proud he'd been, a small boy sleeping alone for the very first time. The room might be spacious but there was barely a spot that was not filled to overflowing with evidence of the passing years. Over time, her son had followed many interests, this shy, sensitive boy with his finely honed curiosity. This summer, it was nature that had taken hold of his imagination – several boards stood at angles to the the wall, displaying leaves of every shape and size and colour, all carefully mounted and labelled. The large wooden desk she'd had the men bring down from the attic stood beneath the window and was piled high with reference books. *The Trees of Great Britain & Ireland* lay open on the floor.

But the toy theatre that had once dominated William's time was huddled against the far wall. Cornford had been skilful in producing a facsimile stage made of wood and cardboard, with a row of tin footlights with oil burning wicks along the front. For years, every penny of William's pocket money had been spent on sheets of characters and scenes. He'd managed to persuade Elizabeth to write several short plays and even help him perform them. Since then, the theatre had been supplanted by other hobbies, as once it had supplanted the regiments of lead soldiers. They were crammed into a battered wooden trunk, along with the clockwork train that had once run the circumference of the room.

But there in the centre was what really mattered – two beds, side by side, and two boys sleeping soundly, exhausted by their day in the sun. How well her son looked! Oliver would never be a favourite with her but it was enough that William liked and trusted him. She allowed herself a satisfied smile and backed quietly out of the room.

At the sound of his mother's approach, William had shut his eyes tightly. He didn't want her fussing over him, asking him why he was still awake, offering to bring medicine to help him rest. He wanted simply to lie there, to lie and watch Oliver sleep. He'd been watching him ever since his friend had drifted into a deep slumber. Olly was stretched lengthways down the bed, the covers thrown to one side. One arm was propped beneath his head, his dark hair a clear contrast to the white linen of the pillowcase. The other arm lay outside the covers, slightly bent towards William and, in the narrow beam of moonlight that crept between the drawn curtains, he could see the small dark hairs on Oliver's arm. They looked soft and inviting, and he felt a strong impulse to reach out and stroke them. It left him confused, disturbed. Olly was his friend. That was the sort of thing you did with girls, he'd heard, though he could never imagine himself touching a girl. You didn't do it with friends. Chaps pushed each other around, cuffed each other's ears in play, but that was different. Everyone did that. What would Olly say if he woke to find his friend stroking his arm? He would think William had run mad and he'd be right.

This was the first time they had ever shared a bedroom, since at school they slept in different dormitories. And they were taught by different teachers, too, so their hours together were precious. They would meet at break times, meal times as well, and after prep if it were possible. It was Olly who had rescued him one evening from Highgrove's biggest bully and that kindly act had cemented their alliance. Since then, they'd become the best of friends. The two musketeers, Olly had called them. How right that had felt; it hadn't seemed to matter then that he didn't fit in, would never fit in. It wasn't just his background that was wrong, it was the way he felt. That was all wrong, too. When his classmates whispered about girls, it made him curl up inside. He pretended to be interested, anything to keep from another beating, but those sniggering conversations made him feel odder than ever. He couldn't imagine wanting to do what the boys spoke of.

He looked across at Olly again, his gaze fixed on the boy's beautiful skin, and was awash with a strange hollowness. Bewildered, he tossed himself to the other side of the bed, his back to Oliver. At school, there were rules to follow, orders to obey, and daily life was cut and dried. But these last few weeks had been different. It was this magical summer that was at fault. That and the beauty and freedom of the gardens. It was being at Summerhayes that was making him anxious. Nothing was cut and dried here. Not with Olly. Boundaries seemed to be dissolving, growing fainter every day. There was nothing to grasp, no certainty to hang on to. How was he to deal with that?

Chapter Five

'Miss Elizabeth! Wake up, Miss Elizabeth. Your father wants you downstairs.'

With the tug at her bedclothes, Elizabeth surfaced slowly from a very deep sleep. She opened her eyes the barest fraction, shielding them with her hand from the brightness in the room. It was gilding the satinwood furniture with its brilliance and had settled in a pool of gold on the embroidered bedspread directly beneath her feet. She glanced at the carriage clock on her bedside table. It was very late. Sunday was no day of rest at Summerhayes and right now she should be at the breakfast table.

'Thank you, Ivy.' She took the teacup the maid was offering.

Between yawns, she sipped at the hot liquid while Ivy's black-clad figure moved quietly around the room, gathering up items of cast off clothing and sorting them for washing or mending. As soon as the maid judged her mistress sufficiently awake, she drew back the curtains, their stencilled linen vivid in the bright sunlight. A vista of soft green and splashed colour crowded in on them.

'It's going to be another fine one, by the look of it.' She smiled at the day's promise.

'That it will, miss.' The girl wore an even wider smile. 'And what dress will you be wearing?'

'I don't know. Nothing special – it's only Sunday service.'

Then she thought again. Would Aiden Kellaway be at church this morning? It was possible, if he had lodgings in the village. It was possible that he'd been in church all these weeks past, but she hadn't known. She shook her head at the thought and then realised how odd she must look. But if she were thinking at all sensibly, he wouldn't be there. He must be a Catholic and would never attend St Mary's. Or he was busy and still working in his spare time on the temple plans. Or he was simply godless. Her mind swung wildly from one proposition to another, until she became quite cross with herself. It shouldn't matter whether he was there or not, but somehow it did and the fact annoyed her greatly. She'd already spent far too long thinking about him.

And far too long growing annoyed. She'd been ruffled by him, ruffled by his assumption that she wasn't happy at Summerhayes, and knowing he was right only added to her annoyance. She wasn't happy. Life on the estate was dull – no one visited and nothing happened. But her dissatisfaction went deeper than that. While she lived here, her art would remain hidden. There was little chance of ever becoming the professional painter she longed to be. In London, it might be different. But then she hadn't been any happier there and had been glad when the Season ended. Plunged into a summer of flower shows and exhibitions, races and regattas, she'd found society frenetic. It was not the London she wanted or needed. She'd danced at ten balls a night, but the mad tempo masked a falsity that struck her acutely. She'd not belonged there any more than she belonged at Summerhayes. But she didn't need a man to tell her that, and a man she barely knew. This morning she would show herself content with her world – just in case he was there.

'I'll wear the Russian green,' she decided. And when Ivy looked uncertain, added, 'The moiré silk the dressmaker delivered last week?'

'I remember – such a handsome dress,' her maid enthused. 'I hung it behind the green cloak, but you'll not be needing that this morning! The colour will show off your hair something lovely though. Will you wear it up?'

'There's no time. Just pin it back and maybe we can find a ribbon to match the dress.'

Ivy went busily to work, pulling the gown from the wardrobe and laying it across the old nursing chair to hang out the creases. Various pieces of underwear were whisked from the chest of drawers and then she was delving into the squat wooden box that sat on the dressing table in search of a ribbon. All the time, the girl hummed quietly to herself.

Elizabeth swung her legs out of the bed. 'You sound remarkably happy.'

'I should be, miss. It's my banns today.'

'Of course, it is. I'm so sorry. I'd forgotten.'

'I don't mind. Neither does Eddie. We don't want a lot of fuss and bother. The next three weeks the banns will be called and then we can lie low for a while.'

'It's September, isn't it? The wedding?'

'We've fixed it for the fifth – we're saving hard.'

Elizabeth knew that money was scarce for them both and had wondered if she dared ask her father to raise Eddie's pay. Cars were still a novelty in the countryside and chauffeurs even more so. But when the gleaming dark green Wolseley had arrived from Birmingham last year, Eddie Miller had performed the small miracle of transferring his driving skills from horse to car. The day he'd donned a motoring uniform of drab grey, together with leather gauntlets and leggings and a visored cap and goggles, he had become an entirely different man from the groom who only weeks previously had flicked his whip at a recalcitrant horse. Surely he deserved reward for that. And reward, if Joshua only knew it, for refusing her request that he teach her to drive this mechanical beast. That had been a step too far, even for a warm-hearted Eddie.

She wanted to help the couple, but she was nervous of tackling Joshua in his present mind. Her father had been mercifully quiet these last few days, but it didn't mean he had forgotten his anger over the derelict lake, and the smallest annoyance could light the spark again.

Aloud, she said, 'Is the bathroom free, do you know?'

'I've the bath running now. Master William and his friend were in and out of there this morning like the shake of a lamb's tail.'

'I bet they were!'

When she walked into the breakfast room half an hour later, it was to find the silver salvers lining the buffet table almost empty. The family had already eaten. She forked a slice of ham and started to spoon scrambled egg onto her plate, but then for the second time that morning saw the hands of the clock. There was no time and she would have to go hungry. She hurried out into the hall, skimming its black and white chequered tiles, and out of the front door where the small family group had gathered to wait.

'You're not driving us this morning, Eddie?' The car stood gleaming on the driveway and Eddie Miller, dressed in his Sunday best, was gently flicking the last spot of dust from its shining chrome.

'Them's my orders, Miss Elizabeth. But I'll be in church, alongside Ivy.'

'Of course you will. Your banns are to be called today.'

His face lit with a warmth she could almost touch. 'It's a special day for sure,' he said, 'and your pa was agreeable to walk. It's not often Ivy and me get to be in church together.'

Ivy, she knew, would make sure her intended went to at least one service on a Sunday. Now that the couple were to marry and occupy the rooms above the motor house, it would be more important than ever to keep the master happy. Not that her father was a devout man, but aping the manners of the aristocracy had become essential to him, and a servant who did not attend church would be a discredit.

Joshua had a detaining hand on Oliver's arm and was pointing upwards to the half timbering on the front façade of the house, lecturing the bored youth on how his personal choice of weathered, unstained oak had so beautifully blended a modern Arts and Crafts mansion into the land-scape.

He stopped mid-sentence when he caught sight of his daughter and walked over to her. 'You've made us late,' he grumbled, but softened the words by smoothing an errant strand of hair from her forehead.

'If we walk briskly, we will be in good time,' Alice said pacifically, unfolding her sunshade. 'And a walk should help curb some high spirits.' She looked pointedly towards Oliver, who, having escaped Joshua's grasp, had taken to kicking loose gravel along the drive and was attempting to inveigle William into a competition.

Her father sounded an irritated harrumph and rammed a felt homburg onto his head. He pointed his cane at the lodge gates ahead. 'Come,' he ordered.

They came, trooping after him down the magnificent avenue of ornamental dogwood, its profusion of creamy bracts just beginning to unfurl their enormous waxy flower heads. Behind the family, the first group of servants, out of uniform but soberly dressed, followed at a respectful distance. She was glad she had worn her second-best boots, Aiden Kellaway not withstanding. It was less than half a mile along a country lane to the tiny village green and the Norman church that overlooked it, but quite long enough for new boots to pinch.

The walk this morning, though, was delightful. Banks of primroses shone yellow on either side of them and beneath the shade of the hawthorn hedge, the deep, sweet smell of bluebells filled the air. Above, swallows skittered across a sky of unclouded blue. She wondered whether this might be the time to broach the subject of Ivy's marriage. The morning was the most beautiful nature could bestow and her father was striding out as though, for once, he had a real wish to attend church. But when she drew abreast of him, his expression was anything but promising and she decided she would wait her moment. All would depend, she guessed, on the meeting with Henry Fitzroy. This would be their first encounter since the lake debacle. The Fitzroys were bound to be in church; they never missed a Sunday, never missed the chance to sit ostentatiously in the family pew. Alice had as much right as they to a seat there, but she never took it. The Summer family sat to the rear; years ago, a tacit agreement had emerged within the congregation that this was where Joshua's family belonged. Her mother did not appear to mind the discrimination and the thought crossed Elizabeth's mind as she entered the church that Alice was glad to be away from her brother. She was scared of him. Why, she didn't know. Uncle Henry had never scared her.

She could see him now. He was a tall man and his head and shoulders were clearly visible through the nodding plumes and feathers of the women's toques, donned for this special moment of a special day. He sat rigidly straight, his glance never deviating from the stained glass figure immediately ahead. The window, fittingly donated by the Fitzroy family, held the image of Jesus in an unusually martial pose. Aunt Louisa sat to one side of her husband and, next to her, Dr Daniels. That seemed odd. It appeared they had a lot to say to each other, small sharp whispers between the hymns or as Eddie Miller's and Ivy's banns were read or as the vicar made his way to the pulpit. She wondered if her aunt or uncle might be feeling unwell, to need the doctor in attendance.

When the last prayer had been said, the congregation trickled from the church to shake the minister's hand as he waited in the porch to greet them. She had thanked him for his sermon and begun to walk along the brick path to the lych gate, when she realised that her mother still lingered by the church door. She looked around and saw her father taking an inordinate interest in several of the more ancient tombstones, their engravings barely visible beneath the lichen. Of William and Oliver there was no sign. They had sat almost entirely silent during the service, and she'd been about to congratulate them on their forbearance, when like two young colts freed from harness, they had chased off, one after another, to the fields that lay at the back of the church. Her mother appeared distracted and seemed not to have noticed.

It was a feeling Elizabeth shared when Aiden Kellaway emerged from the stone porch and came up to her. She had not seen him in church, had hardly dared look for him. And now he was here, in person rather than in thought, and she was most definitely distracted. He looked a good deal smarter than when she'd encountered him in the Italian Garden, though his hair had not remembered it was the Sabbath and still waved wildly across his forehead.

'Good morning, Miss Summer.'

Her mother turned sharply at the unfamiliar voice and she became conscious that Alice's eyes were fixed on them.

Her colour mounted. 'Good morning, Mr Kellaway. I hope you are well.' She tried for a neutral tone.

He gave a small nod. 'And you, Miss Summer?'

'Indeed, yes. And how is your work progressing?'

'Well, I thank you. And yours?'

'My work?' She sounded bewildered.

'Your painting.'

That left her more bewildered still and very slightly affronted. Art was not work, not in her world. It was an acceptable hobby for a young woman, that was how her family thought of it. And most other families, too. There were women, she knew, who'd escaped the straitjacket, a few who'd attended art school and were even painting for a living. Laura Knight, for instance – she'd heard her spoken of last year in London. But they were exceptional and she was not. At Summerhayes, she remained alone in sensing the true nature of what she did. Alone in knowing the passion that gripped her. But it was a secret, brooding passion, and one she had never shared.

'It's going well,' she stuttered, thinking of the lake scene now emerging from the canvas in her studio. 'But tell me about the temple.'

'Tomorrow we raise the first of the columns – it's an important moment. We should have a good idea then of how the finished building will look. But I fear the lake will be a blot on the picture.'

'The stream is still dammed then? I'm sorry to hear it.'

She was burbling. She must sound ridiculous but she had to say something. For days, she'd allowed her mind to conjure an image of him, hear his voice, imagine a conversation. Now faced with the reality, she was flustered and flailing.

But he treated her remark seriously, or had the good manners to do so. 'As far as I know, the situation remains the same. Though I sense there may be moves afoot.'

'In what way?'

'I've a feeling it's to break the dam that has been constructed, though I know little of what's planned.'

It was probably as well to know little. Breaking the dam sounded altogether too grave, but his words reminded her that her father had yesterday been closeted with Mr Harris and several of his men for some hours.

'You must pay the Italian Garden another visit,' Aiden was saying, 'and see the temple as it rises. There's an excellent view from the summerhouse and the pathway around the lake has now dried completely. We have been lucky with the weather.'

'It would be good to see it,' she said impulsively.

But then checked herself. Would she go? She found herself looking into a pair of misty green eyes and thought that she might. Her mother would be shocked by such forwardness, and her father disapprove heartily of her mingling with men he considered servants. But the chance of a small adventure was enticing.

She became conscious that Aiden was looking at her in the same intent way that earlier she'd run from, and found herself trying to fill the silence that had grown between them. 'At least today you can forget about the temple. Sunday must be a day of leisure, even for you.'

He smiled down at her and she grew warm beneath his gaze. 'Will it be meat and pickles for lunch?' she gabbled. She'd remembered the supper he'd spoken of and there was something that appealed to her in that simple meal.

'No, indeed.' His eyes lit with laughter. 'On Sunday, Mrs Boxall treats her lodgers to a feast – a leg of lamb at the very least. A trifle singed around the edges, but nevertheless roasted meat. And, if we're lucky, a slice of Sussex Pond pudding to follow.'

She was about to ask him how such a pudding tasted, when her mother called to her. Whatever had distracted Alice, it was not weighty enough for her to ignore her daughter's protracted conversation. 'Elizabeth,' she called sharply, 'I need you here.'

She was apologetic. 'Enjoy your meal, Mr Kellaway.'

'And yours too, Miss Summer.'

'Who was that?' her mother asked, as she reached her side.

'One of the men working on the temple, Mama. He is apprenticed to Mr Simmonds.'

The information seemed unwelcome. 'You should not

be talking to him for so long,' Alice scolded. 'Your place is beside me.'

She felt the familiar wash of suffocation, the familiar burn of annoyance. But any urge to challenge her mother died when Henry Fitzroy and his wife emerged from the church, their son and his tutor a step behind. Dr Daniels was at the rear of the small party. She hadn't noticed Gilbert in the church, but of course he would have been there. Her young cousin was too small and too quiet, altogether too quiet. She saw her aunt bend her head towards her son, the large plumes on her headdress almost smothering him. Louisa was looking extraordinarily smart, she thought.

'Greet your uncle and aunt, Elizabeth,' her mother almost hissed into her ear.

'Good morning, Uncle Henry, Aunt Louisa,' she said obediently.

Henry stopped mid-path. 'Good morning.' He doffed his hat abruptly and then went to move on.

'Henry, we need to speak to you.' Her mother sounded bold. 'Louisa, you too. On a private matter.'

The doctor by then had drawn level with them and looked surprised, but he bowed a polite farewell and walked on. Louisa, looking equally surprised, hustled away her young son and his instructor, then took up position in the lea of her husband, casting an uneasy eye at him. Elizabeth, too, was uneasy. It looked very much as though another confrontation might be looming – Joshua's anger over the destruction of his lake still burnt brightly – but surely not on a Sunday and not on consecrated ground.

While she was trying to make sense of the situation, her mother turned back to her. 'Go and find William,' she said abruptly.

She blinked. She had never heard Alice sound so commanding. And hadn't she just been instructed to stay by her mother's side? 'Go!' Alice urged, when her daughter remained where she was.

She gave the slightest shrug of her shoulders and went.

Chapter Six

'What is all this?' Henry said roughly.

'We are hoping the unfortunate events of the last few days can be forgotten. Are we not, Joshua?' Her husband's marked reluctance to join them had sent her spirits sinking. 'Are we not?' she asked again, a little despairingly. At that, he gave the required nod, but without conviction.

Henry drew himself to his full height, his chest resembling a pouter pigeon in full strut. 'The events, as you term them, Alice, are not in my view the slightest bit unfortunate. They follow from your husband's determination to purloin water from my estate.'

Joshua took a step forward. 'The water is as much Summerhayes' as it is yours,' he began dangerously.

Alice stepped between them. 'Please, there has been too much argument already. Henry, you have made your point, I think. We are kin and we should not be quarrelling in this way.'

'Kinship appears to mean nothing to your husband –' again her brother refused to use Joshua's name. '– but he would do well to remember the importance of family connections.'

'Such connections mean a lot to both of us,' Alice protested, 'and particularly now.' She looked across at Joshua.

Why wasn't he helping her? He had promised to play his part, but instead was standing blank faced, a pillar of granite.

Louisa, who until this moment had remained a silent onlooker, suddenly expressed an interest. 'Why now?' she asked, glancing up at her husband as though seeking his approval.

She is hoping for scandal, Alice thought. Her sister-in-law might come from a high-born family, but she had always an ear for gossip, with conversation that would fit her for the servants' hall.

'We wish to talk to you about Elizabeth,' Joshua put in unexpectedly. 'She is your niece, after all.'

'I'm well aware she is my niece.' Henry's chest expanded further. 'Are you hoping that she will beg me for water, now you are prevented from stealing it?'

The blank face had gone. In its place, Joshua's lips tightened and Alice could see his knuckles grow white from the effort of keeping his hands at his sides.

'It is something entirely other. She needs to be married,' he said tautly. 'At least, Alice seems to think so.'

'And we would like her to marry with honour,' Alice interjected.

'Ah.' Henry was beginning to understand.

'You have the contacts, or so Alice tells me,' Joshua said loftily. Then, unable to maintain his indifference, the bitterness spilt out. 'You may have contrived to exclude me from society in a most underhand fashion, but I trust you will not treat your niece as shabbily.'

'My niece is a lady,' Henry said deliberately. 'As is your wife.' Joshua's knuckles whitened further. 'I would naturally treat them as such, and if you are looking for a suitable match for Elizabeth, it may be that I can help.'

Alice could see the calculating look in her brother's eyes, a look she knew from old. Most often it was accompanied by a charming smile, and Henry could be charming if it gave him advantage. He had charmed Papa into permanent indulgence from the day he was born; even their astringent mother had buckled beneath the onslaught: his concerned brow, his gentle voice, the smile which said it understood. But if you watched him carefully, and his sister always did, his eyes gave him away. Today, he appeared willing to swallow his rancour and agree to find a suitor for Elizabeth because it meant influence, and even greater influence if that suitor were from a distant branch of the family. It was a disturbing prospect but she must swallow her fear and do this for her daughter. The Fitzroys dotted any number of family trees, from the highest aristocracy to the lowest squire, and Henry was the only person likely to produce the right man.

'That is very good news, is it not?' She turned to Joshua, but her husband merely grunted.

'For myself, I think it an admirable idea,' her sister-in-law offered. 'Elizabeth lives a secluded life, and must meet very few young men. And suitable husbands are scarce at the best of times. We would hate our niece to be reduced to marrying badly. To a man of business, for instance.'

She seemed to find comedy in the words, a spasm passing across her face and leaving her lips disagreeably twisted. Alice surprised herself by a strong desire to slap her sister-in-law, but was thankful that Joshua had stayed silent. It was a silence, though, that teetered on the edge, and she knew he dared not speak for risk of an uncontrollable rage. Still, she tried to think fairly. Louisa had said only what Joshua himself had declared a few days ago.

Henry nodded a dismissal and took his wife's arm. He was making ready to leave when the vicar, half walking, half running along the churchyard path, arrived in their midst and put out a detaining hand. He was breathing heavily. 'May I trouble you? Is the doctor still here?'

'He left minutes ago,' Henry answered abruptly. 'What ails you, Reverend?'

The vicar was still finding it difficult to breathe and did not answer directly. 'Then I must send for him,' he puffed. 'Ah, Mr Summer.' He'd caught sight of Joshua standing in the shadow of a large gravestone. 'You are the very man I need.'

'I thought it was the doctor you sought.'

'Yes, yes,' the vicar said a trifle testily. 'But he is one of your men, Mr Summer. Dumbrell, I think his name is. He is quite badly injured.'

'Dumbrell injured? How can that be?'

'He has a bust head. There has been some kind of con- tretemps. It's difficult to make sense of the man's words but it appears there has been a fight – over a dam?' Henry stared at the vicar, disbelievingly. 'He and his fellows, as far as I can gather, were attempting to demolish it but then a gang of men appeared and thought otherwise.'

'But we did it, Mr Summer. In the end, we did!' A man caked in mud, blood streaming from a large wheal across his forehead, staggered into view.

'We did it,' Dumbrell repeated. 'And them bastards from Amberley – begging your pardon, ladies – they couldn't stop us. That water is flowing neat and pretty. Your lake'll be full in no time, gaffer.'

'What!' Henry was now the one who looked as though

he would erupt into uncontrollable fury, while the smile on Joshua's face spread slowly from ear to ear.

'Good man, Dumbrell,' he said. 'We'll get the doctor to you immediately.'

'*Good man?*' screamed Henry. 'You'll not hear the last of this, Summer. But you have heard the last of any help you might think to extract from me.'

'You need not concern yourself, my dear chap. We find we don't require your aid after all. My money will do the work. It saved your neck years ago and now it will buy Elizabeth a far better husband than any you might propose. Your sister may still have a weakness for her old home and think Amberley important, but in truth the place no longer matters. The Fitzroys no longer matter.'

Henry was gobbling with rage but her husband, Alice could see, was enjoying his triumph to the full. He went on remorselessly: 'And while we're speaking of county matters, Reverend –' he turned to the vicar who was looking distressed and perplexed in equal measure, '– I feel it may be time for you to consider a change. You will be aware that mine is the premier estate in our beautiful part of Sussex. It seems only right, therefore, that I offer Summerhayes as a setting for the village fête.'

'But—' the vicar began.

'I know, I know. It has always been at Amberley, but, as I say, times change. The fête has surely outgrown its origins, and though I grant you Amberley may have a faded appeal, I think such an important event in our local calendar, should be allowed a more modern stage. It is Summerhayes, after all, that has the money to make it the very best.'

The vicar tried again to speak, but was steamrollered into silence. 'Consider for a moment!' Joshua boomed.

'The Summerhayes lawn is so much more spacious than Amberley's and the gardens are in full flower. I am more than happy for the villagers to wander the entire estate if they so wish. I am certain that your parishioners would be most eager for the opportunity. What do you say?'

'Well, yes,' the vicar stammered. 'It's a most generous offer. But Mr Fitzroy—' He broke off. Henry had turned his back on the group, and was marching down the path towards the churchyard gate, his wife stumbling to keep up with him.

'Well?' Joshua raised an enquiring eyebrow.

'Thank you, Mr Summer,' the vicar said weakly. 'I'm happy to accept on behalf of the fête committee.'

Chapter Seven

June, 1914

They had spent all morning building a ramshackle shelter deep in the Wilderness and now they were unsure of what to do with it. William stood back and considered it from a distance. He had to admit it looked a little odd, a boy-made structure dropped out of nowhere into this wild place, besieged on all sides with lush plantings of every kind of foreign shrub. Behind them, drifts of bamboo masked from view the pathway that wound its way through the Wilderness. And behind the massed bamboo, row after row of tree ferns and palms, an ever-changing profusion of shades and textures. As a small boy, he'd had a particular love for the tree ferns. He would fold himself into a ball and hide beneath their long wavering fronds, then wait for Elizabeth to track him down. She would be forced to search long and hard and, when she found him, he would most often be asleep, curled into the fern's green heart.

Oliver swished at the towering vegetation with a broken tree branch, one of the few left over from their labours. 'Are we going to camp here or not?' he asked moodily.

William looked uncertainly at his friend. Oliver was a boy who liked action but he wasn't himself at all sure how wise camping would be. 'There are all kinds of animals prowling through the Wilderness at night, you know.'

'Don't tell me you've got cold feet.'

'How would we manage it anyway?' he defended himself. 'We'd have to sneak bedding from the linen cupboard. And apart from lumping it all the way down here, can you imagine how we'd get it from the house unseen?'

It was midday and the sun was directly overhead. Oliver wiped a sweaty hand over his forehead. 'Well, we need to use it in some way. I haven't spent the last three hours killing myself for nothing.'

He was right, William thought, it was stupid to build the shelter and then not use it, but he wished Olly would sometimes be a little less forceful. 'Sorry,' he mumbled.

Olly shrugged his shoulders, but when he saw William's downcast face, his mood changed and he walked over to his friend and gave him a hug. 'What we need first is something to drink. Then we'll be able to think straight.'

'I'll run back to the kitchen and grab some lemonade,' William said eagerly. 'Cook won't mind.'

'Take care that your mother doesn't see you then, or she'll send you on some tedious errand.'

He thought it more than likely. He knew his mother would be looking for him. 'I'll have to go up to the house and see Mama, in any case. I can bring the lemonade back with me.'

'Why? What's happening?'

'The doctor is there.'

'So? What's that to do with you?'

'He has to listen to my heart and he's coming this morning.'

Oliver frowned. 'What's wrong with your heart? You never said you were ill.'

'I'm not. Not any more, at least. But Mama insists that Dr Daniels comes every month.'

His friend pulled a face. 'What's the matter with parents? Wouldn't life be perfect without them?'

'Pretty much,' William agreed. 'But I'll get it over with – it's only a five minute check – then I'll sneak into the kitchen and bring some grub as well as the lemonade. We can have a proper picnic.'

'Great idea, Wills. That's what we'll do with the shelter – it will be our daytime retreat. Somewhere we go when we don't want to be found.'

William began to wade through the shoulder-high grasses, walking in the direction of the invisible path, but then stopped. He put his hand up to shield his eyes and tried to focus through the shimmer of heat. 'Look there,' he called back to Olly, 'through the bamboo. It's my sister, isn't it? What's she doing down here?'

Olly pushed his way forward and the boys stood shoulder to shoulder, peering intently through the jungle of greenery. 'I don't think she wants to be found either,' William said thoughtfully.

Oliver stood on tiptoe. 'I can just make her out. She's in deep blue. But who's that she's with?'

'I think it's one of the architects. He works for Mr Simmonds. He was in church on Sunday.'

They stood, silently watching the distant tableau. Olly gave a low whistle. 'She certainly seems interested in him.'

'Do you think so?'

'Stand this side of me. You'll get a better view.' Elizabeth was clearly visible from the new position. She was standing beneath the laurel arch and Aiden Kellaway was by her side. They were talking animatedly to one another.

William's mouth drooped at the sight. 'She better not get too interested,' he said in a glum voice.

'Why, what's the matter? Don't you fancy him as a brother-in-law,' Olly teased. 'She could marry him, couldn't she? If he wanted to.'

'I don't think so.'

'But she's old.'

'Old enough, I suppose, but our parents would never agree to it. In fact, Mama would be furious if she saw her talking to him. Elizabeth has to marry someone a lot more special, I think.'

'In what way special?'

'Someone who is important.'

'You mean someone who's rich.'

'Not necessarily. Father would supply the dibs, I guess. But someone from an old family. That's what he wants.'

'Then he's a snob.' Oliver was definite in his judgement.

William simply nodded. He was tired of the conversation and the heat was making him drowsy. He was also perturbed. A dark shadow had seemed to flit across a sky that was cloudless, though he could not say what it might be or why it worried him. He forgot Dr Daniels and his stethoscope and collapsed into the hollow the boys had made, settling himself under a tree fern as he'd done so many years ago. Oliver followed suit. The quest for lemonade was temporarily abandoned. Overhead, the sun was a glowing ball, shepherding the exhausted boys towards sleep. His eyelids were almost closed when he sensed a wavering at the corner of his sight.

He sat upright, his eyes wide. 'Look, Olly, isn't that the

most fabulous butterfly?' The amber wings fluttered closer. 'And look at those splodges of black. It seems to have veins on each wing. But how beautiful it is.'

'Do you know the name?'

'I'm not sure. I think it may be a kind of fritillary. It's large enough. I'll have to look it up when we get back.'

'Shall I catch it for you? Then you can put it in your collection.'

'No!' he shouted. 'Leave it be.' And he cupped his hands around the butterfly to bring it closer, entranced by its fur-like body and its bright orange wings.

Olly came to kneel beside him and cupped his own hands beneath his friend's. 'It is beautiful,' he said, 'and it likes you.'

William smiled a rare smile. 'It likes its freedom better.' He opened his palms and allowed the insect to flutter away, but Olly's hands remained enclosing his.

'I'm never going to marry,' William said staunchly.

'Nor me,' Oliver agreed.

Chapter Eight

Aiden touched her gently on the shoulder and she turned and followed him, through the arch and into the Italian Garden. She found herself looking at a transformation. No longer did the flagged pathway circle a muddy shell but instead a wide expanse of water, its calm surface ruffled here and there by the eddying of the river that nurtured it. For a moment, the glint and glimmer of water beneath the bright sunlight, its occasional plunge into the shadow of sheltering trees, dazzled her. Then she lifted her eyes and saw across the lake's shining mirror the temple that had begun to rise. It stood, delicate and poised, on a platform of levelled white rock. Two marble columns were now in place, their carved scrolls boldly outlined against the bluest of skies.

She was rendered almost breathless. She had not truly believed her father when he'd claimed this garden would prove his most spectacular yet.

'It will be magnificent,' she said in the quietest of voices.

'It will,' Aiden echoed.

Except for the slight ripple of lake water, there was complete stillness in the garden. She wasn't certain she was completely comfortable with it. The stillness was almost unnatural.

'Where are all the men?' she asked, suddenly conscious of their absence.

'Eating lunch.'

'Why not here?'

'It's too enclosed and far too hot. They'll be in the orchard – plenty of shade there beneath the fruit trees. Let's hope tomorrow is a little cooler. We'll begin to lift the remaining columns then and it's heavy work.'

'And after that…?'

'After that, there's the interior to finish, though that's likely to take a little time.'

'Have you plans for it?'

He gave a rueful smile. 'Your father wanted murals to decorate each wall. He was pretty insistent, but I think Jonathan has finally persuaded him against. It's the damp. We'll proof the building as best we can, but water is insidious. It will find a home within the walls and any mural will last only a few years. Instead, we've commissioned a number of reliefs by a local sculptor – classical motifs in the main – and we're hoping that Mr Summer will approve.'

'It sounds as though you've weeks of work ahead. It's a huge undertaking.'

'It is, but when we're through, you will see the most wonderful garden ever.'

She looked up at him. The green eyes had lost their mistiness and were sharp with excitement. 'You really love this place, don't you?'

'Why wouldn't I? It's exhilarating. I've only ever worked in towns and here there's space and freedom and so much beauty.'

A slight flurry among the leaves made her look across at the temple and its guardian trees, but it was an instant only before the garden's stillness had closed in on them once more.

'You come from a city then?' She was prying again, but she wanted very much to know.

'If I come from anywhere,' he answered equably. 'I've lived for years with my aunt and uncle in London. In Camberwell. My uncle owns a small shop there, and when I'm not at lectures or sitting examinations or working on commissions, I help out.'

'He is the uncle who arranged your apprenticeship?'

'The very same.' He looked down at her, a mocking expression on his face. 'And before you steel yourself to ask, my aunt and uncle came to England years ago. Like many Irish people, they faced the choice of leaving home or starving.'

His tone was light but she knew his words were anything but. 'I don't know much about Irish history,' she confessed.

'It's better that you don't. It doesn't make a pretty story.'

'But you still have relatives there – in Ireland?'

He took her by the elbow and steered her towards the bench in the summerhouse. For a while, they sat in silence looking across the lake until he said, 'My mother and father are dead but I have brothers.'

She was surprised. He seemed so self-contained, so much a man who had made his way in the world completely alone. 'Do you ever see them?'

'We've gone our different ways,' he said shortly.

That was a part of his story, but a part he was unwilling to tell. At least for now. She tried another tack. 'So where will you go after you've finished at Summerhayes?'

'I'm not certain. I've had one or two offers – through

Jonathan. They're jobs that would give me independence, but they're small projects and a little uninteresting.'

'Isn't small the best way to start?'

'Possibly, but I'd rather think big from the beginning.'

She smiled at his earnestness. 'Big, like Summerhayes,' she murmured.

'Indeed. It's been brilliant. Passing examinations is one thing, but you can't beat practical experience, and being on site with Jonathan has been a hundred times more valuable than sitting in a dusty office working from drawings.'

His enthusiasm was catching, but she found herself asking, 'How likely is it that you'll gain a large commission?'

'Most unlikely. This country can be a closed shop. Canada would be different though.'

She was startled. 'Canada!'

'I have a cousin in Ontario. That's eastern Canada. He writes to me that Toronto is a city that's growing all the time. It's one of the main destinations for immigrants and there's a huge amount of new building. The sky could be the limit, he said.'

'And do you believe him?'

'Why not? Canada is a new country. It's also very large.'

She felt a strange emptiness. Since their meeting in the churchyard, she had seen him only once. He had brought to the house the architect's final drawings for her father to lock away in his safe, and they'd met in the black and white tiled hall. A brief conversation only, interrupted by Joshua's emergence from his smoking room, but enough for her to want more, to have time to talk with him, time to know him.

She scolded herself. He was her father's employee and a chance-met acquaintance; she would be foolish to think him anything more. Imagine her family's reaction if they were ever to become close. But they wouldn't – and it shouldn't matter to her where he went. Instead, she should be cheering him for his ambition, for the passion he owned for his work and the new life he wished to build. His sense of adventure was something she understood. It was what she loved in her father, what she would wish for herself, if she were not a girl.

She wanted to know more of his cousin, but she'd already asked far too many questions. So she sat quietly by his side, enjoying the coolness of flint and stone. The summerhouse afforded a welcome retreat in what was becoming another broiling day.

'My cousin sailed from Ireland several years ago.' It was as though he had divined her thoughts. 'There was no future for him in Galway. He's working on the railway in Canada and rents a small house for his family on the outskirts of Toronto. He's offered me a room until I find my feet.'

'It seems you've already decided your future.'

'Not yet. Not quite.' He looked at her as though he wanted to say more, but then abruptly changed direction. 'And what about *yours*? Do you intend to stay here?'

'You asked me that before.'

'And I never got an answer. Your father is making Summerhayes a life's work, but it's his life, not yours. You have your own creativity. Don't you want the world to share it?'

She pulled a face. 'How very grand that sounds! I paint for myself, that's all.'

'You should want more. I saw one of your paintings. I'd say you need some formal training, but you're certainly not the dauber you claim. Women are beginning to be taken seriously as painters, you know. You should go to London, enrol in one of the art schools. The Slade perhaps.'

She knew about the Slade. Someone she'd met last year, on one of the interminable morning calls she'd been forced to make with her mother, had told her with a shocked expression that women students there had actually been allowed to draw a semi-clothed male. Right now, that was an uncomfortable image, and she found herself challenging him more strongly than she intended. 'Are you trying to organise my life? How did you see a painting of mine?'

'It was hanging in the hall when I called last week.'

Her father's portrait, of course. Joshua had been so pleased with it that he'd had the picture framed and insisted on hanging it with his most precious trophies, the Tiffany wall lights he'd bid for at extortionate cost. And Aiden Kellaway had taken note of the artist's name, written very small and in the furthest right-hand corner of the canvas. The man was certainly acute.

'I'm happy to stay an amateur.' Her tone verged on the brusque.

'Then just go to the city and enjoy its pleasures. You're very young to be hiding away.'

'I'm not hiding,' she said indignantly. 'And I've been to London already. I told you.'

'And you didn't like it?'

'Not much.'

Four months of hedonistic pleasure filled with parties and receptions and dances, and with no time for painting. She couldn't deny it had been exciting, but the excitement had been gossamer thin. Beneath it always a feeling of being demeaned, of having her essential self disregarded, chipped away bit by bit, day by day. The buying and selling of young women, that was the truth of the Season.

'Why did you go?'

'Papa was keen that I was introduced to polite society,' she said blandly.

'Polite society,' he mimicked, and she giggled.

'I shouldn't laugh. It cost him a great deal of money and I turned out a disappointment.'

'How is that?'

'I didn't "take", as the saying goes. I think I was a little too different – maybe a little too candid.'

'I think maybe you were, Miss Summer.' He seemed to find it amusing. 'Or may I call you Elizabeth?'

'I imagine you can. We seem acquainted enough to be discussing my prospects of making a good marriage.'

'So that's what the foray into polite society was all about. Presumably, you didn't advance your "prospects"?' He was still grinning.

'I received two proposals, if that's what you mean,' she said tartly. 'I turned them down.'

He nodded as though he could not imagine her giving any other answer. 'I dare say you were in trouble for that.'

'For a while. Papa fretted and fumed. Told me I was an ungrateful girl, but in the end I don't think he minded. Not really. It's true he spent a lot of money but he's a generous man.' *For all his irascibility*, she could have added.

'And you are his darling.' It was a statement of fact.

'I suppose so,' she said, blushing a little.

'I don't think he'd want you to be talking to me. Your mama certainly didn't.'

The scene at the churchyard came vividly to mind, her mother frosty and unusually forceful. What had that been about? First, she'd been instructed to greet her aunt and uncle, then commanded in no uncertain terms to disappear. She'd been baffled and just a little threatened. That evening as Alice had sat over her needlework, she'd questioned her mother closely, but received no satisfactory reply.

'I talk to whomever I want,' she said resolutely, bristling from the memory.

'Those are brave words.'

'I am brave,' and for the moment his presence gave her the strength to believe it. 'Though not so brave,' she amended, 'that I can afford to disappear for hours.'

'Then you'd better go, and I had better return to work. Mr Simmonds will be back shortly from his quarry visit, and I should at least look industrious.'

She rose to go and, as she did so, he caught hold of her hand; she allowed her palm to rest in his. 'Will you walk this way again?' he asked.

'I might.'

'Soon?'

'Perhaps tomorrow,' she hazarded, and he looked gratified.

'Tomorrow,' he said, and she sensed his eyes watching as she walked away. There was the slightest tilt to her hips, the cluster of pleats that fringed the silk poplin skirt swinging from side to side.

Joshua was waiting for her at the top of the terrace steps, propped against an enormous urn of sweet-smelling cosmos, their pink and white faces swaying in the slight breeze. It looked as though he had been waiting a long time.

'Where have you been?' The beauty of the flowers had done nothing to soothe and his frown was etched deep.

'Just walking.' She drew abreast of him but avoided meeting his eyes.

'You shouldn't walk alone. You know I am always happy to keep you company. You must ask me. It's a long time since we walked together.'

'We'll walk another day, Papa. And please don't worry. I took a very small stroll and they *are* our gardens. How can I come to harm?'

'They may be our gardens, but still—'

He stopped suddenly. A floating grey skirt had appeared around the corner of the building. Alice had barely reached the top of the terrace steps when he turned on her. 'Your daughter has been out this last hour. Did you know that? Why are you not with her?'

Alice ignored his outburst. 'I was with Dr Daniels. If you recall, he is here for William. I came to tell you that the doctor is leaving. You may wish to say goodbye.'

'Daniels, that old woman,' he muttered. 'Both of you fussing over the boy. There's nothing wrong with him, I tell you. You're encouraging him to be sick.'

As if to prove him right, William chose that moment to fly out of the side door and down the terrace steps, his brown limbs at full stretch. 'Sorry,' he panted, weaving his way between them, but not before Elizabeth had spied a crumpled cloth beneath his arm and what looked suspiciously like half a loaf poking out of it.

'I have to go. Olly is waiting.'

All three of them looked after the rapidly disappearing figure. It was Alice who broke the silence. 'I am not saying he is sick, simply that we should continue to be careful.'

'Rubbish! There's nothing wrong with him.'

When he appeared about to deliver another lengthy diatribe, Elizabeth seized the chance to slide quietly away and make for the house.

Chapter Nine

Joshua glared at the spot she had been minutes before. William was supplanted by a more urgent consideration. 'About Elizabeth '

Alice sighed inwardly. What about Elizabeth? she asked herself. She seemed unable to exercise control over the girl. Her father should be the one to hold her in check, but his fondness kept him from any meaningful restraint.

'Surely, woman,' he was saying, 'it can't be beyond your wit to keep watch over her. Keep her amused so that she doesn't feel the need to stray.'

'It's not amusement that Elizabeth needs, Joshua. It's purpose. A finishing school would have helped,' she couldn't stop herself adding.

She waited for the next outburst, but instead he seemed deep in thought, prodding so savagely at the lawn with the briar stick he carried that Alice feared the gardeners would be called on to lay new turf.

'There are times,' he said heavily, 'when I wish we had stayed in Birmingham. Elizabeth would have had purpose there. The women were… different. More serious. The wives and daughters of the men I knew – they would have been her friends. They would have kept her busy, interested in the world. Given her something beyond dabbing at canvases in an attic. *And* they would have found her the right husband.'

This final shot went over Alice's head. In her mind, she was back in Birmingham and hating it. Fifteen years she'd lived there, and for the entire time she had felt adrift. The friends, the contacts, Joshua spoke of were industrialists, factory owners like himself. They inhabited a world wholly foreign to her and had wives who were just as foreign. Women who gave gossipy and uncomfortable tea parties or, worse, were terrifyingly intellectual. Joshua had taunted her that she was too great a lady, too conscious of her family name and thought herself above their company. It wasn't so but she could never have told him the truth. She was scared of the women, thoroughly scared. Her meagre education, the narrow vision with which she'd been raised, the privileged life she'd led, were poor preparation for holding her own with females who thought nothing of conducting literary soirées in their homes or debating the latest philosophy. They were wives who joined the Women's Slavery Society or attended public meetings on women's suffrage and urged her to accompany them. They made her feel stupid and pointless.

And Joshua had not helped. He'd been incapable of understanding her plight and treated her with a growing abruptness. Even when she'd given birth after years of disappointment, she had been made to feel a failure. A girl rather than the boy that was expected. In time, of course, things had changed. Joshua had grown to adore his daughter and to dismiss the son when he arrived, as hardly worth his attention. His partiality was understandable. She thought Elizabeth too headstrong for her own good, but the girl's spirit and energy were a true echo of her father's.

When her husband had finally gained ownership of his Sussex acres, she'd felt blessed. For weeks, she had sailed aloft on a tumultuous wave of relief. Until she'd returned. Then came the realisation that she'd find no more congenial company in the countryside of her birth. Her brother had made sure that neither Joshua nor she would find a place in county society. The great and the good had decided for themselves that Joshua was unbearably vulgar, but her brother had made sure with a whisper here and a nudge there that he was seen as dishonest too. A counterfeit. She had buckled beneath the assault, but Joshua hadn't. He was a strong man and he'd needed his strength. He'd used it to shrug off the mantle of social pariah and create instead the most magnificent gardens in Sussex. They were his triumphal fanfare, a declaration that he had arrived.

Her thoughts had been wandering badly. Joshua was still complaining and she had heard barely a word. She struggled to look suitably abashed when Ivy saved her the trouble by appearing at her shoulder. 'Beg pardon, ma'am. But you have a caller.'

'I know,' she said shortly. 'The doctor.'

Why could people not leave her alone? First, Elizabeth, then, Joshua, now, Ivy. Her hand crept to the back of her neck. She had the strangest impulse to tug hard at her hair and bring the whole magnificent edifice tumbling around her shoulders. An attempt to break her bonds? she wondered. If it was, it was far too feeble and very much too late.

'No ma'am. Dr Daniels left ten minutes ago. He said not to bother you or Mr Summer, but he'd be back to check on Master William next month. It's Mrs Fitzroy that's in the drawing room.'

'Mrs Fitzroy?' Alice looked blankly at the maidservant.

'You can go,' Joshua growled. 'She's your sister-in-law, not mine. I'll have nothing to do with that family. In any case, I need to see Harris. I want to talk to him about plants for the fête. The more exotic, the better. And cut flowers – vases and vases of cut flowers. We must make sure the whole of Sussex will be talking about the event for months.'

He would take a grim satisfaction in greeting the county's old families and rubbing their noses in his wealth. They might own more land, but that was their only source of treasure, and its value had depreciated hugely over the last twenty or thirty years – ever since the great depression. There was no money to pay taxes, no money to pay the new threepence a week insurance for each of their dwindling band of servants. Joshua had the upper hand.

She supposed it was some kind of poetic justice, though one that left her indifferent. He had ploughed thousands into the estate but had garnered back as much money and more. Under his management, the once failing Home Farm of the Fitzroys was a thriving enterprise, producing all its own livestock and cereals. There was honey, too – she could vouch for its excellence. And wax from the hives and building timber from the coppiced area he'd planted. There was no doubt he'd proved as successful at farming as he had at button-making, and the estate had grown rich as a result. Now his moment of glory had come: Summerhayes would be a showcase of all he stood for.

She watched him stomp away to consult the head gardener. It would be an interesting conversation. Joshua might be allowed to design pleasure gardens but when it came to produce – the vegetables, the herbs, the soft fruit and flowers – Harris's word was law, and his master knew it. Reluctantly, she made her way back into the house and had barely reached the drawing room when she was met by Louisa teetering on the threshold. Her sister-in-law was wearing yet another rich ensemble. She blinked in surprise at the shirred silk taffeta hat with its large jet ornament and two huge black plumes that on their own must have cost a fortune. Where did her brother get the money to pay for Louisa's falderals?

'I was just coming to find you.' The woman sounded petulant. 'I thought that maid of yours must have forgotten my message.'

'Ivy has just spoken to me,' she said calmly. 'What brings you here, Louisa?'

'It wasn't you that I wanted to see, in fact. Though, of course, it's always a pleasure,' her sister-in-law added rather hurriedly.

'Is it?' She would not normally have spoken so bluntly, but the longing to be alone was becoming unbearable and Louisa was the least welcome of visitors. The appalling scene in the churchyard was still vivid in her mind.

She found her sister-in-law advancing on her, a determined smile pinned to her face. The woman reached out and clasped both of Alice's hands between her gloved fingers. When she spoke, there was an attempt to infuse warmth into her words. 'I know there are problems between our families, Alice, but there is no need for us to be at odds. It's really the men who have the problem, isn't it? We should not allow their disagreements to spoil our friendship.'

She had not been aware of a friendship. Louisa had married her brother the year they'd moved to Summerhayes, or what would become Summerhayes. From the start, she had been aloof. After all, she had married a Fitzroy of Amberley, while poor Alice had had to settle for a

Birmingham factory owner. That was fourteen years ago and the situation remained unchanged. At best, it had been an uneasy relationship. She always felt tense in the other woman's presence, as watchful of Louisa as she was of Henry. She had a premonition that if ever she relaxed her guard, her family would suffer the consequences. Joshua was intemperate, his actions hasty and ungoverned, and it was up to her to protect her children. Her husband could lead them into disaster. He did not know her brother as she did, he did not truly appreciate, even after all these years, the damage that Henry could do. Her brother had hurt more people than she could remember – the servants he'd told tales of, the friends who'd mistakenly thought him an ally – wreaking havoc with a smile and a nod and a quiet word. And sometimes worse. Right now, he would be brooding long and hard. He would not let this latest incident – the breaking of the dam – go by. He would repay the insult. Eventually.

Louisa had released her hands and was holding her at arm's length. 'What on earth is the matter, Alice?'

She realised then that for a long time she had been standing silent and dazed. She must pull herself together. It was happening too often these days. 'If you didn't come to see me—'

'I came for the doctor,' Louisa interrupted. 'He promised to send a prescription to Amberley, but it must have slipped his mind. My nerves have never been good, you know that, and since this recent trouble between our families, they've been completely on end. But Veronal always does the trick.'

'I'm sorry to hear you've been unwell.' Alice doubted the truth of this, but in any case what was her sister-in-law doing chasing across the countryside to find Dr Daniels?

'Would it not have been an idea to call at the pharmacy? They're sure to sell Veronal.'

'Yes, yes,' Louisa huffed. Her nerves seemed to be getting the better of her once more. 'I'm sure they do sell it, but that wretch – the new pharmacist – insists on a prescription. I sent my maid to the surgery to collect one, but she is utterly useless. By the time she got there, she'd forgotten what it was I needed. I've been forced to come looking for the doctor myself. Is he here? I heard in the village he was heading this way.'

'He was, certainly, but he left a while ago.'

Louisa looked disconcerted. She walked over to the window and glared into the distance. Then, as suddenly, her face cleared and she turned back to Alice, who had remained standing in the doorway.

'Did you call Dr Daniels? I hope you're not ill yourself. Or is it Joshua?' For a moment, she seemed truly concerned.

'We are both well, thank you. The doctor was here on a trivial matter. A brief check on William, nothing more.'

As soon as she said it, Alice wished she hadn't. She had never spoken of William's weak heart to anyone, not from the moment he was born in this very house.

'William? But he's the picture of health.'

'He is, isn't he?' She could not prevent a surge of pride. 'And that's how we wish to keep him.'

'So why does he need Dr Daniels to visit?'

This was the reason she should have said nothing. To reveal vulnerability in the family was foolish. But Louisa was looking directly at her, her brow creased into small furrows, and she could think of nothing to say but the truth.

'William has a weak heart, or at least he used to have when he was a baby. He seems nowadays to have grown out of it, or so the doctor thinks. But we like to make sure that everything continues well.'

'But, of course. My dear, what a worry that must have been for you. You've never said a thing about it.'

Alice was already regretting her words. Even if she had been close to Louisa, she knew she would have said nothing. The boy's fragility was real, whatever Joshua might argue, but that was not something the world or the Fitzroys should know. William would inherit the Summerhayes estate and with it everything his father had worked for. He was gentle, breakable, and as unlike Joshua as it was possible to be. But he would need to be strong, or appear strong, to hold what was his against a covetous uncle.

She schooled her face to lack expression. 'I've not mentioned it before because we have never wanted William to feel in any way a special case. And it has worked. He is a strong boy now. I hope you will keep to yourself what I've told you, Louisa.'

'Of course, my dear. You can trust me.' But even as she said this, Alice knew that word would be travelling back to Amberley in a very short while. Louisa was Henry's creature.

'I'm glad I came,' her sister-in-law continued. 'I've been thinking about this stupid disagreement between our husbands. Could we not do something to stop it?'

'What did you have in mind?'

'If I were able to persuade Henry to attend the fête at Summerhayes perhaps…?'

For a moment she was genuinely touched by the other woman's concern, but then common sense reasserted itself. There would be a good reason behind hcr suggestion. The crafty look on Louisa's face told her that: her sister-in-law did not do plotting very well. But it was possible it could be turned to Elizabeth's advantage.

'I suppose that might help,' she said thoughtfully.

'Your brother is obviously unhappy,' Louisa continued in queenly fashion, 'but Joshua was quite right when he said that Summerhayes is the better venue. Henry will need some persuading, as I'm sure you know, but I will do all I can. If I'm successful and he agrees to come, can you persuade Joshua to meet him halfway? It could be very helpful to you. I know you are both concerned for Elizabeth's future, and I would like to think that together we can manage an excellent marriage for her.'

It was surely worth a try. If Louisa could smooth the way, then it was possible the right husband could still be found. Elizabeth's marriage was not something she could dismiss as easily as Joshua, and since this latest quarrel with the Fitzroys, she had been nagged by a sense of inadequacy. Every day she had begun to think the matter more urgent. A moment ago, Joshua himself had seemed to realise his daughter enjoyed far too much freedom. It might persuade him to meet Henry in a more conciliatory mood.

'It sounds an admirable plan,' she said, her voice infused with a new energy, as she ushered Louisa to the front door.

'Splendid.' Her sister-in-law beamed approval.

In retrospect, Alice was not sure how comfortable that made her.

Chapter Ten

Ivy always knew where to find her sweetheart, but for once he was not tending his beloved Wolseley, but cleaning shoes. The boot boy must be ill, and it was just like Eddie to help out.

'Are you sure it will be all right?' she asked without preamble. He'd promised to ask Mr Summer if they could put fresh paint around Eddie's apartment.

He gave her a lazy smile. 'Don't fuss, Ivy. It will be fine.'

'You haven't asked him, have you?' She didn't want to sound cross but she couldn't stop herself.

'Not yet, but I will. In any case, why would he mind us making the old place look better?'

'He's got fixed ideas of what he likes and don't like,' she said darkly.

'Three rooms above a motor house? C'mon. It's not likely.'

'Then why haven't you asked him?' She felt her arms rising to her hips to rest akimbo. Like an old fishwife, she thought, annoyed with herself.

'There's not been the opportunity, honest. I'll drop it into the conversation, casual like, when I can.'

'And when will that be?'

'I'm driving him to Worthing this morning. He's off to

collect some antique he's bought – a Japanese vase, Imari, or something like that. He'll be in a good mood. I'll do it then.'

'And mebbe at the same time you could ask for a couple of days off after the wedding?' Her voice was gentler now.

He put his polishing cloth down and got to his feet. 'You don't stop, do you?' He grinned down at her, reaching out to tuck a stray lock of hair behind her ear. 'I'm beginning to wonder what I'm marrying. I'll be pecked to bits before I even get to the altar!'

'I'm sorry, but I get anxious.' She looked around then, and seeing the coast clear, reached up and kissed him on the cheek. 'I don't mean to nag, Eddie, really I don't, but I get that worried things won't work out for us.'

'Why shouldn't they? We'll have a bang-up wedding and a bang-up home. The jammiest, you'll see.' He narrowed his eyes against the sun. 'And I've a mind to ask an extra favour.'

'Yes?' Her gaze widened with anticipation and that made him laugh.

'Don't get too excited. But I've been thinking. My ma can't come to the wedding, you know that, but what if we went to my ma?'

Her face fell. 'How would we do that? She lives miles away.'

'How else?' He turned and pointed at the sleek green beast dozing in the wedge of sunlight.

Ivy gasped. 'You'd never dare to ask!'

'Watch me, girl. For you, I'd dare anything.'

He laughed again and his arms went round her waist, cradling her tight, and swinging her so high into the air that he lost his footing and they tumbled to the ground, landing on the cobblestones in a giggling heap.

'You'll want to keep your jobs, I'm supposing.' It was Ripley glaring at them from the rear door.

Hastily, they scrambled to their feet. 'Yes, Mr Ripley,' they said in unison.

*

Elizabeth looked wistfully out at the busy scene below. A large marquee had already been erected on the huge spread of lawn and a stiff breeze was whipping to a frenzy the flags flying proudly at each of its corners. A sprinkling of smaller tents, too, had begun to lace the perimeter of the grass, the noise of mallets on wooden staves sounding clearly through the first-floor window. If she pressed her forehead hard against the glass, she could just make out Cornford working at his bench, sawing the planks with which he'd construct a temporary dais. And to her right, Mr Harris teetering on the tallest of ladders with one of his boys holding its feet, while he strung bunting from tree to tree. There were men everywhere, it seemed – scurrying, carrying, calling to companions. A few women, too, who had come from the village and were setting up stalls from where tomorrow they'd sell toys and fruits and home-made sweetmeats.

This morning her mother had insisted on her company in the morning room, and she had spent the last few hours reading while Alice sewed. But every so often, she had laid aside the book and glanced longingly through the window. If she were not allowed to escape completely, at least she might do something practical. Perhaps join the scene unfolding below. She could run errands for the women on their stalls or organise refreshment tables for the big tent. Mrs Lacey was busy enough without having a marquee foisted on her – the housekeeper would welcome her help, she knew. But she was not allowed to be useful. Her function was purely decorative and her mother's morning room was where she must spend the day.

Her spirits had been high when earlier she'd watched Joshua leave for a drive to Worthing. He had wanted her to go with him, but she'd excused herself on the pretext of a lengthy journey. His pursuit of another precious vase for his collection was likely to take some time. With her father absent and the gardens filled with noise and movement, she'd hoped to slip from the house and make a swift visit to the temple. But her mother had swooped on her directly they rose from the breakfast table, and she'd had no opportunity. She wanted to speak to Aiden, wanted that he attend the fête tomorrow, for amid the hustle of the fair they could surely meet and talk unnoticed. She had barely seen the young man these last few weeks, now that her walks had been curtailed and Joshua's presence constant. Her father seemed always to be just out of sight but sufficiently near to be aware of her every move.

Unless she could get a message to the young architect, he wouldn't come. Perhaps it was as well that he didn't; she found herself wanting to see him a little too much, and it worried her. Last year, she'd returned from London clear in her mind that her world needed no man. She certainly didn't want to marry. She looked at the Pankhurst women – they led splendid lives, lives of power and excitement, and not a man in sight. And really, why should she want to see Aiden Kellaway so much, since she'd met him for a matter of minutes only? Yet she knew she did.

She was fascinated. He was like no other man she'd encountered: not the awkward boys at the few local dances she'd been permitted to attend, or the fulsome young men of the London Season with their smooth tongues and uncaring hearts. Aiden stood apart and his difference entranced her. She loved his misty green eyes, his soft brown hair, the lilt in his voice. Or was it his intelligence, the way he could cut through pretence and divine what was real, what was important? He was clever, that was certain, but it wasn't that either. Was it then his enthusiasm for life? Or the sadness she'd glimpsed behind the things he didn't say? Perhaps it was all those things.

She had drifted through the past few weeks wearing what she hoped was an impassive face, but all the time she'd been fighting a joy, that despite her best efforts, bubbled within. It was silly, ridiculous, but oddly liberating. Liberation, though, could play false, and her new sense of freedom might well end in disaster. If she doubted the danger, she had only to remember that the friendship with Aiden was not one she could admit to, let alone proclaim. She would do well to stay heart whole.

'Come away from the window, my dear,' Alice urged. 'If you lack employment, why not work on your embroidery? It's an age since you last took it up.'

She looked with dislike at the half-finished tablecloth tossed to one side. French knots and satin stitch had long ago lost their appeal and she couldn't prevent an audible sigh.

'What is it?' Her mother was immediately anxious.

'Nothing, Mama. I am a trifle tired, that's all,' she lied.

Alice was nested comfortably deep in the wing chair that was her favourite, but at this she put aside her crochet work and folded her hands in her lap. She is preparing to offer me unwanted advice, Elizabeth thought in irritation, but still she could not prevent a stab of pity. Her mother looked old and careworn beyond her years.

As a child, she had instinctively sided with her father. He'd been the one to pet her, to buy her the most expensive toys or take her to the most exciting places. Once, when they'd been living in Birmingham – though now she could hardly remember it – he'd taken her to a factory he owned. The noise of the machines had been like thunder in her ears but it was a thunder that produced miracles – the smallest, most beautiful buttons she had ever seen: tortoiseshell and jet, ivory and glass, silk and abalone, the latter hand-crafted from the fragile Macassar shells fished from East Indian seas. She still had a linen bag full of Joshua's exquisite designs. No wonder she had thought him king of the world.

It was her mother who had been the enemy, who had made her do things she didn't want to do, or stopped her from doing things she did: *Pull up your stockings, Elizabeth*; *Smooth out your dress*; *stop running*; *sit quietly*. For years, her mother's unhappiness had barely touched her. Until lately. Lately, she had begun to realise just how much Alice had suffered.

She picked up the hated tablecloth, hoping to deter any homily, and had placed just one listless stitch when the door flew open and her father marched into the room. He was back already. The excursion to Worthing had been unusually swift and this visit to her mother's morning room even more unusual – she couldn't remember the last time she'd seen him here. Almost certainly, there was more trouble brewing. She had a moment of panic, thinking someone had told him of the few meetings she'd had with Aiden, a chance observer that neither had noticed.

It was not the young architect, though, that was on her father's mind, but Henry Fitzroy. Joshua strode across the room to glare down at his wife. At any moment, she thought, Alice might disappear from view, shrinking into the very fabric of the chair.

'He's coming, did you know that?' When his wife did not answer, he raised his voice. 'Henry Fitzroy. Your dear brother. He's coming to the fête.'

'That is surely good news,' Alice said at last. There was only the slightest tremor to her voice.

'And how do you come to that conclusion?'

'If Henry attends, it will say he is happy for us to hold the fête. It will be an endorsement. An approval of Summerhayes.'

'What kind of rubbish is that?'

Alice blinked. 'It's hardly rubbish. If Henry attends a fête that his family has hosted for centuries, he will recognise our right to be here, your right to create the gardens. Recognise that it's just for us to take water from the stream.'

Elizabeth was unconvinced by her mother's logic, but at least it seemed to be circumventing Joshua's immediate rage.

'If you like to see it that way.' He grunted in a dissatisfied fashion.

'I think we should. Being at odds with Amberley is pointless, and if we have the chance to talk to Henry, it could prove useful.' Elizabeth saw her mother give him a meaningful look, but Joshua merely grunted again.

She must interrogate Alice on that look, and was deciding on the best time to broach the subject, when the heavy crash of a body against the wood panelling of the morning-room door brought the conversation to an abrupt halt.

'What the devil!' Her father spun round.

'I'll find out what's going on,' she said quickly, abandoning the embroidery to a nearby chair.

On the other side of the door, she almost tripped over Oliver's prone body. His face was pink from exertion and he had a rugby ball clutched between his hands. William's head was just visible at the top of the stairs.

'Go outside,' she ordered. 'At once. And take that ball with you.'

'They don't want us outside.' William arrived on the landing, out of breath.

'And why would that be?' She could take a fairly accurate guess.

'They said we were getting in the way,' Oliver offered, scrambling to his feet. 'They were quite cross, actually.'

She tried to look severe, but couldn't prevent a smile. 'And people in the house will be quite, too, if you make much more noise. Why don't you go to the Wilderness – lose yourself there? I'll come and call you when lunch is ready.'

Oliver shrugged his shoulders. 'I suppose. C'mon on, Wills.'

'Before you do...' Elizabeth looked at their innocent faces and took a decision. 'William, could you do something for me?'

'What is it?'

'Come to my room and I'll explain. Oliver can go down to the kitchen. Cook has made at least a hundred pork pies for the fête. Tell her I said you could have one each.'

'Thanks,' Olly enthused. 'You're a top-hole sister. I wish I had one.'

She wondered whether *William* would think so once she'd spoken to him.

Chapter Eleven

Ten minutes later, William emerged from Elizabeth's room pushing a small piece of white paper as far down his trouser pocket as he could. He wasn't at all sure that he agreed with Olly's claim of her being 'a top-hole sister'. Right now, he wished he were sister-free. He loved Elizabeth – when he was very young he'd worshipped her – but what she wanted him to do was wrong. Yet she had asked him so plaintively that he'd had no alternative but to agree.

He met Oliver coming out of the kitchen, his right cheek bulging with pork pie. 'Here, I've got one for you. Let's go to the retreat and stuff ourselves.'

They skirted the lawn, making sure they kept a distance from the men who were still hard at work, then bounded along the path that led beneath the pergola, eager to get to their hideaway. It was another warm day and the slight breeze was welcome. In addition to the pork pies, Oliver had managed to secrete two large bottles of lemonade and filch a chunk of plum cake from the larder when Cook had her attention elsewhere. Evidently, there was serious eating to be done.

In front of them rose the beautiful curved wall, dear to William since infancy, its face to the south, its espaliered apricots, pears and plums beginning to form their fruits for a late-summer picking. He felt a swell of love for the garden. Life at Summerhayes could be dull and, when it wasn't dull, his father's short temper made it unpleasant. But the garden never failed to calm. It was what he missed most when he packed his trunk for a school that knew nothing of the beauty his father's despised money had created. And it was the garden he enjoyed most when once more he returned home. Wandering its acres, noticing new flowers, trees that had grown, bushes that had spread. It was like getting to know an old friend all over again.

'What did your sister want?' Olly asked, as they jogged past the outbuildings.

'Just something she asked me to do for her.' He tried to sound unconcerned.

'What?'

'A message. She wanted me to take a message.'

'Sounds exciting. Where is it?'

He trundled to a stop and pulled from his pocket the scrap of paper, already dented and a little dirty around the edges. Before he could stop him, Olly had reached out and plucked it from his fingers.

'"I hope to see you at the fête tomorrow. I'll be there. Elizabeth,"' he read aloud. 'Not much excitement there.' He sounded disappointed.

William retrieved the message and stuffed it back into his pocket. But his friend hadn't given up. 'Who's it for, anyway?' Then, as the truth dawned on him, added, 'Not that chap – the chap working on the temple?'

He nodded miserably. Olly gave one of his low whistles. 'Why are you looking like that? It is exciting, after all.'

'It's not exciting, it's wrong,' he said stubbornly.

'Don't be a spoilsport. True love and all that. We have to help.'

'You'd better not get involved, Olly.' He was alarmed. 'My father will send you packing at the slightest excuse.'

'I know. That's why it's exciting. Come on, let's have an adventure. Let's help your sister find the love of her life.'

Unwillingly, William allowed himself to be dragged along the path through the Wilderness and towards the Italian Garden. He glanced over his shoulder, looking longingly in the direction of their retreat. He should be there, eating plum cake, not playing at messenger. It would lead to trouble, he was sure.

They had almost reached the laurel arch, when an unearthly howl filled the air, overwhelming the small, friendly sounds of the gardeners at work beyond the hedge. He clutched at his friend's arm.

He saw Olly look at him curiously. 'It's only dogs. Where are they, do you think?'

'There are dogs at Amberley. It must be them.'

'They sound much nearer than that.' As they stood beneath the arch, the howling intensified and then there was the sound of threshing undergrowth and of branches being broken.

William's face had grown white.

'Hey', Olly said, 'it's just hounds by the sound of them.'

'I hate dogs. Any dogs.'

'Do you?' His friend sounded genuinely interested. 'I've never met anyone who hated dogs.'

'Well, I do. They give me nightmares. Let's go.'

'But what about the message?'

'That can wait.'

'The animals are nowhere near,' Oliver protested. 'We

can whizz into the garden, find this chap, and whizz out again.'

There was a louder sound of trampling and then one of the gardeners working on the beds around the lake let out a yell. 'Them blasted hounds. They'm got out somehow.'

'See them orf, Joe,' another voice joined in. 'I don't want them buggers in here.'

That was enough for William. He turned on his heel and rushed a few yards back along the path, then threw himself into the middle of the Wilderness, barging through high grass, between palms and beneath tree ferns.

'William!' Olly called out. 'You're going in the wrong direction.'

But he had been made heedless by terror and charged on unthinkingly.

'It's over there,' Oliver was yelling, pointing in an easterly direction, but his friend did not hear; his mind filled with a compelling need to reach the retreat and hide within its shelter. Not that it would have hidden him for long. Any hound worth its weight would have nosed him out in no time. But he wasn't thinking straight, and when at last he looked up and saw where Olly was pointing, he quickly changed direction and leapt over the last few yards of long grass and literally threw himself into the small cave they had constructed.

A bewildered Oliver had started to follow his friend when a rumbling ahead stopped him in his tracks. The various pieces of wood they had gathered and so carefully lashed together appeared to be wobbling dangerously. And then they were tumbling. Like a waterfall. Planks, branches, enormous logs, came crashing to the ground, until half of the retreat was no more than a pile of timber, with William lying beneath it.

'Oh, my God,' Oliver breathed, rushing towards the mound of wood, yelling at the top of his voice for help. He grabbed the nearest plank and tried to manoeuvre it away but it had stuck fast beneath so much other heavy timber. 'Help!' he yelled again, his voice verging on tears.

Within seconds, one of the men working in the Italian Garden was bounding towards him, shoulder to shoulder with Davy, a fellow gardener and a huge wrestler of a man. And behind them, Joe Lacey and Aiden, still holding the theodolite he had been fixing into a new position.

'We'm a problem here, and all,' one of the men said, coming to a panting halt beside Oliver. 'Young master's beneath that lot. How do we get him out without hurting him worse?'

'We'll need to move the wood plank by plank,' Aiden said, 'and be very cautious. The whole structure could fall otherwise. That piece over there first, I think.'

Piece by painstaking piece, they worked their way down the pile of timber, until they could see William's two legs. He had dived to the back of the retreat, where the roof was still intact, but he appeared horribly still. The men began to work even more slowly, holding a collective breath when they removed the last huge piece of wood and laid it to one side. Then Davy and Joe Lacey grabbed William by the boots and, with a sharp pull, dragged him clear of the tottering structure. Olly immediately threw himself to the ground and cradled his friend in his arms.

'Let me look.' Aiden bent down, pushing Oliver gently to one side. 'The boy is breathing but I don't like his pallor. Can you men rig up a stretcher?'

In a few minutes, the men had lashed three of the wooden planks together and gently lifted William onto its hard surface. The movement woke the half-conscious boy and his eyes opened.

'Sorry,' he said dazedly.

'Don't try to speak, lad,' Davy advised. 'We'm getting you up to the house.'

The men lifted the stretcher between them and were about to find their way back to the path, when William tried to sit up.

'You must lie still, quite still,' Aiden said. 'The doctor will need to check you over but, hopefully, there won't be broken bones.'

'The message,' the boy murmured.

'Here.' Olly plucked the paper from his friend's pocket and pushed the crumpled missive into Aiden's hands. 'This is for you.'

'Okay to go now, Mr Kellaway?' Davy asked.

'Yes, do,' he said uncertainly. The men set off for the path and Aiden was left standing in the middle of the Wilderness, the scrap of paper clutched in his hand.

*

'It was deliberate. I'm sure it was deliberate.'

William lay sprawled across his bed. Dr Daniels had come and gone and pronounced him uninjured, except for several cuts and bruises and a heartbeat that was not quite regular. Now he was feeling very tired and slightly bemused. 'What do you mean, "deliberate"?'

Oliver sat cross-legged on the floor, looking up at his friend with bright, enquiring eyes. 'We roped the wood together as tightly as possible. The retreat couldn't have just fallen apart.'

'Maybe the ropes weren't as well tied as we thought.'

'I used my best knot on every piece of wood – it was a clove hitch.'

'But even so.' He picked at the counterpane, wishing Olly would stop playing detective. But his wish was in vain.

'Look!' his friend demanded, yanking a piece of rope from his pocket. 'I took this after they stretchered you up to the house. Just look at it.'

He looked. The rope seemed to have a clean cut but its edges were very slightly frayed.

'See? I bet you anything it's been sliced by a knife. And if I went back to the retreat, I reckon I'd find other cuts in the rope we used.'

'That could have happened from the rope rubbing against wood.' His protest was feeble. He had a bad headache and his heart still jolted occasionally.

'It might have happened with one knot, maybe even two, but all of them? You dive into the retreat and brush against the walls and then, *Bam!*, the structure collapses. I don't think so.'

'But who would do such a thing, even for a joke? They would know that cutting the rope was dangerous.'

'Someone who doesn't like us?'

'But who?'

'I don't know. The gardeners maybe. They're fed up with us. They're always moaning we're in the way. And the head chap – Harris, isn't it? – he gave me a real chewing over yesterday for picking apples before they were ripe.'

'Harris would never do such a thing. He's known me

since I was a baby. And neither would any of the men – they rescued me, remember?'

'Then who else?'

'Maybe you're wrong.'

'I'm not!' Oliver was adamant. 'Someone did it and they did it to hurt us, or to hurt you.'

He was more bewildered than ever, more weary than ever. He closed his eyes and lay back on the pillows. 'No one would want to hurt me,' he said quietly.

Oliver's expression said clearly that he knew he was right, but he didn't again contradict his friend. Instead, he said, cheerfully, 'The fair should be fun tomorrow.'

'Except that I won't see any of it.'

'Why ever not? You'll be fine by the morning.'

'The doc says I have to rest for two or three days. My heart has had a shock, and I need perfect calm. Mama will make sure I stay in this room.'

'But the fair…'

'*You* must go, Olly,' he said swiftly, opening his eyes again. 'There's no need for you to miss it.'

Oliver looked torn. 'I'd rather stay here with you. It won't be any fun on my own.'

'Of course it will. There'll be lots of stuff to buy and stalls where you can try your luck. We were going to win a coconut, weren't we? You can do it for me.'

The boy brightened. 'I could, I suppose. I could go for an hour and come back with a coconut. We could have a feast here. As long as your ma lets you eat it.'

'Good idea,' William said, and closed his eyes again. In minutes, he was asleep.

Chapter Twelve

Alice saw her brother long before Joshua spotted him. He was still at some distance from them, but moving at a leisurely pace through the fête, his wife, elegant in blue crêpe, draped across his arm. Today promised to be the hottest yet. The thermometer had stood high from early in the morning and, by midday, most of the stallholders and not a few of the visitors were seeking whatever shade offered. But Henry, dressed in a suit of French serge and sporting a grey silk waistcoat, appeared unmoved. Not for him the crumpled handkerchief dabbed ineffectually across a perspiring brow. He was the grand seigneur, Alice reflected, bowing to one person here, greeting another by name there, occasionally stopping at a stall to purchase some small item from a gratified owner. It was as though this was Henry's fête, which in a way it was. The venue had changed, but the proprietor had not. Local loyalties were too strong for that.

She sensed her husband's bulky figure draw close. He had arrived while she was watching their Amberley visitors, and she was sure he was sharing her thoughts. By any measure, the event was a success. But she knew Joshua. He would be fizzling beneath the surface, unsure exactly whose success it was. She felt her mouth dry and her fingers twitch. She hadn't realised how nervous she would be. If only the two men could meet in a spirit of conciliation, but that was next to impossible. Elizabeth's future was their sole connection and her one hope was that it might produce at least a temporary peace.

'Good afternoon, Alice.' Her brother doffed his hat in greeting. 'A fine day. And a fine turnout.'

'A fine setting, too,' Joshua could not resist adding.

'Indeed it is,' Louisa said smoothly and, for once, Alice was grateful to her. 'And so much to interest people. It's such a shame that William is missing all the fun. We heard he was unwell – I do hope he feels better very soon.'

Alice's face became very still and she took a while to answer. 'Thank you. You are very kind. William is still a little indisposed, but I assure you, it is nothing serious. His friend is with him.'

'These boys, eh,' Henry said, 'always up to mischief.' His attempt at joviality was unexpected and jarring and Louisa once more moved to smooth the ruffled surface.

'We came across some very clever sideshows as we strolled through. And the village band seems in fine form. But it's far too hot to walk any longer and I know you are wishful to talk about Elizabeth before we return to Amberley.'

Joshua's face creased into a scowl but Alice was encouraging. She was eager to leave the subject of William behind. 'An excellent idea,' she said.

'And a pressing one, too, it seems.' Her sister-in-law gestured towards an open space to one side of the marquee. The crowds here had temporarily dispersed and two figures were etched clearly against the tent's canvas, their shadows merging one into another and spilling across the grass.

All four stared in the direction she had indicated. Henry was the first to recover. 'Who the devil is he!?'

Joshua's scowl had deepened to such proportions that his entire face was consumed by it, and when he spoke, his voice was so tightly controlled it barely seemed to touch his lips. 'The boy works for my architect. Kennedy or Kendall or some such name.'

'He is Kellaway,' Alice said.

'His name hardly matters.' Henry exuded disapproval. 'It's who he is that matters. And if he works for your architect – Simmonds, isn't that the man? – he will be a mere apprentice.'

'I believe so,' his sister murmured despairingly.

'In other words, a man with no money and few prospects.'

'He may have prospects.' Joshua's intervention came as a surprise to his auditors, though Alice could have foretold it. Her husband would never allow a remark to pass unquestioned, that a working man had no prospects. His own rise from poverty was too deeply ingrained in his consciousness.

'No *real* prospects, Joshua,' her sister-in-law coaxed, throwing an anxious glance at Henry. 'There is no reason to suppose that Mr Kendall will not do well in his trade, but is that what you want for dear Elizabeth?' When Elizabeth's parents were silent, she said, 'Of course not. You want so much more and why should you not? Elizabeth is *worth* so much more.'

'He'll be going soon!' Joshua snapped. 'I've told Simmonds to send him packing as soon as the boy is no longer needed.'

'Good, that's good, but in the meantime –'

'In the meantime, Elizabeth will be kept busy.'

'As she is today,' Henry remarked superciliously.

'Let us not have hasty words,' Louisa said. 'Henry, you must explain our plan and, if Alice permits, I will bring to an end this improper tête-à-tête.' Before Alice could give permission, her sister-in-law had released herself from her husband's arm and begun to weave her way through the crowds to where Elizabeth and Aiden stood deep in lively conversation.

*

Elizabeth had walked out of the house and into the fête half an hour previously. She was nervous. This was the only opportunity she'd had in days to speak to Aiden and she wasn't at all sure that he would come. She wasn't sure if he had read her message or even if William had managed to deliver it before his accident. But she was here and waiting, while at the same time she tried to hide in plain sight. She'd made certain she was seen wandering among the stalls, sampling the sweetmeats, trying her luck at shove ha'penny, and been careful to speak to anyone she knew. She was just turning away from exchanging greetings with the postmistress, when she saw him. Her heart gave a curious little pinch. He was lingering outside the marquee, clearly expecting someone, and she hoped that people hadn't noticed. She looked around. Summerhayes was transformed that day, the crowds buzzing from stall to stall, the air filled with shouts and laughter, and the low hum everywhere of people enjoying themselves. Nobody would take heed, surely, not amid this hive of conviviality.

A strange energy swept through her. She walked quickly to his side, but no sooner had she reached him than she was overcome by awkwardness. This was the most embarrassing of situations and she had created it. She had asked a man she barely knew to meet her. What must he be thinking? She had offered no explanation in her note, other than she wanted to see him. He would think her fast. Perhaps she was, perhaps she was turning into the hoyden her mother predicted. She felt herself growing hot from her toes up and cast around for something to say.

'The fête is proving a great success.'

'It certainly looks it.' He gave her the familiar half-smile and her heart pinched again. She forced herself to look away, gesturing with her arm to indicate the spread of crowded stalls.

'My father is very pleased with the way the day has gone,' she added desperately.

'I imagine he must be.'

He was not helping. He was standing so close to her that she could see the lines at the corners of his eyes, so close that she could smell the freshness of his skin.

'I'm glad you came.' The words were blurted out and immediately she wanted them back; her forwardness at sending the message was tormenting her. But he made no mention of it. Instead, he continued to look at her, thoughtfully, steadily, the half-smile still there.

'How could I not come?' He made their meeting sound the most natural thing in the world.

He bent to retrieve the handkerchief she'd dropped, where it lay unnoticed on the trampled grass. As he did so, his hair fell across his forehead in a soft sweep of brown, and she felt an impulse to reach out and stroke it back into place.

'How is your brother today?' he asked, handing her the small piece of linen. 'He gave us quite a scare.'

His question came as a lifeline. With an effort, she managed an even voice. 'He gave us a scare too. He's suffered no obvious damage, thank goodness, but his heartbeat is a little irregular. The doctor thinks it best that he rest for a few days. He is very disappointed that he can't be here.'

How serious her brother's heart defect was, she had no idea. Alice had always been keenly protective while her father ignored the problem, in the same way as he ignored William in general. He was blind to his son's gentle soul, she thought, and blind to William's true nature. She wondered whether her mother was too.

'Poor William,' Aiden said. 'It was one of the worst things that could have happened.'

'It was, but I must thank you for coming to his rescue. If you hadn't been there, he might have been badly injured.' She was feeling more secure now.

Aiden shook his head. 'It's the gardeners you have to thank. They did the hard labour. But it was fortunate they were working close by.'

'Is the new garden finished?'

'Almost, though this hot weather has made working there difficult for the men.'

She thought he might suggest she visit again to see the temple in its full glory, but she was glad when he didn't. It felt good to be with him here in the fresh openness of a sunny day. The Italian Garden was beautiful, there was no doubt, but something about it was wrong. It was her imagination working too vividly, she supposed, but she could never feel wholly at ease there.

'Are you all right, Elizabeth?'

She looked up to see concern in his face and realised

that she'd been frowning fiercely. 'I'm fine. It's nothing – a silly fancy.'

It was the second time that he had used her given name, and it had come as naturally as everything else between them. The impulse to touch surged again. She wanted to reach out to him, reach out and cement the bond she felt, but that would be stupid.

'Have you had time to look around the fair yourself?' she asked brightly.

'I came to see you, not the fair.' His hand moved towards her. In what seemed like slow motion, he reached out and sought hers.

Then, a voice from over her shoulder, a voice coming between them. 'Elizabeth, there you are, my dear. I've been looking everywhere for you.'

Aunt Louisa. In a second, Aiden had melted away and, from the corner of her eye, she saw that he was making his way towards the exit that led to the village. She'd had no time with him, no time to talk, to work out what was in her heart. Just a few whispered words in farewell.

Her aunt readjusted the dashing hat she was wearing. 'A wonderful day, isn't it? Your father has done us proud.'

She was too busy trying to order her thoughts to answer. What was Louisa doing here? Surely the Fitzroys could not have come to the fête? But then Gilbert sidled into view, tugging at his mother's skirt and asking for pennies.

'You should ask your father, Gilbert. I am carrying very little money.'

He cast a scared glance in Henry's direction. 'Please, Mama. Papa is busy.'

Louisa tutted impatiently. 'Oh, very well. But this is all I have.' She dipped a gloved hand into the mesh purse she carried and brought forth a handful of coins, which she pressed into the pair of small, sticky hands.

'Spend wisely,' she admonished.

It seemed that the Fitzroys had overcome their fury to attend the day, but how the breach with her parents had been mended and why, Elizabeth had no idea. It was all very puzzling. Her aunt offered a few more platitudes to which she barely responded, and then the woman was gone and she was alone again. She watched as Louisa zigzagged a path through the crowd, travelling in the same direction as Aiden. Evidently, her aunt, too, had no wish to stay at the fête.

Chapter Thirteen

'I suppose Simmonds knows of your concern about the man he employs?'

Henry had continued with his questions ever since Louisa left, and Alice worried that he would antagonise her husband so badly that Joshua would walk away. There was certainly a snap in Joshua's voice when he answered. 'He knows that I don't want the boy on my estate a minute longer than is necessary. In any case, Kellaway will go of his own accord pretty soon.'

Henry's face expressed disbelief. 'I doubt it. If he did, he would be ignoring his most obvious advantage. And, for a man in his position, that would be unlikely.'

'The boy is Irish, or so Simmonds tells me.'

'So...'

She could see Joshua relax. She sensed he had felt disadvantaged throughout this encounter, but now he wore a superior smile.

'Do you not read the newspapers?' he drawled. 'They are full of the unrest that's brewing. Ireland is a tinderbox. You have only to think of the Curragh. A mutiny! British officers threatening to resign rather than subdue a rebellion against Home Rule! That was a bare three months ago. There will be civil war in Ireland – in weeks. The government is already talking of some form of partition. The country will be in turmoil and Kellaway will run for home.'

'It's possible,' Henry conceded, 'but by no means certain. What is more certain, however, is the solution I'm proposing. I trust you'll both find it satisfactory.'

'You've found someone,' Alice rushed in.

'I haven't found someone, Alice,' he responded tetchily. 'I have spoken to a man we both know. Giles Audley. If you remember, he is our second cousin.'

'I do remember. Of course, I do. But he is a widower.'

'And pray what is wrong with that?'

'He is a little older than Elizabeth,' she said uncertainly.

'All the better to control her. And, by the look of it, she needs control.'

'I haven't seen Giles for years.'

'Nor have I, but I am happy with what I have found. He went abroad after his wife died, but is settled back in Sussex now. He's a capital fellow. Nephew to the Earl of Pevensey.' He said this with satisfaction.

'And he wishes to marry again?'

'Naturally, or we would not be having this conversation. I have spoken to him of Elizabeth and he liked what I had to tell him. I feel they should meet as soon as possible. Louisa and I have discussed the matter and decided that an informal gathering might be best for a first meeting – a tea party perhaps. It will be long enough for them to enjoy some conversation together but short enough for it not to become awkward.'

'I think that's a splendid proposal.' She hadn't expected her brother to exercise such subtlety, but perhaps she should not be surprised. Henry was a chameleon after all. 'Joshua?' She looked anxiously at her husband.

He nodded an unwilling assent. He was shrewd enough, she knew, to see through her brother and recognise his manipulation, but the lure of marrying Elizabeth to a relative of the Earl of Pevensey was enough to suspend his suspicions. Money, land, title: they were the badge of belonging.

'Very good. Then it needs only that Louisa arrange a convenient day. Where is she?' He scanned the lawn, still crowded with parishioners eager to spend their halfpennies. Aiden Kellaway and Elizabeth had vanished, but so, it appeared, had Louisa. 'Where the devil is she?' he repeated.

'She may have returned to the carriage,' Alice suggested delicately, while having her own ideas where Louisa had gone. 'The heat has become quite overpowering.'

Henry looked unconvinced. 'I must find her. I will bid you goodbye.'

When he had gone, she said wonderingly, 'Tea at Amberley.'

Joshua huffed. 'Nothing so wonderful about that.' But she knew he was pleased. It was the first invitation to Amberley they had ever received. The first time since her marriage that she would return to her childhood home. It warmed her heart.

'Amberley doesn't matter,' she said quietly. 'What matters is Elizabeth. I remember Giles Audley as a very pleasant young boy. A gentle boy.'

'He'll need to be a good deal less gentle if he's to wed our daughter.' The pride in Joshua's voice belied his truculence. He looked past his wife at the figure of Ripley making his way towards them and holding aloft a silver tray.

'I have to admit when Henry first mentioned the name, I was concerned.' Her words drifted unnoticed in the air.

'Giles must be forty if he is a day. But I'm sure Elizabeth will like him, and his seniority will allow him to guide rather than rule her.'

Her husband had taken the folded newspaper from the tray and was scanning the front page. A deep frown scarred his forehead.

'If you say so,' he said vaguely. 'But we may have more pressing problems than Elizabeth. Look at this.' He handed her the newspaper, pointing at a bold headline: ARCHDUKE ASSASSINATED.

Alice read aloud the statement, then looked bewildered.

'Why are you so worried? It's very sad, but what has it to do with us?'

'That's precisely what people up and down the land will say, but I am not most people. Read on a little.'

'"Archduke Franz-Ferdinand, heir to the Austro-Hungarian throne, and his wife, Sophie, were today shot dead in Sarajevo by a Bosnian Serb student." Where is Sarajevo?'

'I imagine we'll find out soon enough, and wish that we hadn't,' he said grimly.

*

Elsewhere in the garden, Oliver was sauntering from stall to stall. He paused at each, looked longingly at the wonderful arrays of sweetmeats, but bought nothing. It didn't feel right to be gobbling cakes when his friend was lying upstairs. In fact, it didn't feel right at all being here without him. He was still convinced that the ropes of their retreat had been deliberately severed, but he could see that the suggestion made William anxious, and Mrs Summer had been adamant that he must say and do nothing that could upset the patient further. So he kept his counsel, while feeling angry that he couldn't help William get better, and couldn't help track down whoever had done this bad thing. He couldn't even buy him a cake. Alice had decreed that her son must follow the blandest of diets until he was on his feet again, and Oliver was uncertain he could reach their room while concealing a large slice of cake. And as for the coconuts they'd been promised, the stall was nowhere to be seen. Maybe the man they'd spoken to had decided the fête was small beer and not worth his trouble or perhaps there was a shortage of coconuts in Sussex. But he would like to take William back something; a prize of some kind.

He toured the stalls again. He would take a chance with the hoopla, he decided. Three times he threw, and three times he was unsuccessful. He was certain the little rubber rings had in some way been fixed to fall short of their target. On to the next stall, where he rolled pennies down a slot, only to find that they always came to rest on a line rather than in the square itself. By the time he'd worked his way to the bottom of the lawn once more, he was almost out of money and feeling despondent. Then he caught sight of a stall half-hidden behind a rowan tree. His last chance – a shooting gallery. He could shoot, he thought excitedly. His father had taken him out several times when they'd holidayed in the country and taught him how to manage a gun.

There was one other person at the stall. The man was firing rapidly at the moving display of china, as though if he shot fast enough, he was bound to shatter a passing cup or plate or saucer. Oliver handed over his penny and weighed the rifle in his hands. A bit too heavy, but he would do his best. High up on the shelf that displayed the prizes, he'd seen a highly coloured box. A jigsaw puzzle. He stood on tiptoe, straining to see its illustration. It was a battle scene, a naval skirmish. The Battle of Trafalgar, perhaps. William liked jigsaw puzzles, though he couldn't be bothered with them; but there was no accounting for taste, and he thought William would like it.

The man alongside him was handing over yet another penny and firing again for all his worth. Oliver took considered aim and his first shot fell short. The same with the second. Before he raised the gun again, there was a shout of jubilation and the man began jumping up and down. He'd hit his target. The stallholder asked him what he wanted and he pointed to a large teddy bear at the back of the stall. When the man behind the counter told him the bear wasn't a prize but belonged to his young daughter, the man pursed his lips and huffed his shoulders.

'I'll take that then,' he said, pointing to the jigsaw puzzle. *No*, Oliver wanted to shout. *That's mine*.

But the puzzle departed with the scowling man and Oliver wondered whether or not to keep firing. None of the prizes that were left looked at all the kind of thing William would like.

By the time he took his last shot, he had got his eye in, and a plate with a particularly garish pattern soon lay shattered at his feet. The stallholder shuffled forward apologetically. All he could offer as a prize, he said, was a tea towel or a picture of Shoreham harbour or a large and ugly floppy doll.

'Her name's Beatrice,' the stallholder said. 'Beatty, that's what my girl calls her. She wanted her, but I said a teddy bear is all you're getting.'

'Give me Beatty, then,' Oliver said gloomily.

*

When he crept into the bedroom half an hour later, having finally succumbed to the temptation of plum cake, William was sitting on his bed, bolstered by three or four pillows, and lethargically turning the pages of a book.

He looked up as the door opened, and beamed. 'Gosh, it's good to see you, Olly. Today has to be the dullest day ever, and this is the dullest book I've ever read.'

'Sorry I've been a while. What's the book?' he asked, sitting down on the edge of the bed.

'Some kind of improving tome. Mama thought I'd like it.'

Oliver gave a "What do you expect?" grimace. 'Better not complain too loudly though. I've got you something even worse.'

'What?' William's interest was peeked.

'Meet Beatrice, Beatty for short.' And he brought the large doll from behind his back and dangled her soft stuffed legs in front of his friend.

William gave a loud hoot of laughter. 'Where did you get that monstrosity?'

'Shush, you'll hurt her feelings. I won her, fair and square.' He jumped off the bed and gave an exaggerated bow. 'Meet the shot of the year!'

'You actually won her. Really, well done.'

Oliver came back to the bed. 'I'm sorry, Wills, there was nothing much left by the time I got to the stall.'

'Don't be sorry. She's perfect. And you won her for me.'

Oliver bent his head and kissed his friend on the cheek. 'I did, William. I won her for you.'

Chapter Fourteen

Elizabeth listened. The house was silent, not a creak on the stair not a restless footstep or a distant cough. She scrambled from her bed and dressed as quickly as nervous fingers would allow. A glance at the bedside clock – nearly midnight. It was time to go. If Aiden had caught her whispered farewell, he would be waiting. This afternoon, his eyes, his face, his outstretched hand, had said all she needed to know. He would be there for her.

And now there was added urgency. He would know nothing of the tea party that had been planned and she must tell him. She'd known nothing of it herself until her mother had broken the news at dinner this evening. At first, she'd made no sense of the words. Then she'd been angry and defiant, feeling her life being plucked from her hands. That was what the parley in the churchyard had been about. That was why the Fitzroys had swallowed their anger and come to Summerhayes today. No wonder that she'd been summarily dismissed both times, or else how would they have parcelled out her future so conveniently? It took a few hours alone in her room before she regained a measure of calm, and realised that outright opposition would only strengthen the powers against her. She'd sat at the floral flounces of her dressing table, taken a deep breath and made a decision. For the moment, she would go along with her parents' wishes. Act the part of a dutiful daughter and play for time, until hopefully they tired of their scheme. Or Uncle Henry did. Or Giles Audley himself.

She would meet Audley just this once and hopefully he would take her in dislike. She wasn't an amazing beauty, if that's what he sought. But she was passable, more than passable, if she were to believe Ivy. Her maid never tired of praising copper tresses that shone and dark brown eyes that sparkled. But Ivy was prejudiced and perhaps Mr Audley, or was it Sir Giles, would not find her so very attractive. He might hate brunettes, or tall, slim young women. He would certainly hate one who appeared fierce and uncompromising. She could spout a passage from one of Mrs Pankhurst's speeches maybe, or discuss the wave of strikes that trade unionism was bringing to the country. Men loathed women who talked politics. He would take flight at that, she was sure. But she needed to tell Aiden what was happening. She was galvanised by an impulse to explain, even to excuse herself, though why it was so necessary she had no idea. It simply was. She didn't want news of the Amberley visit to trickle out unannounced. And it would be common knowledge soon enough, since no one from Summerhayes had visited that house for as long as folk could remember.

Very carefully, she opened the window a fraction then threw a pair of soft walking shoes down on to the gravel beneath. They landed with an unusually loud thud and for a few seconds she held her breath. But the house and its inhabitants remained unstirred. She hoisted her skirt as high as its narrow cut would allow and clambered on to the windowsill. Then swung a leg out of the window to find a footing on the horse chestnut, whose branches grew so close as almost to embrace the house. She leant forward and grasped the spar of wood, pulling herself completely into the tree. From here, it was a matter of minutes before, branch by branch, she had climbed her way down to the ground.

She tiptoed across the gravel and onto the soundless grass, walking swiftly to the rear of the house. From here, she could see that most of the fête's attractions had already been packed and returned to the village. Mr Harris and his team had taken down the marquee, too, and cleared much of the detritus left by visitors, though traces of the day's celebrations were still scattered across the lawn. She picked her way carefully through the trail of lost belongings, discarded posters and boxes awaiting removal. It had been a lively event and it would take a while for Summerhayes to regain its calm perfection.

She increased her pace, feeling the minutes flying too fast. Aiden must not think she had failed him. *Midnight*, she'd said in a single breath, and it was nearly that now. There had been no time to say more, no time to fix a meeting place. But if he came, he would be in the Italian Garden, she knew. She told herself to be brave; she had nothing to fear while he was with her. Quickly, she passed beneath the overhanging roses now in full bloom, the warm night air heavy with their perfume, and through the kitchen garden where the scent of sweet peas supplanted that of the roses. For all kinds of reasons, it was a night to savour. She walked on, aware of the silence that was never wholly silent. Always the slight rustle of leaves, the scurrying of small creatures, the fluttering of an unquiet bird. But the bustle of the day was over and the world belonged to her, and to one other.

He was waiting for her beneath the laurel arch. Together

they walked to the summerhouse and the seat overlooking the lake. Across the water, the temple rose grand and stately, its marble pristine in the moonlight.

'You came,' she said.

'Did you think I wouldn't?'

'I didn't know if you had heard me. Or understood.'

He didn't answer but reached out and this time took her hand between his. Her heart gave another of the small thuds she was getting used to. She found herself adrift in a world of emotions that she had never before encountered, her senses so finely tuned they caught every fleeting sound or smell or touch. She could have sworn just then that she'd heard the slightest crackling of branches, as though the trees across the lake had become curious about the interlopers and decided to investigate. But that was foolish.

'I'm sorry my aunt intruded on us so rudely.' She kept her hand in his. 'She can't have realised we are friends.'

'On the contrary, she realised it only too well. She has no wish for us to be friends. She is intent on saving you from a dreadful fate!'

His tone was light and she wasn't sure whether to smile or not. 'That sounds very slightly mad.'

'Not mad at all. In fact, highly practical. She is concerned you don't become too close to a man who would prove the worst possible suitor – or almost the worst. I am without pedigree, without money and I work a trade.'

'But you're a professional man,' she protested, aware that she was not disputing the idea of his being her suitor.

'I can claim a profession, certainly, but in your aunt's eyes, in your family's eyes, I'm as suspect as any man who hammers a nail or wields a scythe. And, even worse, I'm Irish. The Irish are troublemakers, or so the English think.'

Only last week, she'd heard Joshua voice similar sentiments and she wasted no time in arguing. Instead, her mind was taken up with this new and wonderful possibility. It was startling to think of Aiden as a suitor, but exciting too. So different from anything she could have imagined. She snatched a quick glance at him. His eyes were narrowed and he was staring across the water at the temple and at its silver shadow floating serenely on the surface of the lake.

'That was an odd business – what happened yesterday,' he said at last.

His remark was unexpected and she hesitated a little before saying, 'In what way?'

'I've been thinking about it and I can't understand why the boys' shelter collapsed in the fashion it did.'

'I doubt there's any mystery to that. It was Oliver and William who built it,' she joked.

He shook his head, a flick of soft brown hair catching the moon's silver. 'But it was secure. I remember checking it the other day when I was walking through the Wilderness. It struck me then that it could be dangerous, if they hadn't roped the wood together securely enough. But they had I'd swear to it.'

'Then it was probably William diving for cover in the way he did. He told me that he'd been terrified by dogs and, in a panic, had thrown himself into the shelter. It couldn't have been strong enough.'

'It should have been.' Aiden remained unconvinced. 'And in any case, why were those dogs running free?'

She looked blank. 'I thought he must be imagining them, but I didn't want to cause more upset by saying so. We don't have dogs, you see. We've not had a dog since the day William was bitten as a baby. It was a pointer we'd brought from Birmingham and I think the change of scene must have upset the animal. My father was eager to replace him with a Labrador. He said the breed would be more docile, but really I think it was because he saw Labradors as the right kind of dog for a country gentleman. Anyway, Mama would have none of it, and for once she won the fight.'

'The dogs that scared William were real enough. They were from Amberley, a couple of your uncle's hounds. They got loose and found their way into the garden. But the men rounded them up pretty quickly and blocked the breach they'd made in the hedge. William wasn't in any danger.'

'He wouldn't have known that.'

'No, he wouldn't,' Aiden said thoughtfully. 'I don't like it that he could be so badly frightened.'

'He has always been a little delicate.'

'Unlike his sister then.'

She gave him a saucy smile. 'You're not aware that I am the most delicate of flowers?'

'A flower, I grant you. But delicate?' Then more seriously, he said, 'Were you in trouble for talking to me at the fête?'

'I had a ritual scolding over dinner, first from Papa and then from Mama when we retired to the drawing room. But I was expecting that. And expecting that my father will be even more vigilant from now on. He'll have to make sure I'm kept busy every minute of the day – it will be quite exhausting for him.'

'Unless he feels there's no longer a threat. He might insist that I go.'

She felt a punch to her stomach and looked at him in alarm. 'Has Mr Simmonds threatened to send you away?'

'Not exactly. But I know that Jonathan has been told in

no uncertain terms that I must leave the minute he has no further need of me.'

She said as airily as she could, 'They do see you as a threat, don't they?'

'Am I not then?' He smiled, and she saw his eyes soft and dreamy in the moonlight.

He was a very definite threat, but she could not bring herself to say so. She crossed her ankles, then uncrossed them, wanting to be honest but not entirely sure what her heart was saying.

'They wish me to meet a relative of my mother's – a second cousin.'

He tensed beside her. 'And why would that be?'

Her answer skirted the question. 'His name is Giles Audley. He is a relative of the Fitzroys, and very well connected. Papa likes that.' The thought had her twist her lips in annoyance.

'And why is it important that you meet him?'

'He is looking for a wife,' she said bluntly. There was little point in shadow-boxing.

'And you are to be the wife?' His voice had a sour edge to it now.

'I think they are hoping so.'

'And you, are you hoping so too?'

'He is a widower and twenty years older than me.'

'That doesn't answer my question.'

She could feel his antagonism but refused to be drawn. 'I've been asked to go to tea at Amberley and meet him. I feel almost sorry for the poor man. He will be expecting a very different girl from the one he's to meet!'

'But you've agreed to go?' He had shifted very slightly

away, and the small distance between them seemed suddenly a chasm as deep as the Devil's Dyke.

'I will go since my parents are so insistent. It won't hurt me to meet him. It's not going to mean anything.' She was trying to bridge the chasm, to recover something of their earlier happiness.

He stood up and shook his shoulders, as though he would free himself of disagreeable thoughts. 'It will mean everything, Elizabeth. It's your future that is being decided.'

'That's nonsense. I decide my own future,' she said boldly, wanting it to be true.

He glanced down at her, a mocking expression clearly visible in the brightness of the night. 'I think not. You may delude yourself into believing so, but the truth is very different.'

She jumped up, stung by his accusation. 'You are horrid.'

'I am honest.'

'Then I prefer delusion.' She turned abruptly away, the long skirt of her dress swishing against the paving.

'Elizabeth—'

But she had gone, whisking her way sure-footedly along the path and out through the laurel arch.

Chapter Fifteen

July, 1914

'You should be wearing the rose crêpe, Miss Elizabeth.'
Ivy was standing in the doorway, her mouth pursed in
disapproval.

She hadn't heard her maid knock. She had been too busy
gazing through the window, and thinking how much she'd
prefer to be walking in the garden. How much she'd like
to escape and go in search of Aiden. She was desperate to
speak to him again. She had been from the moment they'd
quarrelled. He'd misjudged her, misprized her resolve, but
she should not have walked away.

'I'm saving it for a special occasion,' she said, turning
from the window with a small sigh.

Ivy tutted. 'What could more special than this afternoon?'

Her maid was as much a friend as a servant, a trusted
confidante from nursery days. Ivy knew exactly what this
visit to Amberley meant, and she clearly intended her
mistress to make a lasting impression. She began to tidy
the dressing table, clattering together boxes and pots and
brushes with unnecessary force.

'I shall wear the pink crêpe at your wedding,' Elizabeth

soothed. 'That's what I call a special occasion. In the meantime, the Russian green can do duty again.'

'You're too kind for your own good, miss,' the girl scolded. 'You should be worrying about *your* wedding, not mine.'

She handed her mistress a beaded purse. 'And I'm not sure when you'll get to wear the dress. We brought the wedding forward, like I told you – Eddie couldn't see the sense in waiting till September – but now Joe Lacey is real poorly with his hand. And he's our best man.'

'What's wrong with Joe? Mrs Lacey has said nothing.'

'She don't want no fuss but Joe's ma has been in and out of their cottage these past few days, she's been that worried. And May has hardly touched her books all week, what with running around for her brother. Joe got caught by one of them nasty, vicious dogs. The day when Mr William had his turn. Joe went to help get the dogs back into Amberley and one of them went for him. His hand is swelled up something bad. But Dr Daniels is coming this afternoon, so mebbe he'll fix it.'

'I've never known the hounds to break loose before and I can't imagine how they came to be in the gardens. I do know they've caused an amazing amount of trouble. I wish my uncle would get rid of them, but I suppose there's no chance of that. He loves hunting too much.'

'Loves killing things more like.' Ivy waggled her eyebrows meaningfully. 'Ask them folks at Amberley.'

Her mistress looked puzzled, but the clock was ticking and there was no time to ask for enlightenment. 'I had better go or my father will have worn out his boot leather pacing the hall. Tea is at four and it's almost that now.'

'I hope it goes well,' Ivy said cautiously.

She hoped so, too, although 'going well' was open to interpretation. Her version would be very different from her parents'. Or that of the unknown Giles Audley. He had no idea what was coming his way. He was expecting to share his tea with an agreeable girl, while the agreeable girl was intent on scaring him into flight. Aiden had suggested that she was a puppet whose strings were being pulled by others. She would show him that he was wrong. She would show them all. This afternoon she would be the one to pull the strings.

*

As Miller turned the car into the gates of the Fitzroy estate, Alice experienced a jumble of emotions. For the first time in very many years, she was coming home. Amberley's battered decor, its old fashioned furniture, its plumbing that never quite worked, were still close to her heart. Louisa might bemoan the outmoded muddle of buildings, and envy her sister-in-law her modern conveniences, but, for Alice, Amberley would always be her true home.

She sank back into the padded comfort of new leather, as the car swung smoothly around bend after bend, until it came to rest outside the turreted porch she knew so well. She gazed hungrily through the glass of the car window. Mullioned casements slept in the afternoon sun, white doves perched on a red roof of weathered tiles and on either side of the iron-studded oak door, the griffins sat proudly atop their pedestals, unwearied by the years. She had loved this house deeply, yet at the time she hadn't truly valued it. It was an oddity of human nature that you never seemed to value what you had. Louisa here in Amberley, for instance, she at Summerhayes. But if she'd known how that deal, made behind closed doors over a quarter of a century ago, would play out, she might have acted differently. She might have fought to stay. None of them could have known, of course, what would happen. Not really. Everyone involved had lost as much as they'd gained. Henry hated the very existence of Summerhayes, yet without it Amberley would no longer be his. Joshua had been denied entry to the society he craved, yet become master of an estate that was near to paradise.

It was for her that the dice had fallen most extremely. After Thomas, she had not allowed herself to think too deeply about what might have been. She had accepted a fate she'd had no power to change. Joshua had possessed sufficient money to make his offer attractive to the Fitzroys. Ironically, as it turned out, he had come into Sussex on the advice of a distant member of the Audley family, one of his customers for whom he'd made exquisite buttons for an evening suit. The man, she'd never known his name, had been aware of Joshua's ambition and known, too, something of the Fitzroys' financial difficulties. It was he who had suggested that the next time Joshua was in London on business, he travel on to Sussex and meet the unmarried daughter of the house. She had had no say in it. She had relinquished whatever small power she'd ever had when she proved incapable of attracting a wealthy husband for herself. Instead, the family had found one for her, and it had been her duty to marry this unknown man and save Amberley for her young brother.

*

Now, *that* brother was waiting for them in the drawing room. Alice glanced around as they entered, and saw with surprise that Dr Daniels was one of those present. She had thought him at Summerhayes, visiting Mrs Lacey's son, but here he was lounging comfortably in the old high-backed chesterfield and talking animatedly to Louisa.

'How very good to see you.' Henry stepped forward to greet them, bonhomie personified.

How agreeable he could be if he chose. And how rarely he chose. Their mother's frequent miscarriages meant that he was a full seven years younger than she, and when he was born – the son and heir finally arrived – he'd been lauded and spoilt by the entire household, while she had been largely ignored. Her role had been that of a subordinate, at the beck and call of a demanding small brother. She hadn't protested, but simply retreated into herself and thereby gained the reputation of being vague and indecisive. It was more, she thought, that she was otherworldly. This world had proved an immense disappointment, and she had needed to find another place in which to exist.

A tall pleasant-faced man had risen from the chair he was occupying next to Louisa, and walked towards them. Henry took him by the arm and, with a perfectly judged smile, made the introductions: 'This is Giles Audley. Giles, my sister Alice – you will remember her – her husband and their daughter, Elizabeth.'

'I'm delighted to meet you.' His voice was mellow and, in contrast to his host, Giles Audley sounded sincere.

Alice's heart lifted. She remembered him only vaguely from family occasions many years previous. He would have been little more than a boy then. But the man who stood in front of her now was surely someone with whom Elizabeth could find little fault. It was of the utmost importance to her that her daughter was happy. She had been fearful that she was visiting on Elizabeth the very treatment she herself had suffered. But Giles Audley was clearly a gentleman in manner and voice, a worthy suitor. She could relax. She was doing the right thing.

She slipped into the upright chair Louisa had indicated. Its ruby velvet was new but the woven tapestry cushion at her back was as old as she. Her mother had sewn it. Alice could remember her sitting in this very room, her head bowed low over the canvas as she worked in the fading light. The oil lamps would be brought early in the evening, but her mother would not rest; cross stitch would follow cross stitch. In all, she must have sewn a dozen of these cushion covers and this must be the one survivor that Louisa had not managed to jettison. There were other remnants of her parents' reign, too. The Victorian sideboard still sat heavily against one wall, and above its carved doors perched a huge and hideous vase beloved by Alice's father, its sickly yellow background aflame with pink cabbage roses.

The maidservant had been busy at the tea trolley and was at her elbow now, offering her a cup. This at least was new. New and expensive porcelain. Royal Worcester. Most definitely not the choice of her thrifty mother.

'So what's the news?' Henry asked, as he took the chair beside hers.

Her eyes flickered with nerves. 'News?'

'From Europe. I've heard some disquieting things that I cannot really believe. Your husband keeps in touch with people on the Continent, doesn't he? What does he say?'

She looked across the room at the long windows that

gave on to the terrace. Legs astride and hands clasped behind his back, Joshua was staring into the distance.

'He rarely speaks of it and I know nothing of Europe,' she confessed, knowing she was guilty of the vagueness Henry so hated. 'You will have to ask him for yourself.'

Joshua must have heard for he turned abruptly and, waving aside the offer of tea, collapsed into a buttoned-backed armchair a few feet away.

'You asked about Europe, Henry. I believe that several countries have called up their reserves. One or two may have closed their frontiers.' His tone was subdued, the familiar bombast absent. He was treading carefully, she thought, determined not to give his brother-in-law cause to complain of his manners during the few hours they were at Amberley.

'But surely, it won't come to war.' The doctor had been busy collecting his and Louisa's empty cups, but on hearing Joshua's words, turned to face him. 'I was reading only the other day that ties between Germany and Britain are stronger now than they've ever been.'

'If we're talking business, certainly,' Joshua responded. 'Britain is Germany's best customer and, after India, they are our second-best market.'

'And if we're not talking business?' Louisa put in.

'Then it's anyone's guess. I think we should be prepared.'

A grey cloud hovered over the gathering, but Henry was not so easily defeated and rallied his forces. 'I don't believe in listening to the gloom mongers.' He looked pointedly at Joshua. 'I'm certain Germany will not worry us. It's far more likely we'll be intervening in Ireland.'

'This issue of Home Rule,' the doctor said eagerly, wanting, it seemed, to be accepted as a member of the group.

'The papers are full of it. I read that both Protestants and Catholics have formed their own military units and are importing quantities of weapons—'

'Gunrunning on a huge scale. Yes, we know that,' Henry said crushingly. 'They're drilling and practising marksmanship quite openly.'

Joshua grunted disdainfully. 'Let's hope you're right and that marksmanship is confined to Ireland. A European war would be another matter entirely.' His tone had hardened. He was an intelligent man, a knowledgeable man, Alice knew, and he would not back down on his beliefs, even within the hallowed shades of Amberley.

'You didn't bring William,' Louisa interrupted in a bright voice, and once more Alice had cause to thank her. 'He must be up and about by now.'

'He is much better, thank you, but we thought it best that he remain at home today. We have his friend staying – I think I mentioned it to you. Together they can be a little boisterous.'

'That's the Jewish boy, isn't it?' Henry had not enjoyed playing second fiddle to his brother-in-law and was ready to attack.

Joshua stiffened at the implied criticism. 'I believe his family *is* Jewish.'

Henry ignored him and turned to his sister. 'It doesn't do you credit, Alice, you know. Intimacy with such a family.'

'We are not intimate with the Amos family. We have merely had their son to stay with us for the summer holidays, as a companion for William.' And I wish we hadn't, she thought fervently. Oliver was a bad influence, though his Jewishness had little to do with it. It was the closeness of the two boys she didn't like. It was unhealthy.

Her brother had moved into full combat. 'It amounts to the same thing. Parents or child. You're giving house room to an alien.'

'That's a bit strong,' Dr Daniels protested.

'I'm not sure I asked for your opinion, Doctor. The fact remains that Jewish immigrants from the Russian pogroms are still coming here. These people don't share our culture or our values. And weren't we supposed to have an act of parliament restricting the influx of undesirable aliens?'

'What's so undesirable about Jewish immigrants, Uncle?'

Elizabeth had sat silent until now, seeming intent on the ebb and flow of conversation, but really, Alice suspected, intent on ignoring Giles Audley.

The question hung in the air, but before Henry could dignify it with a response, Elizabeth continued, 'I realise that a dislike of foreigners is part of being insular, part of being British, but when you speak of aliens, you're talking of a highly cultured people. Their civilisation is a great deal older than ours.' She paused just long enough to get everyone's attention. 'Or perhaps that's why you find them so undesirable? Their civilisation makes you feel inferior.'

The silence in the room was so intense that the proverbial pin could easily have been heard. Henry glared at his niece while Louisa fiddled nervously with the folds of her dress.

Giles Audley, taking stock of the situation, started up from his chair and walked towards Elizabeth. 'The weather is very pleasant today, Miss Summer, and I wonder if you would you care to walk in the garden?' In an instant, he was offering his arm and she had little option but to rise and take it.

Alice breathed again. Mr Audley was the gentleman she'd taken him for.

Chapter Sixteen

'Shall we walk in the rose arbour,' he asked, as they emerged through the French windows.

'I really don't mind.'

'The blooms are not at their best at this time of the year, of course, but their scent lingers. And it should be cooler there than on the terrace.'

'I am happy to walk wherever you choose.'

She knew she sounded ungracious and, for a moment, regretted it. The afternoon had been difficult enough and she had just lobbed a hand grenade into the genteel assembly. Not that she was sorry about that. Genteel it might be, but thoroughly false. Now, though, she was being curmudgeonly to this perfectly pleasant man, who was guilty only of trying to smooth the feathers she'd ruffled, including her own. He must be finding the situation as trying as she. She stole a sideways glance at him, seeing the greying at his temple and the creases around his mouth. She wondered about his past and what kind of life he had led. She couldn't ask. That would be to enquire of his dead wife, an intrusion as insensitive as it was ill mannered. In turn, he couldn't ask her what he must want to know. Why had she seemed willing to contemplate marriage with a widower, but appeared now to be decidedly against such a union? Politeness held them in its iron band.

'Do you get up to London often?' she asked at last, unable to maintain her *froideur*.

'Very little these days. My wife loved the social whirl, but since her death I've hardly been to town. I've thrown myself into managing my estate instead. It may be small but there's a constant need for oversight.'

The subject was in the open after all. 'You didn't share your wife's enjoyment of London then?'

'I was content enough to accompany her whenever she fancied a trip to town. What made Lavinia happy made me happy, too.' Then seeming to sense he might have been clumsy, he said, 'But you, Miss Summer. You must often be in London.'

'I've only made one visit. Last year – I was presented at Court.'

'A rare honour. How did you find the experience?'

They had reached the rose arbour and he stood back to allow her to pass through the stone arch, but, once inside, the sense of abandonment hit her hard. The garden was in disarray. Weeds tumbled between bushes, and the roses themselves looked old and weary, their petals a trifle ragged, as though they had grown tired of waiting for a human touch.

When they were again walking side by side along the path that bordered the arbour, she answered his question.

'I found London frantic and the presentation tedious.' She would be honest. What had she to lose? To her surprise, he laughed out loud.

'If being presented at Court was tedious, what do you make of today?'

'Family events are never exactly riveting, are they?'

She'd brushed away his question, but he had no intention of allowing the subject to drop. It was clear he wanted to discuss what had led them both to Amberley on this sunny afternoon. 'I'm afraid this feels very awkward for you – this meeting with me.'

She blushed very slightly. 'It's as awkward for you.'

'I'm an old warrior. Nothing much fazes me these days. But you are still very young, at the beginning of your life. Back there—' and he jerked his head in the direction of the house '—I was worried you'd been brought here as a sacrificial lamb.'

It was her turn to laugh out loud. 'I don't think I'd ever be a sacrificial anything. In fact, I rather think I'd be the one wielding the knife.' They'd paused beside a splendid Damask rose and she smelt its heavy drenching perfume fill the air around them.

'And what knife are you wielding this afternoon, apart from decimating your uncle?'

'That doesn't count. I've yet to start. I haven't quite decided where.'

'My goodness, that alone sends me trembling.'

She looked up at him, seeing the slight twist to his mouth. 'I'm sure it doesn't. But it might make you reconsider whatever plans you had in mind when you came here.'

'Reconsider? You mean, make my escape while the going is good.'

She liked him. He was candid and direct. 'I could give you a flavour of what you've escaped,' she offered.

'I'm intrigued.'

'Well, I could quote Emmeline Pankhurst at you: "If it is right for men to fight for their freedom, and God knows what the human race would be like today if men had not, then it is right for women to fight for their freedom and the freedom of the children they bear." '

'Impressive. So you're a suffragette?'

'In thought only.'

'It might be best to stick to thought. I believe that even ladies of good family are landing in prison these days.'

'That's not what worries me. It's that I don't approve of some of their actions,' she said judicially. 'Trying to get into Buckingham Palace to mount a demonstration seems sensible to me, but what is the point of slashing the "Rokeby Venus"?'

'Or of dying beneath a horse's hooves?'

'Exactly. It doesn't invalidate their demands though.'

'And that is the vote. But do you want it? Many women don't, you know.'

'I want equality and a vote is part of that. I want the freedom to decide my own life, just as you and most other men do.'

'It's a noble aim but I fear it will be some time coming.'

Her face puckered. 'I'm not sure. The suffragettes are stepping up their actions all the time. Something will have to give.'

'Yes, I know. Planting bombs and burning churches. But they're likely to be overtaken by larger events. Strife in Europe is what will do for them. The government will be too intent on keeping us safe from that whirlwind to have much time for votes for women.'

'You agree with my father then? You think that Britain will become involved in whatever trouble is brewing?'

'Not if Asquith has any say in it. But our country is bound

by treaty to intervene if Belgium is attacked, and there's no knowing how present troubles in Europe will be resolved.'

She felt a shadow grasp at her and was unsure of what it meant. These last few hours the gloom of war seemed to have come closer, a strange echo of her family's unhappiness and the darkness of her own future.

'Elizabeth.' Her mother's voice sounded from a distance, and then Alice's figure appeared framed in the stone archway, her head bobbing this way and that as she tried to locate her daughter.

'I'm here, Mama.'

Her mother moved along the path towards them, seeming more flustered than when they'd left her. 'I hope you will excuse us, Mr Audley,' she said, 'but my husband is wishful to leave.'

'Giles, not Mr Audley, please,' he said. 'We are cousins, are we not? And you must have known me as a small boy.'

'I did… Giles… very briefly. And now we have renewed our acquaintance, I hope we will see a great deal more of you.' She looked up at him, raising her hand to shade her eyes against the late-afternoon sun hanging low in the sky. 'Perhaps you would care to visit us at Summerhayes?' Elizabeth noticed that her mother deliberately looked away from her. 'You must come to dinner.'

'I would be delighted.' Giles Audley said, with a wide smile.

Chapter Seventeen

The next morning, Elizabeth walked out of the breakfast room and into an altercation. That in itself was not unusual, but this time it was her mother embroiled in argument with the head gardener. Mr Harris was in no mood to listen to Alice's complaint that the house flowers had not been changed for three whole days. He was still fully occupied putting to rights the ravages visited on his beloved Summerhayes by the recent fair.

Her mother's voice was developing a dangerous quaver and she thought it time to intervene. 'I'm sure Mr Harris has a hundred and one things to think of, Mama. Why don't I cut the flowers for you?'

'It is not your place to do so, Elizabeth, and besides, it's already growing hot and you shouldn't be outside. Your complexion will suffer.'

'I won't be gone long and I'm not so fragile that I can't withstand a little sun. Mr Harris is very busy today and all *I* have to do is splash a little paint around.' The flippancy was a betrayal of her art, but in the interests of peace it was a price worth paying.

Harris tipped his cap. 'Thank you, Miss Elizabeth. I'd be most obliged. The calla lilies are looking beautiful, ma'am. A vase in the hall would be splendid.' Now he knew himself released from the pettifogging chore, he was eager to placate his mistress.

Elizabeth found her sun hat squashed behind several old jackets in the hall cupboard, then walked quickly down to the tool shed and selected what looked to be the sharpest pair of secateurs. There was just a chance that she might see Aiden on her way. But by the time she'd walked through avenues of dahlias and delphiniums and gladioli, she'd seen no one and could only suppose that the men were working by the lakeside or in the greenhouses to the east.

She had reached the calla lilies and stooped to begin her task, when the voices reached her. Even from this distance, one had a familiar ring. She straightened up again, screwing her eyes against the sun and made out two blurred figures walking through the arch of the Wilderness and into the walled garden. As they drew nearer, she could see that one of the figures belonged to Giles Audley. She hadn't been wrong about the voice. But what was he doing here so early in the morning and completely unannounced?

He shook his companion's hand and turned to walk along one of the gravel paths that bisected the walled garden. He was evidently making his way to the house. But when he saw her standing watching him, he paused, and then came on towards her. She thought he looked a little sheepish as though caught out in some minor mischief.

'Good morning, Miss Summer. You're at work early, I see.'

'And you too, Mr Audley. This is a surprise. I didn't hear the door knocker or I would have accompanied you down to the garden.'

'I didn't knock. I'm afraid, I'm something of an intruder,'

he said guiltily. 'I came from Amberley, through the back way.'

She was puzzled. 'The back way?'

'There's an old path, did you not know? It's become a little overgrown now but it's still passable. It leads to a disused entrance to the lower part of this estate. I think it must have been blocked at one time, but the brickwork has crumbled here and there. The path comes out just behind the lake, in the middle of the trees, in fact.'

She took some minutes to digest this. She'd had no idea there was any way into Summerhayes from the lower end of the estate and she was pretty sure that none of her family had either. And what about Harris and his men? Were they aware? At times this summer, she'd felt a disquiet she couldn't explain and now it grew more intense.

'I'm sorry, I can see I've startled you. I don't usually pay calls in this irregular fashion. I do hope you'll forgive the intrusion.'

'You have surprised me,' she admitted. 'But why come that way?'

'I wanted to catch Simmonds before he went off on his day's travels, and I knew he'd be working there.'

'You need Mr Simmonds? You need an architect? Are you building a temple, too?'

His laugh was a trifle self conscious. 'Nothing like that. It just seems like a good time to refurbish Wych Hall – that's my home – and your father recommended Simmonds. I thought it sensible to speak to him while I'm in the district.'

'What's wrong with Wych Hall?' She knew she sounded suspicious, but she couldn't help herself.

'There's nothing wrong with the house. It's just a little tired, I suppose. My wife has been dead ten years and to be honest I've done very little with it since. I let it out while I was abroad and my tenants were a bit careless, and since I've been back in Sussex, all my energies have gone into setting the estate on its feet.'

'So what has brought on this flurry of housekeeping?'

Her suspicions were mounting. Perhaps Audley's desire to refurbish his house was a genuine impulse. Or perhaps it was something more. Before the tea party at Amberley, she'd hoped he wouldn't like her. But he had, and their ease with each other in the rose garden could have misled him into thinking that, despite her bold words on female freedom, she was willing to contemplate marriage. On top of which, there was the dinner her mother had promised. The space in which she moved seemed to have got smaller these last few hours. Had Aiden been right then in saying her life had already been mapped out and she would have little say in it?

But there was nothing in his expression to suggest subterfuge. 'It's simple enough,' he said easily. 'It was seeing other people's homes and realising how shabby I've allowed mine to become. I've the money after all, to make the place a great deal more comfortable, so why on earth don't I do it?'

If Amberley were his standard, Wych Hall must be shabby indeed. And was that a hint that if she married him there would be no lack of money? As if he knew what was passing in her mind, he said, 'Amberley is a little old fashioned but it's very agreeable. And your father was keen to show me what he's done at Summerhayes. I understand your house is very modern.'

'Bang up to the minute,' she agreed. 'And Papa will be delighted to give you the conducted tour. Make sure you admire the stained glass – it's everywhere, but he's particularly proud of the panels in the dining room. They illustrate the seasons and are quite beautiful. Oh, and the inglenook fireplace in the drawing room. The tiles are William de Morgan's. But don't praise too heavily when my mother's around. She prefers her old family home, but tries to keep it a secret.'

'I could see yesterday how much she loved Amberley. Her gaze was never still. I gather she hasn't been back to the house since she left to be married.'

He was diplomatic, she'd give him that. 'Things have been a little difficult between the families,' she said, practising her own diplomacy.

'Yes,' he said thoughtfully. 'Your uncle is a forceful character.'

'As is my father. It doesn't make for peace. But I hope you won't let Uncle Henry bully you.'

'There's no chance of that. No one persuades me into anything I don't want.'

Was that a message for her? Was she what he wanted? She'd hoped that her lack of interest had been clear, but the warmth of his smile suggested otherwise. Things were moving too quickly and the sooner he left the district, the better.

'Are you staying long at Amberley?'

'I arranged to stay a few days, but I'm thinking now that I might extend my visit. Your aunt and uncle have no objection and it will give me a chance to consult with Mr Simmonds properly. Shall we walk up to the house together?'

'You must excuse me for the moment. I still have flowers to cut for Mama.'

'I hope we may meet later then.' He smiled a goodbye and walked towards the pergola. She watched him as he disappeared from view. Things were definitely moving far too quickly.

*

She escaped from the house as early that evening as she dared. William had been persuaded to take another message and now, shadow-like, she stole through the garden. The peacocks roosting in the trees that bordered the lawn chattered irritably. It was a mystery to her why her father insisted on keeping such bad-tempered birds. It could only be to lend Summerhayes an aristocratic air. As swiftly as she could, she glided past, anxious for them not to begin their loud calling.

She could feel her body ache with tension. Would Aiden be at their meeting place? She wasn't sure he would come. She'd discovered from talking to Joe that he had gone that afternoon to the sculptor's studio to help load the carved reliefs that would hang on the interior walls of the temple. It was fatiguing work and he might choose to go back to Mrs Boxall's indifferent cooking rather than return to Summerhayes. He must certainly be out of charity with her, after she'd run from him in anger. More than anything now, she wished that she hadn't. He had spoken the truth as he saw it, and after this morning's encounter with Giles Audley, she had begun to share that truth. She should not have taken such quick offence. But she had felt insecure, her nerves jangled by fear of the coercion she might meet at Amberley. Fear that, despite her brave words, she would not be strong enough to resist the pressure brought to bear by her family.

Audley's visit today had increased that fear. He was a

pleasant man, someone with whom she could talk easily and honestly. Not a man who would bully or harass her into something she did not want. He had been charmingly frank about his late wife. It was evident he'd loved her dearly and she might well be the reason for his wishing to remarry, for there were no children to consider. He had been happy in his marriage and it was clear that he hoped to repeat that happiness. But it would not be with her. It wasn't that he was unattractive. He was a distinguished-looking man. And it wasn't that she had thought him out of sympathy with her – quite the opposite. But none of that mattered when her heart was leading her elsewhere.

He was in the summerhouse, looking out across the lake, and must have caught the sound of her skirt on the paving because he jumped up and came swiftly towards her.

'I'm sorry.' He reached out for her hand.

'Isn't it me who should be saying sorry? I flounced off like a silly schoolgirl.'

'Well, yes.' His face broke into a wide grin. 'But you do flounce very well.'

Still holding her hand, he led her back to the wooden bench. For some minutes, they sat side by side, neither of them speaking. The slightest night breeze rippled the surface of the lake and there was a whispering in the trees. Now that she knew there was a hidden entrance not far distant, her discomfort grew. She must take Cornford to one side as soon as possible and ask him to block it. She would need to be discreet; if she announced the news at large, it would embarrass Giles Audley as a trespasser.

When Aiden spoke, his voice was serious. 'I hope you'll believe me when I say I had no wish to offend you, Elizabeth.'

'I do believe you. And you were right in what you said. I think I knew it and that's why I behaved badly. I was worried, fearful that I was walking into a trap.'

His grip on her hand intensified. 'I should have been more understanding. I know what it's like to feel trapped.'

She pulled away from him in surprise. 'You? But you're a man and can marry as you wish.'

'Marriage isn't the only kind of prison, you know.'

'I'm sure not, but why would *you* feel trapped?'

'That maybe the wrong word. Let's say my choices have been constrained.'

'By what?' He was being mysterious and she didn't like it.

'By my family. I've not gone home to Ireland because they've made it impossible.'

She was taken aback, and in the pause that followed, he said, 'You asked me once about my brothers and I'd no wish to speak of them then. But I want you to know the truth. You deserve it.'

'If you're sure.' She was uncertain she wanted to know the truth. Aiden was as perfect as a man could be – did she really want the doubtful details of his past?

'Yes, I am sure. I haven't seen my brothers since I left Ireland, but that doesn't mean I haven't heard of them or their doings. They belong to a nationalist movement, the Irish Republican Brotherhood. It's dedicated to achieving Home Rule for Ireland.'

Since she'd met Aiden, she'd made sure to read every piece of news coming from that country. It seemed right to her that Ireland should be free; in her mind, its fight for independence marked a clear parallel with women's struggle for the same. There had been several fervent arguments with Joshua, who had nothing but disgust for the Irish vipers, as he called them.

'I've heard of the movement,' she said cautiously.

'It's a secret society, but it's common knowledge who belongs and what their mission is. Members sign they are willing to use force to further the cause and a small band of them already have – bombings and shootings mainly. My brothers count themselves as part of that band.'

She gave a small gasp and her hand flew instinctively to her mouth. Then she turned to look at Aiden: his face was set and almost white in the light of the half-moon.

'I'm sorry. I thought I could keep from telling you, but I find I can't. I don't want to have secrets.'

His confession had shocked her, but he was struggling and needed reassurance. 'You were right to tell. Secrets only fester and destroy.' She thought of her parents, of her uncle and his family, and the secret arrangements they'd made that had produced only misery.

'Do you see now why I have no contact with them?'

She nodded in a mechanical fashion, still trying to absorb what he'd told her. 'It's better that way,' he went on. 'I understand why they feel the way they do, but I can't condone their actions. And, for their part, they'll never forgive me for not returning to Ireland once I was full grown and had the chance. They despise me for selling out, for going over to the enemy.'

'Living in England doesn't make you the enemy,' she protested.

'That's not the way they see it. For them, you're either one thing or another, black or white.'

There was little more she could say, and she'd begun to

retreat into her thoughts when she heard again a rustling of the trees. This time, slightly louder. 'What was that?'

'The wind? It's getting up. I wouldn't be surprised if we had a storm tonight.'

Of course, it had to be the wind. But she did not like this garden. It was as though its situation far from the house, enclosed and solitary, had drawn to it all the secrets, the dark impulses that existed in Summerhayes, and trapped them in a still suffocation.

'You haven't told me what happened at your tea party,' he prompted.

It was an effort to put to one side her troubled feelings but she launched gallantly into her tale. 'You would have been proud of me – I refused to have my strings pulled. It was quite a gathering: my parents, my Uncle Henry and Aunt Louisa, the doctor even. I don't know why he'd been invited. Perhaps they thought I might faint at the sight of Giles Audley and Dr Daniels' services would be required.'

'And were they?'

'No, they were not! Mr Audley turned out to be most gentlemanly and made no attempt to coerce me. And he didn't seem the kind of person who would be coerced himself.'

She waited for Aiden to respond, he'd asked for an account, after all, but he remained mute. The seconds ticked by. An owl hooted from the trees beyond and another answered. The ghostly sounds travelled through the long silence. She was confused, not knowing how to break a quiet that was becoming ominous.

In the end, he was the one to break it. 'You sound as though the tea party was enjoyable.' His voice was flat. 'I imagine you'll meet him again.'

She could have said that Audley was a horrible man and that she would be whipped before she agreed to another meeting, yet she had wanted to speak truly. No secrets, they had agreed. But now she was wondering if she had made a mistake.

'My mother has invited him to dinner at Summerhayes. I don't know if Papa has agreed or if the rest of the company are invited. But, whatever happens, when I meet Giles Audley again, it will mean as little as it did yesterday.'

'And why is that?'

'Because I choose it to mean as little.'

It was suddenly very important to convince him and, without thinking, she reached out for his hand and rubbed it against her cheek. He loosened himself from her grasp but moved closer so that she could feel his warmth through the thin silk of her dress. 'So is there someone you choose to mean more?' The question was provocative.

She looked into his face and her smile was equally provocative. 'I really cannot say.'

'Then it's best we don't talk.'

His hands were in her hair, his fingers twirling the fine copper strands into small corkscrews. Then he drew her face to his. She saw his form blur as his mouth came closer. His lips were on hers, hard and warm. For a moment, she struggled, but only for a moment. She sank into him, wrapped around by his arms and pulled into his chest. He kissed her hair, her cheeks, the smooth cream of her eyelids, and then found her lips again. She was kissing him back, over and over again, her mouth soft and open to his.

'What are we doing?' she asked between breathless kisses.

'Whatever it is, it feels very good,' he said, and kissed her again.

Chapter Eighteen

The breeze that in late evening had wound its way through the Italian Garden, had in the night become a gale, bringing with it torrential rain, which hammered on the windows and spooled across the flagged stones of the terrace. William climbed onto the window seat and looked out, his nose pushed hard against the glass. The glorious summer garden they'd known had been obliterated and in its place was a cold, damp landscape.

'No chance of getting out today,' he said gloomily, surveying the wind-tossed greenery and the almost vertical rain.

He was feeling edgy and ill tempered. Olly had suggested they build another shelter, this time within the house, perhaps in one of the forgotten attics, but the idea hadn't appealed. He had no wish to build another shelter. Ever.

'So what do we do this morning?' Oliver asked

'How should I know?' He jumped down from the window seat and started riffling through the stack of magazines by his bed. 'You don't like doing puzzles. You don't want to read a book or help me label specimens.'

'We could kick a ball.'

'And where precisely did you have in mind? The drawing room?'

'C'mon, Wills. Don't be such a grump. We could take a ball up to the top floor. We wouldn't bother anyone there.'

He felt guilty. It wasn't Olly's fault that something had changed for him, that unfamiliar feelings were pushing for escape. At times, times like today, it was difficult, painful even, to keep them imprisoned. Every day, it seemed, he'd fallen more deeply under his friend's spell, and all he'd come to want or need was to hear Olly's voice, follow in his footsteps, enjoy his adventures – and touch him. But that was something he mustn't think of. It wasn't done. It was definitely not done. He'd heard stories, of course he had, but they were just stories. He must stop feeling this way. It wasn't Olly's fault that bad weather meant no fishing or digging or rampaging through the Wilderness; not Olly's fault that the energy he'd regained was seeking a new home.

Without looking at his friend, he said, 'We can't go up to the attics. My sister is there.'

'What now? It's very early.'

'She doesn't sleep late – most often she's up before me. And then she goes to her studio. Since she went to tea at Amberley, she's been painting every day.'

'Do you think that means anything?'

He didn't want to think it did; didn't want to think what might be happening to Elizabeth.

Oliver threw himself down onto the rug and sprawled lengthwise beside him. 'She asked you to deliver another message yesterday, didn't she? Was it because she wanted to meet him again?'

He bit his lip. He had taken the last message yesterday morning, a day after the Amberley visit, and he'd hoped it *was* the last. He knew his parents would disapprove; in fact, they would be furious and punish him severely. But it was Elizabeth he worried for. He loved her dearly. She was five years older than he, but she had been his friend and ally all his life. He didn't want her in trouble and he had a premonition that Aiden Kellaway, nice chap though he seemed, meant very big trouble.

'Let's go and see her,' he said suddenly. Oliver's words had triggered a deep misgiving. If his sister had met Kellaway last night, what might have happened?

'Won't she mind us barging in?' Oliver said. 'Artistic temperament and all that.'

'She's not that precious. But she *is* a good artist. At least I think so. I think she's good enough to be a professional.'

'You mean sell her work for money?'

'That's what professional means, you chump.' And he ruffled his friend's hair in a loving gesture. In return, Olly ruffled his and for a moment they clasped each other tight.

*

Elizabeth was working hard on a seascape. It was a view of the shore at East Head, the sand dune spit at the entrance to Chichester harbour. The family had visited the beach the previous summer and, although it hadn't been a particularly happy experience, the light on the sea, the rippled finger of sand, had etched itself into her mind and needed expression.

Especially now. It was keeping her from thinking of other things, dangerous things. She had kissed Aiden last night, and been kissed by him into recklessness. She wasn't ignorant. She had read about desire, but that had been mere words, something that happened to other people, characters in a book perhaps, but not to girls like her. Now she knew differently. Last night, she had been overwhelmed by a longing like no other, to hold this man, to touch him, caress him. It had been the most wonderful feeling, yet the most terrifying too.

She had never wished to live the kind of life her mother had, dancing to another's tune. She had kicked against the very idea, even though she'd known that for a girl like herself there were few options but marriage. Then, in London, in the midst of a frenzied Season's revelry, a small window of escape had appeared. She had begun to dream that one day she might become a professional painter. Laura Knight had done it. The woman had earned her own living for nine years before marrying, so why not her? She had the imagination, the creativity – if she could get formal training, if she could further develop her skill... But the obstacles had been huge and the flame that had once burnt bright slowly faded.

And then this summer she'd met a man who had made her see differently. Made her consider anew the struggle to carve a life for herself. Made her feel that anything was possible. And she had stopped struggling, stopped kicking, and started loving. That's what her heart had been telling her these past weeks: she had fallen in love.

She was broken from her reveries as William and Oliver shuffled into the room and leant against the door frame, one on either side, recovering from the climb up the steep, narrow steps.

'And what do you two want?' she asked in an amused voice.

They wore a slightly dejected air, as though, for the moment, they had lost their bearings. For weeks they'd run free through acres of garden, but now found themselves trapped and tamed within four walls.

'We thought we'd come up and help you,' Oliver announced grandly.

She raised an eyebrow. 'You paint then?'

'Gosh, no.' He seemed horrified at the suggestion. 'But maybe we could clear up a little.' He waved his hand around the room at the jumble of outcast furniture, the quietly mildewing heap of old curtains, and a discarded stair carpet lost in one corner.

'Clear up? If your room is anything to go by, I doubt it.' Their faces took on an even more dejected look, and she took pity on them. 'I suppose you could mix me some paint, if you want to be useful. I mean to use this greenish-blue cerulean for the sky, but I need a slightly deeper blue for the sea.'

William loved the job of mixing paints, though his efforts were not always successful. Over time, though, he'd improved and, even when disaster struck, she had been able quietly to dispose of the result. She had always been his friend, playing games to amuse him, shielding him from their father's anger, helping him with the schoolwork he found so difficult. She had grown quite proficient in Greek, a fact that had bemused and scandalised her dear governess, when Miss Tremloe first discovered her pupil deep in *The Odyssey*. Study of the classics was not for girls, she'd declared. It was boys' learning and should be left strictly alone. Cookery, needlework, household management, these were the subjects that were important. But domestic topics bored Elizabeth to distraction. She had inherited her father's quick intelligence, his energy too, but with no outlet for either. Ancient Greek had filled the gap. And with her diligent translations, her brother's homework had never failed to pass muster with Mr Binks – such a silly name for a very serious young man – though William himself had known little more of the language after three years' study than when he'd first begun. Binks was not the most patient of tutors, a little too handy at wielding a ruler she remembered, and her help was certainly needed.

But when William was despatched to school, Ancient Greek was despatched along with him, and she'd had to find another way to satisfy her restlessness and channel a passion she barely understood. From then on, all her energy had been poured into art. She had always loved to draw and to paint but now she became an ardent devotee, wielding her brushes with newly discovered fervour. And the wonderful thing was that she had not to excuse herself, since painting was viewed as eminently fitting for a young girl. An interest of which even Miss Tremloe, now long gone, could not have disapproved.

'Use the cerulean as a base and then experiment – there are several other blues you can try. And zinc white. There's a spare palette behind you and use this linseed oil as a thinner.' She handed them a small cup of liquid.

The boys rolled up their sleeves and, heads bent, carefully made their way around the tubes of colours. Five, ten minutes passed in deep concentration. Then, 'What do you think of this?' William offered her a startling blue.

'You might tone it down a little,' she said tactfully. 'Can you remember the sky when we visited East Head beach?'

'When Papa lost his temper with those boys playing cricket?'

'Yes,' she sighed, 'when Papa lost his temper.'

'I can sort of picture it. It was more wispy than real blue, I think. We can tone this colour down, can't we, Olly?'

'Absolutely.'

Two heads again bent diligently over their shared palette and, in ten minutes more, had produced a very tolerable light blue.

'That's not at all bad,' Elizabeth complimented them. 'If you'd like to attempt a beigey blond for the sand...'

But Oliver wasn't listening. He had climbed onto an old chest that stood against one of the walls and was balancing on tiptoe, looking out through the wide skylight. 'It's stopped raining at last,' he said excitedly. 'We can go out.'

She glanced up at the window. Leaves that had been torn from the surrounding trees were pasted to its glass. 'The wind is still blowing hard,' she warned. 'And everywhere is thoroughly wet.'

'The wind won't matter.' Oliver was buoyant. 'And look, the sun is coming out.'

It was more a hope than a reality, but, as if to prove her wrong, a bright beam of sunlight channelled through the skylight and hit the floorboards at the far end of the room.

'See, it's getting better.' William was already at the door.

'If you must go out, stay away from the Wilderness. Stick to the upper lawn, or your clothes will be soaked.'

'But there's nothing to do on the lawn. It's boring.'

She caught sight of several poles protruding feet above one of the many tea chests that stored the relics of their family life. 'How about a game of croquet? We used to play.'

'Yes, we did,' William's face was bright with anticipation.

'I'm not sure if it's too windy but it's worth a try.' She pointed to the tea chest. 'Whether the set is still complete, I've no idea.'

They were into the chest before she'd stopped speaking, pulling out mallets, and a collection of hoops, and finally red, blue, black and yellow balls. 'I'm sure it's all here,' her brother said, 'though I think there were some flags. But how do you set it up?'

'I'll do it for you. As long as I can remember how. And we won't worry about the flags.' She dropped her brush into a jar of turpentine. 'I need some fresh air right now. Come on, let's go.'

Chapter Nineteen

It took her a while to remember the exact layout of the court, but, with the last hoop in place, the playing rectangle was as accurate as she could manage; she stood back to admire her handiwork. Her father had bought the croquet set when they'd first arrived at Summerhayes, a diversion for the children while they waited for their new home. An old manor house belonging to the Fitzroys had been pulled down and its palatial successor not yet fully completed. They had lived in a small apartment at the rear of the building, but the lack of space hadn't seemed to matter. The rooms had been cosy and they'd spent most of their time together, her father coming and going, full of plans, full of new and ever more extravagant ideas. It was a period, she thought, when they'd come closest to being a happy family. Her mother was delighted to be back in the countryside she loved, and with a new baby to keep her company. She'd spent hours tucked away with William, out of earshot of the heavy machinery that scared him, while Elizabeth followed her father around the estate, listening avidly as he mapped out plans for a garden that would trump all others. He had been at the peak of his powers then; after years of punishing work and worry, he'd sold his Birmingham factories for a vast sum. He had acquired the perfect family, acquired a rural estate that he could mould to his liking, and a modern mansion built to his specifications.

But how badly life had gone from there. Not all at once, it was true. But, as time passed, the family's isolation became clear. They were cut off from any kind of social life, too grand for the village and not grand enough for Amberley. There was a forcible turning in on themselves, with bleak results. Her father's expansiveness took on a hollow ring, as, month by month, he'd known himself excluded from the club he thought he'd joined while her mother had retreated from any shared life, guarding the boy she adored from Joshua's growing frustration with an heir who disappointed.

The damp was seeping through the thin soles of her shoes and she quickly corralled the coloured balls into a cluster, dredging from memory the rules she thought must be the most important. The boys seized a mallet each and began swinging wildly at one ball after another. She gave a small laugh. 'It's not that easy, is it?'

A few practice shots later and Oliver threw down his mallet and disappeared into the house, reappearing in minutes with Beatrice in his arms.

'We must have an umpire, and here she is!' he proclaimed, installing the large doll at the top of the terrace steps, where she languished in an ungainly slump.

The match began and it was evident that both boys were playing to win, tackling the game with verve. One round complete and Oliver was slightly in the lead. Cock-a-hoop, he began a victory dance around the lawn but while he wasn't looking, William equalised the score.

'Hey, you can't do that!' Oliver yelled. 'It wasn't your turn!' He marched up to the terrace steps and appealed to the doll. 'Is that fair, Beatty? C'mon, old girl, you're supposed to adjudicate.'

But William was already taking his turn at dancing around the lawn. At the sight of him, Olly began to laugh uproariously, then joined in the victory celebrations, clasping his friend in a bear hug, and they proceeded to whirl together in and out of the hoops. She noticed Oliver's face as they danced. Love was so clearly written there that she felt afraid for them both.

When they returned to play a second round, she thought she would leave them to it. Her feet were now thoroughly wet and her arms chilled. She turned to go back into the house, but had barely taken a step when chaos enveloped the small party. Before she knew it, something brown and terrified had streaked by her and then a dog appeared, tearing towards them at full speed. And not one dog, but dogs, dozens of them, it seemed. Howling and snarling in frustration that their prey had mysteriously disappeared. They were in a frenzy, bounding over each other this way and that, and giving vent to angry growls as they did so.

At the first sound of the hounds, William had frozen to the spot. He stood paralysed, his mallet still raised as though ready to strike the ball. It was as if boy and mallet were permanently carved in stone. The hounds, milling angrily in a pack, caught sight of the raised stick and decided, in the absence of any other enemy, to attack it. As the hounds leapt up, scrabbling against the boy's body, William let out a thin scream that pierced the still sodden air. The eeriness of the sound galvanised Oliver into action. He ran from one side of the lawn, waving his arms at the dogs, while Elizabeth charged at them from the other. But no amount of arm waving was going to see the pack disperse. The dogs continued to jump and snarl at the wooden stick, clawing at William's legs, his arm, his body.

'*Drop the mallet!*' Olly yelled frantically.

But William could not. It was doubtful that he even heard his friend. He stood stock-still, as though in a trance, his face ashen, his chest rising and falling rapidly. Elizabeth was terrified that his heart would burst. Did hearts burst? she thought wildly. She tried to fight her way through the pack to take the mallet from him and throw it to one side, but the hounds were a huge, heaving barrier and she was beaten back.

Out of the corner of her eye, she saw Oliver dart back to the steps. He picked up the cloth doll and ran back on to the lawn, waving it wildly above his head.

'Here. Here!' he called. 'Look what I've got for you.'

Something in the timbre of his voice made the hounds' ears prick. Several of them at the outer edge of the pack looked in Olly's direction. For an instant, they stood staring at him then launched themselves forward. Oliver threw the doll into their midst and retreated. The rest of the pack, seeing some of their number tossing an object that looked uncommonly like prey, ran to join the tussle. Snarling and snapping, the dogs dismembered the doll, piece by piece, until not a scrap of her was left intact.

Elizabeth edged her way around the sated dogs to get to her brother's side, and had just reached him as a posse of gardeners, who had been working on the kitchen plots, appeared at the edge of the lawn. Aiden was just behind them, with Mr Harris in tow.

The younger man ran to her side. 'Let me take him,' he said urgently, and grasped William by the arm. But the boy remained frozen to the spot.

'What's happened to him?' she sobbed.

Aiden put his arm around her and gave her a swift hug. It was the briefest caress, yet at that terrifying moment she knew with complete certainty that she wanted this man by her side, always.

'He'll be all right,' Aiden said. 'He's in a stupor that's all. Self-protection, I imagine, but we must get him inside.' He lifted William off his feet and half slung him over his shoulders.

She ran ahead, up the stone steps, to open the glass doors leading into the drawing room, and almost collided with her uncle, stepping out onto the terrace, a white-faced Alice immediately behind him.

'We heard the noise,' he said.

And saw that hug, she feared silently.

'William, my poor dear boy,' her mother cried, as Aiden appeared at the top of the steps, Oliver in tow. Alice launched herself at the prostrate figure, frantically smoothing his hair and kissing his cheeks. William was not a large boy but Aiden had begun to stagger beneath the burden.

'Shall I carry him up to his room?' he managed to ask, his breath coming in spurts.

'Yes, yes, please do, Mr Kellaway. But I must go with him.'

She scurried through the French windows, following on their heels, but almost immediately turned round to her daughter. 'Elizabeth, please ring for Dr Daniels to come immediately.'

'You must keep calm,' Henry was saying in a hearty voice. 'The men have things under control.' Elizabeth turned her head and saw that between them the gardeners had managed to round up the pack and were driving them back the way the dogs had come.

Alice was looking too. 'But why...?' she began.

'No idea,' her brother answered. 'Unless your fences are not secure.'

'This is the second time your dogs have found their way into the garden.'

'Then I suggest you send your carpenter on a reconnaissance mission. Don't fuss, Alice, there's no harm done – except for a ruined doll.'

'But William—'

'The boy will be fine. You mollycoddle him. Joshua is right about that at least.'

*

Several hours later, Elizabeth tiptoed out of her mother's room. Alice was sleeping heavily, thanks to the draught administered by Dr Daniels. William, too. Wearily, she climbed the stairs to her studio. What a truly terrible morning it had been. She must pack away her paints, for there was no possibility she could work again that day. She was filled with an odd, queasy feeling and needed time to think. Her heart was beating faster than usual and she put it down to the shock she'd sustained. But it was more than that. There were things she didn't understand, yet she could feel herself flinch at the idea of probing too deeply. The questions, though, kept coming. Why had those dogs escaped for a second time? Her uncle claimed that the Summerhayes fences had to be faulty but surely, after that first intrusion, Cornford would have made sure they were secure.

And why had Henry been here talking to her mother? It was to do with Giles Audley. It had to be. There could be no other reason, since to her knowledge her uncle had never before crossed the threshold of Summerhayes. He had come to quiz Alice on the dinner invitation, she was sure. Come to make certain it still stood and that preparations were already in train, though the date was fixed for several weeks hence. Her uncle, though, would be eager to seal whatever arrangements he'd made with Audley. He would be doubly eager, now that he had seen Aiden. Seen the way the young man had instinctively comforted her. Henry would be outraged and determined to bring the alliance he'd negotiated to a satisfactory conclusion. Satisfactory to him. She packed away the last tubes of paint and sat down in the old bentwood rocker. What could she do? How should she behave now that the net was drawing ever closer? But it didn't have to be that way. There was rescue at hand. More than rescue, a different future – of adventure, of new horizons, of uncertainty, if she could find the courage to reach out, grab hold and ride the storm.

She closed her eyes, trying to relax, but almost immediately a small scratching caught her attention. Mice? They were not unheard of in the attics. There were enough soft furnishings abandoned here to make comfortable bedding for a family of mice and keep them from hunger. The scratching became louder. Reluctantly, she rose from the chair and walked towards the sound. The creaking of floorboards as she walked seemed to cause alarm, because the scratching abruptly ceased. She stopped opposite a discarded console table – they'd had that when they'd first moved to Summerhayes, she remembered, when they were living in just half a dozen rooms. A thick blanket covered the table and, bending down, she very carefully lifted one edge and peered into the darkness beyond. Two bright eyes stared unblinkingly back at her. This was no mouse. She reached in and hauled out the small, brown body.

A rabbit. The little creature lay in her arms, panting with fear. Rhythmically, she smoothed its fur, every so often gently stroking its long ears, and all the time talking quietly to it. Soon the small heart beat a little less fast. This was what the hounds had been chasing, the streak of brown fur she'd barely glimpsed as it ran for its life. In its terror, it had bolted through the open window and as far into the house as was possible. But the rabbit presented her with another puzzle. It was tame, used to people, or it would never allow her to nurse it in this fashion. So how had it escaped from its hutch, and how had the hounds picked up its scent?

She gave up the puzzle, and instead fixed her mind on what she should do. It might be possible to trace the rabbit's owner, she supposed, but it seemed a long shot. Meanwhile, she must find a place for it to live. Perhaps Cornford could make a hutch? William would love the small animal. It might even hasten his recovery. Once her mother was rested, she would ask Alice if they could keep the rabbit, at least until they found the true owner. In the meantime, she would take it down to William's room. Oliver could look after the little creature until William woke. It would be something to delight him, to distract him from the horrible memories of today.

When she opened their door, William was still asleep, with Oliver lying close by him on the same bed. He lifted his head at the sound of the door opening and put a finger to his lips. She nodded. She had no intention of waking her brother.

'I've brought a present,' she whispered, and showed Olly the rabbit.

'He's a beauty,' Oliver said, taking the little animal in his arms and stroking him gently.

'I'm going to ask Mama if we can keep him. I think William would love him as a pet – until he goes back to school at least.'

'He would.' Oliver beamed at her. 'It will help. He'll need help, you know.' And he turned towards his friend and, with his free hand, stroked the boy's cheek.

Chapter Twenty

'Joe's hand will likely mend, thank the Lord,' Ivy said, 'though he'll be laid up for a while with a bad fever.' She was packing the chest of drawers with neat piles of newly delivered laundry. 'But he'll be fine to walk down the aisle in a week or so. And come to the party afterwards.'

'Do you really want to marry so soon?' Elizabeth had wondered at the haste, but the girl seemed unperturbed by the change in her plans.

'Of course I do, miss. The sooner the better. We'll have some time together – you know –' two pink spots dotted her cheeks, '– before Eddie has to go, if he does.'

'Go where?' Elizabeth looked blank.

'It's all this talk. Not in the village – no one knows anything there – but when Eddie was in Worthing the other day, people were saying there'll be a war here. I dunno who's fighting who. As long as it's not us. But if it is, Eddie says he has to do his bit.'

Ivy's words were a shock. She'd been as indifferent to the news as the villagers, but without their excuse. At the breakfast table this morning, her father, hidden behind a double spread of the *Daily Telegraph*, had growled out one piece of bad news after another. Several days ago, she'd gathered, Germany had given its support to Austria-Hungary,

and was now threatening to declare war on Russia. The
situation in Europe was very serious, she could see that.
Serious maybe, but dreamlike as well. What had any of it
to do with ordinary people? Very little, it seemed. Ordinary
people weren't concerned that the London Stock Exchange
had closed this very morning or that a wave of panic had
swept the business world. The upper classes weren't much
concerned either. Life for them flowed on without interrup-
tion. This summer was like every other English summer: the
Derby had been run and won, Royal Ascot had come and
gone, the Chelsea Flower Show admired, the Wimbledon
championships cheered and the regatta at Henley staged
in all its glory. For virtually everyone in England, the bel-
ligerence in Europe seemed far away and unimportant, but
here was Ivy bringing forward her wedding in case her new
husband should leave to fight.

She looked up from the book she'd been trying to read
and saw that her maid had not left the room, but was standing awkwardly in the middle of the carpet and fidgeting
with her starched apron.

'Is there something else, Ivy?'

'I know you won't want me to say this, but I have to.'
She worried what was coming.

'I want to say thank you,' Ivy rushed out. 'I know it
were you that persuaded the master to give Eddie and me
a present. Money,' she added.

Elizabeth jumped up from her chair and took both the
girl's hands in hers. 'I'm glad my father came up trumps. I
hope he was generous.'

'More than generous, Miss Elizabeth. It's enough for
a real good party and some sticks of furniture that we're

needing. We'll be going down to the Horse and Groom straight after the ceremony. You'll come, won't you?'

'I wouldn't miss it for the world. I told you, I've been saving the pink crêpe for the very day.'

'And I've saved the lovely frock you gave me months back. It will be my wedding dress.'

'The blue velvet?' It could prove a difficult choice in sweltering weather, but she kept her qualms to herself.

'Eddie has never seen it,' her maid said happily, 'and I'll make sure he don't until the day I walk up the aisle.'

'And what is Eddie wearing? Not his chauffeur's uniform, I hope,' she teased.

Ivy's face puckered. 'To tell the truth, it were a bit of a problem. Your pa's gift was very generous, but we reckoned that by the time we'd bought enough beer, not to mention the food and the new bed, there wouldn't be over much left for Eddie's suit. But his mother made him new trousers – she used to be a seamstress, you know. They're black and very smart. And your young man has given Eddie his best jacket.'

'My young man?' It was her turn to flush pink.

'Mr Kellaway. He's been so kind. He had a new jacket made for when he graduates as a proper architect. There's some kind of ceremony, I think. And the jacket is ever so smart, but it fits Eddie something perfect. So he's given it to him for the wedding. Just like that. Eddie will give it back, I know. But isn't that kind?'

'Yes,' she said faintly. 'Very kind.'

*

When Ivy had left, she crossed to the window and stood looking out, hoping the quiet beauty of the garden might help her regain poise. The weather had settled and cotton-wool clouds high in the sky signalled another lovely day, but she found little consolation in the sunlit landscape. Ivy's parting words had jolted her severely. Were her feelings for Aiden so obvious? They must be, if her maid knew of them. And Eddie would know too, and probably the rest of the indoor staff. And what of the gardeners? She was appalled. How did they know? How had they guessed? Ivy had shared her mistress's life for very many years, but she would never have confessed to the girl what was in her heart. She had not spoken of her feelings to anyone. At the margins of her mind, she knew that she was flirting with a future that, if it should happen, would sever her from her family and from Summerhayes. How could she have spoken of that? How even consciously acknowledge it? Yet she must have given herself away – in looks, in gestures. That hug of Aiden's, a simple hug, but one loaded with significance. And if it were loaded with significance for her, why not for those who had witnessed it?

A knock at her bedroom door stopped the carousel circling in her mind. Oliver was standing on the threshold.

'How is William?' was her immediate question.

It was two days since the attack, but apart from a fleeting visit, she hadn't wanted to disturb her brother. The more he was able to sleep, the quicker his health would improve. And though her mother had come to the breakfast table each morning, she'd not been able to ask her for news of William. Alice had recovered sufficiently to peck at a slice of toast, but it was clear she was still deeply upset and throughout every meal, had remained sunk in thought. There had been no mention of Saturday's events and, since

Joshua was choosing to ignore the incident, his wife and daughter were forced to ignore it too.

'He's much better,' Oliver said cheerfully. 'Actually, a great deal better. I think the rabbit is doing the trick. He's spent an hour grooming it this morning.'

She smiled. 'I hope the rabbit doesn't mind.'

'Not a bit. Mr Cornford is going to make him a hutch, but in the meantime he loves being with us. He's lapping up all the attention. Or maybe I should say *she* is?'

She looked at him questioningly. 'We don't actually know how to tell,' he confessed, 'but we've called it Beatrice, so she has to be a girl.'

'Beatrice – in place of the doll?'

'Exactly. They've both been lifesavers.' Oliver moved further into the room and walked towards the window. 'You've a smashing view from here, haven't you?'

'Yes,' she said, looking out with him over the acres of rolling lawn. In the far distance, she could see the old fig tree that grew against a warm curve of south-facing wall. Apricots and pears, cherries and plums, hung there in abundance, some already fruiting, others yet to come. 'The gardens are looking splendid. And the weather is perfect. Do you think William will venture out today?'

'I'm going to encourage him. Perhaps best if we avoid the lawn. We can stay on the terrace or in the walled garden. He should be happy there.'

He walked back to the door, but then fidgeted a while with the handle. She wondered why he didn't leave and was about to suggest an errand he could run, when he said abruptly 'I've already been out this morning, you know. I couldn't sleep – I'm still a bit queasy after what happened.

Anyway, William was sleeping peacefully, so I crept out early and walked right through the gardens to the very end.'

'Yes?' She wondered what was coming.

'Mr Kellaway was there. Mr Simmonds, too. They're putting the finishing touches to the temple.'

She found herself growing hot again. It was ridiculous in front of a fourteen-year-old boy.

'The thing is, Mr Kellaway gave me a note.' Her flush turned bright red. 'It's for you.' And Oliver reached into his shorts pocket and dragged out a crumpled slip of paper.

'Thank you, Olly,' she managed to say, though her voice sounded tight and unnatural. 'It was kind of you to bring it to me.'

'I didn't let anyone else see it,' he assured her.

She must be almost crimson by now, she thought, and made haste to usher him out of the door. 'It was very kind of you,' she repeated to his disappearing figure.

This was turning out to be a morning of surprises. She took the note back to the window and spread its creases flat. *I need to see you,* she read. *Tonight after dinner. I'll work late.*

Her stomach did a small churn. What had happened for him to summon her in this fashion? He must know how difficult it was for her to slip away, but here was this terse, uncompromising note asking, demanding in fact, that she do so. *I need to see you.* It had to be something serious, something threatening. Another bad surprise.

*

Dinner that night was a subdued affair. And interminable. Five courses served by Ripley at a glacial pace. The boys had already eaten their evening meal in the kitchen. Earlier in the day, they'd gone for a short excursion through the gardens, but William had been too tired to stay out long. His heart had suffered considerable stress and it would be a while before he regained full health. His return from the Wilderness, white faced and breathing unevenly, had been enough for Alice to declare him in need of more rest. His malady offered a perfect excuse to rid Summerhayes of its unwanted guest, and Elizabeth was surprised that her mother hadn't suggested Oliver bring his stay to an end. But if Alice had been tempted, she had evidently decided against. These days William only truly came alive when he was with his friend, and her mother must know that only too well. But an early bedtime was the price, hence their meal amid the clatter of servants. The boys would have been happy enough, she thought, preferring the warmth and informality of the kitchen to the agony of a protracted and largely silent dinner.

At last, the meal was over and her mother suggested they retire to the morning room until tea was brought in at ten. It would be an evening, as so many others, of desultory conversation and the hated embroidery, and she had more pressing things on her mind.

'I have a bad headache coming on, Mama.' She put her hand to her forehead in what she hoped was a convincing gesture. 'I think I'll go to my room, if you don't mind. I might even sleep – I didn't have much rest last night.'

'You have my sympathy.' She imagined her mother must have spent an equally restless night in which dogs and boys hurtled through Summerhayes, a trail of blood and broken bones in their wake. 'But if you're retiring early, Elizabeth, so will I. We should both feel better in the morning.' Alice paused at the foot of the stairs. 'This business with the dogs… it's so dreadful and… so very odd. And now there's the dinner party. I'm worried to death.'

It was unclear whether it was the dogs or the dinner that was concerning her mother most, but then she went on, 'Mrs Lacey is very efficient, I can't fault her, and I know Cook will be wonderful about the extra work, but I feel I will have to check everything myself, two or three times over.'

'It will be fine, Mama,' she said reassuringly. The creases on her mother's face had deepened perceptibly and she looked ready to sink with fatigue.

'And will *you* be fine?' Alice asked anxiously. 'About the dinner, about meeting Mr Audley again?'

She gave her a quick hug. 'You are not to worry. All will be well,' she promised.

But how well? After the euphoria of those midnight kisses, fear had taken hold. Genuine fear. Fear that her life was unravelling and that she had lost control. Until Aiden's caress had seemed to make everything simple again. As she'd clutched at her stupefied brother, he had put his arms around her, gently, casually, in a gesture that said *you are already mine*. And if that were so, she was standing at the very edge of a precipice. It wasn't simple at all.

She pulled a chair up to the window and sat watching as the golden circle of summer sun sank below the horizon. In its place, a soft mist, hovering inches above the ground and turning the air gauzy and indeterminate. She sat and watched, then watched some more, as the world turned a gradual grey. In her ear, a tapping sound had started up. It was highly irritating and she looked around for a way to stop it. Then she saw that it was her own fingers making the noise, playing along the windowsill. She had been too hunched in thought, too bound by tension, to realise. Something was wrong, badly wrong, she guessed, or Aiden would never have risked another message. She needed to know the worst and this waiting was unnerving. But she dared not leave yet. Her mother might well be asleep – judging by Alice's face when she'd left her, she almost certainly was – but Joshua would still be in his smoking room, cigar in mouth, and downing his customary snifter of warm brandy. Tea addled the insides, he maintained, and unless his women folk were present, it rarely passed his lips. Ripley would be bringing no tea tray tonight.

There was a creak outside her bedroom door. Her father, it seemed, had decided on an early night too. Smoking cigars and drinking brandy alone couldn't be a great deal of fun. But they were a badge that Joshua chose to wear, a badge that signalled he'd arrived, that he was part of a world where a country estate was one's calling card.

She steeled herself to wait longer but, when after another twenty minutes, there was no further noise, except for the creaks and groans of wood panelling as it settled for the night, she decided to take the risk. She tucked her shoes into one hand then edged her window open. Climbing out, she blessed the wonderful chestnut tree. It was as though it had grown to full strength and so conveniently close, for her alone.

Chapter Twenty-One

He was halfway along the path through the Wilderness when she saw him, as though he'd come to speed her passage to whatever news he carried.

'I'm sorry.' Her breath was coming short. It was almost a mile from the house and she had hurried all the way. 'I had to wait until everyone was asleep.'

'It doesn't matter. You're here now.' He put down a bag of books and tools and, before she could protest, enfolded her in his arms. She heard her breath becoming more ragged still and knew she must disentangle herself, and quickly.

'I couldn't be sure that Oliver would deliver the message,' he said, when they stood apart once more. 'He might have lost it. Or you might have chosen to ignore it.'

Nothing would have stopped her from seeing him tonight, but she kept the thought to herself. 'As you see, he was an excellent postman. William has taught him well.'

'And how is William? I seem always to be asking you that.'

'He's recovering, but I think it will be a long time before he's back to his normal self. That's not why I'm here though. What was it you wanted to tell me?'

'Let's find a seat first.' He turned to thread his way back

through the avenue of tree ferns, heading for the Italian Garden, but she reached out and stopped him before he'd gone a few paces.

'Can we talk somewhere else?' The top of a palm tickled her head and she brushed it aside. Palms held no fear for her; it was the furthest stretch of the garden that she found threatening.

'The lake is looking very beautiful tonight,' he tempted. 'Why don't we go there?'

'I'm sure it looks magnificent, but I'd rather we talk somewhere else – the walled garden perhaps?'

In the half-light, she could see him puzzled by her disinclination for their earlier meeting place. 'If it worries you, certainly... but why?'

She felt uncomfortable attempting to explain. Said aloud, it sounded foolish. 'It's as though... the trees are listening.' She stuttered a little as she said the words.

He paused and looked at her, the crooked smile back. 'And the fruit and vegetables won't be listening?'

She let his teasing go without comment. She deserved it. Put like that, her fears sounded stupid. But whenever they'd met in the Italian Garden, she had sensed some kind of presence there, and it was not one that was benign.

In single file, they walked out of the Wilderness and into the kitchen garden, following its gravelled path through row after row of potatoes, beans, carrots, onions – just about every vegetable that could be planted. Mr Harris and his team were miracle workers, feeding not just her own family but every man and woman employed at Summerhayes. Beyond this bounty, the old brick wall stood guard, its outline clear even in the dimmest of light, cutting a horizontal against a partially cloudy sky, its surface bearing fans and espaliers heavy with harvest. Nearer still, and she could feel its warmth drawn from the day's sun. A wooden seat had been set in a niche at the furthest point of the wall's curve, and she led the way to it.

The smell of ripe apricots settled around them. Aiden stretched out his legs. 'It's another beautiful evening,' he remarked. He seemed almost too relaxed. She'd thought from his note that he had urgent news, but if that were so, he appeared in no hurry to divulge it.

Instead, he said, 'The hedges have been trimmed and Mr Cornford has a team erecting a solid barrier along the entire boundary with Amberley. It will take them a fair while to finish the job, but William should feel comforted.'

'As long as it prevents another invasion. He can't afford any more scares.'

'Then we must hope it works.'

'You don't sound very sure.'

'If I'm truthful, I'm not. There are ways and means of getting around any barrier.'

She was disconcerted by the edge to his voice. 'What do you mean?'

'I've been doing some thinking. The first time the hounds ran free, I thought it odd. They'd never done that before. It was only two or three of them, then this time it was the whole darn pack. Don't you think that strange?'

She had thought it strange, but hadn't wanted to admit it. Speculation might lead to a dark place. 'I suppose it's possible that the same two or three dogs found their way back into Summerhayes, but this time they led the rest of the pack. Whatever gap existed must have been made bigger by the sheer force of numbers.' It was what she had been telling herself.

'I agree, but the dogs had to have been free to do that. I'm no countryman, but surely hounds are kept in some kind of enclosure. They're not allowed to roam, are they? And wouldn't you think that after the first incident, those responsible for the animals would make sure they were very firmly contained?'

She felt a spurt of impatience. Was this the news that had brought her running here? Surely not. The light had almost gone, but, sitting so close to him, she could see the misty green eyes had darkened with excitement.

'So what are you saying?' she forced herself to ask.

'I'm saying that someone deliberately let those dogs out. Maybe deliberately encouraged them into the Summerhayes garden.'

She was startled but only for an instant. The suggestion had always been there at the back of her mind, but so far she'd refused to contemplate such a possibility.

'I was working inside the temple at the time and I saw nothing,' he went on. 'But I heard the shouts of the men and came out to see what was going on. I caught a glimpse of two of the dogs disappearing into the distance. They looked as though they were chasing something.'

What Aiden didn't know could only add weight to what, until this moment, had been unthinkable. But she had to be honest. 'They were – chasing something,' she said. 'They were chasing a rabbit.'

'That's not exactly unusual,' he mused. 'It's what dogs do. They could have nosed out the rabbit on the Amberley side of the border, I suppose, and chased it through to here. But that still means they had to be roaming free.'

'It was a tame rabbit.' Better to confess the worst.

'Tame! Then it *was* deliberate.' His expression was one

of complete conviction. 'Someone released a tame rabbit and allowed the dogs to chase it.'

'How awful. It could have been torn to shreds.'

'But it wasn't? Or at least I saw no signs of bloodshed on the lawn. Just a clutter of rags.'

'The clutter was once Beatrice, a doll that Olly won at the fête.'

He gave a wry smile. 'Poor Beatrice.'

'Don't worry, she has risen again,' she reassured him. 'The rabbit has now become Beatrice.'

'You found the poor creature then?'

'I did. She'd run up two entire staircases, looking for sanctuary, and found it in my studio. I gave her to William, so he has a new love in his life. Mr Cornford has been very busy making her a hutch – in between erecting fences.'

She hoped they could bring the topic to a close, but it seemed that Aiden was intent on talking of Amberley. She had no wish to follow him there, no wish to probe further. But he was on a mission to lay bare the wickedness he suspected.

'Someone did this, Elizabeth, but who and why?' She spread her hands wide in a gesture of resignation. 'You have no suspicions?'

When she didn't answer, he said, 'I think you have. And they're very likely my suspicions, too. But why would your uncle order the hounds to be released and give them prey to chase?'

Because he likes killing things. Ivy's words came to mind, but she shook herself free of them. 'There is no reason,' she said stoutly, 'and that's why I won't believe it. The dispute with Summerhayes over water for the lake has been settled, maybe not to my uncle's advantage, but it's settled. And there's no other reason to think badly of him. The idea that he would deliberately loose his hounds makes no sense.'

'Unless he wanted to frighten William.'

'What!'

'That's been the result each time, hasn't it? Your brother has been scared half out of his wits. Does your uncle know how panicked he is by dogs?'

She had no notion but shook her head in denial, as though hoping to shake the idea from her mind.

'And don't forget the retreat the boys built,' he continued inexorably, 'that didn't collapse of its own free will. The binding ropes were almost certainly cut.'

He sprung up from the seat they shared and began to pace back and forth in front of her, scuffing and crunching the gravel as he did. He seemed indifferent to the noise he was making. 'So William has been the target. He has to have been. And it's worked well, hasn't it? He has spent days in bed or resting. His constitution has been weakened, which is what your uncle has been about.'

'That's completely insane.'

'Yes, it is. Completely. But then Henry Fitzroy is not exactly well balanced, is he? When we first met, you told me of the emnity between Amberley and Summerhayes. You said that anything your uncle could do to upset your father, he would. For the last three months, I've heard much the same thing from a number of people. Mr Fitzroy, it's generally known, is an angry and jealous man.'

'But what has that to do with my brother? William is no threat to him. He has a son of his own – Gilbert.'

'It's not William himself. It's the future he represents. He is the heir to Summerhayes.'

'You're accusing Uncle Henry of trying to hurt William because he'll inherit Summerhayes?'

'Your brother has a weak heart. A minute ago, you said that he must suffer no further scares. Doesn't that tell you something?'

She felt herself twisting her hands together so hard it hurt. 'That is a shocking thing to say and I won't believe it. In any case, if William didn't inherit, I would. My father has two children, or have you forgotten?'

He stopped his pacing and sat down beside her. Her figure had grown stiff with anger that he'd dared to suggest her uncle could be guilty of such wickedness. But then he reached out to stroke her hair, his fingers moving slowly down her cheek. 'How could I forget you?' he whispered. 'But...'

There was a long pause and, when he spoke again, his voice had lost its softness. 'Your uncle is organising a husband for you, isn't he? A marriage to one of his own kin, which will anchor you firmly within the clutches of the Fitzroys. If your brother were to come to harm, you would be tied to their apron strings. In fact, neatly trussed.'

She jerked away from him. 'I cannot listen to one more word, Aiden. I came to meet you tonight because it seemed most urgent that you see me. But if this is the reason, I'm not prepared to hear more. The whole notion is a sick madness.'

His mouth tightened. 'I understand your loyalty, though I think you're mistaken. But I'll say no more. Instead, I must tell you why I asked you to come – not your uncle's wrongdoing as it happens, but something more important perhaps, at least to us.'

So there was urgent news after all. She put her hand on

his arm, pulling him a little closer, spurring him to speak. It seemed to take him a while before he could find the words, but then they came, simple and shattering. 'Next week, I will be leaving Summerhayes.'

'Leaving?' In that moment, she felt immensely fragile, unsure even of the wooden seat beneath her. 'You mean that your work here is finished?'

'Not quite, but as good as. I am to complete the temple interior - Jonathan has been allowed to keep me until Wednesday next, but after that I must be gone. Your father is his client and he has no choice in the matter.'

Her father had done this? Or was it her uncle who'd made sure that Aiden was dismissed before his contract ended? If so, the caress Henry Fitzroy had seen must be the reason. Could the man beside her be right after all? Henry would not want an intruder on the scene, not when he hoped to marry his niece to Giles Audley. No, she told herself vehemently. There had to be another explanation.

'What will you do?' Her voice was hollow. Her whole being was hollow.

'I can stay on with Mrs Boxall for a short while. I've money to pay the rent for a few weeks, but after that I'll need to find work.'

'In town?' There was the slightest hope that he would return to London. At least in the capital, he would be only a few hours away.

'In Canada.' She had known it, known it was what he'd say. The hollow grew ever larger.

He turned towards her, his face close to hers, his voice gently persuasive. 'I mentioned my cousin to you a while ago. Do you remember? I've had another letter from him, urging me to book my passage to New York. He's convinced there are wonderful opportunities in Toronto for someone with my skills. The city is growing fast and needs professional men.'

She was too dazed to speak. Meeting Aiden was always difficult but once he left Summerhayes it would be almost impossible. After Wednesday next, she might never see him again. The fact was slowly sinking in. But what had she expected? His touch, his kiss, the dreams she had played with these past weeks, what had they really been worth? Deep down she had always known they were destined to tread a different path, yet she'd refused to accept it. She had carried on dreaming, of a future in which Aiden Kellaway would be part of her life. Would be her life.

'You know that war is creeping closer. Wouldn't you want to stay and fight?' It was an underhand thing to say but she was battling for her happiness. If it would keep him close a little longer...

He looked at her askance. 'War may well come, but who would I fight for?' he said evenly. 'This isn't my country, remember.'

'England may not be your country, but you're still British. You could fight in the British army.'

'No, Elizabeth. If this country goes to war, and please God it doesn't happen, other Irishmen will fight for Britain that's for sure. But not me.'

'Because you hate the English,' she said bitterly.

'No, how could I? I've lived among them half my life. The hatred, if hatred there is, will be on the other side. If war is declared, I'll almost certainly be interned. There'll be no fighting for me, just a prison cell.'

'I don't understand.' All she understood was that she felt more miserable than she'd ever done in her entire life.

'I'll be considered an enemy, someone likely to help the Republicans in their plots against this country.'

'But you haven't seen your brothers, you haven't spoken to them, you haven't even written to them. They have nothing to do with you.' There was bewilderment in her voice and in her face, and he put his arm around her waist and nestled her against himself.

'Things change in war. Justice becomes rough and ready. Any man who is the slightest risk to the state will be suspect. Not immediately, it's true, but over time. And if the fighting goes badly, it will be a good deal quicker.'

'But how would anyone know who you are or where you were?' She was clutching at wisps.

'Everyone will have to register. There'll be no chance of escaping, and my name and place of birth will be like a red flag. It won't take long for the authorities to link me to troubles over the water.'

'And Canada is the answer?'

'It is.' He hugged her tight, and the warmth of his touch hurt her more than she could believe possible. 'I've thought long and hard about it. Canada is the answer, and to more than a possible war. After all, the conflict might not spread. It might stay in mainland Europe for all we know. But the idea of making a new start in a country that is young and energetic and growing, I find that exhilarating. A country where it won't matter if I'm English or Irish or anything else, as long as I work hard to make a good future.'

'And your cousin will help you?'

'He has a spare room and is happy for me to stay until I have the money for a house of my own. And he has contacts. He's a railwayman and meets a great many people, prospective clients. He'll introduce me. And with the experience

I've gained and the professional certificates and Jonathan's testimonial, I'm certain to find work.'

'When will you go?' The question was wrenched out of her.

He made no answer for a while, and when he spoke it was to say, 'Isn't it the grand dinner very soon? Joe Lacey has been telling me his mother is being driven half mad by yours. Apparently everything – the house as well as the food – has to be perfect for this Audley fellow.'

The sudden plunge into a dinner party she'd almost forgotten forced her to push her misery away and summon every atom of stoicism she possessed. Her heart had been chopped into very small pieces but she would not show it.

'From what I know of Mr Audley, I doubt he'd want the fuss.'

'Well, he certainly seems to be getting it. And what about you?'

'I don't want the fuss either. I don't want the dinner. It will be a dreadful evening.' And for the first time, she realised fully how very dreadful it would be.

'Why so bad? I thought you liked him.'

She couldn't say what was in her mind. That very shortly, the crux would come. It was too near the dark scene that Aiden had already painted. Her mother and father, her aunt and uncle, would be ranged against her, expecting, pressuring. Very shortly she would be faced with an ultimatum. And she would have to say no.

'I like him well enough, but—'

'But perhaps not quite well enough,' he finished for her.

He pulled her to her feet and cupped her face in his hands. He was looking down at her, a long slow glance, seeking what was in her heart, she thought. Then he bent his head to kiss her full on the lips. A great rushing torrent of emotion, dammed until now, found its escape. She put her arms around his neck and kissed him back. His mouth was hard on hers and for minutes on end it seemed, they kissed as though their whole world depended on it.

When they finally pulled apart, he said, 'Marry me.'

Chapter Twenty-Two

August, 1914

Alice was in a state of high tension. She stared at the note that had come from Amberley, uncertain whether to feel anxious or insulted. How had it come about that she was expected to invite the doctor to eat with them tonight? It must be Henry's idea, a way of discomfiting her, or more likely, she thought, tight lipped, Louisa's. Both of them must know it was unacceptable. A physician or solicitor might be asked to take tea, but the only professional men who should be invited for lunch or dinner were officers, clergymen or diplomats. Deciding she felt insulted, she tore the note into small pieces and threw it into the wicker basket.

There were plenty of other papers on her desk: list after list to ensure this evening's dinner was perfection. For the last hour, she had been wondering whether to read them for what must be the twentieth time. The decision on food had been easy, at least at first – Joshua hired an excellent cook after all – but then the doubts had begun to set in. Was the choice she'd made sufficiently elegant to serve to such an important group of people, on such an important occasion? She had gone through the menu over and over again, until the relative merits of various soups and seafood, game and garnishes had resulted in abject confusion. That was when Cook had taken that particular piece of paper from her hand and said, severely, 'Mrs Summer, I will produce a dinner for your guests that you will be proud of.' And then she had planted herself in front of the new gas-fired cooking range, her hands fixed firmly on expansive hips, and waited for Alice to leave the kitchen. That list had been abandoned.

But there were others. What should she do about the wine? Joshua showed not the slightest interest, much preferring beer or his nightly snifters of brandy. She had to turn to Ripley for help, but could she trust him to choose the right wine for the right course? Sherry went with the soup, she knew, but when did you serve hock or burgundy? It had never before been a worry. As a girl, she'd had no responsibility for the household, and since her marriage had never entertained formally. The few invitations the family had extended during their early years at Summerhayes had been rebuffed, sometimes with a polite excuse but at others, simply ignored. That had put an end to invitations and an end to any pretensions she might have had as a hostess. Eventually, Ripley had taken matters into his own hands and ordered what he assured her were the most acceptable wines.

No sooner had the food and wine been settled than she was plunged into an agitated conference with Mr Harris over the flowers. He'd become quite irate, telling her that he hadn't grown cut flowers for thirty-odd years without knowing exactly what to produce for a dinner party. There would be vases in the hall and the drawing room, all of them filled with godetia and cosmos and zinnias, along with the delicate froth of gypsophila. The inglenook fireplace would be the setting for a huge basket of fresh-picked roses. He could already see it in his mind and it would be nothing short of perfect. She had emerged from that encounter pink-faced and slightly dishevelled, only to walk into a confrontation with Mrs Lacey – the last of an endless succession, it seemed.

When she'd dared to venture to the housekeeper's quarters, the woman had shown even less forbearance than Mr Harris and, in Alice's view, had verged on rudeness.

'I intend to use this table covering, ma'am,' Mrs Lacey had said, when she saw the anxious face in the doorway. She pointed to a lace-trimmed white damask cloth, ornamented with drawn work, that lay folded and pristine on the severely polished work table. 'And beneath it, we'll have a silence cloth and then this silk lining.'

'Should it not all be white?' she had suggested tentatively.

'No, ma'am. Some colour showing through is best. And the tint of the lining is very delicate. There are napkins to match, you see, and we'll have these fine lace doilies put under the service plate.'

'They're a little small.' She couldn't stop herself saying it. 'Don't we have a larger size?'

'We do, ma'am, but they are of a different pattern.' Mrs Lacey's tone clearly indicated she was losing patience. 'These will afford a large enough space for a butter plate, a soup bowl and one spoon. All other silver will be set in place as it's needed.'

'And the silver is where?' Alice astonished herself with her temerity. Only terror of the evening ahead could have prompted her to ask.

'With Ripley,' the housekeeper answered abruptly 'He has cleaned soup spoons, forks for the seafood and the ice cream, knives and forks for the meat courses and, before you ask, ma'am, he's organised tumblers and wine glasses and the carafe for chilled water.'

Alice had turned tail and fled.

But she was left with one more list, the only one in the end for which she was solely responsible. It was by far the most challenging: the evening's seating plan. She must decide who was to sit beside who, and where exactly they were to be positioned around the table. She supposed Joshua should be at the head and Henry at the foot, or should she be seated at one end? If not, should she be next to her brother or her husband? Should Elizabeth be facing Giles Audley or seated beside him? Where should she put Louisa, and where Dr Daniels? And, as for William and Oliver – she blanched at the idea that they might be included, and decided to consign them to the kitchen once more. Not that they'd minded a jot when she told them. Oliver had looked at her with his cheeky grin and said, 'That's all right, Mrs Summer. William and I will be fine together.'

Together. That was the problem. They never left each other's side, and since William's illness, their closeness had become even more intense if that were possible. For a very short while, she'd contemplated writing to Mr Amos – the family apparently had no telephone – and asking him to collect his son as soon as convenient. She couldn't tell him the truth, that she sensed the boys' friendship was in some way not right. She would have to manufacture an excuse. She could write there had been a family emergency, and she had been called away. But it had been only minutes before she'd realised the plan was impossible. As soon as Mr Amos got to Summerhayes, he would realise there was no emergency and that Oliver was being sent away.

He might even assume it was because they were Jewish and the Summers were responding to pressure from their neighbours. She'd gone quite cold at the thought.

For a short while, her hopes had risen when William fell ill. She had thought that Oliver would grow bored with a friend who had little strength for their previous rough pursuits, and would himself ask to leave for home. But he had stayed, negating all her preconceptions. Stayed and spent hours with William in their shared room, helping her son put together his nature collection, or reading books with him, or even doing the despised jigsaw puzzles. A part of her was grateful for his not abandoning William, but for a boy of such energy and wicked humour to be so thoughtful, so kind, so loving, made her uneasy.

When the two did venture out, it was to take relatively sedate strolls on the terrace or around the lawn, since William could not be persuaded to walk much beyond the outbuildings. She had found them one day in the tool shed, William giving his friend a lecture on how every implement should be used. She hadn't realised he was so knowledge-able. She wished his father had overheard the conversation: he might be forced then to reconsider his view of William as a futile heir. Joshua, of course, had noticed nothing of the unlikely friendship blossoming beneath his eyes. He was blind to nuance. In his book, William was behaving true to form. He was a weak child, a disappointing son, a mother's boy. The fact that his son now spent most of his time far from Alice appeared not to have dawned on him. He was far too concerned with the events in Europe to give much attention to his family. Every day he brought bad news and today was no exception.

She looked up as he erupted through the door, waving

the morning paper. 'The country is done for now. Germany has declared war on France and invaded Belgium.'

He plumped himself down on an occasional chair, overflowing its basket weave seat and threatening its spindle legs with imminent collapse. 'And Woodrow Wilson has made it clear the United States will stay neutral. There'll be no assistance from that quarter.'

She felt her husband's gloom filling the space. 'But do we need assistance?' she ventured.

He looked at her as though he were a scientist who had just discovered a strange specimen in his laboratory. 'Have you any idea of the odds we'll face?'

She hadn't and it all seemed so far away. She glanced through the window. It was another day of brilliant sunshine, a fresh breeze was blowing and fat, fluffy clouds billowed across the sky. For weeks, England had basked in the sun and the surrounding countryside glowed. It would be the most beautiful autumn and she knew from the servants' chatter that local farmers were expecting a prolific harvest. The idea of war seemed inconceivable.

She made a feeble attempt to keep the world at bay. 'But it's Belgium that has been invaded, isn't it? We have the English Channel between us.'

He leant towards her, impatience stamped on his face. 'We've signed a treaty guaranteeing Belgian neutrality. And last Sunday, sent a letter to the French ambassador pledging to support France if Germany attacked them.'

'But why? Why do we have to be involved?' It seemed to her that the most sensible course of action was to leave the Continentals to get on with things on their own. If they wanted to squabble, it was hardly England's business.

'That's what treaties are for, Alice,' he said slowly, as

though explaining to a small infant. 'We're committed. We can't escape trouble. Don't you ever read the newspapers? Britons living on the Continent are fleeing in their thousands. They're abandoning businesses to get home as soon as possible. Trainloads of them at Charing Cross and Victoria. See here, what it says.' He jabbed at the front page. 'They've travelled for hours and they're telling tales of harassment and sometimes outright hostility. It's clear they've seen some horrors, too. Mark my words, within days we'll be in the thick of it.'

'I hope Summerhayes won't be affected.' Life for Alice would always be played in a minor key. It was the small scale that mattered. The small people like herself, who were picked up by tides they could not control and thrown hither and thither.

'We'll all be affected. Can't you get that into your head?' He shrugged his shoulders in despair. 'You seem to have no more idea of what we're headed for than the Bank Holiday crowds on Brighton beach. They might be a little more subdued than usual, but they've no real understanding of what's coming.'

She was suitably chastened but also frightened. Seeing the expression on her face, he said with heavy humour, 'Comfort yourself with the fact that at least we have a common enemy now – the Hun. The suffragettes have laid down their little hatchets and union leaders are no longer talking strikes.'

She hardly heard him; fear of the future had taken hold. She half rose from her chair and then sat down abruptly. 'We must think what's best to do. We're so close to the coast here that we could be in real danger. The Germans could be on our beaches in no time. There are already refugees in Steyning. Mrs Lacey saw them and thought they must be Belgians. They were talking a strange language.'

'If the Germans do invade, it's far more likely they'll land on the east coast. Yarmouth or Cromer.'

'They might come south,' she said timorously. A whole new raft of anxieties had descended in a matter of minutes, and the dinner party had drifted from sight. 'Perhaps we should move. For a while at least.'

'What are you talking about? Where on earth would we move to? Back to Birmingham?'

'Somewhere in the countryside,' she said quickly. Even the Germans might be preferable to a return to Birmingham. 'North of London maybe.'

'We're moving nowhere,' he said forcefully. 'If they invade, we stay and fight.'

'But, Joshua…'

'Not another word. Where is your backbone? Think of the brave men on the *Titanic*. That was the Empire spirit at work. And the way Captain Scott and his party met their death only this year.'

She thought about them and it didn't seem to make it better. 'The children – William, Elizabeth.'

'Elizabeth will be married very soon and Audley will keep her safe. As for William, he'll be miles away, back at school.'

She kept herself from pointing out that having a son miles away at a time of national emergency was hardly comforting. The mention of Giles Audley had brought to mind yet another anxiety, one that so far she had managed to suppress in the hectic preparations for the evening.

'About Elizabeth's marriage…' she began. 'Do you think it's an entirely sensible thing at the moment?'

His stupefied gaze suggested that the laboratory specimen had climbed out of the test tube and suddenly begun to speak. 'What's got into you today? For God's sake, you're giving a dinner for the man this very evening. Giving it so we can get the marriage settled.'

'I know,' she said miserably, 'but I'm not sure it's what Elizabeth wants.'

'Elizabeth doesn't know what she wants. And what she thinks she wants has nothing to do with it. It's a good marriage. She'll adapt soon enough.' He heaved himself out of the inadequate chair and thumped to the door.

Alice was left to fret. Her husband appeared to think the match was a deal already signed and sealed, and tonight was simply a celebration. The lure of an aristocratic connection was blurring his vision, but it wasn't blurring hers. Their daughter was unpredictable and Alice knew the alliance was far from finalised. Elizabeth had certainly seemed to like Giles Audley. When she'd come upon them in Amberley's dilapidated rose garden, they had been talking together as though they were old friends, and her heart had lightened at the sight. But since that day, she'd been unable to coax a word from her. Elizabeth had remained resolutely silent on the subject. Every time she had tried to raise the matter of a future wedding, the girl had smiled gently and then almost imperceptibly melted away. It had been like trying to catch a will o' the wisp. There had been no outright refusal to contemplate Audley as a husband, but neither had there been the enthusiasm of a bride in the making.

And her concerns had multiplied tenfold when she had seen the Kelloway boy put his arm around her daughter, and seen Elizabeth sink into him for comfort. That moment had brought back memories of Thomas. Unwelcome memories:

the same attraction, the same likely disaster. It had been deeply worrying and still was. Her mind skittered around the scene she had witnessed. There was that whole dreadful business of the dogs. She'd tried to push it from her mind, but she sensed something bad was going on. Henry had laughed it off. He always did. From his earliest years, he'd laughed off whatever awful things had happened around him. Derided accusations, deflected suspicions.

She laid aside the seating plan. Like the food and the flowers and the wine, it was simply a distraction from more important problems. If Elizabeth refused Giles Audley, what would happen to her daughter? Might she be tempted by the young man who had been working at Summerhayes, tempted to jettison all she'd been taught to value? Or might she reject the whole notion of marrying? She had once, Alice remembered rather too clearly. Now the spectre was emerging from the shadows again. Might Elizabeth begin to talk once more of setting up as an artist, of earning her living by her own hand? It didn't bear thinking of. And then there was Henry. If Elizabeth refused Giles, how would her brother react? What would he say? What would he do? That was probably the most frightening question of all.

Chapter Twenty-Three

While her mother wrestled with that evening's entertainment, Elizabeth spent the day in her room. She was safest there from intrusion. The studio was too open to unwelcome visitors and she doubted she could have painted a brushstroke this morning. There was a tension running through the entire household and she felt it acutely. She had heard Joshua's announcement, the news that could determine their country's fate, and so had everyone else. They were all waiting for the unspoken blow to fall. And she had a distinct reason to hide away. She had no wish to meet Alice and be subjected to an interrogation ahead of this evening's gathering. For days, she'd slid from her mother's conversation. She had seen Aiden only once since he'd left Summerhayes, but it made no difference. She could not marry Giles Audley. She should have put a stop to the fantasy days ago, but she had clung on, hoping the idea would die a natural death. She knew that when she refused him, she would meet a wall of resistance and be made to suffer hours of persuasion. Persuasion that would turn to hostility and then to anger, that she'd rejected a perfectly decent man when no other plan for her future was to hand.

She'd had a plan once, but it had withered in the days

and months after she'd returned to Summerhayes. She hadn't wanted to go to London, but her father had insisted. He'd wanted the world to know that a man born into the poorest of families and reared in the slums of Birmingham, had a daughter grand enough to be presented at court. Elizabeth's Season was to be a masterstroke for both of them. But when she'd returned home, unapologetic that she'd rejected two sterling offers of marriage, he'd been furious. She had been equally angry and announced that she would never marry, never be beholden to a man. And when her father had jeered at her and asked her how in that case she proposed to live, she had told him she would be an independent woman, and thrown into the fray the idea that had grown in significance during those tedious months of the Season.

It was a gauntlet cast at her parents' feet and their reaction had been so averse that she had never dared speak of it again. The notion that their daughter might work for a living seemed at first to bemuse them, then when they realised she intended to earn money as an artist, they'd been rendered dumbstruck. When finally they'd found the words to condemn the project, she'd been left in no doubt what her future would be if she were ever to leave the family home and try for an independent life. She would be rendered penniless; it was for her own good, her father had said, that she realise this. How then could she even begin? She had no money of her own and no knowledge of how to sell her work in order to raise sufficient rent for a single room. Her retreat from the dream she'd carried was craven and she'd spent months scolding herself for lacking courage, but that had altered nothing.

Until Aiden Kellaway had arrived in her life. She had

been attracted to him from the very beginning, but she could never have envisaged a future together. For weeks, she could only guess at his feelings, but she knew now that he loved her and wanted to be with her. Wanted to be her husband. Her hostility to marriage was no more. She wanted to wed him; it was so evidently right. Aiden's love had transformed her vision of the life ahead. Yet, had it? She would not be allowed to marry him. She was still not of age and her father would refuse his consent. And if she were to marry without consent and by special licence, what then? He was a skilful architect. He was energetic, enthusiastic, primed to make a good life. But he was at the outset of his career and it would take time to build a secure future. Even if that future had lain in London, their marriage would have been a leap in the dark for them both. But it didn't lie in London. He was going to Canada. She understood his reasons clearly enough, but Canada! An unknown land, a pioneer country, thousands of miles from home and family. Thousands of miles from Summerhayes.

'I'll find work,' he'd reassured her and she believed him. 'I'll find enough to keep us in good heart. You won't live as lavishly as you do here, but I'll make sure you've every comfort I can give you.' His words had torn her heart in two.

'I'd be a burden,' she protested, 'a millstone. I'd contribute nothing – just a few daubs on canvas. If it wasn't so sad, it would be laughable.'

He'd taken her by the shoulders then and given her a gentle shake. 'Don't dare to speak of burdens. We'll be a team. I'll design the buildings and you will paint the pictures to hang on their walls.' He raised her hands to his lips. Then his mouth found hers again.

'And that's not just a dream,' he murmured, when he finally broke away. 'You'll sell your pictures without a doubt. I've seen them – they're good. They're very good.'

Whatever he might say, it *was* a dream, an enticing picture of a shared life, loving each other to the full, labouring together to build a future. The very stuff of dreams.

'I'm travelling to Southampton the day after I finish my work here. I need to book the first available passage to New York. Then from New York, I'll make arrangements to travel on to Ontario.'

The dream died. He was going. He was going, but she was not. Her ties to family, to Summerhayes, were too strong for her.

'I can't do it,' she whispered in a broken voice. 'I can't leave my family.' At the best of times, she would find it impossible, but now with William ill and war on their doorstep, how could she abandon them?

Her whisper died into silence. He'd slipped off the seat then and knelt on the gravel beside her. His expression was grave but his eyes were filled with love. He had taken one of her hands in his, and then the other, and gripped them tightly. 'I understand that what I'm asking is enormous. I truly do. But you must understand, too, that I cannot stay here, or my life will be over.'

They had remained like that, hands clasped, Aiden kneeling by her side, for minutes on end. When finally he spoke again, his voice rang with fierce sincerity. 'If you marry me, Elizabeth, I will honour you and care for you. I will love you more than I can put into words. But I cannot stay.'

*

His words had been with her ever since. They'd buzzed and bounced their way through every thought, one minute tormenting her with the promise of happiness, the other taunting her with reality. The sun was still flooding her bedroom and the fresh, clear air of evening spilling through its open windows, when at precisely six o'clock, Ivy appeared at her mistress's door. Her maid's appearance signalled it was time to dress for the most difficult dinner of her life. She had only herself to blame for her predicament. She should have been bolder and braver and put a stop to the pretence days ago.

An hour earlier, she had snatched a glance at her mother's seating plan and seen that she had been placed opposite Giles Audley. She would be required to talk to him across the table, talk to her neighbours on either side, on everything and nothing, to smile and to laugh as though there were little more at stake than a good dinner and a glass of wine. But all the time, she would be conscious that at any moment she must find the words to disappoint the kindly man who sat opposite. And all the time, too, shimmering and dark, a much greater pain, the knowledge that she was losing the man she loved. The man she could not marry.

Ivy was in boisterous spirits. 'It will be Saturday, Miss Elizabeth,' she said a trifle breathlessly. 'We've just this minute arranged it with Vicar.'

She looked blank. 'The wedding,' Ivy prompted.

'This Saturday? You've brought it forward again?'

'We had to.' For a moment the girl's face clouded. 'But Vicar has been that kind. He says, in the circumstances, he's happy to marry us at short notice. And Eddie's checked with the Horse and Groom and they don't mind a bit.'

'But why the rush?'

'You've not heard then? Your pa don't stop talking about it.'

'You mean the news of Belgium?' She couldn't see how that would make Ivy and Eddie marry at such breakneck speed.

'There's an ultimatum. I think that's what it's called. If Germany don't respond by midnight tonight, we'll be at war.'

'And Eddie wants to go and fight? Surely he doesn't have to?'

'No, he don't. But he won't rest till he's enlisted. He comes from a soldier family,' she said sadly, as though that were sufficient explanation.

Elizabeth was stunned. Since her father's dismal announcement early this morning that Belgium had been overrun, she'd been closeted in her room and heard nothing more.

'What about the other men?' she asked.

'They'm all talking about it. They'll be marching to the recruiting office soon enough, you'll see... I've run your bath, miss,' Ivy remembered suddenly.

She walked across to the girl and gave her a hug. 'Don't despair. The ultimatum might work and then Eddie won't need to leave.'

She was needful herself for it to work. If there were no war, Aiden might be persuaded to stay. They could steal away, obtain a special licence and marry somewhere – London perhaps. They'd find a room and Aiden would get work and she might sell a few pictures. Eventually, her family would see what a wonderful husband she'd won, and accept her marriage. They'd be happy for her and everyone would be reconciled. But she knew she was whistling in the wind.

When she emerged rosy-faced from the bathroom, she saw that Ivy had laid out the cream silk her father had bought her for the London Season, together with a pair of flimsy cream sandals.

'The dress is a little grand for Summerhayes,' she remonstrated. 'I think we'll have to find another.'

Ivy shook her head. 'We can't do that. Your ma wants you to look the very best. She says this evening is a big occasion for you.'

'More like a big occasion for my mother. It's the first party she's thrown in all the time we've been at Summerhayes.'

'Mistress is in a right tizzy, to be sure. But you'll still want to look your best.'

She gave up the argument. 'The cream silk it is then.'

Ivy draped her figure in layer after layer of undergarments in a resigned silence. A corset to compress the waist and hips, a square-necked camisole, and then a pair of frilly knickers buttoned at the waist. Silk stockings with their attendant garters came next and finally a lawn petticoat laid out in a circle on the floor. She stepped into the centre and Ivy lifted the petticoat up and buttoned it at the waist. At last, she was ready for the dress.

'That's some beautiful.' The girl stood back and gave a happy sigh at the finished picture. 'Shall we use the gold and rhinestone comb?'

'If you like,' she said indifferently, walking over to the window and looking out at the scene she loved. The air might be soft but the greenness of the world had largely disappeared beneath a harsh sun, and the once verdant lawn was now bleached and tired.

She walked slowly back to her dressing table. Her hair was brushed into a shining mass, then piled high on her head and swept into a soft swirl with the gloriously ornamented comb to fasten it. Her mother could not complain of her appearance tonight. She was expected to look as though she had made an effort, and the ornament, the hair, the flowing silk dress with its ruched lace bodice encrusted with beads spoke effort loudly.

She'd been uncaring of the final effect, but when she looked into the mirror, she was pleased with what she saw. Although her figure was slender, the cream dress clung to her curves in a sinuous fashion and its décolletage was tempting rather than obvious. She wished it were Aiden who would see her tonight. Her maid fastened the matching gold and rhinestone necklace around her throat and she was ready.

She took up the beaded evening bag and gave the girl a kiss on the cheek. 'Next time, you must let me work as hard. I shall dress you for your wedding and make you the bride of the year.'

'I couldn't let you do that, miss.' Ivy was scandalised.

'You could – and on Saturday, you will.'

A gong sounded from below and, with a small sigh, she whisked herself out of the door. Ivy was left shaking her head but there was a pleased smile on her face.

Joshua was waiting in the hall, impatient as always, his foot tapping loudly against the black and white tiles and his fingers beating a tattoo along the console table. The evening light poured through the front door, illuminating its swirling design of textured glass, and splashing the hall with pools of bright colour. Its beauty went unnoticed by him. He was on edge, she could see, despite the indifference he'd affected whenever this evening was mentioned.

'Good evening, Papa,' she said primly.

At the sound of her voice, he turned around and stared at her. Then continued to stare, his gaze fixed, as though she were someone he'd never seen before.

'You look so beautiful, Elizabeth,' he said at last.

'Don't I always?' she teased.

'Yes, but…' He cleared his throat, seeming for an instant to be overcome by feeling.

She hoped not. She needed to play a part this evening, but she'd no wish to raise expectations that it was for real. Before she could say anything to depress his spirits, Alice had drifted down the stairs towards them. She hardly glanced at her daughter but floated on towards the dining room, her face creased with anxiety.

Eizabeth followed and found her mother walking around the table, first one way and then the other. Fiddling here and there with a knife, a spoon. Creasing the starched napkins to a stronger crease. Putting the already straight chairs, straight.

'Mama, it looks beautiful.'

And it did. The silver gleamed on starched white damask, crystal glasses sparkled and caught fire from a sun low in the sky, and Mr Harris's small pots of roses tripped colourfully down the centre of the table. She breathed in their deep, sweet perfume and thought it heavenly.

'Come into the drawing room,' she coaxed. 'Maybe a small glass of sherry to steady your nerves?'

Her mother's nerves looked as though they would need a whole bottle of the spirit, but Alice would have none of it. 'Sherry with the soup, Elizabeth,' she said, but allowed herself to be steered into the drawing room, where she perched on the very edge of the sofa, primed and ready to fly.

Chapter Twenty-Four

A bell clanged and Alice started up, as though she were a jack escaping its box. Ripley could be heard tramping to the front door, but her mother was already in the hall and greeting Henry and her sister-in-law effusively. Dr Daniels was close behind. Louisa, Elizabeth noticed, was wearing a particularly revealing dress and her scent was powerful, mingling with the heat of the sun that poured through the coloured glass. That perfume would prove a serious challenge to the roses.

When Giles Audley arrived, he greeted her as an old friend. But his gaze, warm and admiring, was not the gaze of a friend, and her misgiving increased sharply. For a short while, the small group were gathered uneasily in the drawing room, none of them quite sure what to say or what to do on such an occasion. When the gong sounded promptly at seven – country hours were kept at Summerhayes – there was an almost audible murmur of relief around the room. Their guests could be shepherded across the hall and into the cool of the dining room.

Ripley, unfamiliar in black tails and bow tie, served the first course immediately, and once bowls of watercress soup and schooners of sherry were on the table, a stilted conversation could begin. It centred, inevitably, on the frightening situation across the Channel and the subject looked likely to continue for some while. Her gratitude was unspoken but heartfelt. With luck, marriage would remain unmentioned.

'No one has been prepared for it, you see,' her uncle said between slurps of watercress. 'There's been talk of war for years, predictions even, but it has still managed to take people by surprise.'

'It's hardly a wonder, is it?' Louisa smiled ingratiatingly at her husband. 'Not when Lloyd George has been at such pains to claim our relations with Germany are more friendly than they've been for years. How he's misled us! This morning, people open their newspapers and suddenly there's the threat of war – not from Ireland, which they might have expected, but from Europe.'

She noticed that her father, who had been the first to warn of a cataclysm, was keeping his lips firmly closed. 'We're assuming that there will be a war,' the doctor said in his high, tight voice. 'We could be very wrong. It's not too late for us to avoid disaster, is it?' Louisa gave him a swift approving glance, while everyone else ignored him and bent their heads over the last of the soup.

Ripley, together with the two footmen hired for the occasion, cleared the dishes, but soon returned with platters of prawns in aspic, baked fish, and a third with a toppling edifice that proved to be a shrimp mousse. Bottles of hock replaced the sherry.

'Dr Daniels is right,' Alice said. 'Nothing irrevocable has happened. We can still avoid a catastrophe.' Now they had reached the second course without misfortune, her mother appeared a little less tense and was evidently feeling sorry for the doctor whose attempt at conversation had been so blatantly dismissed. 'You know that special prayers were said on Sunday,' she went on brightly. 'They may well be answered.'

'We've been caught out, there's no doubt,' Henry opined, ignoring his sister. He took a long draught of cooled wine. 'We should have seen it coming when Austria issued its ultimatum to Serbia and tried to humiliate them. But we took no notice. We preferred to be bystanders.'

She could have pointed out to her uncle that he'd been contemptuous when her father had voiced just those fears, but she said nothing. Keeping Henry Fitzroy happy this evening was what mattered.

'You would have thought we'd have worked it out though,' her uncle blethered. 'That ultimatum made certain that Russia would defend Serbia, and then, of course, Germany and France were bound to be pulled in on one side or the other.'

'Like a dormant volcano that has erupted unexpectedly,' the doctor said, to no real point.

Her father was forcing himself to remain silent, but in the presence of such obvious ignorance, the effort was causing his colour to mount alarmingly. She glanced across the table at Giles. He gave a small smile, but then returned to the sweetbreads and cutlets that Ripley had just served. His appetite appeared unimpaired by the tensions bubbling not so far below the surface. The two of them had not exchanged a word since the meal began, but she had no quarrel with that. Any postponement of the difficult conversation they must have was a happy one. Long may the talk of war continue, as long as Joshua's temper could bear it.

The burgundy certainly wouldn't improve his temper. He rarely drank wine and, when he did, he was liable to become more belligerent than ever. This evening, he'd had to endure comments that would have shamed a child; comments that were crass and vapid and on a subject he felt himself entitled to judge wisely. But there was more insult to come, though this time it arrived silently. Ripley was carving the roast beef while the two footmen offered an unending line of vegetable dishes to each guest in turn. She saw that for the first time Henry, seated at her father's right hand, had noticed the hired help and his face was suffused with disdain. She hoped her father hadn't noticed. The absence of a butler was for Henry entirely predictable. Summerhayes managed on half the number of servants than was common for such a large estate; it was only what one would expect from a button manufacturer, his expression seemed to say.

Burgundy was doing him no favours either. 'We shouldn't despair,' he intoned. 'Even if war comes, it's sure to be a short campaign. Harsh but short. It will be all over by Christmas, you'll see. This country has been unbeaten for years. Our young men will be champing to get to grips with the enemy. And you can trust the aristocracy to be at their head, leading the charge.'

'Donkeys leading other donkeys into carnage,' her father muttered, having decided, it seemed, against neutrality.

In response, Henry banged his wine glass down on the table. A crimson pool spread across the white damask. 'That's bloody unpatriotic,' he blustered. Louisa dared to make a shushing sound and reach across to lay a restraining hand on her husband's arm. It was not going to restrain him. 'But then I wouldn't expect anything else. Your people –' he almost spat the words, '– would allow the Kaiser to trample all over us, as long as he let them continue churning out their profits.'

Joshua's anger had turned to ice and his voice cut a cold swathe through the thick quarrelsome atmosphere. 'You need to get your facts right, Henry. The Royal Navy might still rule the seas with its battleships and cruisers, but our engineering lags way behind Germany's and we have the army to prove it. It's too small and far outflanked by Germany's battalions. Any rational person can see that it's ill equipped to fight a modern land war, let alone overcome an enemy twice its size in a matter of months.'

Henry pulled his face into an ugly scowl, but it did nothing to deter his brother-in-law. 'My people, as you term them, are far from unpatriotic. But they have heads on their shoulders and know only too well that a foolish war will bring economic chaos to this country.'

'Foolish!' Alice visibly jumped at her brother's bellow. 'You call standing up to the Kaiser foolish? That's the talk of a socialist.'

'And yours is the talk of a man who knows nothing.'

There was no attempt now to hide the contempt each man harboured for the other. 'I suppose you were in Trafalgar Square two days ago?' Henry jeered. 'Waving placards with your fellow socialists.'

'I wasn't but I would have been happy to be there. They have every right to protest. And they represent the mood of much of the country – the mood of people a long way from the bubble in which you live. I'm no socialist, God dammit, how could I be, but fifteen thousand demonstrated that day against going to war. The government should take notice. You should take notice. But then that number means nothing to you. They're only workers, aren't they, people who graft a living with their hands?'

'As you did,' his brother-in-law sneered.

'And proud of it. I worked day and night to become a man who could buy a factory. Then another, and another. A man who was trusted enough to make money for others. What have you ever done, apart from holding out your hand?'

From the foot of the table, Alice was darting frightened glances from one to the other, her hands twitching uncontrollably. She looked on the verge of tears. Elizabeth was about to go to her when Ripley and his minions appeared with the game course, moving deftly around each guest while studiously ignoring the hostility ricocheting across the table.

While her father and uncle had been engaged in battle, she'd noticed Louisa grip her cutlery more tightly with every escalation in Henry's fury. Her eyes had been fixed doggedly on the square of white tablecloth immediately beneath her plate, her gaze never deviating an inch. But now in the fidgety silence that followed, her aunt seemed released from the spell that had fallen on her and was taking the opportunity to whisper in the doctor's ear. Whatever she said, seemed to please him. He must be the only happy guest, Elizabeth thought. This was the most miserable dinner she had ever eaten: the sound and fury of claim and counterclaim was wretched, the pretence that this was a genial family party equally so. It was war by any other name. She toyed with the small slices of duck that Ripley had served her, and chased a few of the accompanying game chips. Whatever appetite she'd had had long gone, and her head felt full to bursting.

Alice had eaten even less well, she could see. Her mother had managed to gain control of her hands, but she was sitting unnaturally in a rigidly upright position. When Ripley appeared again, her head clicked to one side like a machine to order, and her eyes followed his every movement. It seemed she could maintain her composure only by checking and rechecking the minor details of the dinner – had the table been cleared properly, was it being relaid correctly with a new tablecloth, with fresh cutlery and glasses? The sweet wine that Ripley was serving along with the pistachio cream and lemon-water ice seemed a particular worry. Not much longer, Mama, she thought.

The hostilities had temporarily abated, both participants too exhausted, or, more likely, too full to continue. She'd thought that Giles Audley might have stepped between the crossfire and attempted to halt the battle, but he had said nothing. Somehow she imagined him more a man of action than words. She wondered, if war came, whether he would volunteer to fight. Perhaps he'd be considered too old for the battlefield.

He must have sensed her thoughts, or felt her gaze, because he looked across at her and said, 'Is all this talk of war upsetting you, Elizabeth?'

'Not as much as if the talk should turn to reality.'

'Your father seems fairly convinced it will.'

'He still does business on the Continent. His contacts there have been warning him for months of the danger.'

She spoke quietly, not wanting to attract attention. The other diners were picking at their desserts and the conversation had become listless but unthreatening.

'Mr Summer runs his own factories then?'

'Not any longer. He sold them years ago, but the present

owners are glad to use his knowledge of Europe. And he seems happy to keep a small link with his old life in Birmingham.'

'That of a country gentleman is certainly very different. Such a change of fortune.' He seemed to marvel at Joshua's transformation. 'He will see the world from two quite different perspectives.'

The thought had never occurred to her. 'I suppose he must. I know he fears what war will do to the workers he knows.'

He leant back in his chair, pushing away a half-eaten ice. 'And not just them. If war comes, it will affect everyone.'

'The young men going off to fight, you mean?'

'Young men from all backgrounds. It won't be just the gallant cavalry galloping to the rescue. If there is conflict, the footmen, the gardeners, the carpenter, everyone in fact, is likely to be drawn into it. And probably the estate itself, too.'

For weeks, she had sensed darkness. Not just a personal darkness but a larger fear, a shadow encroaching on the sunlit days that had only slowly taken form. It had shimmered in the background, at first hardly noticed, but imperceptibly growing in intensity. And now it hung over Summerhayes itself.

'If there *is* war, what will happen to country estates like this?'

'It's anyone's guess. There are many already struggling to pay death duties, but a war could be the final straw. Think of it, if a father dies and his heir is killed too, the estate will suffer a double hit. Whoever is left – sons, grandsons, distant cousins – won't have the money to carry on. They'll need to sell the family silver bit by bit, and that includes the land that makes the estate what it is.'

'So the world we know will die?'

'It might not mean complete extinction,' he tried to reassure her. 'It might simply be that there are fewer estates and less money and staff to run them.'

Her father had the money, but if there were no one left to maintain Summerhayes, his fantasy could be over. He had chosen to ape a mode of life, it seemed, when it was already too late. In different ways, both he and Henry belonged to a past disappearing before their eyes. It was men like Aiden who were the future.

'In any case,' Giles went on, 'there might not be much of an estate to run if the military becomes involved.' She frowned at him. Was that meant to be reassuring? 'They'll want land for their training camps, and local councils will claim any unused fields for food production. Then there's the livestock. They'll need to commandeer that and to cut timber from the woods.'

'You've really thought it through.' She was admiring, though she had no wish to flatter him.

'I was a soldier as a young man. It gives you an idea of what will be required.' So she hadn't been wrong about that. He was a man of action.

'And a house like this would be requisitioned?' The words trembled on her lips. It was a devastating prospect.

'It's hard to say. Country houses would certainly be expected to supply accommodation for hospitals and training, but hopefully Summerhayes would be spared.'

'I hope so, too. It would kill my father to lose it.'

'Try not to worry,' he said warmly. 'The war isn't yet

certain and things will go on much as usual – for a while at least.'

'One of our men, Eddie Miller – he's our chauffeur – is already talking of joining up. Poor Ivy. She's to be married to him on Saturday.'

'I'm sure he'll be around for some time yet. Conscription is bound to be delayed. There's a deep-ingrained hostility to it in this country.'

'He intends to volunteer.'

'Does he? Good man. That's the kind of spirit we'll need if war does happen.'

She leant forwards across the expanse of starched white cloth. 'Tell me the truth. You *are* expecting war, aren't you?'

'I won't disguise the fact that the situation looks very grave. You don't proffer an ultimatum unless you mean to enforce it.'

'Perhaps the government shouldn't have issued one. Perhaps they should have waited.'

'They had little choice. As a nation, we are bound by treaty to support those countries that Germany is invading.'

'And if we didn't meet our pledges? There are plenty of reasons why Britain shouldn't. We're an island and it's not our quarrel.'

'A treaty is a legal document,' he remonstrated gently.

'That's not the point though, is it? It's not so much about the law. It's all about honour. Not losing face. That's such a male notion.' Her complexion was flushed. The talk had made her feel angry and powerless.

'Are you saying that women don't possess a sense of honour?'

'I'm saying that in a difficult situation they're willing to compromise.'

He shook his head. 'With a force like the Kaiser's, there is no compromising.'

She suddenly became conscious that no one else around the table was talking, and that their conversation was being marked and approved by a phalanx of smiles. Even the doctor exchanged a knowing look with her aunt. It was beyond embarrassing. Ripley could not have appeared at a more opportune moment. Fruit and nuts arrived along with the port; it was time for the ladies to retire to the drawing room and await the tea tray. The men were permitted their cigars now, though she noticed her father offered no invitation to his smoking room. That redoubt might lack the stuffed fish and heads of game common to most, but it was an entirely masculine domain. Above all, it was Joshua's private domain and he guarded it ferociously.

Chapter Twenty-Five

'Giles Audley is such a gentleman, don't you think?' Louisa asked over the teacups.

'I imagine he must be, since he's related to the Fitzroys.' Elizabeth's answer was deliberately obtuse.

What made a gentleman anyway? Was it breeding, or money, or good manners? Or a mix of all three? If so, neither her father nor Uncle Henry would qualify. But if it lay in honesty, in integrity and kindness, then Aiden was the true gentleman.

'I mean,' her aunt explained painstakingly, 'that he is gentlemanly in his conduct and bearing. And so handsome for a man of his age. He is a splendid prize.' She stroked the expensive sunburst china thoughtfully.

'And one already awarded to another woman,' Elizabeth couldn't resist saying.

Louisa reached out for her hand. 'Oh, my dear, you mustn't worry over that. She mustn't, must she, Alice?' she appealed to her sister-in-law. 'Giles's dear wife died many years ago and, of course, there are no offspring to make things difficult.'

'If anything,' her mother chimed in, 'it should give you confidence. He evidently loved his wife deeply and, by all accounts, he was a very good husband.'

Louisa nodded sagely. 'He has an excellent pedigree,' she agreed. 'And that's what we want for you, Elizabeth, to be in the hands of a good man – particularly in a world so unsettled as this.'

She prickled with distaste at being so blatantly pressured. She could have said to her aunt that she had no wish to be in the hands of anyone. Except that it wasn't true. But, for the Fitzroys, they would be entirely the wrong hands.

'My maid has chosen a good man,' she said, attempting to deflect the conversation. 'She is to marry him on Saturday.'

'How nice,' Lousia said indifferently. 'But hardly something that should concern you.'

'On the contrary, I'm worried for Ivy. *Her* future looks very uncertain. Her new husband intends to join the fighting if it happens and I want to make sure she has a wedding day to remember.'

Her aunt looked horrified and Alice made haste to intervene. 'Elizabeth has had Ivy with her since the nursery, you know. It's natural for her to be concerned for the girl.'

Louisa took a visible breath. She seemed to be readying herself to denounce this treason, but when she spoke it was on a different subject entirely.

'I was surprised not to see William at dinner. It's an excellent idea, I think, for a child to be trained in etiquette within the family, and William is well on the way to being a young man. Gilbert will certainly be eating his dinner with us very soon.'

'If you remember,' Alice said, 'we have a friend of William's staying.'

'But still, my dear, could they not both have come? I imagine it would do the friend a power of good, particularly coming from the background he does.' She paused. 'William is well, I suppose?'

'Perfectly.'

'I wondered. Henry was saying only the other day that his health must be a worry for you both. It would be quite shocking if he became a permanent invalid.'

Elizabeth's pulse tumbled uncomfortably, but before she had time to analyse exactly why, the door opened and the men drifted in, one by one. In the end, they had not sat long over their port. She could not imagine a conversation between the four; the atmosphere must have been more awkward even than when the women had been present.

Giles Audley made for the chair nearest her and sat down. She was sharply aware of another round of approving looks filling the room. She was suffocating beneath this weight of expectation and longed to flee. But there was no escape. Not yet.

'I've been thinking about what you said,' he began.

'You haven't been talking then?'

He pulled his mouth into a grimace and his eyes flickered with amusement. 'The conversation wasn't that easy, shall we say.'

'It hasn't been easy here either. So what were your thoughts?'

'Not great ones, I'm afraid. But your worries over your chauffeur – it may not be so very bad. You heard what your uncle said. He's sure that any conflict will be short and sharp and over by Christmas. Eddie and his compatriots could be back to celebrate with you.'

'If he comes back,' she said thoughtfully. He looked nonplussed. 'I don't mean he wouldn't return to Ivy, but I wonder how willing he'll be – how willing any of the servants will be – to return to the kind of life they have here.'

'I can't imagine they wouldn't return,' he said in a surprised voice. 'Think of the emotional stake they have in the family, in the estate. All servants do. Quite often, you know, they feel the house belongs to them as much as it does to you.'

'But they would have seen a different world, a wider world. Once they're convinced they can sell their skills elsewhere, and for greater reward, they may not be quite as keen to return.'

He tilted his head, weighing her words. 'It's true they'll be of value to the army. A number of them will know how to shoot and most can use tools. And there'll be others who can drive horses or even motor vehicles. But I still think you'd see your men return. Their jobs would be kept open for them and no doubt, when they got back, their wages would rise. There are already tales that some farmers are offering their labourers higher wages to keep them. And employment as a servant is secure, don't forget. One should never underestimate the lure of security in a harsh world.'

'But theirs is already a harsh world, isn't it? I'm not sure that once they've tasted freedom, they'd want to come back. Our servants are mainly from the village, but factory work would certainly pay them more. And once the traditional link is severed, it would be for good.'

'I think you're being unduly pessimistic. Your family are good employers. A position at Summerhayes would be a great deal to give up.'

She took a while before she answered. 'We treat our people as well as anyone else, but there's no disguising that their lives are hard. They work from dawn to dusk. We have electric light, telephones, a motor car, but even in a modern house like Summerhayes, the chores are unending. Being a servant is little better than being a drudge.'

'Those are the words of revolution, Elizabeth. I wonder, is this Mrs Pankhurst's influence? I know she's preached that the women's vote could mean a government that would help both workers and women.'

She'd read that speech and been heartened by it, but in truth it was meeting Aiden that had given her a new sensitivity to the lives of working people. Previously, their existence – even Ivy's – was something she'd taken for granted.

She ignored his question and asked instead, 'Would you be willing to fight?'

He gave a droll laugh. 'Willing, but whether they'd have me is another matter. I wouldn't be conscripted that's for certain – I'm too old. But volunteering would be different. I was once in the cavalry, like most of the young men I knew, and, if I should ever volunteer, a cavalry regiment is where I'd go.'

'This war, if it happens, will not be a war for horses.' Joshua's strident tones broke through their talk.

'And surely you would not volunteer.' Alice was following in her husband's footsteps. 'Not now, of all times.'

Elizabeth had been engrossed in her conversation with Giles and had not noticed the room grow quiet around them. Now she realised that every word they'd said had been overheard. It was as though the company were silently encouraging them, nudging them forward, urging them to bond over this talk of war. It was ridiculous. Yet here was her mother posing a question to Giles Audley of what he intended for his future.

'In all probability, Mrs Summer, I won't volunteer,' he answered her mother placidly.

'Absolutely not! You'll have far more important things on your mind, eh, Giles?' Her uncle had rediscovered his social manners since leaving the dining room, but the familiar smooth polish had leached into a cordiality that was horribly false.

'That will depend,' Giles said easily, without specifying exactly what.

Every person in the drawing room seemed to be looking at her, as though she were an icon in gold, giving off lustrous light, to be gazed upon in wonderment. Even Giles became conscious of the extraordinary attention the two of them were attracting, and for a moment his easy manner slipped. He made a business of clearing his throat.

'I hope to call on you tomorrow, Mr Summer,' he managed to say.

*

'He'll be here tomorrow,' Joshua said with satisfaction later that evening. 'Good. That's one thing we can settle, if nothing else.' Most unusually, he had come to Alice's room before going to bed. Her elderly maid was still unpinning her hair, but she dismissed the woman immediately.

'When do you think we should have the wedding?' she ventured, swivelling around on her dressing stool to face him.

Elizabeth had seemed interested in her suitor and happy to talk with him, but Alice's doubts over her daughter's future had not entirely subsided. One could never tell with Elizabeth. All Alice could do was to cling to a hope.

The dinner had been one of the worst trials of her life and she could only pray that the terrifying evening had been worth the pain.

'We'll have it as soon as possible,' Joshua declared. 'There's no point in delaying and, even at short notice, we can put on a splendid party.' She could see that he was already imagining Summerhayes decked in bunting. 'You'll have Mrs Lacey to help you. Together, you'll manage well enough. Tonight was a good show, Alice.'

She flushed with pleasure at the unexpected praise. 'It wasn't the most comfortable experience,' she hazarded.

'Only because your brother is an arrogant snob, and pig-headed to boot.'

'I don't think he understands the situation in the way you do,' she said placatingly, though in truth she had little understanding of it herself. The idea of a looming war still seemed unreal.

She saw her husband look at the small clock on her dressing table. It was ten minutes to eleven.

'We'll know the worst very shortly,' he said. 'Midnight Berlin time, that's when the ultimatum expires. Most of us know already. Nobody expects Germany to get out of Belgium. Despite what Henry says, the country has sensed there's something bad coming. There'll be people in the Mall tonight, you'll see. It's a warm evening and they'll be converging on Big Ben and singing, "God Save the King".'

From deep in the hall, the chimes of the grandfather clock struck eleven. 'That's it. The die is cast,' he said solemnly. 'At this very moment telegrams will be winging their way around the world, telling our ships to begin hostilities against Germany. Can you imagine it?'

She couldn't. Her mind was remote from far-flung ships

or even the crowds in London. It was the personal that once again struck a chord. 'I do hope Giles won't think of signing up to join the cavalry.'

'He'd be a fool if he was. They'll be mincemeat,' he said crudely.

She looked alarmed and his impatience spilt out. 'Don't fuss, Alice. Audley was quite clear. He won't be wandering off to war if he gets married. A wedding will stop him from any nonsensical idea of joining up. We'll organise it for a few weeks' time – you should be able to manage that – and then both of them will be anchored here. They can make their home at Summerhayes. No need for a separate establishment.'

He began to walk towards the door, but then paused as a happy thought struck. 'We're bound to lose men from the estate, even if your ignorant brother is right and the conflict is over in months. I'll need help in running Summerhayes and Audley is the man to do it. He comes from an old country family; he'll know the ropes. Having him as a son-in-law will be just the ticket.'

'I hope Elizabeth thinks so,' she risked saying, and received due punishment.

'Sometimes you talk utter nonsense! Of course, she'll think so. You can see she's delighted with the match. The two of them never stopped talking the entire evening.'

Alice kept silent. She dared not say what she was thinking, that unceasing talk was hardly a guarantee of lifelong commitment. In many ways, just the opposite. She'd watched Elizabeth's face as she had sat chatting. It was open and friendly, interested in what Giles was saying, but there had been not a shred of love in it.

'They'll get married,' Joshua declared, brooking no argument. 'And very soon.'

'Of course they will,' she agreed. But her husband had stomped from the room without hearing her or hearing the quiver of doubt in her voice.

Chapter Twenty-Six

The boys had enjoyed their evening watching Ripley and his fellows rushing in and out of the kitchen, arms sagging beneath precariously balanced trays, and with faces schooled to blankness as they prepared to do battle in the dining room.

'There's a right to-do upstairs,' Ripley announced, dumping the remains of the roast beef on the wooden worktop. 'You should hear 'em going hammer and tongs.' His sober face lit with the ghost of a grin.

'Never mind that now.' Cook, flushed and out of breath, scattered commands. 'Grab that platter of duck, Mr Ripley, and you – Jim, isn't it? – you'll need to follow with the game chips.'

William, comfortably ensconced at the trestle table, could feel only gratitude that he'd escaped the hammer and tongs. His poor sister had not and he dared not think how his mother was coping. It wasn't something worrying Oliver. With his mouth still full, he reached out for a final spoonful of mash to go with his last bit of steak-and-kidney pudding. 'This is amazing potato,' he said in a muffled voice.

'Looks like it, Master Oliver,' Cook said tartly, 'You've managed to eat most of our supper, too.'

Oliver looked abashed and began to apologise when

Cook gave him a friendly tap on the shoulder. 'Don't worry, lad. By the look of it, there'll be plenty over from the dining room. With all those shenanigans going on, the mistress for one won't be eating. And after all my hard work.' She gave a weary sigh, and began to pile up the plates they'd scraped clean.

'You know *we* appreciate your hard work, don't you?' Oliver said.

'I do that, and I've baked you both a lemon sponge to prove it.'

'Gosh! Thanks, Cook.' William jumped up and hugged her. He carried the cake to the table and cut them two large slices. Then carefully topped up their glasses of ginger beer.

'Yes, thanks,' muttered Oliver, his mouth once again full.

'The ladies have gone to the drawing room,' Ripley reported a few minutes later, kicking the kitchen door shut behind him. 'As soon as the men have drunk their port, we'll clear the table. They won't be there long. They can barely manage a word between 'em.'

'Then it's time you two were gone.' Cook nodded a dismissal. 'We've still a deal of work to do getting this place cleaned up.'

There was a crash from the other side of the kitchen. 'What are you doing with that pan?' she yelled at a scullery maid, who was chasing a large aluminium dish around the Belfast sink.

'Time to go, Wills.' Olly winked at his friend and scraped back his chair.

'Let's go by the back stairs,' William said. He had no wish to meet his parents or his parents' guests. They must be avoided at all costs.

As soon as they reached the bedroom, he burrowed in the old toy chest and brought out a battered box. 'Look what I found the other day when Mama made me stay in.'

'Ludo?' Olly looked disdainful, but then his competitive spirit got the better of him. 'Bet I can beat you at it.'

They spread themselves across the floor and, before long, true to his word, Oliver was victorious. 'We'll play draughts next,' he decided. 'That should give you a chance. You're good at draughts and you need to win some of the time.'

William smiled at him and Olly smiled back, warmly, secretly, as though they were part of a conspiracy together. But draughts proved to be as much Oliver's game as ludo and, in desperation, he pulled the box of Chinese chequers from under the bed. '*This* is your moment, William. Chinese chequers will be it.' The game that followed was fought with vigour, but finally William was able to give a victory 'Hurrah!'

'Did you let me win?' he asked suspiciously.

Olly reached out and smoothed his friend's cheek, then punched him lightly on the shoulder. 'Maybe a little. Tonight I'm super champion, but you can have your revenge tomorrow.' He scrambled to his feet, grabbed his pyjamas and toothbrush, and made his way to the bathroom.

William slowly packed away the chequers. He had begun to crumple into tiredness: winning had been hard. He put on his pyjamas and climbed into bed, then lay there, unmoving, watching the door for Olly to come back. Olly was the very best friend he could ever have. More than a friend though. That must be true, or he'd not be plagued by a yearning he couldn't lose, one that left him empty and adrift. He knew he shouldn't feel this way. Friends didn't, did they? They didn't want to *kiss* each other. His body stiffened at the thought. He'd always refused to form that word in his mind, but now he had and felt himself trembling. He had to stop thinking like this, had to stop imagining how it could be. It couldn't.

The effort to subdue his imagination made him tireder than ever and, by the time Oliver returned from the bathroom, he was almost asleep. Fatigue muffled him in its thick dark blanket, and he was hardly aware of his friend moving around the room. But then Olly came over to him and knelt beside the bed. William opened his eyes. Was there something wrong?

'It's okay, Wills,' Olly whispered. Then he bent over and brushed his lips against his friend's face. William's fatigue slipped away, miraculously disappeared, and all he wanted was to pull the other boy into his arms. He wanted it so much and he thought that maybe Olly wanted it, too. But it was a step too far. Chaps didn't do that sort of thing, at least not the chaps he knew. What would his father say? What would Olly's father say?

But Oliver was fearless. He bent his head again and, this time, his kiss was not for William's cheek, but full on his lips. William's body quivered. He thought that now his heart might truly burst. He didn't care. He raised his head, and cradled Olly's face between his hands. Then he kissed him back. Full on the lips.

*

A narrow streak of sunlight had nudged its way through a gap in the drawn curtains, its bright beam circling the pillow on which William lay and travelling upwards over flocks of papered bluebirds, landing at last on the dark wood cornice above. William tossed himself to the other side of the bed and saw that Oliver was already up and about. His friend was an early riser and the sun-filled morning must have tempted him outside. He would be walking, running – leaping in all probability – through the length of the gardens. William longed to have the same energy. Longed to be out there with Olly, but he was weary. Even now, lying flat on his bed, his arms and legs felt as though anchored by cumbersome weights. It was an effort to push back the bedclothes and swing himself to the floor. He mustn't be feeble; he mustn't let Olly down.

He didn't dress immediately, but sat on the window seat and gazed out at the perfect day beyond. His mind's eye was elsewhere, savouring again and again the most perfect moment of his life. Last night he and Oliver had kissed, kissed properly, and as soon as they had, he'd realised that this was what he'd wanted for weeks. At that moment, all the jagged pieces of his world had slotted together into one splendid whole. But this morning it was different. The memory was still magical but he'd been left even more uncertain. Because he'd wanted that kiss so much, because it had felt the best thing ever, didn't make it right. And what would happen now? How were they to go on? He was still thinking, when the door was thrust open and Oliver himself bounded into the room.

'Guess what?' His friend was almost dancing with excitement.

'You've been down to the lake.'

Olly came to a halt, temporarily distracted. He had to think for a moment. 'Yes, I've been down there. Mr Harris is supervising the fish. Well, not the fish, of course, but the men putting the fish into the lake. Bass and bluegill.'

'There's going to be angling? But who's going to fish? Pa wouldn't know one end of a rod from the other.'

'I've no idea,' Oliver said impatiently. 'It's not important. But this is. We're at war.' His eyes were wide and sparkling with excitement, and when he saw William's mouth drop open, he said, 'Yes, really, Wills. Something about a deadline being passed. Your pa's newspaper is full of it. I went into the kitchen – I thought there might be a slice more of the lemon sponge going and Ripley was ironing his paper. He let me look at it. It was on page seven. "England defied by Germany" and then just below, "England's Declaration of War Against Germany!"'

'Gosh!' William said. 'What happens now?'

'It said that the King has issued a message to the Fleet, telling them they're the shield of Britain.'

'Gosh!' William said again.

Oliver climbed on to the window seat and settled himself beside his friend. 'Mind you, the Fleet didn't much help the minelayer I read about. It was sunk yesterday by the Kaiser's ships. And don't say gosh again.' He ruffled his friend's hair. 'You need to get dressed. There are stirring deeds afoot!'

'But we won't be part of them. We're too young to join up. I wish we could.'

'It might be fun,' Oliver agreed. 'On the other hand, we might get our heads blown off.'

'But we'd be together.' He looked shyly across at his friend and wondered if he remembered last night.

'We can be together anyway,' Olly said, hugging him tight.

He had remembered, William thought, and he was right, they could be together without risking their lives in battle. At school, though, it wasn't a real togetherness. There were too many unkind eyes, unkind voices. But it was better, far better, than not having Olly at all. He was the only thing that made school endurable. With Olly by his side, he could bear the disdain, the contempt, for having a father in trade.

'C'mon,' Oliver hurried him, 'you're missing all the fun. Stirring things are happening at Summerhayes, too.'

He didn't know what Oliver meant but he thought that he should.

'What if I told you that your sister is getting married?' his friend goaded.

'I'd say you were talking rubbish. Elizabeth doesn't want to get married. She said so only a few days ago.'

'I reckon she must have changed her mind then. Where will she live, do you think?'

He ignored the question. Olly was being deliberately provoking, but there was a dread in him, deep down, that somehow his taunting might contain truth. 'Who would she marry anyway?' he demanded petulantly. There was a pause while his friend's eyes teased him. 'Not Aiden Kellaway?'

'No, stupid. The man that's here now, talking to your father. Ripley says his name is Audley. Do you know him? Ripley says he's a relative of your mother's.'

'Of my uncle's, more likely.' It was an instinctive response.

But how could there be a man, any man, wanting to marry Elizabeth? He'd heard nothing of it, not from the servants, not from his mother, not from Elizabeth herself. If Oliver were right, stuff had been happening of which he had no inkling. So what to make of those notes that his sister had asked him to deliver? What to make of the architect fellow? Aloud he said, 'Audley sounds a familiar name, but I don't think I've ever met the man.'

'He's downstairs right now, so let's take our chance.'

'We can't just barge in.'

'No, but we can eavesdrop. The balcony has some very clever fretwork – useful too – we'll be able to hear and see without being spotted. At this moment, he's probably falling to his knees and begging your sister for her hand.' Oliver gave a melodramatic sweep of his arm and clutched at his heart with one hand. 'Let's creep down,' he urged, 'and find out what's going on.'

Chapter Twenty-Seven

Earlier that morning, Ivy's breathless appearance in her room was the first intimation Elizabeth had that Giles Audley was in the house. When she heard her maid's knock, she was midway through exchanging a dress of figured cotton for a paint-spattered smock. This morning she was bound for her studio, intent on distracting herself. She hated to treat her work in this way, as a diversion – it deserved so much more – but losing herself in paint was her sole refuge. She knew what was coming. She couldn't pretend that she didn't. But with a force of will that surprised her, she had tried to blot it from her mind. It was Aiden's words that were filling her head and her heart: *Marry me*. Words of hope, of joy, words that at one minute could lift her spirits to the sky and at another cast her into complete dejection. She wanted nothing more than to spend her life with him, but she couldn't. She couldn't leave her home, her family, her country, and travel into the unknown. She lacked the courage to break free. Or, more kindly, she lacked the ruthlessness to abandon what she loved.

She looked up to see Ivy fidgeting in the doorway. 'I'm glad you've come,' she greeted her. 'You can help me with this smock. The back fastenings always defeat me.'

The girl cleared her throat. 'I think mebbe you should change back again.'

'Why would I do that?'

She knew the answer almost before she asked the question. She'd heard Giles Audley's declaration that he would call today. And now she was sure that he was here, ready to lay his circumstances before Joshua, and ask her father's approval to their marriage.

'It's Mr Audley, Miss Elizabeth,' Ivy said quietly. 'He's downstairs and wishes to speak with you. Here, let me help you dress again.'

The moment had come at last. She must find the strength to face the battering that awaited: the zealous persuasion, the censorious stares, the furious voices. She would be forced into the tightest of spaces to defend the choice she was making. But she would hold the line. She would not marry a man she did not love.

Down the golden oak staircase, a breath away from telling Giles the news he didn't wish to hear. Or maybe – she grabbed at the thought – he might wish to hear it after all. He might be relieved. Perhaps he, too, had been pushed into this. She could imagine the way her uncle must have managed the affair, cajoling, exhorting, even coercing his younger relative towards a marriage he'd never before considered. Perhaps the promise Giles Audley had made last night to her father had been his way of buying time. If so, he had bought himself a few hours only.

Ripley had shown him into a room known rather grandly as the library. It certainly possessed the necessary shelves and the books to fill them, but apart from these and a few ancient copies of *Punch* and a tattered Badminton series explaining the intricacies of different sports, there was precious little else. The one or two chairs that had found their way here were horribly uncomfortable. The room faced north and rarely caught a glimpse of the sun. It was a sober and gloomy place, a perfect setting for the scene they were about to play.

'Elizabeth.' He strode forward to grasp her hand. 'How are you?'

*

'You refused him!'

She stood at one side of the desk and tried to regain the sense of purpose that had temporarily deserted her. Her father, his face blotched, the loose skin around his jowls visibly shaking, had half risen from his chair. He lunged towards her, as though he would drag her across the desk's wooden surface and into his large, angry hands. She fixed her eyes on the mantelpiece above his head and swallowed hard. The ornamental clock, a square of Delft blue tile, showed it was barely midday.

'I didn't actually refuse him,' she said quietly. 'I didn't allow him to propose.' She had spared Giles that humiliation at least, but if she had thought it might improve her father's temper, she had been wrong.

'You turned him down before he could even ask you!' Joshua bellowed. 'What is wrong with you, girl?'

She didn't attempt to answer. Whatever was wrong with her, it wasn't something her father could fix. He continued to shout into the silence. 'Here was a decent man, an honourable man, who would have made you a good husband, and you refused even to hear him out!'

A decent man who would have smoothed your path into the

social circle you so much covet. But it was disloyal to think in that way; whatever defence she mounted, must be her own. Her father's face was still contorted, still frightening. She fixed her gaze again on the blue and white clock. 'I don't love Giles Audley, Papa, and I can't marry him.'

'Love! What has love to do with it?' He abandoned his lowering pose and pushed away the ladder-backed chair to walk around the desk. Instinctively, she took several paces back, but when he spoke again, his voice was quieter. His face, too, was a little less blotched, and she drew a small breath of relief.

'You must rid yourself of these stupid, romantic fantasies, Elizabeth. They are not worthy of you. Remember – you're no longer a child. You're a grown woman and you must begin to act responsibly.'

'So marrying a man for whom I have no feelings is acting responsibly?' Now the first shock of Joshua's aggression was over, she was touched with anger herself.

'You lie. You do have feelings for the man and don't deny it. You like him. I've seen the two of you chattering away twenty to the dozen.'

It was what Giles Audley had said himself barely half an hour ago. *I'm a disappointed man. A bewildered one, too. I thought we got on famously.* But liking a man, enjoying his company, was a world away from loving him with a barely containable passion. Her father would never understand; he could never have loved so.

He was by her side now, close enough for her to see the worry in his eyes. 'I do like him, Papa,' she agreed, 'but not enough to spend my whole life with him.'

Her father seemed to disregard this scruple. 'Is it because he's a widower?' He reached out and stroked her hand with a gentleness that belied his previous fury. 'If so, my dear, you should disregard it. And disregard the difference in ages between you. Age brings sense and reason. And since the man has been married before, he'll know the demands that marriage makes. He's likely to be an even better husband.'

I can understand your reluctance, Giles had said wryly. *I'm a good deal older than you and a widower to boot. I'm not exactly an enticing marriage prospect, am I? Until I met you, I hadn't seriously considered marrying again. But being with you has made me happy. Enough for me to think we could make a good future together. That I could make you happy, too.*

'I've not refused him because he's a widower or because he's a good deal older than I.'

Her voice cracked. The effort of containing her frustration was taking its toll. Her father had married without love, a marriage of utility, and refused to understand why anyone would not do the same. For him, it was simple. Her future was best secured by marriage to a man like Audley.

'If that's not the problem, what is? What else do you want? He's a good man, he has independent wealth, he admires you and likes your company. That surely should be sufficient.' When she made no reply, he dropped her hand and went to stand behind the desk once more. A barrier, she thought. A barrier to any real understanding between us.

'A person cannot always have exactly what they want in life. This is a lesson you need to learn,' he said now.

'What did *you* want, Papa?' she dared to ask.

'What!' His exasperation had returned.

'When you married Mama. What did you want? Whatever it was, it didn't happen, did it?'

His face was wiped of expression. 'You will speak of your

parents with more respect. You have been given a good life, you and your brother. Neither of you have lacked a thing.'

'Except a happy home.'

'Now you're talking namby-pamby drivel. A happy home! How many of those do you know? They don't exist. What does exist is shelter, food, clothes. I grew up with none of those things, but you have never known a life without them. For years, I worked every hour God gave me and you have been the beneficiary. You have been gifted everything you've ever needed. Last year, I spent hundreds of pounds on a London Season, and what did you do with it?'

'I refused two proposals.' She said it defiantly.

'And now you can chalk up a third. Feel proud of yourself. But don't think there's another bridegroom in the wings who will be more to your liking. You've had your chances and they won't come again. Be ready to wither into an old maid.'

It was his trump card, she could see, but she took the threat calmly. 'If I must, I will.'

'You don't know what you're talking of. A woman who stays unmarried knows nothing but misery. As you'll find out. She is despised by all, my dear – by men and by other women, too.'

'But not by herself. And that's what matters, at least to me.' She could feel herself grow taller with the words. 'I have to do what feels right.' If she could not marry where she wished, she must find her way to an independent life. With barely a pause, she spat out her challenge. 'The fate you prophesy, Papa, is not inevitable. I could escape it. If I became a respected artist, I'd be celebrated rather than despised.'

'You have taken leave of your senses,' he muttered.

She took a step towards him, her chin jutting. 'You think I cannot paint?'

'You can paint all right, but be recognised by the world? Sell your pictures? That's an illusion. You had better think again.'

Her father's dismissal hurt, but more hurtful still was the knowledge that he was right. It *was* an illusion. She could paint all she wanted, but without connections in the market, without patrons, a woman artist cut a lonely figure. Attitudes were changing, but only slowly. There might come a day when women artists lacking the genius of a Laura Knight might still gain acknowledgment. But that day would come too late for her. There was no future; in every way, she was rendered bereft.

Joshua must have sensed the deep unhappiness crowding in on her. He walked back and took her hands in his. 'This is getting us nowhere, Elizabeth. You must reconsider your decision, if not for me, for yourself. It is a good future you are being offered. If you marry Giles Audley, you'll be free to paint to your heart's content. He won't object, I'm sure. It's perfectly acceptable for a lady to pursue such a pastime. He might even find a small market for your work.'

He was trying to be kind, but every word he uttered stoked an angry blaze. Just as Giles Audley's had. *Would it not be easier to be an artist if you were married? I have no animosity to lady painters. And I have the perfect space in my house that I'd willingly assign to you as a studio. I have some strings, too, that I could pull, some influential patrons who might come calling if I asked.* Giles had been trying his best to win her over, but if she were tempted to waver, he could not have said anything more to stiffen her resolve than the notion that she be given a space in which to perform for an audience whose praise had already been purchased. She would be little better than a circus animal.

'In the meantime,' her father was saying, 'let me speak to your uncle. Once Audley tells him the news, he will not be well disposed, but we can smooth things over. As for Giles himself, he will understand your change of mind. You're still a young girl, still trying to find your way in life.'

She was an empty space it seemed, to be labelled as the world wished. At one moment, a grown woman exercising reason and responsibility, at another a giddy girl so capricious that in seconds she could change a life-altering decision.

She bit down on her lip so hard that it hurt. 'I may be trying to find my way, but I'm quite able to know which path I don't wish to follow. And I don't wish to marry. Ever.'

His eyebrows rose ceilingwards. 'That is a nonsense.'

'But it's not. I won't be deflected, even if I have to make a lot of noise to follow my choice.' There was satisfaction in confounding him.

'More suffragette rubbish, I don't doubt. Of course you want to marry. All women do.'

'I don't.'

'I know what it is,' he said, in a small flash of understanding.'It's that young jackanapes I've seen you talking to.' She could not prevent the fire from creeping into her cheeks. 'There, I'm right. If that's your plan, you can forget it. There is no chance that I will ever give my permission for you to marry a man like that.'

She was raging inside; she wanted to beat her hands hard against his chest. Instead, she schooled herself to mockery. 'A man like that?' she echoed derisively. 'What do you know of him?'

'I know he works with his hands and that is sufficient.'

'He works with his hands and with his brain. He's a craftsman. But what would it matter if he were a humble gardener and grew cabbages for a living? If I loved him.'

He swooped on her then, catching her by surprise, seizing her by the arms and shaking her forcibly. 'You will not marry him or anyone like him. Do you hear? I've not struggled to get where I am, only for you to bring shame on me, not while I have the breath in my body to prevent it. And if you dare go against my wishes, you'll not have a penny. Then we'll see how your craftsman gets on, with a wife hung around his neck and working for a pittance.'

'You had a craft once. You worked with your hands, made beautiful things, and taught others to do so. But then you turned your back on that gift and squandered it pursuing a foolish fancy. Aiden won't make the same mistake, you can be sure.'

Her father's colour had risen to an alarming degree. 'The man has gone from Summerhayes. Gone for good. And you will not try to find him.'

She had had enough and turned to go, but he shouted after her, 'And what am I to say to Henry Fitzroy? You have spurned the match we asked him to make. He will consider his reputation damaged. That is your fault. You've deceived him and you've deceived me.'

At this, she turned back. 'I've deceived no one. The marriage was entirely your idea. And I don't care what Uncle Henry has to say. If you're wise, Papa, you won't either. If you're wise, you will have nothing more to do with him.' Aiden's warning was sounding loud and clear in her mind.

'And what is that puny threat supposed to mean?'

'He is a dangerous man.'

Her mother had slipped around the door without either of them noticing. Joshua caught sight of her at that moment. 'Did you hear that?' he said mirthlessly. 'Your brother is dangerous.'

His wife's silence was eloquent, if he had chosen to listen to it. Instead, he blustered on: 'I have news for you, Alice. Our daughter has just announced that she will not marry Giles Audley after all. Better than that, if she can't have her way, she'll not marry at all.'

Her mother's expression was filled with sorrow. 'Elizabeth, consider— '

'Oh, she won't consider. She's far too arrogant to listen to advice. Why don't you tell her, my dear, what it feels like to be left on the shelf?'

Alice turned a horrible white and clutched the door handle for support.

'Do you see your mother's reaction? Not pleasant, is it?' he went on. 'You would do well to think again. Time is what you need, my girl, time and space to think again.'

He walked towards the door, his shoulders stiff with outrage, then stopped sharply. 'A school, I think. That's the solution. One of those places your mother is always bothering me about. A school that will keep you out of trouble and, with luck, teach you to respect your parents' judgement.'

'But you said— ' Alice began.

'Yes, yes, I know,' he said irritatedly. 'But it's what you've always wanted.'

'But, surely, Joshua, it's too late? Europe is in turmoil.'

'Not Europe. And what a good job I didn't listen to you,' he said with satisfaction. 'No, not Europe. But as far away from Sussex as possible. Scotland might be the perfect place. I'm sure they will have institutions that will be only too happy to discipline young ladies and imbue them with the right ideas.'

And, looking pleased that for the moment he'd had the last word, he swept out of the room, leaving Elizabeth and her mother confronting each other.

Chapter Twenty-Eight

'I must talk to you. Please stay,' Alice heard herself pleading.

Her daughter, who had been halfway out of the door, retraced her steps, her feet dragging and every lineament of her body expressing reluctance. 'If this is about Giles, there is nothing to talk about. I've already said it all – to Giles himself and to Papa.'

'Then you must let me have my say.' She sank wearily into a leather chair and Elizabeth was forced to follow suit. 'I must ask you to think again,' she said, with as much resolution as she could muster, then leant forward and took her daughter's hand. 'You have allowed your heart to do the talking, but your papa is right. There comes a time in everyone's life when they must listen to their head.'

'You are saying that I should commit myself to a man for whom I've no love? I cannot do it. I am not you.' There was scorn in her face.

'You should not judge harshly, Elizabeth. Whatever I have done has been guided by my duty to others.'

'Duty?' Her daughter almost choked on the word. 'And that is your advice, that I should marry from duty?'

'There are no easy choices, my dear.' There had been none for her. She took a deep breath. She would share what she had never thought to speak. 'I knew a different life once, one of which you have no idea. I fell in love. Very much in love, but I had to accept that it was not to be. I could not marry where I wished.'

She saw the stunned look on the girl's face and there was a long silence before Elizabeth found her voice. 'Why not?'

'I was very young, younger than you are now. The man I had set my heart on was not acceptable to my family.'

'And so you gave him up?'

'I had to. I had to do my duty,' she repeated.

'And that was to make an unhappy marriage.'

The scorn was back and Alice braced herself to meet it. 'I know what you think of the marriage I made, but you see only part of the truth.'

'Really? It seems clear enough to me. You married to bring money into Amberley. But that hardly applies in my case, does it? Summerhayes needs no money. The estate is wealthy enough.'

'It wasn't only money that was in question. I needed a home of my own and that is true for every woman, even today when girls enjoy so much more freedom. I'm convinced the home you would make with Giles Audley would be a happy one. You enjoy his company – I've seen that for myself. And he enjoys yours. You are already friends and, given time, friends can become sweethearts. I've known it happen.'

'But it wouldn't happen for me. I like Giles enormously, but not in a way that would make our marriage a happy one. If I cannot marry a man I love, I will live alone.'

Alice's heart sank to somewhere around her feet. She had hoped Elizabeth had forgotten that foolish idea, but here it was again. Her daughter's desire for an independent life still burnt bright. 'My response is the same now as when you spoke of this before,' she said as firmly as she could. 'In my opinion, you have become far too influenced by the views of those whose lives bear no resemblance to yours.'

'Mrs Pankhurst says that as long as women consent to be unjustly governed, they will be. I don't consent. I want the freedom to choose my own life.'

'Mrs Pankhurst says a great many things,' she said tartly. 'Most of them impractical. A single life is not one to be envied. You will find yourself disregarded and a burden to others. How can you wish for that?'

'I've no intention of being a burden to anyone.'

Elizabeth's tone was proud and defiant and she knew she must step carefully. 'This is unwise talk, my dear,' she chided. 'You must believe me when I say that I cannot see any way in which you could support yourself.'

'Apparently, you have as little faith in my talent as Papa.'

'I have faith in you, but I know the world. And I know that what you are proposing – if indeed you're serious – is impossible. You would not be able to support yourself from art alone.'

'Then I'll stay here and become the old maid that Papa has prophesied.' The girl's voice was becoming harsher with every exchange.

'Would you really wish to stay here and live as his pensioner? And think, when we are gone and William inherits, what then? Will William's wife want you here? Of course, she will not.'

She saw a startled look cross Elizabeth's face and pressed home her point. 'You must have a home of your own and Giles Audley can provide one. Will it be so very bad? We are not asking you to commit yourself to a thoughtless or unkind man. Giles will make you a good husband.'

The echo of her father's words were sufficient to push Elizabeth into action. She started up from her chair and marched towards the door. 'I don't care how good a man he is,' she flung over her shoulder. 'Can't you both understand? I don't wish to be married to him, or to anyone.'

Alice jumped up too, following close behind. 'But that's not true, is it?' she asked gently. She had not wanted to mention him, but it seemed that she must.

Elizabeth's lips were tightly mutinous and she was forced to risk her daughter's anger once more. 'Do not think that we are ignorant of your friendship with the young man that Mr Simmonds employs.' She could not bring herself to give him his name. 'It is a friendship that will find no acceptance in this house, or anywhere else. And you must know that. He has been sent away, and not just from Summerhayes, if Mr Harris is correct. He has been asked to leave the village. You will not see him again, my dear, and you must stop thinking of him.'

Elizabeth let go of the door handle. 'What do you mean, he has been asked to leave the village?'

Her daughter was past pretending, Alice thought, that Aiden Kellaway meant nothing to her. 'I believe that he has been asked to vacate his lodgings.'

'Mrs Boxall's cottage?'

'Yes.'

'My uncle owns that cottage, does he not?'

She said nothing. The authority Henry exercised in the district was not without its compensations. But then she looked at her daughter's face, and her heart hurt. Elizabeth was trying so hard to maintain a blank façade, while she struggled with emotions that must be tearing her apart.

'My dear girl,' she said in her gentlest voice, 'it is an impossibility. The young man has no money and whatever prospects he has are for the future. For his own sake, you should forget him.' There was a pause while she gathered courage. 'When I let Thomas go,' she said in the quietest of voices, 'I did it as much for him as for me. He could not afford to encumber himself with a wife from such a different world – and neither can your young man.'

'And what if my young man should think differently?' Her voice had only the slightest break in it.

'Then he would be very foolish. Papa will never agree to your marriage. And if you are thinking that one day you will be twenty-one and can marry at will, I doubt the young man will wait that long. He will marry a girl from his own background, and that will be far better for him.'

It was infatuation on both their parts. And perfectly understandable, she thought wistfully. They were two beautiful young people, it had been a beautiful summer spent in beautiful surroundings. But spent against a backdrop of threat, constant and always growing. The temptation to snatch happiness while it offered would be difficult to resist. But she could not allow herself to show weakness. Elizabeth's future depended on her mother's ability to remain stern.

'If you marry to displease us,' she warned, 'your father will withdraw any financial help. You do know that? And he will make sure that on his death you do not receive a penny. Is that what you want?'

'The money is nothing to me.' The girl paused very slightly, but when she spoke again, there was a catch in her voice. 'What would hurt me is to lose Papa's love, and to lose yours.'

'Then be guided by us. Do the sensible thing and make Giles your husband.'

Elizabeth did not respond and her whole being looked weary and defeated. Alice hated to see her daughter so distressed and clung to the hope that her words might bear fruit. The girl walked to the door and out into the hall, barely able, Alice could see, to contain the unspilt tears.

'I'm going to my room, Mama,' she said over her shoulder.

Chapter Twenty-Nine

'Did you hear all that?'

The boys had been bent double, looking through the fretwork of the oak bannister down into the hall, but on Elizabeth's departure, Oliver jumped up buzzing with excitement. From their vantage point, they had been able to see through the open study door and to hear every word of the highly charged dialogue.

'Elizabeth is being sent away.' William said the words faintly, drawing them out as though with luck they might disappear into the ether. It was the one thing he remembered from what had been said, the one thing his mind repeated incessantly. When he stood up to join his friend, he was forced to lean against the bannister for support. His face was as white as his mother's.

'Phew!' Oliver was still bouncing. 'Your old man certainly has a temper. I thought my father was bad enough but—'

'She's going away. That's what Papa said.'

'Looks like it, old chap. But don't get down. I'm here.' He gave him a rough bear hug.

William could only manage a sad shake of the head. Whatever Oliver said, he wouldn't always be here. He would be leaving Summerhayes soon and if William had read the signs correctly, his friend wouldn't be invited back.

His mother didn't like him and, as for Joshua, he liked no one – except Elizabeth. And Elizabeth was deserting them. She wouldn't be here when he returned for the holidays. Elizabeth who was his friend and his shield. For weeks, he would be alone at Summerhayes, except for Alice. She would be unable to protect him from his father. And the two of them would have little to say to each other. It had been different when he was a small boy. Things had been simple then, but not any longer. How could he ever make his mother understand who he'd become? He would be truly and utterly alone, and his soul withered at the knowledge. If Olly should leave him, too... On impulse, he turned towards his friend and grabbed hold of him, clinging as though he would never let him go.

Then shaken and disorientated, he allowed Oliver to lead him by the hand, down the two flights of stairs to the basement and into the kitchen. All summer, bad things had been happening at Summerhayes. Accidents that couldn't be explained: the shelter he and Olly had built collapsing into firewood, those wild dogs rampaging through the garden right up to the house, the meetings between his sister and the architect, meetings that were secret and forbidden, and now Elizabeth's banishment. And horrendous things were happening, too, just a few miles across the sea. Now that England was involved, they could happen here as well, in a country that had always felt so safe. Everything was going wrong this summer. Well, perhaps not everything, he conceded, feeling Oliver's firm clasp on his hand. But the world he'd known seemed to be trembling on its axis.

'What's up, Master William? Cook greeted him cheerfully. 'Lost ten shillings and found a penny?'

'He's a bit upset,' Oliver responded for him. 'He needs feeding up. That lemon cake would be fine.'

'It might be if someone hadn't eaten it already.' Cook fixed him with a minatory look.

If there was anything less that William wanted, it was food. But he knew Olly meant well; for his friend, food made things right.

'I don't have lemon cake, my treasure.' Cook turned to him. 'But I could knock up a Battenberg in no time.' He saw his friend's face brighten. 'Except –' she rummaged in a cupboard, '– I seem to have run out of almond paste, dang it.'

'It doesn't matter—' he started to say, when Olly interrupted: 'We can go to the village and buy some, if you like.'

'That'd be champion. The cake'll take no time to rustle up once I get the paste. And you shall have the first slice, Master William.'

He didn't want to go to the village. He was too exhausted in mind and body to walk even a yard. Oliver could go by himself. He would sit in this comfortable kitchen and watch Cook at her business. She was halfway through preparations for that evening's dinner and the smell of roast lamb filled the warm space.

'We can take the bicycles,' Oliver said eagerly. 'We haven't been out on them for an age, have we, Wills? And it will be quicker than walking.'

'A nice bit of fresh air, Master William, that's what you're needing most,' Cook decided, emptying a glass jar of a handful of coins. 'Here. This should be enough. And, Master Oliver, don't touch that plate – the Eccles are for the master's tea. Go on, off with both of you now.'

Shooed from the kitchen, Oliver led the way along the

passage and out of the servants' door. Eddie was busy in the courtyard, washing down the Wolseley.

'What are you two young monkeys about?' He barely looked up from the pail of water.

'We've come for the bicycles,' Olly said.

'Have you now? Then you'd best check the tyres. Those bikes haven't been out for weeks.'

'They seem all right.' Oliver had walked into the motor house where the bicycles were stored and bent to examine the two machines leaning against the wall. 'They're okay, aren't they, William?'

He agreed, though he'd hardly glanced at them. He had no interest in a ride, to the village or to anywhere else. But when he wheeled the bicycle out into the courtyard, he remembered how proud he'd been of this birthday gift just two winters ago.

'If you're going to the village, best take the long way round,' Eddie advised. 'They've been cutting the hedges in the lane this morning and there's muck and branches everywhere.'

When they'd wheeled their bikes on to the drive, Oliver said, 'It's a good idea of Eddie's to take the road. There's a great slope we can fly down all the way into the village. The hill must be half a mile long.'

'And a great slope to climb up again,' William muttered gloomily.

Olly didn't hear him. His friend was already halfway down the drive and he was forced to clamber on his bike and follow suit. Once out on the road and riding freely, the sadness that seemed to have seeped into his very bones began slowly to drift away. Perhaps, as Cook suggested, the fresh air was helping. Or perhaps it was simply leaving

Summerhayes behind. The bad feeling within its four walls upset him greatly. But he knew that to keep strong he mustn't think of it. The situation wasn't dire, he comforted himself. Elizabeth might be sent away, but that didn't mean she wouldn't come back. And, as for the unexplained accidents, nothing bad had happened to him for days, for weeks even. And this afternoon the sun was shining, the sky was without a cloud and the air filled with the scent of wild honeysuckle. He would enjoy it.

Even by road, the village was only a mile distant, and they were soon at the peak of the hill that Oliver had spoken of.

'This is it, Wills,' he said. 'We should try freewheeling. It will be brilliant. I'll go first.'

'You'll need to use brakes,' he warned him. 'At least from the halfway mark, otherwise it gets dangerous. I know, I've tried it before.'

'We'll see.'

His friend's cheeky grin was worrying but he had to let him go. Oliver was too determined, too headstrong, to attempt to control. He gave him a minute's start then pushed off himself. It was wonderful, like sailing on the wind. The tarmac sped beneath his wheels and hedgerows on either side rushed past as though they had not a minute to spare. Ahead, Olly's figure was hunched over the handlebars, his hair blowing this way and that as the hill fell away. Halfway down, William had reached the speed where he knew he must apply the brakes or end in trouble. He squeezed the metal lever on his right, but nothing happened; he squeezed the lever to the left, but nothing again. He pressed both together as hard as he could, but still he was flying forward at a frightening speed, and all the time gaining momentum as the hill snaked its way downwards. Over and over, he pulled on the brake levers. He was going to crash, he was certain.

The village was straight ahead and any minute now he would cross the road that ran at right angles. He prayed there would be no pedestrian, no cyclist, coming that way. There wasn't. It was a car that appeared out of nowhere, right in his face it seemed and, giving up any effort to control the bicycle, he threw up his hands in despair, expecting any minute to feel the impact of hard metal. Instead, the bike slewed sideways, bumped up and over the grass verge, and landed with him beneath, deep in the ditch that ran alongside the road.

He heard voices and footsteps hurrying towards him. At least he was conscious. Olly's frightened face peered over the grass bank and into the ditch.

'Let me get there.' It was Dr Daniels. It had been his car. That was all right then, he thought stupidly.

Frank Daniels clambered up on to the verge and pulled the bike free, tossing it to one side. Then he bent forward and stretched out an arm.

'Can you grab my hand, William?'

He grabbed. Slowly, he managed to stumble to his knees then to his feet. With the doctor on one side and Olly on the other, he found himself hauled roughly out of the ditch, over the grass bank and onto the road. He was covered in leaves and twigs and Oliver had begun brushing him down when the doctor pushed him aside.

'Let's have a look at you, young man. You've taken a very nasty tumble.'

A nasty tumble was not how he'd have described it. His body felt as though it had been on the rack, one of those instruments of medieval torture, but he said nothing and allowed Dr Daniels to prod and poke him from head to foot.

'Nothing broken, I think. I should take you back to my surgery, though, and listen to your heart.'

'I'm fine. Really, I am.' He was embarrassed at the fuss.

'Then we'll leave it for now. You'll have some bruises tomorrow but I'd say you were a very lucky boy.'

He tried to smile but he knew it was a wan effort. 'Come on,' the doctor said briskly, 'we'll load up the bikes and I'll drive you back to Summerhayes.'

'But we haven't got the almond paste yet,' Olly protested, evidently seeing the Battenberg disappear from sight.

'Never mind the almond paste. William needs to be home.' And the doctor picked up Oliver's bicycle and heaved it into the open boot of his car. 'You should have checked your brakes before you left,' he said severely, and grabbed the second bike to stow it in the same fashion.

'We checked the tyres but not the brakes,' Oliver admitted, 'but— wait a minute!' he said urgently. The doctor had lifted the bicycle high in the air, but now let it fall with a thump on to the road. 'What now?' he said impatiently.

'Look!' Oliver was pointing at the back wheel. A thin metal cable still ran to the rear of the bicycle but the small caliper that should have forced the rubber block to press against the wheel when the brake was applied, had been badly bent.

'It's damaged,' the doctor said indifferently.

'It's not just damaged, it's been twisted out of shape.' Oliver was excited. 'And look it's happened on the front wheel too. And it's not just the calipers. The thick rubber blocks have been cut almost in two. No wonder the brakes didn't work.'

'The blocks must have worn out,' the doctor insisted. 'They obviously needed replacing.'

'That can't be right.' Oliver never feared to argue with an adult if he thought he was right. 'William's bike is nearly new.'

Dr Daniels shrugged and began to lift the bike again, when Olly blurted out, 'It's been damaged deliberately.'

'Nonsense!' the doctor exclaimed. 'Why on earth would anyone do that?'

William swallowed hard. Olly's eyes were on him, intent and full of meaning, but he kept his silence. It could have been an accident, he told himself, as he squashed into the front of the car beside Oliver and the doctor. No one said a word until Dr Daniels had deposited boys and bicycles outside the motor house once more, and taken off down the drive.

'Well…' Oliver began.

But he didn't want to hear it. No more conspiracies please, his mind was pleading and, before his friend could launch into his latest theory, Cook appeared at the rear entrance. 'Sorry,' he said, 'we didn't manage to get the almond paste.'

'Never mind, my love. I don't blame you taking the lift when it was offered. That hill from the village is some steep. I heard the car and came to tell you – Mrs Lumley has sent over your favourites.'

'Who is Mrs Lumley?' His companion was temporarily distracted.

'She's the cook at Amberley. When I'm home, she bakcs something special for me every week. I expect it's macaroons.'

'I don't like macaroons,' Oliver said, disappointed.

'But I do.' William gave a rare smile and went through the door and along the flagged passageway to the kitchen. Astonishingly, he found himself hungry. It must be all that fresh air. And he hadn't been badly hurt, had he? He was just aching and sore. A macaroon or two would put him right.

Chapter Thirty

In the middle of the night, he woke feeling wretchedly ill. He was going to be sick. He sat up quickly and tried to swing his legs off the bed. He must get to the bathroom. But his stomach was heaving and somehow his feet couldn't find the floor. Before he could stop himself, he gave a loud '*whoop!*' and a stream of vomit flooded his pyjamas, bed-clothes and much of the bedside rug.

'What's going on?'

Oliver sat bolt upright, blinking in the beam of cold moonlight that had edged its way between the curtains. Then he realised his friend was in trouble and threw himself out of bed, rushing to William's side.

'Ugh!' He had nearly trodden in the mess.

'Sorry,' William could just about mumble. Then, 'Go away. I'm going to be sick again.'

This time when his stomach had stopped its pitching, he was wet with perspiration. 'Need to get to the bathroom,' he ground out.

Oliver put his hands under each of his friend's arms and hauled him out of bed, trying to place his feet on a dry patch of carpet. Together, they limped along the landing, but almost immediately they reached the bathroom, William began to vomit again.

'I'm going to get your sister.' Olly sounded seriously worried.

'No,' he gasped. 'Mustn't. She's already in trouble.'

'But she's the best bet. Your ma will fuss so and make things worse. Stay there, I'm going to fetch her.'

He didn't have much choice, he thought, his head once more over the toilet bowl.

*

When Elizabeth opened her door to a frenzied tapping, she stepped back in surprise. 'What on earth…?'

'It's William, he's ill. You've got to come.'

She didn't pause to ask questions, but grabbed her wrapper from its hook and followed Oliver along the length of floral geometry that carpeted the landing. The door to the bathroom was open and William was sitting on the toilet seat, his head drooping, his face beneath the harsh electric light a ghastly shade of grey.

'He's been sick.'

Her nose had already told her that but she simply nodded. 'Very sick,' Olly went on. 'And it's all over the bedroom.'

'Stay with William,' she commanded. 'I'll sort it out.'

Oliver hadn't exaggerated. The mess was beyond anything she could clear on her own. She scurried up the stairs to the servants' quarters and crept into Ivy's room. Her maid, as always, was intensely practical. Within minutes, the girl had grasped the situation and dressed quickly. Together they ran down to the basement for buckets of water. It took nearly an hour to clean the room sufficiently well for William to return and, even then, they were forced to throw the stained rug out of the window to deal with in the morning. Ivy fetched clean sheets and remade the bed while Elizabeth returned to the bathroom. Oliver was sitting on the side of the bath, while William was exactly where she'd left him.

'He's not been sick again,' Olly said cheerfully.

'Good. It's probably safe now to get you back to bed.' But when her brother tried to stand, he was so weak that both she and Oliver had to put their arms around him to keep him from falling.

'Be brave,' she urged. 'Just a few steps along the landing and we'll have you lying down.'

Progress was painfully slow but at last he was climbing between clean sheets. Ivy had left a small bowl of lavender water and she set about sponging her brother's face. The smell of the lavender, sweet and refreshing, filled the room and she was relieved to see the grey retreating from William's pallid cheeks.

'Better?' she asked after a while.

'Lots,' he answered. 'But you shouldn't be here.'

She was puzzled. 'Why ever not?'

'They might not like you to talk to me.' She guessed he must mean their parents.

'That's silly,' she said bracingly. 'Of course, we can talk.'

'But you're going away. To school.' His voice broke and she saw tears forming in his eyes.

She put the bowl down and put her arms fully around him, hugging him close. His body was stick thin, she noticed. He'd lost weight in the days since the dogs had attacked.

'Was it worrying about me, that made you so ill?'

He shook his head.

Oliver bounced up from the adjoining bed. He'd been

unusually quiet. 'I reckon it was those macaroons. The ones Mrs Lumley sent over.'

'It couldn't be,' her brother protested feebly. 'Mrs Lumley bakes them most weeks for me when I'm home.'

'They're the only thing you ate and I didn't,' Oliver persisted.

'Could it have been the macaroons, William?' she asked. She felt very slightly sick herself. She didn't want to think what that might mean.

'They tasted a bit different,' he admitted, 'but I'm sure there was nothing wrong with them.'

She couldn't share his certainty. He didn't want to make a fuss, worried no doubt that he might get Mrs Lumley into trouble, but the macaroons had come from Amberley and that fact was a great bell tolling trouble. Ivy had told her this evening about the damaged bike – the servants all knew of it – but she had put that down to a lack of maintenance. Until now.

At all costs, though, she must avoid scaring William. She set off down another track. 'Are you eating properly? Not cakes, I mean. Good food that will make you strong?'

He hung his head. 'To be honest, I don't feel too hungry these days.'

'So where does all the food go that Cook serves you in the kitchen? No, don't tell me – Oliver, I suppose.'

Oliver's protest was muffled by the bedclothes, but William gave a shy grin. 'I guess so. Some of it at least. But—'

'But nothing. You have to eat. I don't know whether there was anything wrong with the macaroons. Probably not,' she lied. 'But you must eat and get strong. And you must stop fretting. There's nothing at Summerhayes to disturb you. The dogs are under control and they won't be coming back. The fencing is done and the stonemason has blocked up the old rear entrance.'

'Are you sure?'

She took his thin hands in hers. 'I'm absolutely sure.'

'I've been having nightmares,' he confessed.

'No more nightmares. And no more worrying about my going away to school. That was just Papa in one of his tempers.'

'But he meant it.'

'He meant it at the time, but you know what he's like. I went against his wishes and he was very angry and threw out the first threat he could think of.'

She got to her feet, ready to go. She could see that he was thinking hard.

'Mama wants you to go to school, too,' he said at last. 'I heard Father say so.'

'She wanted me to go to school in Switzerland. She's wanted that for a long time. But now war is raging, it's completely out of the question.'

'He said Scotland.' William was stubborn.

'And where would they find to send me in Scotland? It's ludicrous. I don't imagine for one moment that the Scots have their own finishing schools, do you?'

'It did sound strange,' he admitted.

'That's because it was strange. Papa was casting around for a place as far away from Sussex as he could find.'

'So you won't be going away?'

She couldn't prevent the slight hesitation in answering. 'That is *not* to be your next worry. I forbid it! I'm here now and I love you. I'll always love you.' She had wriggled out of a promise to stay, but if William realised this, it wasn't clear.

'You'll marry Giles Audley and live at Summerhayes?' he asked eagerly.

'I can't marry him, William. I don't love him. But it will make no difference to us, I promise. I'll always be your friend, married or not.'

*

It was nearly dawn when she returned to her room. Wearily, she climbed into bed but could find no rest. There had been a day of upset and now a night. Yesterday, she had bolstered herself for the interview with Giles, even imagined its aftermath, knowing her father would bully and Alice entreat, but the reality had been so much worse. And it hadn't changed her mind one jot, even after her mother's extraordinary confession. For a moment she'd been stunned – the idea of her mother in love was so foreign – but the moment had passed and she knew she would never act in the same way. Alice had done her duty as she saw it, but her own duty was very different: it was not to make the same mistakes as her parents had.

Yesterday's raking wouldn't be the end of it. She would have to face the inquisition again and again, and face it alone. Aiden was going away and could not help. After the dreadful morning, she had longed to see him, feel his arms around her, hear his voice. They'd arranged a rare meeting in the late afternoon as soon as the men had packed away their tools and left for home. He was to cycle from the village; he'd wanted to know how she'd fared at the dinner party, but it hardly seemed worth the telling. She'd arrived at their meeting place without incident, though at that time of day it was difficult to slip from the house unnoticed:

the light was still bright and people still on the move. The minutes had ticked slowly by and there had been no sign of him. She'd made a fair guess why. Mrs Boxall would have shown him the door within hours of Giles returning to Amberley with his tale of rejection – her uncle would have seen to that – and Aiden would need to find a resting place for the night. After an hour, she could stay no longer. Her mother might come knocking on her bedroom door, armed with yet more reasons why she should accept Audley's proposal. When she'd turned back towards the house, her spirits had been very low.

But not nearly as low as now. It seemed impossible to believe, but William had again been the target of malice. The faulty bicycle might still be accidental since the boys had hardly used the machines this summer, and for long periods of time while William was at school, they were never ridden. But even if that were a mishap, she couldn't believe the same of his illness. She'd seen him very briefly on his return from the village yesterday evening, and he'd seemed well. Tired and bruised it was true, but otherwise unaffected by the crash. Was it possible that overnight he had caught some horrid illness that made him sick? And he had been so very sick. She hardly thought so. It had to have been the food he'd eaten, and since the macaroons were the only thing that Oliver's immense appetite had balked at, they were where guilt must lie. They had come from Amberley, but there was no way Mrs Lumley could bear responsibility. She was a good friend of Cook's and a good friend of the Summers. Someone else must have tampered with the cooking, that was the only explanation.

By now her head was hot and aching, as she tried to take in the enormity of what was happening. Her own young brother was being systematically hunted down and weakened. No one else in the house appeared to have eaten the cakes, but if others had and fallen ill, they would have recovered swiftly enough. For William, though, the bouts of nausea had put untold pressure on his body. Sickness alone would not cause permanent damage, but for a boy with a weak heart, it could have severe consequences. If the measure of poison that had been added to the macaroons – and she was speculating here – had been a little larger, goodness knows what they would be facing this morning.

William was in danger, it was clear, but how to protect him? She could spell out her suspicions to her mother and she thought she would be believed. Alice had been frightened of her brother for as long as Elizabeth could remember, and she'd begun to see her mother might have good reason. But her father would scoff at her, scoff at them both, and take no action. For him, his heir was a weakling and they were silly women who fussed unnecessarily. She could hear him now, saying that all his son needed was a spell of hard discipline. But no amount of discipline, no amount of hardening, could combat an evil intent on destroying the young boy. Aiden had been right all those weeks ago. She hadn't wanted to listen to him, had stopped him when he claimed that the boys' retreat in the Wilderness had been rigged to collapse, that Amberley's dogs had been encouraged to invade their gardens.

She hadn't wanted to listen, but he had been right all the time. A clear plan was emerging, its origins somewhere in Amberley. She was to be married according to Fitzroy wishes and, at the same time, her brother made weak and helpless. Yesterday morning, she'd been expected to accept Giles Audley's proposal; yesterday afternoon, William had crashed his bike and then been made deliberately sick. That was the plan, and it would have moved smoothly ahead except that she hadn't accepted Giles. Her refusal had thrown the project into disarray, and if her uncle really were the villain she was imagining, how would he react? What would he do next?

Chapter Thirty-One

Alice had risen that morning almost as early as her daughter. By seven o'clock, she was sitting at her desk and gazing despairingly at the letter she had started an hour ago. She roused herself to concentrate. Focusing hard on the inky characters, she noticed that she'd written the same sentence twice. Her hands unsteady, she tore the paper in two, and reached for a fresh sheet. *Dear Henry*, she wrote again, and then stopped, discarded the second piece of paper, too, and stared hopelessly ahead at the pale peach wall and the Sickert painting of a Venice church. What could she say to her brother that would explain Elizabeth's conduct? What would in any way mitigate the offence? Her daughter had shown a gross lack of respect for her elders' judgement and, in particular, for Henry's judgement. It was not a transgression that could be easily excused.

Since yesterday's catastrophic events, there had been silence from Amberley. But she wasn't deceived by the seeming calm; it was the silence itself that was frightening. She knew her brother would be furious, as angry with her as he was with Elizabeth. And ferociously angry with Joshua. They had asked him for help and out of the kindness of his heart, as he would see it, he had given it. He had produced Giles Audley, the perfect bridegroom. And instead of receiving grateful thanks, instead of luxuriating in a lordly condescension, he had had his choice rejected. And by a nineteen-year-old whose knowledge of the world was a shadow of her uncle's.

Alice felt quite ill at the thought of the encounter she must have with her brother. And iller still, when she considered the reprisals he might exact. And there would be reprisals, if past experience was a guide. As a boy, he had cut her favourite dress into shreds when she'd refused to hand over the tennis racquet she'd been given for her birthday. He'd lied to their father that she'd stolen money from Mrs Lumley's kitchen fund because she'd screamed when one of his horrible school friends had tried to kiss her. And, darker still, he'd killed her cat – she was sure of it – because she'd inadvertently broken the glass case containing the sticklebacks he was keeping. But all that had happened when he was a boy. He was a grown man now, a civilised man. What could he do, except in various small ways, make their life unpleasant? And the family would weather whatever was coming: the petty insults, the spreading of rumours, the trivial acts of bad faith. After all, they had done so for years.

Dear Henry, she wrote a third time on yet another fresh sheet. *We are so sorry…* A light footfall sounded outside her door and she jumped up. Elizabeth. She hadn't seen her daughter since yesterday's dreadful interview. Dinner last night had been a solitary affair – Joshua at one end of the table and herself at the other, both of them mightily relieved when the meal had come to an end. And she had little hope that Elizabeth would appear for breakfast this morning. She needed to see her; if she could talk to her again, perhaps exert a little more persuasion, a letter to Henry might not be necessary. She might even be able to write an entirely different missive.

She opened the morning-room door in time to see a skirt of bright blue cotton disappear up the stairs.

'Elizabeth,' she called. The skirt stopped moving, hovering three steps from the top of the staircase, then disappeared in a swift movement. She sighed. She would have to write the letter after all.

*

Elizabeth wasn't the only one to miss breakfast. After the rigours of the night, the boys had slept late, much to Olly's consternation, but, by midday, Ripley had retrieved matters by serving them a modest luncheon in their room. When Elizabeth looked in on them, they had just finished eating. She thought that William still looked unusually pale but he assured her that he was feeling a good deal stronger. The old theatre had been pulled from its hiding place and various pieces of scenery scattered across the floor. He and Oliver were about to spend the afternoon working on a new play. She was relieved; he could come to no harm here.

She wished them well with their project and walked back to her room. She would spend the next few hours here, safe from any new attempt at coercion. She settled herself to read and it was a while before she realised she'd read the same page several times and was getting nowhere. It was the fault of the print, she decided. It was dancing crazily across the page, dancing to the tune of a mind that couldn't be still. Today, surely, Aiden would come. In a short while, she would slip from the house and wait in the garden once more, near to the lane that led to the village. She wanted so much to be close to him, to confide in him her worries. But if he came, what could he do? And if he pressed her again to marry, what could she say? She loved him, of that there was no doubt. But the thought of leaving the home she knew, the brother she cared for, filled her with dread. And now she was convinced that William was under attack, it had become impossible.

She put the book aside. The house was silent. The servants' work must be done for the moment and they were taking a well-earned rest. William would be in his room, planning with Oliver their next great work. Her parents would be in their respective hideaways. She heard the chimes of the grandfather clock, way down in the hall. Four o'clock. Teatime. But there was no rattle of cups. No one had called for tea. It was as though the house were holding its breath. And for what? She'd expected her uncle to arrive on the doorstep as soon as the news reached him that she'd refused Giles Audley. Giles was staying at Amberley and her uncle would have known immediately the outcome of his protégé's mission. But there had been no sign of Henry Fitzroy yesterday or today and, as far as she knew, no message from Amberley. It was strange for her uncle to remain so quiet. Her father had shouted and threatened her with exile to a non-existent school, her mother had tried soft persuasion and painted an unhappy picture of life as an old maid. So where was Uncle Henry in all this?

If making William sick *had* been his doing, perhaps that was sufficient punishment, but she thought not. His scheming was twofold. It included her and she was the one who had destroyed his plan. There would be trouble, she was sure, but what and when? A black shroud hung over

Summerhayes, but for the moment she must put it out of her mind. She must escape the house again and hope for Aiden to come. She must tell him her place was here, tell him he must travel alone.

At five o'clock, she put on a light coat. The French linen should keep her warm enough on a day that had remained overcast. Summer had temporarily retreated, the weather adding its own touch of grey to the gloom within the house. She would need to be swift. In an hour, Ivy would be knocking on her door, expecting to dress her for dinner, and she would not be allowed to miss another meal.

She stole down the stairs. The house remained uneasily silent, the hallway empty, but the smell of warm dough rising from the basement signalled that the kitchen staff were still hard at work. Slipping out of the side door, she was in time to see the last of the men gathering their tools and making their way out on to the lane that led to the village. She took cover beneath a nearby elm and waited until they'd disappeared from view, then stole past the bothy and past Mr Harris's office, to reach the tool store which stood adjacent to the lane. A small part of her had expected her lover to be there, but there was no sign of him. Could he have gone away already, gone away without saying goodbye? Her heart gave a sharp twinge and she scolded herself into sense. He would never do that. Then an irrational panic washed over her. Was he unwell or injured, or had he been lured away? Perhaps he'd been physically manhandled and forced onto a train. If so, he could be miles away by now. But she was allowing her imagination too much licence.

Her skin was prickling, with cold as much as with disquiet. The linen coat was no match for the chill of early

evening and she decided she would wait in the shed.
Five minutes passed, then ten. She became increasingly
anxious, peering through the cobwebs that draped the
mottled glass of the window. From here she had a view
of the vegetable garden, rows of kale and cabbage, carrots and onions, and pyramid after pyramid of runner
beans now flowering wildly. A sound came to her and
she crouched down. If anyone from the house found her
here, she would be in deep trouble. Her father would
draw his own conclusions and take action; most likely to
despatch her immediately to his friends in Birmingham.
For all Joshua's love for her, she knew he was determined
that she obey his wishes, and her father's determination
was not to be gainsaid. But it was the sound of a bicycle
on gravel. One of the gardeners returning for a forgotten
bag, or Aiden himself?

A figure blocked the doorway and her heart jumped –
with relief, with delight. He ducked beneath the low lintel
and she saw the worry lines creasing his forehead. 'You're
here! How good to see you!'

'And to see you.' She had thought to keep distance
between them, but found herself walking towards him,
drawn against her will.

'Not without difficulty though.' He pulled her into his
arms and when she made no protest, kissed her soundly.

'What difficulty?' she said into his shoulder.

He stepped back. 'Several of the Summerhayes' men
were on the road and I had to avoid them. I spent a lot of
time in the ditch along with the bicycle.'

'I hadn't thought of them being on the road.'

'Nor me, but then we're not natural conspirators. And
shouldn't have to be,' he added.

The thought of conspiracy made her ask, 'What happened, Aiden? My mother said that Mrs Boxall asked you to leave.'

'She did, but with a great many apologies. She said all the right words – that I'd been a model lodger and so on – but certain things had come to her notice and unfortunately she couldn't allow me to stay. I imagine the "certain things", as she put it, had come to your uncle's notice, too. He's her landlord.'

'I know he is. But when did this happen?'

'Yesterday afternoon. I had my bags packed and was out of the door before supper.'

'But where is your luggage?'

That made him laugh. 'You didn't think I'd come to meet you balancing a suitcase on my handlebars?'

'I didn't know if you would come at all,' she said in a low voice.

He took hold of her roughly and she was aware of his warmth encasing her. 'How could you think I wouldn't?'

'I wasn't sure what had happened. I didn't know where you were.'

'I found a room at the the George in Kingston.'

'But that's miles away.'

'A little over two miles, that's all. It was the cheapest place I could find. Luckily, Jonathan was generous when he bade me goodbye. He didn't like being told to send me packing. Thanks to him, I've enough money to stay a few days more.'

'And after that?' she asked, even though she knew what he would say.

'After that, it's Canada.' He pulled from his inside pocket a small cardboard envelope. 'See. Two tickets for a passage on the *Mauretania*. It's a Cunard ship and sails in four days' time. The route goes via Queenstown – that's on the south coast of Ireland – but from there we'll speed straight across the Atlantic to New York. Like an arrow. Seven days in all and we'll be there.'

Her head was whirling. 'You bought me a ticket. You expect me to come?'

'Why wouldn't I? We belong together. You know that, Elizabeth.'

The speech she'd prepared disappeared without trace and she was left grasping for a straw to cling to. 'But we're not married. I can't travel with you as an unmarried woman. And I can't marry without my father's permission, and he won't give it.'

'Of course he won't. I never expected him to. But there is such a thing as a special licence. That's what Niall – he's my cousin – is procuring. He and his wife will stand guarantors for us and, when we reach Toronto, we can be married without the need for banns.'

She was too dazed to make any kind of reply. 'Are you fearful for your virtue?' he teased. 'Don't be. You'll have a single cabin on the ship. The money has stretched just far enough to travel Second Class, though it means we'll have few savings left. But it will be worth it. It won't be as crowded or insanitary as travelling Third. You're at the very bottom of the ship there and everyone is seasick. And when we dock at the East River pier, passengers in Third Class will be shipped to Ellis Island for a medical. While we, my darling –' and he put his hands around her waist and twirled her around, '– will be free to disembark.'

He was talking as though it had all been settled. But it hadn't. She felt her heart tearing itself from its moorings, and dashed against the hard rock of old loyalties. Her hands clasped at the skirt of her coat. It was as though she needed something, anything, to hang on to, and she twisted the linen this way and that until it revealed a spider's web of deep creases.

'I can't come with you,' she said in a broken voice. 'I can't leave Summerhayes.'

He looked at her long and searchingly. He was trying to understand, she thought, but the green eyes showed him perplexed. 'I know I'm asking much of you, but if you believe we should be together, you will come. Everything is arranged. Niall has been busy finding me work. He's had several enquiries already. And he'll look out for an apartment for us. It might be small but it will be a start.'

'Why have you done all this?' she asked desperately. 'Why are you so sure? I never agreed to marry.'

'You love me,' he said simply, 'and I love you. What else is there?'

'But love isn't always enough, Aiden, and I can't go.'

'It's a choice you must make.' His voice was soft, wistful. 'The day after tomorrow is Ivy's wedding. I'll be at the church, I'm one of Eddie's supporters. Your father may be able to dismiss me from his estate and your uncle throw me out of my lodging, but neither of them can prevent me from attending a wedding. Tell me then. One single word, one whisper. And I'll be at the lodge gates at twelve the following night with a pony and trap.' He stroked her cheek with one finger. 'More arrangements, you see. With a farmer this time, Jack Roberts from Hedge End. He's been sworn to secrecy. We'll leave the trap at Shoreham and catch the train from there to Southampton. Bring only a small valise – there'll be no space to carry more.'

'You're suggesting we elope.' How stupid she sounded. What other course was open to them, if they were to marry? The 'if' went unspoken and floated between them.

'It's an elopement,' he agreed, 'and I wish that it weren't. But it's one that promises a new future. Be brave, Elizabeth.'

*

It wasn't until he had gone that she realised she'd said nothing of the dinner party. Nothing of Giles Audley's proposal. It was as though they no longer existed. And, for Aiden, they didn't. He was fixed on the future, one he expected her to share. But he had no idea of the predicament her family faced; that was something else she had failed to mention. She would not cloud his life by confessing their troubles. She must let him go, leave him free to fly.

Chapter Thirty-Two

Alice was deeply worried about her son. She had learnt from her maid how ill William had been the night before last – the servants always knew everything – and although she had wanted to scold Elizabeth for not waking her at the time, she hadn't done so. She must tread carefully. She was terrified that, if provoked, the girl might storm from the house and carry out her threat to set herself up as an artist. Alice had horrible visions of a garret somewhere in Brighton. Instead, she'd gone quietly to work, asking Cook to prepare a few special dishes and having the boys' meals sent to their room. But how much William had eaten was uncertain. He had a delicate constitution and his sudden illness, following the quarrels of the past week, had upset him badly. The healthy boy of a few weeks ago had become a thin shadow of himself, and it broke her heart to see it.

This morning he'd come down to breakfast but then sat with an empty plate, while Oliver made his busy way around the buffet, heaping his dish with bacon and kidneys and fried potato cakes. She'd tried to persuade William to eat at least an egg, but he had shaken his head and reached for a slice of toast. He'd taken a single bite only, before he rushed from the table, saying he felt sick.

She called the doctor immediately, but his telephone rang unanswered. This would have to be the very morning, she thought, that Eddie Miller had taken the car to Shoreham to collect packages from the London train, and she was reduced to sending Joe Lacey to the surgery on foot. Since then, she'd been wandering between drawing room and hall for what seemed like hours. The boys had retreated upstairs. She had to admit that Oliver was a good friend: he'd immediately broken off his own hearty breakfast and gone with William to their room.

But when at last the knocker sounded and Ripley made his dignified progress to the front door, it was Louisa she glimpsed over his shoulder. The doctor, thank goodness, was close behind.

'Good morning, Mrs Summer.' He handed his hat and gloves to Ripley and, bag in hand, made for the stairs. 'I'll go up and see Master William now, shall I? I'm sure there's not too much wrong.'

Alice and her sister-in-law were left looking at each other. 'Your man passed us on the road,' Louisa said by way of explanation. 'Dr Daniels was giving me a lift home and we saw the poor man trudging towards the village.'

'Thank you for stopping for him. It was lucky he met you.' Lucky for William at least, but what was Louisa doing in the doctor's car and dressed in her finest? Alice wasn't sure she wanted to know the answer.

The maids would still be cleaning in the drawing room so instead she led her visitor to her private retreat. 'Can I offer you some refreshment? You must be very thirsty.'

'Parched, my dear. After yesterday's gloom, it feels hotter than ever. A glass of lemonade would do nicely.'

When Ripley had left for the kitchen, Louisa said casually,

'You must wonder why I am travelling with Dr Daniels.' Alice shook her head, but her sister-in-law seemed intent on justification. 'I had a few errands in the village, you see. I walked there from Amberley, but then the sun became so hot, I really couldn't face the walk back. I saw the doctor just setting off on his rounds and begged a lift with him.'

With a dozen servants at Amberley, it seemed odd for Louisa to be running her own errands, and doing so in a gown of the palest pink silk and a hat aflutter with matching feathers. It was the biggest hat that Alice had ever seen. But she couldn't think too much about it. Her whole mind was concentrated on the room above.

'I'm sure the doctor is right, and there's not too much wrong with William,' she said hopefully. 'It may be a chill to the stomach. Yesterday was remarkably cold after all the hot weather we've had. It can be disturbing to the system.'

'And William's system is very easily disturbed.'

Ripley entered the room at that moment with a tray of lemonade and Alice was forced to bite back a sharp retort.

'He'll shake off the chill in no time, I've no doubt,' she said quietly, when the footman had left them.

'I'm sure you're right, my dear, but William does appear prone to illness.'

'He's prone to being extremely scared, if that's what you mean.' This time she couldn't refrain from a stinging response. 'The Amberley hounds have terrified him – twice.'

'Perfectly dreadful accidents. I can't tell you how sorry I am, but it won't happen again, you can be sure. I would have thought, though, that by now he would be fully recovered from any shock.'

Alice took a sip of the lemonade before she answered.

'He has almost forgotten his fright, I think, but he is a sensitive boy.'

'I know he is. We both know it. And it must be such a worry for you. And for Joshua, too, of course.'

Alice was trying to gauge her meaning when her visitor went on, 'Your husband has built such a wonderful house here and the gardens are superb. Everyone I speak to says the estate is prospering amazingly well and the home farm doing magnificently.'

'Joshua is a good businessman.' As you are anxious always to remind me, she thought.

'Indeed. And I'm sure that William will follow in his footsteps.' Alice wasn't at all sure, but she would never admit to such a doubt. 'I do feel, though,' Louisa continued, 'Henry too, that it's more important than ever that Elizabeth makes a good marriage. If William should be too delicate, shall we say, to manage the estate, Elizabeth's husband would be key to maintaining Summerhayes.'

She bridled. 'I'm sure when the time comes, William will manage the estate very successfully.'

'I'm sure he will, my dear. But one never knows what is round the corner. It's such a shame that Elizabeth was unable to accept Giles's offer. He would be perfect – for her and for Summerhayes.'

Since Alice thought much the same thing, she was left with nothing to say.

'Do you think she might change her mind?' Louisa ventured.

She couldn't prevent a small sigh from escaping. 'Elizabeth can be very stubborn and when she has set her mind against something, it is almost impossible to make her think differently.'

'The question of her marriage is too important for stubbornness.' Her companion was sounding an uncomfortably strident note. But then she lowered her voice and said, 'Perhaps if I spoke to her?'

'Oh, no,' she said involuntarily. 'I don't think that would help at all.'

Louisa replaced her glass on the gate-legged table. 'I understand the problem you face, I really do. But the young man that Elizabeth has set her eyes on is completely unacceptable. You must see that.'

Until her sister-in-law spoke, Alice had not realised how widely the news of her daughter's infatuation had travelled. Louisa's words shocked her, but she managed to say, 'I'm well aware of how improper such a union would be. You can be assured that whatever friendship Elizabeth has enjoyed with this man, it is now over.'

'But is it, my dear? You know that he is still in the area?'

She didn't know and the news, if it were true, was most unwelcome. And even less welcome coming from Amberley. 'He no longer works at Summerhayes,' she protested, 'and I understood that Mrs Boxall had asked him to leave his lodging.'

'She has, and no other villager will house him, you can be sure. Henry will make certain of that. But there are other villages in the district where he cannot exert such influence. You should take particular care of Elizabeth at this time.'

She felt herself growing hot. She needed no instruction on how to be a good mother. 'I hope you are not suggesting that I cannot care for my own daughter.'

'Not at all,' Louisa soothed, 'but there is much at stake. The young man in question has a lot to gain by inveigling himself into Elizabeth's heart and a lot to lose if she tells him goodbye. He will be persistent, you can be sure. And he is an attractive man. I met him at the fair – do you remember – and I could see immediately why she was so charmed. And girls are not as they were in our day, Alice. They have a great deal more freedom.'

'They still need to respect their parents' judgement.'

'I agree completely, but many do not. Elizabeth is a modern young woman. She is lively and intelligent and has doubtless been imbued with all kinds of free thinking.'

'If she has, it is not by me. Times may have changed, but young women still need to make a satisfactory marriage.'

It was her sister-in-law's turn to sigh. 'You are right, of course. But the wish to follow one's own path in life, to choose an attractive partner for oneself, is most understand-able, is it not?'

Alice stared at her. She had never before heard Louisa talk in this fashion. Her sister-in-law flushed a little self-consciously. 'Understandable or not,' she said in a firmer voice, 'we cannot allow it to happen. While this young man is still living close, we need to be on our guard.'

Forewarned was forearmed. She would speak to Joshua immediately. Banishing their daughter to Scotland was a wild idea, but arranging a protracted visit to Birmingham might be the saving grace. They could send Elizabeth to Joshua's friends. A month, two months, and this Kellaway boy might have faded from her mind. And certainly from the district. He would run out of money and would need to find work elsewhere.

A slight cough behind them and the doctor appeared in the doorway. 'As I thought, Mrs Summer, nothing too much to worry over. The boy's nerves are fragile and he seems to have suffered an upset recently. I think you'll find that is the cause of his sickness.'

It was what she had thought. William must have overheard the frightful quarrel between Elizabeth and her father, heard Joshua threatening to exile his sister. It would be enough to send him spinning. Her face cleared as a new thought made its appearance. William could go to Birmingham, too – there were still several weeks of the summer holidays left. Oliver could go home and William could accompany his sister.

'Keep him as calm as possible,' the doctor was saying. 'A day resting, I think, in preparation for tomorrow. I know he'll want to be at the wedding. I must be getting on now, it's a busy morning. Mrs Fitzroy, are you ready to leave?'

Louisa rose immediately. 'Are you sure you don't mind driving me to Amberley, Doctor?' She smiled up at him from beneath the wide brim of her hat. 'I wouldn't wish to be a trouble to you.'

'You are never a trouble, Mrs Fitzroy,' he said gallantly.

Alice watched the two of them walk to the doctor's car. Scattered images of the past few weeks, shifting and undefined, flickered through her mind. She couldn't say precisely why, but they made her feel uneasy.

*

Elizabeth saw the doctor's car drive away and was dismayed. She'd thought her brother over the sickness and could only imagine that he must be so thoroughly rundown, that he'd been unable to shake off the last vestiges of illness. But when she put her head around his bedroom door minutes later, she saw that his face had a smidgen of

colour and he was about to eat the small lunch specially
prepared by Cook. She was relieved. She blamed herself for
not watching him more closely, but yesterday's encounter
with Aiden was all she'd been able to think of. In all but
name, that meeting had been a farewell to the man she
loved, and in the hours since, the pain had been indescrib-
able. She would see him in church tomorrow, walking by
Eddie's side, but they would not speak. She couldn't say
the word he wanted to hear. Her decision was made and
there was no turning back.

Someone had drawn the blinds and the boys' room was
enticingly cool, its bluebirds swimming in dark shade. The
sun had returned today with a vengeance and a thick haze
lay over the gardens, but neither of them would be venturing out. The doctor had decreed that if William wished to be
at Ivy's wedding tomorrow, he must rest today. And he did
want to be, she knew, very much. Eddie was a particular
favourite. So he was doing as he was told and, in friendship,
Oliver had followed suit.

Olly had stacked their empty plates on the tray and was
now engaged in digging deep into the trunk the Summers
had brought from their old home. He spread the lead soldiers he found across the carpet and the boys set about
creating opposing camps, one on either side of the room.
As she watched, they were soon deep in battle strategies.
She wasn't sure how restful the activity was, but it was
keeping William happy. She looked at them, their heads
bent purposefully over troops of brightly painted horses,
and they seemed no more than small boys still playing
with toy soldiers. Yet she knew that at other moments,
they could be disarmingly adult. She had seen the looks
they exchanged at times when they thought no one was

watching. There was nothing childlike about those looks. Olly was a staunch friend, a loving friend, but that was the problem. Too loving for both their sakes. Why was life so very complicated?

Chapter Thirty-Three

Life was simple for Ivy. She needed to see the man she was about to marry; she had no idea why it was important to see him just that it was. The servants' supper was ready but before Cook called them to the table, she managed to slip out unnoticed to the courtyard. Eddie was rounding the corner as she arrived. He looked pink in the face and his uniform jacket was unbuttoned.

She pointed a finger. 'You better not let Ripley see you like that. He'll ban you from going to your own wedding!'

He strode across the cobbles towards her, fastening the jacket as he did. 'I've been running, that's why – to the Horse and Groom and back. I had a few minutes spare and thought I'd check that everything was fine for tomorrow.'

'And is it?' She bent down and finished the row of buttons for him.

'It is, my lady. All arranged, and it's a slap-up meal the landord's putting on.'

'Is he doing the roast he promised?'

'He is, and not any old roast at that, but half a pig. I persuaded him to splash out. He were a bit reluctant at first, but once he got the order for the beer, he saw things differently.'

'I hope you've not ordered too much. We don't want rowdiness.'

'It'll be like Goldilocks. Not too big and not too small, but just right. I can't invite the lads to my wedding, Ive, without giving 'em enough beer, can I?'

'I suppose not,' she said a trifle doubtfully. 'And the meal will be ready for us straight from church?'

He took her left hand, waggling the fourth finger back and forth. 'As soon as the ring is on this pretty little finger, we'll be off to the Horse and Groom for a feast. So stop worrying.'

'I've stopped, honest, I have. I just feel all jumbled up, it's that exciting.'

'There's a bit more excitement, too, that you don't know about. Remember I mentioned mebbe going on a little jaunt? Well, we are!'

'You asked to borrow the car? You really did?' Her face was one wide smile.

'I really did. *And* we've got two days off to enjoy it. The gaffer wants a few errands run but there'll be time enough to get to Bracklesham and give Ma a couple of rides out. And plenty of time for other things.' He gave her a wicked smile.

'And what would they be?' she asked, affecting innocence.

'I've no idea,' he teased. 'But we'll find out together.'

She blushed a fiery red and turned to go. 'I'll see you in church then,' she said at the doorway.

For a minute, he looked a little uncertain. 'Talking of church, Ivy, love, I'm not really sure about the jacket.'

She walked back to him. 'The one Mr Kellaway has leant you? But it's a beautiful jacket.'

'I know it is and I know it cost him a lot of money. But, when I tried it on last night, I felt a bit stupid. I dunno why. Mebbe because I'm always in uniform. Ma has sent up the new trousers and I wondered if you'd take a look at them both? I want to look good for you.'

'You'll look wonderful,' she said warmly, giving his cheek a gentle stroke. 'But, if you like, I can meet you later. Before I help Miss Elizabeth to bed.'

His face cleared. 'In the garden then. Nine o'clock?'

'Nine o' clock. I'll be there.' And with a swift kiss on his lips, she disappeared into the house.

*

Ivy arrived to dress her mistress for dinner full of the plans that she and Eddie had made. The girl chattered twenty to the dozen as she gathered together the evening's finery, and Elizabeth didn't stop her; she was glad of the distraction.

'Your pa has been that generous. We're going for two whole days and he's given Eddie the car to drive – yes, really.' She nodded her head vigorously when her mistress looked surprised. 'We can take Eddie's ma out and about. That's something she can't ever do on her own.' She slipped the simple gown of blue satin over Elizabeth's head. 'She can't walk much, you see. It's her left leg, Eddie says. She had a bad fall and now it won't work at all.'

'Does she live in Sussex?'

The maid looked nonplussed. Her world was bounded by house and village. 'She lives a fair distance. Chichester way, I think. Mebbe it's Sussex.'

'It is,' Elizabeth assured her, 'and it will be wonderful

for Eddie to see his mother, and to introduce his new wife to her.'

Ivy dived into the bottom of the satinwood wardrobe and brought out a pair of embroidered slippers. 'Will these be all right?'

She nodded. 'So no more laundry to sort or tea to bring or dresses to iron? You'll be as free as a bird, at least for a few days.'

The maid took up the hairbrush and began to pull it through a painful knot. 'Your hair do get in a tangle, miss,' she scolded. 'I'll make sure to brush it slowly though. There's a few errands that Mr Summer wants done around Chichester way, but they'll not take long. Then we can do whatever we want.'

'It sounds wonderful.'

She tried to sound enthusiastic. Ivy's wedding signalled a huge change and it was not one she was looking forward to. The two girls had grown up together and over the years had confided some of their innermost feelings, but once Ivy was married that would stop. Her maid would move into the flat above the motor house, as modern as the mansion it aped, and delight in being its mistress. She would be Mrs Miller, a wife first and a confidante second. A poor second at that. They would live different lives, there would be secrets they couldn't share, and the understanding between them, if not broken, would be constrained. Tomorrow she would go to St Mary's and see Ivy married, and feel more lonely than ever. She would go to St Mary's, but not say the word that could make her own dreams come true.

Her maid put the finishing touches to the twist of copper hair, then glanced into the mirror and saw the expression on Elizabeth's face. 'You should tell me to be quiet,' she said. 'Here's me chattering on and you must be worried to death about Master William.'

'William will be fine, I'm sure. It's just taking him a while to get back on his feet. But he'll be at the church tomorrow. He wouldn't miss seeing his favourite chauffeur get married.'

Ivy beamed. 'It will be some wonderful to have you all there, and our work mates, too. Everyone we care about. It may be one of the last times we'll all be together.' She laid the hairbrush back on the dressing table and was suddenly very quiet.

'There will be plenty of other times,' Elizabeth rallied her. 'And plenty of good things to come.'

'I hope so. But Eddie hasn't forgotten about signing up to fight, and I know it won't be long before he's off to Worthing. They've set up a recruiting office there.'

She was taken aback by the news. She'd known that Eddie Miller was keen on doing his bit for king and country, but if she'd thought about it at all, it was to imagine that once married, he would wait a while before volunteering. But then she remembered her father saying days ago that the trickle of volunteers making their way to the recruitment centres was not nearly enough. If the war continued after Christmas, conscription would be necessary.

'He still means to fight?'

'Yes.' Ivy looked at the floor, but Elizabeth could see her lip trembling. 'I can't dissuade him. Not that I'd try. He says there'll be a battle in France. Our chaps are heading for some place called Millhouse or mebbe it's Mullhouse? They're only a small force and likely it will go bad for them. The army will need new blood then.'

She shivered at the phrase. 'I don't suppose Eddie will be

the only one to answer the call.' It was supposed to sound comforting, but she rather feared it didn't.

'Joe is going, for sure. He's signing up with Eddie, though his ma is dead against it. And the other men – Eddie says they all feel the same.'

Would Giles Audley be making his way to a recruitment centre, too? He had joked that he was too old to be conscripted, but now that his marriage plans had fallen apart, he might think to volunteer and rejoin the cavalry.

'Summerhayes will look pretty odd if every man decides to enlist,' she said a little shakily.

'Not just Summerhayes, either. I reckon everywhere will look pretty odd. The war will change things.'

Ivy was right. It would change things. She had been so concerned with her own small drama that she'd barely registered what was happening in the wider world. She knew that Britain was at war, of course. The declaration had come the night of the fateful dinner party, but since then she had taken little heed of newspaper headlines. The world had continued to turn, men had continued to fight in countries not so very far away, and continued to die there, too. She'd known for a long time that the fingers of conflict were reaching towards them. Now, finally, they seemed to have arrived at Summerhayes and life would alter for them all.

'I'm meeting Eddie tonight,' Ivy confided, regaining a little of her former bounce. 'He's putting on his wedding outfit for me. I've to give it my blessing.'

'Should he be doing that? Isn't there some kind of taboo?'

'That's the bride. The bridegroom mustn't see the bride in her dress before the wedding, but I think it's different for a man. You don't think it will be unlucky, do you?' she added anxiously.

'Don't worry, I'm sure to have got it wrong. It's sweet of Eddie that he wants you to approve. And stay as long as you like. I can see myself to bed.'

'It's silly really. He's bound to look the cat's whiskers. He's got your – he's got Mr Kellaway's jacket – and the trousers his ma has made and sent up by carrier. And I've saved up and bought him a spanking new shirt and collar.'

'He'll look splendid.'

'He will that,' the girl said, entranced at the thought.

*

Ivy lingered beneath the rose arbour. The day had been very warm and the flowers, still in full bloom, filled the air with a drowsy scent. The entire garden seemed to be laying its beauty at her feet. That was silly, she knew, but she couldn't help feel that the world was a wonderful place. She found herself tapping out a rhythm with her foot, unable to stop her body responding to the excitement within. Tomorrow. The day was coming at last. For two years, she and Eddie had been waiting for this, the very best moment of their lives. She would not think beyond the wedding, beyond the honeymoon. She would give herself to these next few hours and make them the happiest she had ever known.

She'd slipped away as soon as the men began to clear dinner. Ripley had given her the nod. He was being unusually kind. All the staff were excited about tomorrow, even the stately Ripley. She looked back along the pergola. Eddie should be here at any moment. When she'd left the house, the kitchen timepiece had shown just after nine o' clock.

That was when they'd agreed to meet and he should be here. Perhaps he was having difficulty with the new clothes. More likely he'd found a fault with the motor car. He'd been working on it off and on all day, wanting to make sure it was in tip-top condition for their journey to Chichester. She imagined how it would be when they left the Horse and Groom, ribbons and shoes tied to the bumper – there wouldn't be any banging pots, Mr Summer wouldn't like that. But then her bouquet thrown to the crowd and she and Eddie covered in confetti.

The air was cooling and she wore only her thin maid's uniform; she paced up and down the gravel path to keep warm. Should she go to Eddie's apartment? No, he'd said he wanted to carry her over the threshold, and she mustn't anticipate the moment. It was another treat to look forward to. She might walk down the garden a little. The pergola was where they usually met but perhaps he'd arrived early and walked on. Or perhaps she'd got it wrong and he'd told her a different spot. What with one thing and another, her head had been all over the place these last few days. She walked slowly through the archway and into the vegetable garden. It was looking magnificent. There was enough food to feed an army here, she thought, then deliberately pushed the word 'army' out of her mind and kept walking. Past the fruit wall and into what Mr Summer called his Exotic Garden. She rarely ventured this far. It was too wild for her liking and it was unlikely Eddie would have said to meet her here. Then she knew. A sudden illumination. Eddie was in the Italian Garden. Of course, that's where he'd be. He'd wanted her to see the new temple. *Proper smart*, he'd said. *We should meet there sometime*.

She ran past what seemed an acre of dense vegetation.

In the gloom, the path was difficult to make out, but she ran on regardless, eager to reach her destination. He must be wondering where on earth she'd got to. Now she was through the laurel arch. The garden here was darker, the surrounding trees cutting out what light there was from a thickly clouded sky. A splash sounded straight ahead. Fish. She knew Mr Harris had stocked the lake though no one had fished there yet. The sound echoed eerily across the empty water and she didn't like it. There was no sign of Eddie, but she was sure now that this was their meeting place and she would wait. He would come.

The minutes ticked by and still no Eddie. The breeze had picked up and was whispering through the trees. They looked very tall, very dark, against the skyline. She didn't like the sound of their whispering either. It was as though they were telling her something she didn't want to hear. At length, she turned homewards. He wasn't coming. Somehow she'd made a mess of the arrangements, and she had to get back to the house or she'd be locked out. Ripley locked the doors at ten o'clock sharp and she risked being stranded in a garden that had begun to feel strangely threatening.

As quickly as she could, she retraced her steps and whisked through the servants' door just as Ripley appeared with a large brass key.

'You lovebirds,' he chided. 'Never know when to stop talking. It was talking, I take it?'

She smiled but said nothing. It was going to be all right, she told herself, making her way to the small, narrow bedroom she shared with the second housemaid. Eddie had been delayed or she had got the meeting place completely wrong. Or he'd changed his mind and gone off with some mates for the evening and forgot to leave her a message. His last night of freedom, she could hear him joke. It was going to be all right. She'd see him tomorrow and he'd explain. She'd see him tomorrow for the very best day of her life.

Chapter Thirty-Four

It was very early the next day when Oliver crept out of the side door, earlier even than usual. He'd not been able to sleep and had spent most of the night tossing in his bed. He wasn't sure why exactly he was fearful, but a nagging concern for William was giving him little rest. Now he was up and dressed, he felt a great deal better. He ran across the terrace and jumped down the circular steps onto the lawn. It was wet and spongy from the night-time dew, its freshness filling the air as he trod across to the rose arbour. He loved this time of day and he loved these gardens. He'd never known anything like them. His house and garden in London were super smart, he supposed, but their cold elegance left him unmoved. Summerhayes was different. It was an enchanted world, a fantasy far removed from the streets of Mayfair, and when he wandered through the gardens alone, he could think that this was his very own kingdom.

This morning, though, he was not alone, despite the early hour. A young boy appeared from the bothy, slow and sleepy-eyed. Oliver had once poked his head into the small two-storey building. He'd been curious to see how the men lived when they attended the night-time servicing of the garden. Upstairs, he'd found a bare-boarded room.

In one corner, a truckle bed with a mattress made of straw and covered in sacking and, in the other, a hurricane lamp. That was it. Below the room was an even smaller space, a dark cramped hole of a place – the thunderbox he'd heard the men call it. Its use became clear when he saw the cement fillet with a wooden seat on top and a bucket below. He guessed that was emptied straight on to the garden as manure. Moss or dock leaves were piled to one side and it had taken him a minute before he realised they were used as paper. There were pencil scrawls on the plaster walls, where someone had doodled while at his business. The room had stunk and he'd quickly backed out into the fresh air, but it was a glimpse into the world of those who made and maintained the paradise he enjoyed.

The young gardener had opened the tool shed and was trundling a huge hand roller towards the lawn. Oliver gave him a chirpy 'Hello' and skipped on his way. It was going to be another perfect day. The sun had just appeared over the horizon and the sky was shading from the wispy grey of dawn to the palest blue. The garden itself was still full of dark shapes. Across the vegetable plot, cane pyramids, smothered in runner beans, threw their shadows slantwise, like rows of black and slightly tipsy soldiers. As he slipped through the archway of warm brick and into the Wilderness, he heard other voices. The gardeners were arriving for their morning's work and would soon be swarming over the vegetable garden and in and out of the greenhouses, eager to finish in time for the wedding. He wanted to put some distance between them. He wanted to be quiet and to think. He would go to the Italian Garden.

He was worried about William. He'd left his friend sleeping but that wasn't concerning. William wasn't the early riser he was. His friend, though, seemed to be sleeping a good deal more these days. Of course, he'd had that dreadful bout of sickness and he was still feeling tired from it. But yesterday, when they'd played baby games with the toy soldiers, it hadn't been long before William had shaken his head to playing any more. He'd shaken his head again when Olly had suggested that instead they work on his nature collection. He'd taken up a book, but after a few minutes had put that aside too. Gone was the boy who had raced around the gardens with him early in the holidays. That seemed another time altogether.

He paused on the path through the Wilderness and looked across at the spread of ferns and palms and bamboos. They'd had fun building a retreat; then he remembered its collapse. There was no doubt that bad things had happened to his friend this summer and William hadn't coped well. And now there was trouble over his sister. He didn't really understand what was going on, but he knew that his friend was fearful that Elizabeth might leave Summerhayes. When he'd taken William's hand last night, he'd felt the rough, torn skin around his fingernails. The boy was literally tearing himself to pieces. He'd held him tight but he hadn't kissed him again, not on the lips, though he'd wanted to, and more. He thought that maybe William wanted it too, but his friend was in such a bad state that he couldn't risk making matters worse. It seemed unlikely Elizabeth would leave, but he suspected she had her own plans and they didn't include William.

He wanted so much to protect him, to help him back to being the boy he'd known only a few weeks ago. He just didn't know how. And in as many weeks, they would both be back at Highgrove. How would he protect him in that brutal environment? A gang of boys had made William's life a misery from the moment he'd arrived in the school, pinching and punching him, cutting up his clothes, destroying his books, calling him vile names. The teachers never intervened. They seemed to take a sadistic pleasure in letting the weaker boys sink or swim. Presumably, they'd suffered the same treatment in the past and stayed afloat. Or perhaps it was because William was trade, and though his money was good enough, he wasn't. So far, Olly had managed to keep the boys at bay by dint of a good left jab and a foot that could kick in the right places, but he feared that wouldn't always do the trick. And then what? All he could hope was that their tormentors would get bored and leave them alone.

The lake looked beautiful this morning. A beam of sunlight had found its way through the clustering trees and was flooding the temple with light. The shadow of its classical pillars waved long across the surface of the water. He thought the temple truly magnificent. He went to sit down on the bench in the summerhouse and for a long time gazed across at its white marble. That man – Kellaway, he thought his name was – he'd worked here and then disappeared quite suddenly. He'd thought him sweet on William's sister but then the man had left with barely a word to her. Or it seemed that way. He supposed he shouldn't be surprised. It was something to do with her being a girl. He didn't understand girls and he didn't want to.

But this Kellaway had been a clever chap, there was no doubting that. Perhaps one day he could build something as brilliant. He'd like that, to see the pencil marks on rolls of paper become this grand structure of smooth marble, and to know that he had created it. He'd have to get qualified, but perhaps William and he could work together – he would do the building, and William could do the paperwork. His friend was good at organising and it wouldn't tax his strength too much. He closed his eyes and the sun was warm on his face. He was travelling through a fantasy in which he and William shared a beautiful home – by a river, he thought – and when they weren't there, they planned exquisite buildings for very rich people.

The sun was beginning to feel warm and the sky look very blue. Cerulean blue, he remembered, from the morning in Elizabeth's studio. That's where she'd found Beatrice hiding. Now not even Beatty could make William give more than a half-hearted smile, and he went days without visiting her, though Olly continued to open her hutch every morning and smother her in cuddles. He would go and find her on his way back to the house. He could sense the sun gathering strength and the enclosed space begin to feel hot and sticky. When he ran a finger around his collar, it was wet to his touch. It was time to move. He opened his eyes and the water's sparkle danced hotly across his sight. And then he saw the log. A log right in the middle of the lake. The gardeners couldn't have worked here recently, or they would have removed it before their master could find fault. Joshua Summer wouldn't like it at all, the way it spoilt the beauty of this, his favourite part of the gardens.

But it was strange that it had fallen plump into the middle of the lake. The trees surrounding the garden were ancient and very large, but they did not overhang the water. So someone must have thrown the log into the lake. He began to feel uneasy. He knew there had been a lot of trouble about this garden and wondered if this was something to do with it. But that would mean another intruder, and nothing or no one could get in now, could they?

He looked again at the log, estimating how hard it would be for the gardeners to pull it out. Then he got up and walked towards the lake's edge. At closer quarters, he saw that it wasn't a log, in fact. It was a bundle of clothes floating on the surface of the water. He bent down and leant in, peering intently. What he saw made him totter to his feet, hardly able to breathe. The clothes had a body attached to them. There was a man floating face down in the lake.

*

Oliver saw Joe look up in surprise as he came racing towards the gardener, waving frantic arms and yelling at the top of his voice. But Joe didn't seem to hear what he was saying until he'd pulled nearly level. He was badly winded and bent double. He took some time to find sufficient breath to croak hoarsely, 'Body... in the lake.' Joe's face was uncomprehending and he had to rasp again, 'Body, lake.'

The gardener took off his cap and scratched his head. 'You mebbe got a touch of the sunstroke, Master Oliver. Better go indoors and lie down.'

But he lunged out and grabbed Joe by the arm, his grip like iron. He kept repeating over and over again, 'Body, body.'

By now, several of the men had downed tools and sauntered over to them. In answer to their questions, Joe said, 'Summat's got the boy in a pucker. We'm better take a look, lads.'

In single file the men trooped down through the gardens and he followed close behind. Now he'd delivered his message, he couldn't quite believe what he had seen. He could have been mistaken and he had to make sure. He would feel a complete idiot if it had been a log. But when the little band reached the lakeside, it was clear he had not been mistaken. The body had floated a little nearer the middle of the lake now, bumping up against the statue of the dolphin. The face had turned slightly to the side and the features were unmistakable.

''Tis Eddie. My God, 'tis Eddie.'

Then all was flurry and haste. Joe and a companion lowered themselves gingerly over the edge of the lake rim. The water was only shoulder high but neither could swim and they were nervous. But the dead man was one of their own and they put their fears behind them. They waded out to the statue, one of them taking Eddie by the shoulders, the other by the feet, and together towed him back to the side of the lake. The third man grabbed hold as soon as they were within reach and, with much effort – Eddie's clothes were sodden and weighed very heavy – they pulled their companion out and laid him on the paving stones.

'Best get up to the house and tell them to call Dr Daniels,' one of them advised, dripping pools of water across the flagged pathway.

'He don't need no doctor,' said the man who had stayed on land.

Joe squelched his way around the prone figure and got ready to lift him. 'Doctor's important. He needs to sign a certificate,' he said knowledgeably. 'We must carry him up anyways and tell Master. But quietly, mind. Ivy can't know.'

'Not yet, leastways,' his comrade said gloomily.

Chapter Thirty-Five

Elizabeth was up and dressed when she heard the commotion: voices, some of them loud, carried through her open window. She ran down the stairs and into the morning room. From here there was a good view of the terrace and of the lawn beyond. Craning her head around the open window, she saw a number of the gardeners huddled together and then her father coming out of the house and looking down at something and shaking his head. His expression was unutterably sad. What was going on?

She ran from the room, along the landing, and down the last curve of the oak staircase. Then across the drawing room, in her haste sending to the floor a hefty biography her father was reading, and out through the glass double doors to join the group on the terrace.

'Go back indoors, Elizabeth,' her father commanded. 'This is not for you to see.'

'But what is it?'

'Go indoors!' he barked, 'and make sure you keep Ivy with you.'

'Ivy? But…?' She had moved closer and could see now what the men were gathered around. A man, a very dead man, it appeared. And then she realised what, who, she was looking at and the full horror of discovery burst over her. Eddie. Eddie Miller.

Her heart had risen in her throat and was beating so strongly that she found it difficult to speak. Dear, kind Eddie. Her father was right though. Ivy mustn't see. But why was Eddie lying dead on the terrace? She saw the runnels of water leaking out from beneath his body and that his clothes were saturated.

'Drownded, miss,' one of the gardeners said.

'In the lake?' Her voice, when she found it again, hardly seemed her own.

'Fell in, poor bugger,' another muttered, and received a stony glare from Joshua.

What was Eddie doing by the lake? He hardly ever went into the gardens. The motor house was his domain, the car his god. He spent every spare hour tending its needs, damp cleaning its leather seats, dusting its chrome, polishing its bodywork. But he hadn't been at the motor house last night, had he? He'd gone to meet Ivy in the gardens to show her his wedding outfit.

She looked at the clothes dousing the flagstones wet. They were his wedding clothes all right: Aiden's new jacket and the trousers Eddie's mother had made. All very smart, or they would have been if they had never seen lake water. *Aiden's jacket*. The phrase stuck and then repeated itself: *Aiden's jacket*. Something made her push past Joe, who was keeping a ceremonial guard over the body.

'Come back here this minute!' her father shouted. 'Do as you're told and go inside!' But she had bent down to Eddie, now face up on the terrace and very gently moved his head to one side. He was so young, she thought, so vulnerable, and there was a large red wheal on the crown of his head.

'Look!' she said. 'He didn't drown. Or at least, he was hit before he went into the water.'

The men crowded around. A low angry murmur erupted. "'Tain't no accident,' one of them said. 'He were hit. Some poacher or summat did this, and him about to marry, too. We'm must get the police.'

She noticed that her father had turned a ghostly white. 'There's no need for the police,' he said. 'The doctor is all we need. Miller must have hit his head on the stone rim as he fell.'

The men exchanged a look. It was clear they weren't sure of this version of events, but the gaffer had spoken and his word was law.

Elizabeth walked slowly away, back through the drawing room, up several flights of stairs, and into her bedroom. She was feeling very ill but she knew she must stay strong. She must keep Ivy away, keep her from seeing such an appalling sight on her wedding day. She'd barely sat down to think what best to do when there was a tap on the door and Ivy herself appeared on the threshold.

'My word, you're up early, Miss Elizabeth,' she said brightly.

'I couldn't sleep.'

'Nor me,' the maid confessed, 'I'm that excited. But there's plenty of time now to get ready. I've brought my dress with me – I hope that's all right.'

She said nothing. How was she to tell the girl?

'Is summat wrong?'

'Yes, Ivy, I'm afraid it is.' Her voice shook. 'There's been an accident. Eddie–'

She had hardly spoken the name when Ivy flew past her and down the stairs. She was beyond Elizabeth's reach in a matter of seconds, and it was only a few seconds more before she heard the girl's anguished wails. She must go to her. Get her to bed, stay beside her until the doctor arrived. Alice would need to know as soon as possible. And the vicar must be told. The whole village must be told. Action, that was what was needed. Action to stop her hands shaking and her mind from flying apart.

*

When all was done and the house was left brooding in the heat of late morning, she shut herself away in her bedroom, slumping into the old nursing chair, her heart full of tears. Eddie had been part of Summerhayes for as long as she could remember. He'd come as a young boy, as under-groom to the frightening maestro who then ruled the stables. In time, he'd become head groom himself, but had stayed the same kind, sweet-natured man. How often had he tried to help her conquer her fear of horses? How long had he spent teaching her in secret to ride a bicycle? And after he'd swopped horses for engines, he'd stayed the same cheerful friend, driving her whenever and wherever she chose. A decent honourable man, a man of whom to be proud. And now he was no more.

She'd left Ivy asleep in Mrs Lacey's room – the doctor's medicine had seen to that – before watching the ambulance leave for the mortuary, bearing its poor, broken cargo. The doctor had signed the death certificate, death by drowning. An accident. There would have to be a post-mortem, but it was clearly an accident, he'd said.

It wasn't though, was it? And her father knew that. It would be well nigh impossible to hit the crown of your head falling from the side of the lake. If you lost your balance and overtoppled, you would fall outwards, straight into the lake and since the water was four-foot deep at the most, even if you couldn't swim, and she didn't imagine Eddie could, you could get to your feet and wade to the side. But not if you were unconscious. If you'd been struck a blow on the back of the head and pitched forward face down into the water, you would drown as certainly as morning followed night. Someone had deliberately attacked Eddie. One of the gardeners had mentioned a poacher, another a vagrant, but she knew without thinking that this was no unknown person who had found his way through the old, hidden entrance. It was someone who knew where that entrance had been, had unblocked it sufficiently to slide into the gardens with the intent to kill. And succeeded.

But why Eddie? What kind of enemy had he made who would want to do this to him? None that she knew of, and if Ivy were able to talk, the girl would be as dumbfounded as she to think of Eddie having enemies. It wasn't supposed to be Eddie though, was it? Throughout this morning, as she'd gone through the motions of advising, consoling, arranging, she'd been pushing the truth away as far as possible. But really she'd known, ever since she saw the jacket. Aiden's jacket. He was the intended victim, not Eddie. And Aiden did have enemies. Or at least he had one, and living on his doorstep. There had been silence from Amberley ever since she'd refused Giles Audley and now she knew why. The silence had felt sullen, sinister even, though she'd taken herself to task for fanciful thinking. But she'd been right. Summerhayes had been waiting for the strike, and here it was. Her uncle – my God, her uncle! – or someone under his direction, had walked into the garden last night with a large piece of wood, had seen the jacket and had struck.

The agitation she'd so far managed to suppress took hold and she began a restless walking from door to window and back again. But how would they have known anyone would be there? They wouldn't, not for sure, that was the answer. To be certain, they'd had to be keeping a regular watch. They'd expected Aiden to return, to meet his sweetheart in the place the lovers usually met – in the Italian Garden. No wonder she had thought herself watched. It was because she had been. And whoever had been watching them then, had watched last night and thought they'd eliminated the one obstacle that stood in the way of her marriage to Giles Audley.

It was as Aiden had prophesied all those weeks ago when William was first attacked. The trouble had started then, around the time that Audley had been suggested as a possible bridegroom. For years, her uncle had seethed impotently while an old Fitzroy home was demolished in favour of modernity, and ruined Fitzroy lands transformed into a profit-making farm and a riot of pleasure gardens that was the talk and envy of the county. Henry had succeeded in isolating the family at Summerhayes, cutting them off from the social connections natural to them, but that had never been enough for him and he'd kept his malice warm. This summer he had found the perfect focus for the resentment that ate away at him. It must have seemed that at last he had the chance to recover his birthright, to recapture the power his family had relinquished. It was hardly possible to believe that Henry would kill to gain his own ends, but she knew it now for the truth.

Her parents had released a maelstrom in their attempt

to find her a husband. One that beneath the sound and fury was driven by a plan as cold as it was precise. She did a quick calculation. Her father was a good deal older than Henry Fitzroy and, in the normal run of things, he would die years before his brother-in-law. Even now, he was not a young man and his temper was erratic. Anything could happen to him at any time, leaving his son vulnerable to whatever manipulation Henry intended. It would be too easy. Already William's heart had been weakened, his confidence lowered. And she – she would be married to someone Henry could exploit, too, perhaps not through weakness but through blood ties. She would be pressured and pressured until she agreed to marry a man of her uncle's choosing. And if Giles were too much of a gentleman to persist, Henry would find another willing relative.

It was a startling realisation. That last night the man she loved had been the intended victim and any man not of Henry's choosing who came too close to her would meet the same fate. That was the warning implied in Eddie's death. The attack had been mistaken, but as a threat it worked nearly as well.

She stopped her pacing and tried to order her thoughts. No wonder her mother had been happy to keep a distance from Amberley. Henry Fitzroy was an evil man and this summer they had invited him into their midst to wreak the havoc he chose. It had been the plans for her marriage that had been the catalyst for so much wickedness and had led, inevitably, to death. Would news of the tragedy reach Kingston? Would Aiden know what had happened? He would be immeasurably sad when he heard, but it would not change his mind. Tonight he would make his way to Southampton, as he'd promised. In hours, the man she loved would be setting sail for a new world, while she stayed to protect her brother.

She walked to the window and gazed out at the landscape she loved, but her eyes saw nothing. How *would* staying protect her brother? The question leapt into her mind unbidden, but once it was there, she couldn't lose it. How would it put a stop to the terror unleashed on Summerhayes? It wouldn't, that was the truth. She would still be menaced with a marriage she didn't want and William would still face threats to his well-being. Even if she fell upon her sword and married the man Henry Fitzroy chose, her uncle would stay William's enemy. And marrying as Henry dictated, she would become his puppet. He would have the power to pull her strings, to arrange her world as he saw fit. She would be his prisoner, and if she were ever to try to cut the ties that bound her, she could expect no mercy. Her uncle had shown himself ruthless. He may not have killed Eddie Miller with his own hands, but he was as guilty of sending the poor man to his death as the hired thug who had bludgeoned on his orders.

The genie had escaped the bottle. Henry had found a way to control her future and, worse still, her brother's. William was a fragile boy, no match even when fully grown for such a man. This summer, Oliver had gifted him an extra strength, but Oliver wouldn't always be there. Her father wouldn't always be there. And then what? Their uncle would seize his chance and strike. There was no way out. Unless…

Slowly, the thought came. There might just be. What if she were no longer here, what if she married far away and had children that were beyond Henry Fitzroy's reach? She could give Summerhayes heirs, but heirs that her uncle could not intimidate. Their presence in the world would ensure the estate would never be his, no matter what happened to William. That was it! If she were to leave, the threats to William, to her family, would surely stop. They must. There would be little point in Henry continuing the vendetta if she had a husband and children he could no longer control. The idea took her breath away. For months, she'd told herself that she must stay to keep those she loved safe. But it wasn't so, was it? To be safe, she needed to be a very long way away. To keep her husband safe, too. Above all, to keep William safe.

But did she have the courage to go? Was she brave enough to hazard her fortune with a man of whom she knew little, except that she loved him. She grasped the windowsill between her two hands. She had to have the courage. It wasn't just for her now, it was for her brother, for her family. She wished she could take William with her, but she knew he would not come, and she doubted he would be strong enough to make the journey. He would fare far better at home with Alice to nurture him. She must find him now, make him understand what had been happening and why she must leave. And ask him one last favour, him and Oliver.

Chapter Thirty-Six

It took only minutes for William to decide what he had to do. He'd always hated being a messenger for his sister, knowing his parents would be outraged if they discovered what he was doing. It seemed to him underhand, not quite cricket, to go against their wishes in that way. But overnight the world had changed, everything was different, and he was convinced now that Elizabeth's future depended on a single message reaching its destination. His own future, too. He could save his sister from disaster and save himself at the same time. She had talked to him and what she'd said had made perfect sense. The shock of Eddie's death was still with him. He'd been bewildered by the news: he hadn't understood why the chauffeur had been in the gardens last night or how he'd fallen into the lake and drowned in a few feet of water. Eddie was young and fit and healthy. Then his sister had told him of the wheal on Eddie's head and her belief that the young man had been murdered, not because he was Eddie but because in the muted light of evening he had looked like Aiden. The chauffeur's untimely death was a spur, if he needed one, to counter whatever wickedness their uncle was planning next.

He must take her message to Aiden Kellaway, for there would be no wedding today, no church where Elizabeth might meet him. Kellaway was staying at an inn in Kingston, well over two miles away, and he wasn't sure if he had the strength to cycle there and back. But he was the only one who could do it. A bicycle was the sole way of reaching the village and it was essential the trip stayed secret. He could travel unnoticed, while a young woman in a tight skirt wobbling her way through country lanes would give rise to unwelcome interest. Aiden was leaving, Elizabeth had said, and her brother must get to him before he vacated the inn.

He had thought Oliver would see the mission as an adventure, as a rare chance these days to have fun, but he found his friend strangely subdued and his reluctance evident.

'Don't you want to come?' he asked.

'I'm not sure we should be doing this.'

He had never before heard Olly sound so uncertain, and it left him grappling. 'Why not?'

His companion kicked the bedpost, then kicked it again. 'You know what happened to Eddie Miller – just a few hours ago. We might be stepping into danger.'

He hadn't thought of their errand as being dangerous, but even if Olly were right, he wouldn't let it stop him. It seemed odd that for once he appeared the braver of the two. 'We'll be fine,' he said bracingly. 'No one will even know where we've gone. We're just taking the bicycles out for an airing, aren't we?'

Olly stopped kicking the bed and sat down hard on it. His eyes were worried, his forehead creased into small lines. 'Think about this, Wills. There's something bad going on here. Someone knew that Eddie would be in the gardens last night. If they were watching him, they could be watching us,' he said darkly.

He had no wish to explain Eddie as a case of mistaken identity, but he could see the chauffeur's death had upset his friend deeply, and he tried to reassure him.

'It's not night. It's broad daylight. If anyone asks where we're going, we'll say we're just tootling round the lanes to get a bit of fresh air. If anyone did try to follow us, we'd know.'

But his companion wasn't convinced and continued to hang back. William was unused to being the decisive one and it made him impatient. 'If you don't want to come with me, just say. I'll go alone.'

'You can't do that. You're not well enough. It's a long way to ride and what if you came over faint or became ill on the way?'

'It's only just over two miles and I promise I won't faint or be sick. Come on, Olly. Be a pal. The bicycle's okay now – Eddie mended it for me.'

He couldn't stop his voice from wavering, and that seemed to decide Oliver. He allowed himself to be shepherded down the stairs and out into the courtyard that housed Eddie's apartment. Both boys looked up at the building.

William's eyes were pricking with tears 'Let's go,' he said roughly.

The first mile was hard on him. He'd hardly been out of the house in recent days and he found himself labouring whenever the lane took an upward slope or became so rutted and uneven that he was forced to hang tightly to the handlebars. But gradually he relaxed into a rhythm and his body responded to the demands he was making. The weather certainly helped. It was sunny and warm but not as hot as it had been, and a pleasant breeze blew through the hedgerows and across grass verges, filled now with cornflowers and meadow rue. It was a day to be out in the open, to enjoy the countryside, a day to be far from the house. He could feel a new strength flowing through him. Once again, it was escaping from Summerhayes that made him happy.

*

His joyful mood endured for the ride to Kingston and back, but no further. As they brought their bicycles to a halt, the world turned black. Joshua Summer strode out into the courtyard. He must have been listening for us, William thought.

His father stood, legs astride and arms rigidly folded, as though to let them go would allow his anger to escape and blow the entire courtyard and everything in it sky-high.

'Where have you been, William?' His voice was passionless but in its very impassivity, there dwelt deep threat.

'Just out riding, Mr Summer,' Olly said swiftly. He had recovered some of his spirits, but the sight of William's father, large and imposing, blocking their path, had made him yearn to see their bedroom very quickly.

'Just riding, eh? An idiot could see you've been riding.' Joshua's voice had lost some of its restraint. 'I'm asking you where you've been.'

'To the village, Papa.' It was William's turn to swallow hard. Mentally, he was crossing his fingers that this would be enough.

But it wasn't. 'What village?'

He could have said any village in the neighbourhood, but incurably truthful, he blurted out, 'Kingston.'

His father's face seemed to harden before his eyes. It was as though, at a single stroke, every contour had calcified into stone. 'Come with me,' he ordered. 'And you,' he said over his shoulder to Oliver, 'go to your room. You will be leaving tomorrow.'

Olly looked scared but lingered still, seeming compelled not to leave his friend, until Joshua turned round to look him full in the face and roared, 'Go!' Then he turned once more and strode into the house, with William following him, a small, obedient lamb.

His father led the way to the library. It would have to be this room, he thought, a dull, dreary space, oppressive in its soullessness. He stopped just inside the door, hoping he could take early flight. Joshua stood with his back to the window glaring across the room at him.

'So you've been to Kingston. And what were you doing there, my fine lad?'

The cold, emotionless voice was back and his courage began to wane. He had to dig deep to answer.

'We wanted a trip out on our bicycles and thought it would be a pretty ride.' His voice came out squeaky and high.

'There are no other villages then that are just as pretty?'

His father was sneering, but he answered as though the question had been put in good faith. 'There are, Papa, but we liked the sound of Kingston.'

'I imagine you did. And did you also like the sound of the George?'

'I don't understand.'

'Oh, I think you do. Answer me, boy.'

He gulped down a breath and imperceptibly moved nearer the door. His father hardly noticed. He was continuing with his accusations. 'You went to the George to see a certain young man, did you not?'

William hung his head.

'Didn't you?' Joshua walked up to him, towering over him, and blocking what light there was from the mullioned window.

'Yes.' His voice was barely audible.

'And you had a message, didn't you?' his father continued, inexorably.

'Yes.' His voice now was little more than a whisper.

'And the message was from your sister?' He simply nodded.

'What was the message?' Joshua barked, the sudden noise echoing around the barely furnished room.

It woke him from the almost catatonic state he'd fallen into and spurred his brain into action, scrabbling to think as quickly as he could.

'It was only to ask the man how he was,' he stumbled.

'How he was! Don't dare to play with me!'

He gathered his courage again. 'I'm not, sir, really I'm not. Elizabeth was worried – after what happened to Eddie. She wanted to make sure her friend was well.'

'And what does Eddie Miller's death have to do with it?'

'I don't know,' he said miserably. 'But she was upset. We all were. We still are.'

His father paced up and down, looking much like a baited bear. He appeared to be getting nowhere and the frustration showed.

'Where is this message?'

Once again, he resorted to stupidity. 'I don't understand.'

'I don't understand. I don't understand,' Joshua mocked. 'Have I spawned a complete fool? Where is the piece of paper you took to this man? Or the message he wrote in return?'

'There is no paper, Papa.' That at least was true.

'Turn out your pockets.'

He dutifully turned his pockets inside out and laid the contents on the library table: a motley collection of pieces of string, a handful of oak leaves, the broken shell of a bird's egg and a solitary boiled sweet, but no piece of paper.

'Where is it?' his father demanded, his anger palpable.

'There isn't any message. I was just to check that he was well and tell Elizabeth, so she wouldn't worry.'

'You expect me to believe that balderdash?'

'It's true, Papa.'

Joshua looked uncertain and William began to hope that he might escape with no more than a thunderous scold. Then a crafty look came into his father's eyes. 'Was this the first message you have delivered for Elizabeth?'

Oh, Lord, he was going to have to confess everything. He couldn't. But when he said nothing, his father made the correct deduction. 'Your silence is confession enough. I won't ask you how many messages you have delivered or how long you have been deceiving your parents in this unpardonable fashion. You are guilty of the worst kind of behaviour.'

He hung his head even lower and muttered, 'I know.' He was in agreement with his father. He had always thought it very bad form to deceive them.

'You have aided and abetted your sister in a friendship that can only harm her,' Joshua intoned. 'You have deliberately gone against your parents' wishes and sought to undermine our judgment. You must be punished.'

Some time in the last few minutes, William had known

he wasn't going to escape. He lifted his head slightly and saw Joshua begin to walk to the locked cupboard that hung between two very large bookcases. Then he closed his eyes. He dared not look, but every sound registered with him – the footsteps to the cupboard, the key jangling on his father's key ring, the sound of metal against metal, the slight creak of the cupboard hinge unoiled for some time and unopened for even longer. Every sound brought him closer to his fate.

'Pull your trousers down and bend over.' His father had returned and he opened his eyes sufficiently to see the tip of a leather strap advancing towards him.

With trembling hands, he did as he was commanded. Joshua had raised the belt in preparation for the first strike, when the door of the library flew open.

'Stop! You cannot do that!'

His father turned in annoyance and William dared to straighten up. His mother was clutching at her husband's hand, trying to wrest the strap from him. 'You cannot do that,' she repeated. 'You cannot beat a boy who is unwell. You cannot hit a sick child.'

'He is neither a child nor sick,' her husband retorted. 'He has just ridden to Kingston to take a message from your daughter to a man she is forbidden to see. What do you think of that?'

'Is that true, William?' His mother's face matched the whitewash on the walls.

'Yes, Mama,' he said unhappily, 'but it was only a small message.' The truth again. 'And it didn't mean anything.' But that, he thought, was most definitely a lie.

'You must apologise to your father for such disobedience,' she urged.

'He will do more than apologise.' Joshua had regained control of the situation and his voice was loud. 'He will be punished.'

'No, Joshua, he is not fit to bear such punishment.'

'If he is fit enough to ride five miles on a bicycle, he is fit enough to be punished. Now go.' He strode to the door and held it wide, waiting for Alice to leave. She had no option but to obey.

Then he strode back. 'Bend over,' he said again, and raised the strap.

*

William's howls of pain were heard up and down the house. The servants stopped whatever they were doing and looked towards the library, then bent their heads once more to the task in hand, their hearts a little sadder. Elizabeth in her studio heard it and clutched the paintbrush she was holding so hard that she broke it in two. She guessed what must have happened and knew it her fault; she could blame nobody else. Alice in the morning room buried her face in an already wet handkerchief. And Oliver, in their shared bedroom, clutched his hands tight and drove his nails into his hand with every stroke of the strap. Three strokes. Three howls of pain echoing across every room. Then silence. A horrid, creeping angry silence.

When William returned to the room, he was sobbing uncontrollably. Olly was at the open door, waiting for him. He guided his friend across the room and then helped him crawl onto the bed, face down.

'Wait there,' he said, though William was going nowhere. 'I won't be long.'

In ten minutes, he was back with a bowl of warm water, a cloud of cotton wool and a small bottle of iodine begged from Mrs Lacey. He very gently eased William's trousers from his legs, then with equal gentleness, rolled down the top of his drawers. Three ugly red stripes had violated the soft flesh and, at the sight of them, Olly had to knuckle away the tears that had sprung to his eyes. One wound was already bleeding and the second just beginning. He bathed the wheals thoroughly, staunching the bleeding and patting them dry. Then, one by one, he kissed each scarlet stripe in turn.

When Olly was through, William rolled on to his side and looked at his friend. Both their faces were streaked with tears. 'Thank you,' he said quietly.

Oliver's response was to gather him in his arms. He stroked his hair and kissed the tears from his face. 'You'll be all right,' he whispered, though inside he was blazing. Then, seconds later, he said, 'He won't get away with this.'

But William was too spent to hear. The boy had closed his eyes and fallen into a troubled sleep.

Chapter Thirty-Seven

Oliver lay awake for hours, listening to the whimpers of pain coming from the adjoining bed. At first, he was too angry to think clearly and too upset to formulate any plan. But then, as his friend settled into a deeper sleep, the whimpers gradually faded and his anger began to cool and mould itself to a cold determination. He would avenge William for the hurt he had suffered. It was scarcely believable to him that a father could punish his son in such savage fashion, and a son who was already in fragile health. And punish him for what? His friend had taken a one word message and taken it for his sister. William had been reluctant, he knew, but he loved Elizabeth and had done what he thought was right. And for that he had been cruelly beaten. His own father would not have stooped to such brutality — he might have been gated for a week and his allowance stopped, but a beating, never. Joshua Summer was an out-and-out bully, and the only way to deal with bullies was to hit them back where it hurt most.

He lay for long hours, thinking how best to punish the man. He hadn't got much time in which to do it. Mrs Summer had written home some time ago, asking when his father would collect him and, just before they'd set off for Kingston, she'd told him that she'd had a reply and that his pa was coming very soon. Then William's father had insisted that he leave tomorrow. The telegram would already have been sent. There was no reprieve from that. And what could a fourteen-year-old do in a mere twenty-four hours that would lay waste the life of a powerful adult?

It took him hours of thinking and rethinking. One plan after another was rejected, until it came to him, and suddenly he felt very good. Good enough to fall into a gentle doze until the first glimmer of light showed between the curtains. Then he was up and silently dressing and just as silently, stealing down the oak staircase. It would not do to wake the household. Within minutes, he had found the key to the side door and turned it noiselessly in the lock. Summerhayes ran like clockwork: every key was hung in its rightful place, every lock oiled regularly. He blessed Ripley for his efficiency.

He was in the tool shed a few minutes later but took time to choose the right implements. In the night, he'd worried that the shed might be locked; Mr Harris, though, evidently didn't fear thieves. Still, he must be as quiet as possible. The young duty gardener, asleep in the bothy just yards away, would be waking soon and by then he must have finished the job and restored his booty. He edged past the spades and forks and wheelbarrows and, from the racks of hanging tools, selected a medium-sized scythe, a steel mattock and a heavy duty axe. That should do it, he thought gleefully. He'd show that brute of a man that he couldn't maim a defenceless boy without suffering just punishment.

The tools weighed heavily on him and by the time he reached the Italian Garden, he was out of breath and needed to rest. But he couldn't linger for long. The gardening staff would begin work shortly and he must be gone before they arrived. The scything was easy, the plants soft and susceptible to the implement's biting edge. He beheaded them with gusto and then was sorry when he saw their stems stunted and withering before his eyes. It wasn't their fault that he was so angry, and he didn't like destroying nature. He knew, too, that William would hate what he was doing. But the plants were a casualty of war, he decided, and he must go on. He might love these gardens, but he loved William more.

The lakeside path didn't make him feel so bad. It was not a living thing. Skilled craftsmen had spent hours building it, but the beauty they'd created was simply a job done. He was comforted by that thought as he set to work with the mattock, systematically breaking the ornamental paving into the smallest of pieces. It proved unexpectedly hard work and he had reached only halfway around the lake when the sun's rays began to infiltrate the surrounding trees. The minutes were whirring past and he should be gone. That thought, as much as the growing warmth, sent dribbles of perspiration down his face. There would not be the time to effect a complete destruction, but when he looked back at what he'd achieved, he felt a glow of satisfaction. The path was all but a ruin. He glanced across the lake at the dolphin and its endless spout of water, and thought how much he'd like a stab at that.

But there was no time and instead he dived into the summerhouse, clambering onto the wooden bench that ran around its interior, and hoisting the axe up after him. It took him five minutes of aiming hefty blows at the roof before the first chink of daylight was visible. He shuffled a few yards along the bench and began wielding the axe at a different part of the roof. The more he destroyed, the easier it seemed to become. It was almost as though the shingles had decided it wasn't worth the fight and were happy for him to do as he wished. What he wished was to do a lot more, but he had to go. With sweaty hands, he gathered up the tools and, using the small strength he had left, trotted as fast as he could through the Wilderness, through the vegetable garden and almost to the bothy door. There were sounds coming from within and, for a moment, he was scared. He held his breath, then glided past the entrance and into the single-roomed tool shed. All the hand tools were kept above a workbench on which to repair them. Very carefully and trying hard not to fumble, he replaced the scythe, the mattock and the axe, one by one, in the exact same position that he'd found them. Then he was out of the door just as the boy emerged from the bothy, yawning and harrowing his hands through a tumbled head of hair.

Oliver melted into the shadows and waited. He knew the gardener would have to check on the greenhouses – Sundays were no exception to the rule – and once the boy disappeared from view, he turned tail and ran towards the house, reaching the side door just as the indoor servants were beginning work. He was within a whisker of being caught. One of the housemaids had come from below stairs with an armful of dusters and brushes, and he was forced once more to melt into the wall. She passed within inches but went on into the drawing room without seeing him. In a matter of seconds, he'd regained the bedroom. William was still sleeping and hardly stirred even when the door clicked shut. He flung himself onto the bed and lay there, breathing heavily. He'd done it. Now he could wait for the fun to begin.

*

It wasn't revenge that had kept Elizabeth awake for hours,
but guilt. Guilt that she had caused her young brother to
suffer such drastic punishment, guilt that she was leaving
him and their mother to face Joshua's ire. Even guilt for
the betrayal she was about to visit on her father. He was
not an easy man, but for her entire life he had loved her
as well as he was able.

That love, though, was no longer a shield. He had known
Eddie's death was deliberate and he must have deduced,
as she had, where the responsibility lay. Yet he had done
nothing to bring the culprit to justice. On the contrary, he
had covered up the crime and persuaded his men to do the
same. She wondered if he'd also realised the true nature
of the attacks on William. And if he had, why he'd chosen
to look away. Why, when he hated Henry Fitzroy, he had
become complicit in his brother-in-law's wickedness. For
an hour or so, she had wanted to march into the smoking
room and demand an explanation, but she knew she would
not get one. Her father had decided on a course and he
would not be deflected.

It seemed incredible that such a highly intelligent man
could refuse to acknowledge the truth, but in his own way,
Joshua was as obsessive as her uncle, and the lure of marrying her into an old family must have taken possession of
his mind. This was his chance to become part of a world that
for so long he'd craved to join, and he would do nothing to
jeopardise it. He was horribly mistaken. Any marriage that
Henry sponsored would ostracise him even further. Once
she was married into the Fitzroy family, her uncle would
find a way of cutting all ties with Summerhayes, and Joshua

would lose his daughter for ever. But she would never be able to convince her father of that.

When she looked in on William and his friend, she felt vindicated. She was doing the right thing. It was early still and they were both sleeping, their faces innocent and unguarded. She walked quietly over to her brother's bed and bent over him. With the utmost gentleness, she stroked a soft finger down one side of his cheek. She would make sure that he reached maturity unmolested, untroubled by threats he could barely understand. Quietly, she closed the door on the sleeping boys, and stole down the oak staircase, golden in the sunlight that poured itself into every corner of the hall. She would breakfast early and hope to avoid her father. The memory of William's howls of pain was still too raw.

But Joshua had been another early riser and, when she walked through the dining room door, he was already filling a plate from the silver serving dishes lining the top of the sideboard. A quick glance in her direction and a gruff 'Good day' was all he offered. The brittle silence spoke more loudly than any words and she longed to turn around and flee back to her room. But she was trapped and would have to make at least a show of eating. They sat at either end of the long dining table, she toying with a piece of toast and her father chewing his way through eggs, sausages and devilled kidneys. The ticking of the large mahogany clock seemed to grow louder with every minute.

She was mentally concocting an excuse, any excuse, to leave – a spurious errand for her mother perhaps – when the door to the dining room was flung back with such violence that it struck the panelling behind. Mr Harris stood on the threshold. Her father looked up from his half-eaten breakfast, annoyance flickering across his face. 'Harris? What the devil is the matter, man?'

The head gardener was a man of few words and even fewer emotions. She saw with surprise that his hands were shaking and that he was kneading the cap he carried with an almost frenzied force. Seeing him so oddly agitated was unnerving.

'Beg pardon, sir,' he began, 'but I had to come up to the house straight away.'

'Obviously you did.' Joshua was terse. 'But why? What has happened to throw you into such a pucker?'

Mr Harris shook his head dumbly, unable to find the words he needed. 'Speak up, man,' Joshua commanded. The master of the house was not in the habit of having his breakfast interrupted and was losing whatever patience he had. 'What has happened?' he asked again.

Chapter Thirty-Eight

'You must come, sir,' Harris managed to say at last. 'You must come and see.'

The man's voice echoed around the room, dull and defeated, as though emptied of all vitality. It was that, more than his words, that made Joshua take notice. She could see gradual foreboding taking hold of her father's face. Without another word, he rose from the table and followed Harris from the room. She went to follow, for uneasiness had given way to alarm. But her father stayed her and she had no choice but to do as he commanded.

For nearly an hour she waited in the drawing room. Its glass doors gave on to the terrace and she had a clear view of a considerable length of the garden. She had almost given up when she saw their two figures emerging from the rose arbour and stopping halfway across the lawn. They were talking, her father giving his gardener some kind of instruction. But it was Joshua's face that smote her. It was ghastly, as though painted from nightmare. She ran out on to the terrace and met him coming up the steps. His feet dragged on every piece of paving, and she wondered if he would ever reach the top.

'Whatever is the matter, Papa?'

The furrows in his face were carved deep and there

seemed to be tears in his eyes. She looked again and was sure of it. She had never before seen her father cry. 'What is it?' she asked, genuinely panicked.

'The Italian Garden is ruined.' The words fell lifelessly from his lips.

'But how can that be?'

He took her arm and leant heavily on it. She could feel the weight of him dragging her down, but she tried to hold firm, too shaken to know what else to do.

'Every plant has been destroyed, scythed to the ground.' The shock of his announcement jabbed at her heart, but now he had begun his tale, he couldn't stop. 'The ornamental paving has been cracked into a thousand pieces. It is ruined, completely ruined. And the summerhouse roof has been so badly attacked that the building is likely to fall to the ground at any minute.'

Her heart went out to him. She had wanted to punish him for his attack on William but this was too much. Who would do such a thing?

'Who would do such a thing?' she said aloud.

'Who indeed?' Still leaning on her, he began to shake his head slowly from side to side. He was like some bewildered and tormented beast, and it made her feel ill to see it.

'Amberley?' she dared to whisper.

He straightened up then and splayed his legs wide, as though in that way he might find a secure footing. 'Not Amberley, no one from Amberley. It can't be. Cornford has built a spiked barrier to ring the entire estate and he told me just yesterday that he'd had the stonemason block an old rear entrance.'

'It's possible that someone dismantled a part of the barrier, or perhaps climbed over it. Someone who was very determined.' The same determined someone, her thoughts were saying, who'd come the night Eddie was murdered.

'Certainly determined,' her father said bitterly. 'But a person from Summerhayes.'

Her mouth dropped open. 'That can't be.'

He'd begun to shake his head again in the dumb fashion she found terrifying. She tried coaxing him to walk towards the drawing room doors, but he seemed unable to move. Instead, he stood, legs still splayed, looking blankly ahead. She'd given up any hope that he might speak again when he said, 'Harris tells me the scythe from the tool shed has been used.' The words were jerked out of him. 'The boy cleaned it last night – it was the last job he did before retiring – but this morning it is green with plant juice.'

The implications of Harris's discovery were appalling. A person who was known to her, someone close at hand, had deliberately destroyed her father's dream, destroyed his life even. She could not bear to think it, and instead delved for what comfort she could find.

'The garden can be put back again. If it can be built once, it can be built again.'

'It cannot. It will never be the same.'

She could see that the ideal he carried in his heart had been vandalised as thoroughly as the garden itself, tainted to such a degree that he would walk away from what had been his greatest desire. For his own salvation, she must try to make him see differently.

'Not the same, perhaps, but a new garden can be as beautiful. Give it time, Papa.'

There was a bitter twist to his face. 'Time is not mine to give. Look below.' He gestured towards the kitchen garden, way in the distance. She could just make out the group of small figures, and it seemed to her that, despite it being Sunday, every gardener on the estate was gathered there. They had collected their tools and as she watched, each man, one by one, laid down the implements they carried.

'Even if I wanted to rebuild, I couldn't. It's men I'd need and it's men I won't have.'

Mr Harris had reappeared at the bottom of the terrace steps. 'They're going then, Harris?' her father asked.

'Yes, sir. Every man jack of them.'

'Going where?' This morning had left her struggling.

'Morning, Miss Elizabeth.' Harris appeared to have regained his customary calm. He doffed his cap to her as though he were seeing her for the first time that day. 'The men are off to Worthing,' he explained. 'The army's recruiting there and they're walking in to enlist. I did hear as there was going to be a Southdown battalion, part of the Royal Sussex. A pals' regiment or some such.' Harris's tone suggested that joining the battalion would be akin to entertainment, a fun day by the seaside. He passed up a leather-bound volume. 'I've brought you the day book, sir. I thought that mebbe you should have it from now on.'

She glanced across at the open page. The last heading was Saturday, 8 August, 1914, and a thick black line had been drawn beneath the list of completed tasks. From now on, it seemed, the day book would remain blank.

Her father half turned to her. 'You see, my dear, it can't be put right. The dream is over.'

He began to shake so violently then that his whole body dissolved into spasms and was in danger of toppling to the ground. She was not strong enough to support his bulk and, seeing this, Mr Harris leapt up the steps with an alacrity that belied his fifty years, and took hold of his master's arm. He guided Joshua through the open doors into the drawing room.

'Call your mistress immediately,' he said to the maid zealously polishing the fluted arches of a mirror. 'The master is in need of her.'

*

After his destructive revel, Oliver had fallen into a heavy sleep, and William had to tug at his arm before he could wake him.

'Are you all right, Olly?' He looked anxiously down at his friend. 'It's not like you to sleep so late.'

Oliver half opened his eyes, then yawned and gave himself a long, lazy stretch. 'I'm fine. In fact, more than fine.'

There was a note of euphoria in his voice that seemed odd, but William ignored it and stepped away from the bed to walk to the window. 'Come here and look. The men are all lined up on the lawn.'

Oliver hung back and that was a trifle odd, too. He would have thought him nervous if that wasn't so silly, and he beckoned to him again, this time more urgently. His friend eventually shuffled over to join him and together they watched as the gardeners moved off, walking two by two, back across the lawn and out to the side gate that led to the road and the village.

'What do you make of that?' William asked.

'No idea, old chap. Perhaps they got wind of your beating and they're walking out in protest.'

He was astonished. 'Why ever would they do that? What happens in the house is nothing to do with them, and in any case I deserved the beating.'

Olly stared at him. 'That's rubbish,' he said hotly. 'How could you possibly deserve to be hurt in that way?'

'I carried a message when I knew it was wrong. I deliberately deceived my parents. Papa was right when he said I was guilty of the worst kind of behaviour.'

Without thinking, it seemed, Olly put out his hands and gave him a rough shake. 'I don't want ever to hear you say that.' William winced at the contact. 'Sorry,' his friend muttered. 'But see, you're still in pain from what he did to you. How can you excuse him? It was barbaric and I'm glad his precious garden is destroyed.'

'What do you mean, destroyed?' Fear pinched at him. Something bad had happened and Olly was at its centre.

'The Italian Garden he dotes on. It's destroyed.'

He stared at his friend unseeingly. Then backed several steps away. 'What have you done?'

'I just took a few tools to it, but enough to make the garden a sorry sight.'

He tottered across the room and slumped back onto his bed, 'How could you, Olly? How could you do that? It was my father's dream.'

'Exactly. That's why. He hurt the one thing I love so I decided that I'd hurt the one thing he loved. And I must say I was spectacularly successful.' He couldn't quite restrain a grin.

William hardly noticed. His gaze was fixed on the faded Persian rug, his shoulders sagging beneath the weight of the misery he carried. 'It's a most terrible thing that you've done.'

'It was a terrible thing that he hurt you.' Olly sounded impatient. 'Why can't you see how badly he treated you?'

'It was my own fault that I got a beating. You must know that. I did a bad thing and I deserved to be punished.' He looked up then, his eyes heavy with resignation. 'Whatever he did, he's my father and I owe him my loyalty.'

'Then you're mad.'

'I'm his son,' he said stubbornly. 'What you've done is unforgivable. My wounds will heal, my father's won't.'

'I hope they don't. And when you've had the chance to mull it over, you'll hope so too. So mull away after I've gone.'

William did not reply, retreating into a world where his friend couldn't follow. Would never again follow. Oliver turned back from the window and came to stand in front of him. 'I'm leaving today, remember? Pa is coming at midday to collect me.' He sounded a little uncertain. 'But we'll be back at school in a few weeks and we'll meet up then.'

But they wouldn't. The ground had shifted and nothing would be the same again. He would see Oliver, but it would be from afar. They would no longer meet as friends, as dear friends, and somehow he must endure school without him. The boy he had loved had gone.

'I bet by the time I see you, you'll be singing my praises!' Oliver's rousing tone emerged flat.

He braced himself to say what he must. 'I won't, Olly. And going back to school will make no difference.' He got to his feet. He was standing inches from his companion and looking directly into his face. 'We can't be friends, not any longer.' His eyes brimmed with unshed tears. 'We can't be with each other any more.'

'What! That's crazy, Wills. I know you're angry with me but I acted out of love for you. You've got to understand that. You've got to forgive.'

'I can't and I can't be friends with someone who has hurt

my father so badly.' He spoke from a well of unhappiness. 'I love him and I have to be loyal.'

For several minutes, Oliver stood immobile, as though pinned to the floor by invisible bonds. Then he found his voice, dull and stupefied. 'You're saying we're not to be friends any more? You can't mean that.'

'But I do,' and the sadness of the world was in his words.

Chapter Thirty-Nine

Two hours after Oliver's departure, the hot weather broke. It had been building for a storm from early afternoon and towards evening the sky mushroomed into a dark, smothering blanket, and the first drops of rain began to patter against the studio window. Elizabeth had been sitting at her easel ever since she'd waved goodbye to the boy and his father. It had been a sad leave-taking, with William nowhere in sight and Olly uncharacteristically withdrawn. Whatever William had said to him had robbed his friend of all spirit.

But it wasn't Oliver and his troubles that were preoccupying her. It was her own. The fear of what lay ahead. When she was with Aiden, the strength of his love sent fear chasing into the shadows. It was when she was alone that it took hold and grew. She found herself unable to work, unable even to place a brushstroke of paint on the canvas. Her small valise was packed and hidden deep in the sandalwood wardrobe, far from inquisitive eyes. Not that there were many. Only Ivy, once more in attendance on her, was likely to discover the bag, but the girl was listless and uncomprehending, a ghost of her former self. Her duties as a lady's maid were carried out as well as ever, but now in mechanical fashion. It would be many months, many years maybe, before she recovered from the tragedy visited on her.

She longed to take the maid into her confidence, to say a proper goodbye, but she dared not. Ivy would never betray her, but the last thing she wanted was for the girl to be subjected to Joshua's savage questioning. The maid must have no knowledge of the mistress's plan. But when it was over and Ivy left in need of a new post, she was confident one would be waiting. Her mother would welcome the girl with open arms. Alice's maid was elderly and would have retired already but for her mistress's unhappiness at having a new woman wait on her. Ivy would fill the role perfectly. The girl had shared most of her life with the family and now had shared with them this most dreadful of summers.

She'd resolved she would keep strictly to a familiar routine and allow no clue to escape of what she intended, but when Ivy came to dress her for the last time, she could not stop herself marking the moment in some small way. 'I'd like you to have this.' She handed her maid the pearl necklace she had been given when presented at court the previous year. In future, she would have no need of such expensive baubles, but it might one day benefit the girl, even if only to sell it.

Ivy gasped. 'I can't take that, miss. It was your father's gift. It was your presentation necklace, that and the earrings.'

'I know,' she answered tranquilly. 'I still have the earrings but as for the necklace – I'd like it to go to someone I care for.'

The maid blushed scarlet. 'I know you feel sorry for me, but you mustn't. You mustn't give it to me out of pity.'

'It's not given with pity, Ivy. It's given with love. Please take it as a remembrance of me.'

Instantly, she wished she could bite back the words. Ivy's diminutive figure had stiffened and her eyes grown too large for her face. 'Remembrance?' she queried, and there was a quiver to her voice.

'Remembrance of our time together when I did the London Season,' she said lightly, trying to recover her mistake.

The girl was thinking back and, for the first time in several days, she smiled. 'That was a fair grand time, wasn't it?'

'It was,' Elizabeth said, 'fair grand.' And then she walked down the stairs to the dining room, readying herself to eat with her parents for the last time.

*

Once dinner was over, the storm set in properly, and a vicious wind fluttered the roof tiles and caroused the brick of the three tall chimneys. The windows in her bedroom were too well set to rattle, but the furious rain beating against their glass made her feel she was under attack. What a night to venture out. What a night to begin the rest of her life.

She allowed Ivy to see her to bed and then settled herself to wait until the house fell asleep. Before long, the only noise to reach her was wind and rain. An hour, two hours, then she was up and dressing herself in the most service-able gown she had. Over this, she put on a summer coat of thick French linen, ankle length, and with a wide enough collar to protect her neck. It would have to do. Her winter clothes were pressed and packed away in trunks, and a visit to the attics to find a heavier garment would have provoked unwelcome questions. She scrabbled in the top of the wardrobe, drawing out an untrimmed velvet poke bonnet. It was the best head covering she could find.

She checked the clock on her bedside table. Five minutes to twelve. Time to go. But she would make a last visit to William. She was relieved to see he was asleep but when she bent down to kiss him, he stirred fleetingly and opened his eyes a fraction. Then he raised his arms and held her in a tight embrace, nuzzling his face against her neck.

'I'll write,' she whispered.

He smiled and fell back into sleep. A note left for her mother in the morning room and one for her father in his smoking room. Then she was sliding the bolts back on the front door and walking out into the storm.

He was waiting for her just past the bend in the drive. A pony cowered beneath what shelter the trees offered, pawing at the gravel, impatient to be off. Aiden, water running off his hair and face, jumped down from the open carriage and enfolded her in his arms.

'We've certainly chosen a night,' he murmured. He took hold of her valise and threw it into the trap, then helped her up onto the seat beside him. Only then did he kiss her.

'We must be off or we're likely to drown before we ever reach the railway station.'

There was a laugh in his voice, but as the trap pulled forward and travelled the length of the drive, he fell quiet. They had reached the lodge gates and, for an instant, she looked back. It was her last glimpse of Summerhayes and her heart splintered. Even on a bleak and stormy night such as this, it called to her to stay. *This is your home*, the voice said. *Why abandon the beauty you have loved all your life for an unknown land, so distant, so alien?*

He reached across and clasped her hand. His touch was warm, comforting. 'You'll be back, don't doubt it. We'll both be back.'

His words helped a little to fill the sudden emptiness, but to divert herself, she asked, 'What will happen to the horse and carriage when we get to Shoreham?'

'There shouldn't be a problem. I've arranged for the trap to stay at the station and a porter to mind the pony. Roberts will collect him when he meets the milk train from London.'

He appeared to have thought of everything and she must concentrate now on enduring a journey that was wilder than either of them could have imagined. But the pony had a good heart and trotted tirelessly through wind and rain, until the skies began to lighten and the rain to slacken. The South Downs, smooth and majestic, rose clear against the sky. She felt their claim on her, felt their need to keep her here, safe from a hostile landscape.

But she would not think of the future; the present was what mattered. By now, they were both thoroughly wet and she wriggled uncomfortably in her seat. 'We're through the worst,' he said hopefully. 'But as soon as we reach the station, we should plunder our bags for dry clothes. Otherwise, we could fall sick and lose our sailing.'

She nodded absently. Now that the storm was no longer a distraction, her mind had wandered back to Summerhayes. It was impossible to escape its pull.

'You must have heard about Eddie?' she asked.

He turned his head towards her, seeking her face. 'I did. Joe came to the inn to tell me the dreadful news.' There was a pause as he weighed his next words. 'Is that what decided you?' he asked at length. 'Is that why you're here?'

'I'm here because I love you, Aiden.'

'Eddie's death must have made a difference though. It was a most shocking thing.'

She admitted as much, but then said vehemently, 'I wanted to come. Always. I wanted to be here with you, you must know that. But I was torn, thinking I owed it to my family to stay. Then Eddie was murdered and the balance tipped. I knew I was no longer safe at Summerhayes. And while I stayed, nor was William.'

'Your brother is a boy of few words, but when he came calling, I reckoned that must be the case.'

'Thank goodness he found you at the inn. I was afraid you might already have left for Southampton.'

'I stayed on to the last moment – there was always the hope you would decide for me. But soon after William visited, I packed up and left. I knew about Eddie by then and the inn no longer felt safe.'

'Where did you go?' she asked in surprise.

'I spent the night in a cottage a village or so away. It was well hidden, so safe enough. As soon as I put two and two together, I knew that I'd been the target and not poor Eddie. And that once whoever killed him realised their mistake, I would still be the target. It seemed sensible to move.'

It was a sober thought, and for a while they travelled in silence until Elizabeth burst out, 'If my parents hadn't decided that I should marry, none of this would have happened. For once, they might have agreed with each other and simply sent me away to school, as my mother wanted.'

He raised an eyebrow. 'If you'd been sent away to school, we would never have met.'

'I know, and that's the wonderful thing that has come from it. But there are so many bad things, too. It was my father asking Uncle Henry to find a husband for me that began this chain of misery. William has been made ill and forced to forfeit the best friend he's ever had. You lost employment and were driven into hiding. Eddie has had his life taken from him – think of that – and Ivy been condemned to a future of service.'

'Can you really lay the blame for all of that on one simple request.'

'All of it. In the end, the request wasn't that simple. When Papa asked for Henry's assistance, my uncle saw his chance, I'm convinced. For years, he's been waiting for an opportunity to move against Summerhayes, and there it was quite suddenly, out of the blue, presented on a plate. Marry Elizabeth to a relative, torment William until he is weak and defenceless, and then wait for my father to die. Or perhaps not even wait.'

The thought had come unbidden. A thought that was as grim as it was new. Seeing her stricken expression, he squeezed her hand again. 'Be glad. We've called a halt to it. We've broken the chain.'

'You're right,' she said at last. And her mood lightened alongside the coming dawn. 'We've broken the chain.'

Chapter Forty

William found his mother in the morning room, trying to create order from the jumble of her sewing box. The storm had finally cleared and the first beams of sunlight were brightening the room. He saw the letter as soon as he walked through the door, but that was because he was expecting it. It was tucked behind an ugly Chinese vase sitting in the middle of the mantelpiece. His mother seemed unaware.

She looked around when she heard his footsteps. 'Come and help me untangle these silks. You're so good at it.'

He went willingly. He'd always been happy in his mother's company and now it seemed more precious than ever. Almost happier with her, he realised with surprise, than with Oliver. He felt safe, consoled and reassured. Olly had been exciting, the feelings he'd induced had been exciting. But worrying, too, and difficult to live with. For all kinds of reasons, Oliver was dangerous. He still loved his friend, he always would, but this was simpler, more easeful.

Mother and son set to work on the tangle of silks. 'Should these go with the pinks?' he asked, waving several skeins of fuchsia and rose thread.

'You can line them up with the pinks or the reds. I don't

think it matters, dear.' She looked over her spectacles, observing him closely. 'How are you, William?'

'I'm fine, Mama.'

And he was, though he knew there was more trouble to come. There was misgiving at the thought of his sister's letter, but he couldn't be sorry that Elizabeth had escaped. He would miss her dreadfully, but his heart told him that she'd been right to seize her chance of happiness and right that she had made them both safer by doing so.

His mother smiled. 'You certainly look a good deal better. And you are over the sickness now?'

'Completely.' And over his punishment, too, though he noticed Alice couldn't bring herself to mention the beating.

'I was wondering about your friend,' she pursued. 'How you felt about Oliver leaving?' He could see that she was approaching the subject as delicately as she could.

'I was sad to see him go, Mama. But he couldn't stay. And I can't be friends with him any longer, not after what he did.' He knew his mother had never liked Oliver and the boy's confession had come as no surprise to her.

She looked relieved. 'I'm very glad to hear you say that. Particularly as you'll not be seeing him again.'

'I'll see him at school, of course, but I don't need to talk to him.'

His courage ebbed at the thought of the difficult encounter to come. And worse, how he'd fare confronting the school bullies without Oliver's championship. Already he could feel himself encircled, hear the animal chants of 'button boy', and the blows buffeting his head.

'No,' his mother said firmly. 'That isn't so. You'll not be returning to Highgrove Academy. I have spoken to your father and he has agreed that you will not be sent back there. Your education is to be completed at Summerhayes. We will find a new tutor for you, a younger man, I think, who shares your interests.'

The news broke on him like a shower of gold, a balm that made his wounds whole. Not to have to go to school, not to face the taunts of teachers and the spiteful kicks and punches of his fellows. To stay home, here in his beloved Summerhayes, with the gardens to roam and his mother to talk with. A Summerhayes no longer darkened by bad deeds.

'Are you happy with our decision?' His mother was still looking concerned.

'Yes, Mama,' he hastened to say. 'Very happy. But why am I not to return?'

'It is a matter of principle. We cannot have you attend a school where boys such as Oliver Amos are accepted. What he did was a wicked, wicked act. The loss of the Italian Garden has destroyed your father.'

Olly would be pleased to hear it, he thought miserably. But his mother's words worried him. 'Where is Papa?' He hadn't seen his father since the beating. He wondered if Joshua, too, had received a letter from Elizabeth.

'Since the garden was laid waste, he has spent every hour in the library. The room seems to chime with his mood. He is sitting there now, staring at the walls and refusing to talk. And he's hardly eaten a thing. At dinner last night, his plate went completely untouched.'

'But he will get better?'

His mother spread her hands in surrender. 'I have no idea. At the moment, he is sunk deep in misery. All we can do is wait and hope. It's important that he recovers soon – now that all the men have left. He needs to find a way of keeping the estate going and, when he does, we must be sure to be by his side.'

She gathered up the last few skeins that William had disentangled and laid them lengthwise along the bottom of the sewing box. 'There. That's a good job we—' she broke off as the door swung sharply back.

Joshua stood on the threshold, his face working uncontrollably. The blank look Alice had spoken of had been replaced by one of fury. 'Have you had one?' He waved a piece of paper at her.

His wife looked bewildered. 'One what?'

'A letter, woman. A letter.'

'I've had a number of letters, Joshua,' she said placidly.

'Not any letter.' His face was slowly taking on the familiar crimson. He darted looks around the room, his gaze coming to rest on the mantelpiece. 'That letter over there. Haven't you read it?'

It was a superfluous question, since Alice clearly had not. She adjusted her spectacles and peered across at the gaudy ornament. Then rose stiffly and walked across to take hold of the cream vellum half hidden behind its bulk.

She tore open the envelope and William waited for the explosion. But his mother said nothing, walking back to her chair and sinking into its depths. She looked a trifle paler than she had minutes before, and her breathing had become a little more rapid, but when she spoke, her voice was steady. 'She's gone.'

'She's gone!' her husband repeated in a roar. 'And with that young villain.'

'Is there any way in which we might stop them?' It was an ill-advised question.

Joshua's lips formed into a sneer. The letter appeared to

have snapped him back to his old self. 'And how precisely do you imagine we can do that, when we don't know when they left or where they're going.'

'I would think it was during the night, though I believed her in her room still.'

'Of course, it was during the night,' His roaring had reached full pitch. 'But in case you hadn't noticed, the night lasts for many hours. If they left at midnight, they will be well on their way to wherever they intend.'

To Canada, thought William. That was where Aiden Kellaway was headed. The man had told him. There was a cousin or some such who could find him work and a place to live.

Alice read the letter again. William noticed that her hand wasn't quite steady, but her voice remained suprisingly calm. 'She says that she will write to us as soon as she reaches her destination. She says that she is to be married.'

'And you believe that poppycock? *She* might be naïve enough to believe it, but surely at your age, you must know the truth. The girl is ruined. Completely ruined.' He stormed to the window and then back again, his face mottled and his lips working furiously. When he came to a standstill, he raised a fist. 'From now on,' he declared, 'she is no daughter of mine. She has cut herself adrift from Summerhayes and that is where she'll stay. I wish to hear no more of her.'

His audience was stunned. Elizabeth was the love of his life. Even the gardens came second in his affections. For a long moment no one spoke, then Joshua, still glowering, stalked to the door. He shot an angry look at his wife. And another at his son.

'You knew,' he accused. 'You knew what she planned to do. Both of you.'

'We did not,' Alice said indignantly. 'How could we have known such a thing? How could we have known that she would take such precipitate action?'

'Yet you don't seem unduly perturbed.' His face assumed a sly expression.

'I may not feel the need to shout, but you can be certain that I am deeply upset. I cannot believe, though, that Elizabeth would serve us in this way unless she had very good reason.' She paused for a moment and then spoke her thoughts. 'We should not have pushed her so hard. Our determination to see her married could be reason enough for her to leave.'

William thought his mother on dangerous ground. And so it proved. 'Good reason!' Joshua yelled. 'Her only reason is to get what she wants.' And he stomped from the room.

'Not unlike her dear father then,' Alice remarked, as the door slammed behind him.

William wondered how much his mother knew or guessed of that summer's doings. Did she suspect her brother of plotting against her family? Is that why she'd received the news of Elizabeth's elopement with such equanimity? If she did suspect, no one would ever know. She would cope alone with the knowledge. For all her timidity, his mother had an inner courage that saw her steadfast against whatever fate dealt.

'I won't ask you if you knew what your sister intended,' she said. 'I shall assume that this letter is as much a shock to you as it is to me.' She gazed at him intently and he found himself unable to meet her eyes. He looked down into his lap and shuffled a stray skein of silk between his fingers.

'Your sister is a headstrong girl,' she went on, 'she always has been. But she is also a loyal daughter, and I know in my heart that she would not have taken such reckless action without good cause. I had hoped that Giles Audley would give her a safe future and, when she refused him, I tried to persuade her to think again. She wouldn't listen. Perhaps she couldn't. Maybe her life had become so difficult that her only option was to take flight.'

He nodded vigorously. His mother was right, though whether she realised just how difficult, he couldn't tell. 'She will write to us,' he said eagerly.

'We must look forward to that.' She gave his hair a gentle stroke. 'In the meantime, we must find some distraction. Shall we do a jigsaw puzzle? I have a new one I've been waiting all summer to do with you. It's called "Woman with Poinsettia".'

She walked over to one of the highly polished chests that lined the room and brought out a large box. 'Just look at these beautiful colours.' She held up the illustration for him to see. 'The woman's hair is an amazing shade, isn't it? Though I think we might find the background a little tricky. It's fairly monochrome and there is little to distinguish the pieces.'

'It will certainly be a challenge, but we'll do it, Mama. We're the experts.'

Chapter Forty-One

They had begun to search for the straight-sided pieces that would make the puzzle's frame when the door flew open once again. This time, though, it was not Joshua, angry and red, but Henry Fitzroy, white and shaken. Alice tensed immediately.

'You have to help me,' he began. 'I don't know what to do. Where to go.' He was an altogether different man from the one she knew.

She sat up straight in her chair but made no move towards him. 'It would be best that you stay calm, Henry, and tell me what has happened.'

'I don't know where to start.'

She could have retorted that the beginning was usually a good place, but she could see that he was in a state of shock and she tried to sound compassionate. 'Tell me what has brought you here.'

'Lister heard a conveyance in the night,' he said. The butler's night-time observations hardly seemed relevant, but she waited patiently for her brother to continue. 'There was a storm, you know.' She nodded encouragingly. 'And Lister got up to make sure the front door was secure. Then he heard the noise. He was sure it was a horse and carriage driving past the gates of Amberley – it was unusual enough for him to report. Do you know anything about it?'

'No, indeed. It seems a strange time and even stranger weather to be venturing out.' She looked as blank as she was able and was glad to see that William's face, too, was expressionless.

'I had thought you might know, but if not…' He wavered on his legs and looked likely to fall. For the first time in her life, she was seriously concerned for him. 'Sit down,' she said, trying for a friendly voice. 'You look unwell.'

He slumped into the nearest chair. Then gave a loud groan that startled both his listeners. 'She's gone,' he said. 'She's gone. Louisa.'

'Surely you must be mistaken. She will be in the village. She will be visiting a tenant. There is fever among the cottagers, I believe.'

He shook his head with a despairing violence. 'That can't be so. She left a message.' He fumbled in his breast pocket and brought out a folded sheet of paper, but when he tried to spread it out, his hands were shaking so much that he was forced to give up and let the white oblong sit in his lap. 'It's for Gilbert, you see.'

'But—'Alice began to say when he cut across her in a voice drained of all life: 'Her woman tells me her clothes are missing.' Then, 'Where has she gone, Alice?'

She had a good idea where, or at least with whom, but she kept the thought to herself. 'I'm sorry I can be of no help. It would be best if you sent one of your servants to make discreet enquiries in the village – and maybe beyond. By now, your staff will know there is something amiss and there is little point in pretending otherwise.'

He seemed hardly to hear her, returning again to the

night's events, as though unable to think beyond that one crucial moment. 'It was certainly a carriage that Lister heard, and she was in it, I am quite sure.'

That was another thing she had ideas about, but again she said nothing.

'Why would she leave?' Henry wailed. 'And why travel alone?'

She had no intention of enlightening him. It was clear to her that Louisa had made off with her doctor and in due course Henry would discover it. But two elopements in one night! That was scarcely believable.

'How could she do that?' he continued. 'How could she bring such shame on me, such shame on the Fitzroys?'

She could not find it in her heart to blame her sister-in-law. For months she'd noticed how happy Louisa had looked in the company of Frank Daniels, happier than she had ever known her. Not that she had been surprised. She could only guess at the life the woman endured at Amberley. For all her faults, she should not have to suffer her remaining days tied to a man like Henry Fitzroy. Even now, he was most concerned with his family's honour. Love, true love, was a foreign country to him. A social manner that was easy, a charm that was shallow, friendship that was manipulative, all these he could do, and far, far worse, but not love.

She went over to his chair and gently urged him to his feet. 'I'm afraid we cannot help you, Henry,' she repeated. 'You must go back to Amberley and start enquiries.'

He stumbled towards the door as though asleep and walking through a nightmare. Then on, to vanish from sight without a word of goodbye.

When he'd gone, she said, 'You will not speak of this, William?'

'No, Mama,' he said, wholly undisturbed. 'But shall we go on? I think I may have found sufficient pieces to make the frame.'

*

From his smoking room, Joshua had a view of the front drive. His mood had changed from sad introspection to outright fury and his own private space seemed best suited to his angry pacing. His daughter had gone. Gone for good. The girl he'd loved and cherished. She had refused the man to whom he had given his blessing and chosen to throw herself away on a poor working man, a good-for-nothing Irishman with little to offer but charm. She had left him without a word, except for these few. He snatched up the crumpled sheet and thrust it into a tight, hard ball. Then he threw it with force across the room.

She would find herself punished, he thought with satisfaction. Did she really imagine that young man would marry her? Could she be that foolish? She would come crawling back, contrite and weeping, seeking forgiveness. He might forgive her, he decided, forgetting his earlier words to Alice. He might, but she would have to grovel first. She would be spoilt goods, no man would have her; she would have to live the rest of her life at Summerhayes tied to her father. And that would suit him splendidly.

The sound of scattered gravel took him to the window. Henry Fitzroy, of all people, was walking towards the Summerhayes' gates. Walking! That was the oddest sight. The man called for his carriage if he so much as wanted to visit his own lodge keeper. But the oddity didn't end there. There was something about his posture that wasn't right.

He seemed smaller, shrunken, his shoulders bowed and his head bent. Something bad had happened to him. Joshua experienced a ripple of pleasure. It was poetic justice. The man had been behind the troubles at Summerhayes, he was certain. He would not allow his mind to dwell on whatever wickedness had been committed, but he was sure his brother-in-law bore responsibility for this summer's evil.

He watched as his enemy trudged bare-headed towards the gates. There was something in his hand. A piece of paper. A letter? Another letter. Had he, too, received bad news? A surge of energy, sudden and compelling, suffused every one of his limbs. It was good to know that Henry Fitzroy suffered.

Chapter Forty-Two

Elizabeth had been frantic to board the ship as soon as they reached the dock at Southampton, frantic to squirrel herself away out of sight. Her anxiety was acute. At any moment, she expected to be discovered and a uniformed figure to leap up the gangway and drag her back onto the quayside. The liner would sail without her, and she would be forced to watch as Aiden slipped from her life for ever. But that had been foolish, a panic brought on by the ordeal of leaving Summerhayes and the fear of a new life ahead. When Aiden had said, reasonably enough, that no one could know where she'd gone, since even the farmer who'd hired him the pony and trap knew only that they were bound for Shoreham station and the railway line could have taken them anywhere, she scolded herself for her timidity and braved the open deck.

And there was plenty to keep her interest. The preparations for departure were frenetic and there were hours of hurryings and scurryings, around the decks and up and down the gangway. Late passengers straggled aboard, forgotten luggage was heaved onto trolleys, the crew scrambled across the ship, making last-minute checks, and case after case of food was delivered to the kitchens, sufficient to feed the ship's company for the seven days they would be at sea. When the *Mauretania* finally cast its anchor and nosed majestically into the English Channel, she felt a frisson of anticipation. A heady mix of nervousness and delight.

Her buoyant mood did not last. Once they had rounded Cornwall and were ploughing the peaks and troughs of the Atlantic, she wished herself safely back in port. The journey to and from Queenstown was not one she wished ever to remember. The seas seemed mountainous to her and the ship not at all steady. She knew her cabin was superior to the steerage of old, but it was as small and stuffy as Aiden had warned. For three days she clung to her bunk, a tin basin by her side, unable to move. Aiden was a regular visitor, bringing her weak tea and dry biscuits, but she was too unwell to take food or drink, and sent him away.

It was not until they were two days distant from the Irish coast that she dared to leave her bunk and try to stand unaided. Very gingerly, she shuffled to the porthole and looked out. The sea still seemed huge, but the waves were a little less choppy and the ship more solid beneath her feet. When Aiden made his morning call, she was persuaded to take a gentle walk. He led her along what seemed like a dozen corridors and up several companionways, all the time clearing a path for her through scattered chairs, mingling passengers and odd pieces of luggage that appeared to have been abandoned. Finally, they came out onto the open deck. She walked over to the rail and took a thankful breath. The wind was in her hair and the sun warmed her face; another deep breath of fresh, tangy air and she began to feel herself almost a new person.

For the first time since they'd left Southampton, she took

notice of her surroundings. 'It's enormous.' She waved a vague arm towards the *Mauretania*'s seven decks and four massive funnels.

'It was the world's largest ship until recently. But are you feeling a little better?' He bent down and kissed her lightly on the top of her head.

'I might just survive.' She felt well enough now to poke fun at herself.

'Then we must cross our fingers the weather continues calm and speeds us on our way. The *Mauretania* is still the fastest ship across the Atlantic and we should be in New York in four days.'

Another four days at sea. She hoped fervently that she could remain upright for that time. Aiden lifted his hand to shade his eyes and she followed his gaze, out across the expanse of ocean, mile after mile of undulating sea, to the smudgy blue horizon and beyond. 'Think of it,' he said. 'We'll be landing in the New World – and soon. It's hard to believe. I would love us to see New York City but we don't have the money to linger. We'll need to be on our way, once we disembark.'

'I don't mind not lingering.' She had become eager to reach her future home.

He gave her a hug. 'We'll take a hansom from the port to Grand Central Station – it shouldn't be too expensive. The trains leave from there twice a day.'

'And when do we arrive in Toronto?'

'The journey will take the rest of that day and most of the night, I'm afraid. It will be a tiresome business for you, especially travelling straight from the ship. But Niall will be waiting at Union Station for us.'

'Your family have been very kind.'

'They'll make us welcome, for sure, and we can stay with them for as long as we like. Take things slowly for a while.'

'Not too slowly, or we'll overstay our welcome.' The wind was turning fresher and the coolness of autumn was in its touch. She nestled into the shelter of his arm. 'We should find a lodging of our own as soon as possible and that might take some time.'

He pulled back and held her at arm's length, smiling as he did. 'There is the small matter of a wedding first, or had you forgotten? But perhaps you were thinking of flouting convention completely?'

She took a while to consider, then pulled his arms around her again and buried herself deep within them. 'Do you know, I don't think I really care.'

'Elizabeth Summer!' He put on a face of pretend shock.

She smiled at his teasing but then shook her head and said seriously, 'I'm not sure I've ever cared. Not about convention. Not for myself. I've always said what was expected of me and always acted in the way I was supposed to – more or less – but that was for my family's sake. I was what they wanted me to be. It was easier than being in a constant quarrel with them. But if I'm truthful, following social rules has never had much meaning.'

'And you've just discovered that?'

'I think I discovered it when I met you,' she said lovingly. 'You taught me to recognise the person I really am.'

'And who is that?'

'A braver spirit than I thought. A person who can do what she wishes with her life, be what she wants. Have impossible dreams and try very hard to make them come true.'

'If I have anything to do with it, they won't stay impossible.' He dropped another light kiss on her head.

Those dreams, though, were taking her far from Summerhayes, and without notice, a swell of sadness flowed across the ocean and caught her unawares. Her mother and brother would be all right, she told herself. They would go on better without her. But her father? She would not think of her father, not right now.

She clutched Aiden's hand hard. 'I may not have liked my old life but I can't forget it.'

'Why should you?'

'I must write home as soon as I can.'

'You will, I promise, as soon as we have a home to write from.' He smoothed her cheek. 'I think you're getting cold – we should walk a little.'

She allowed herself to be guided along the busy deck to the rear of the ship. It was a fair distance and, by the time they reached the stern, she was feeling tired. She was still weak from the three days of sickness. She stood close by Aiden's side, both of them leaning against the white-painted rail, and watching the waves furrow and cream in the ship's wake. A flight of gulls screamed and dipped overhead.

'Some day, we'll return,' she said wistfully. 'When this war finishes.' She loved him more than she could express, but a part of her would for ever dwell at Summerhayes.

'We will, and I guarantee your family will greet us with open arms. Even your father. As long as I've made my fortune by then!'

'A mere trifle,' she said gaily.

'A trifle,' he agreed. 'Compared to this.' He put his arms around her and, taking no heed of a passing sailor, kissed her long and tenderly.

HQ
One Place. Many Stories

The home of bold, innovative
and empowering publishing.

Follow us online

 @HQStories

 @HQStories

 HQStories

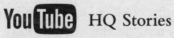 HQ Stories

 HQMusic

HQ_SM

Dervla McTiernan was born in County Cork, Ireland, to a family of seven. She studied corporate law at the National University of Ireland, Galway, and the Law Society of Ireland, and practised as a lawyer for twelve years. Following the global financial crisis, she moved with her family to Western Australia, where she now works for the Mental Health Commission. In 2015, she submitted a story for the Sisters in Crime Scarlet Stiletto competition and was shortlisted. This inspired her to complete the novel that would become *The Ruin*. She lives in Perth with her husband and two children. Follow Dervla 🐦 @DervlaMcTiernan.

Praise for *The Ruin*

'A future star of the genre' Chris Brookmyre

'This one was a winner for me!' Alex Gray

'A very fine novel ... excellently written' Marian Keyes

'Heartbreaking and heart-stopping in equal measure!' Caz Frear

'Loved every page.' Sam Blake

'Fans of Tana French will love McTiernan's expertly plotted, complex web of secrets that refuse to stay hidden' Karen Dionne

'Absolutely brilliant. Wonderful characters, authentic setting, and a sublime, twisty plot' *Irish Examiner*

'Intelligent, compassionate and believable' Sinead Crowley

'*The Ruin* is a terrific read!' Liz Nugent

THE
RUIN

DERVLA
McTIERNAN

sphere

SPHERE

First published in Australia in 2018 by HarperCollins
First published in Great Britain in 2018 by Sphere
This paperback edition published in 2018 by Sphere

1 3 5 7 9 10 8 6 4 2

Copyright © Dervla McTiernan Ltd 2018

The moral right of the author has been asserted.

A CIP catalogue record for this book
is available from the British Library.

ISBN 978-0-7515-6931-5

Printed and bound in Great Britain by
Clays Ltd, Elcograf S.p.A.

Papers used by Sphere are from well-managed forests
and other responsible sources.

MIX
Paper from
responsible sources
FSC
www.fsc.org   FSC® C104740

Sphere
An imprint of
Little, Brown Book Group
Carmelite House
50 Victoria Embankment
London EC4Y 0DZ

An Hachette UK Company
www.hachette.co.uk

www.littlebrown.co.uk

THE
RUIN
DERVLA
McTIERNAN

sphere

SPHERE

First published in Australia in 2018 by HarperCollins
First published in Great Britain in 2018 by Sphere
This paperback edition published in 2018 by Sphere

1 3 5 7 9 10 8 6 4 2

A CIP catalogue record for this book
is available from the British Library.

ISBN 978-0-7515-6931-5

Printed and bound in Great Britain by
Clays Ltd, Elcograf S.p.A.

Papers used by Sphere are from well-managed forests
and other responsible sources.

Sphere
An imprint of
Little, Brown Book Group
Carmelite House
50 Victoria Embankment
London EC4Y 0DZ

An Hachette UK Company
www.hachette.co.uk

www.littlebrown.co.uk

To Kenny, my partner in crime. Thank you for the Thursday nights, for the log-lines, and the laughs.

To Kenny, my partner in crime. Thank you for the
Thursday nights, for the log-lines, and the laughs.

Ní scéal rúin é más fios do thriúr é.

An Irish saying, meaning 'it's not a secret if a third person knows about it'.

The title of my book can be read in English, or can be given its Irish meaning. In Irish, Rúin means something hidden, a mystery, or a secret, but the word also has a long history as a term of endearment.

Dervla McTiernan